THE
ONE MAN

ANDREW GROSS

MACMILLAN

First published 2016 by Minotaur Books

First published in the UK 2016 by Macmillan
an imprint of Pan Macmillan
20 New Wharf Road, London N1 9RR
Associated companies throughout the world
www.panmacmillan.com

ISBN 978-1-5098-2281-2 HB
ISBN 978-1-5098-0866-3 TPB

1 3 5 7 9 8 6 4 2

A CIP catalogue record for this book is available from the British Library.

Printed and bound by CPI Group (UK) Ltd, Croydon, CR0 4YY

Visit **www.panmacmillan.com** to read more about all our books
and to buy them. You will also find features, author interviews and
news of any author events, and you can sign up for e-newsletters
so that you're always first to hear about our new releases.

*To my father-in-law, Nate Zorman, for the stories
told and for those that still remain inside*

CONTENTS

Recent reports both through the newspapers and through secret service, have given indications that the Germans may be in possession of a powerful new weapon which is expected to be ready between November and January [1944]. There seems to be considerable probability that this new weapon is tube alloy [i.e., uranium]. It is not necessary to describe the probable consequences which would result if this proves to be the case.

It is possible that the Germans will have, by the end of this year, enough material accumulated to make a large number of gadgets which they will release at the same time on England, Russia and this country. In this case, there would be little hope for counter-action. . . . This would place particularly Britain in an extremely serious position but there would be hope for counter-action from our side before the war is lost, provided our own tube alloy program is drastically accelerated in the next few weeks.

MANHATTAN PROJECT PHYSICISTS EDWARD TELLER
AND HANS BETHE TO ROBERT OPPENHEIMER
AUGUST 21, 1943

THE ONE MAN

PROLOGUE

The private room is on the fourth floor of the Geriatric wing at the Edward Hines Jr. Veterans Administration Hospital outside Chicago, bent, old men shuffling down the hall in hospital gowns with nurses guiding them and portable IVs on their arms.

The woman steps in, in her mid-fifties but still young-looking, smartly put together, in a short, quilted Burberry jacket and olive cowl, her dark hair in a ponytail. She sees her father in a chair, looking smaller to her than she'd ever seen him before, frailer, even in the two months since the funeral. For the first time, she can see the bony lines of his cheeks coming through, yet still with that remarkable full head of hair—graying, but not yet white. He has a blanket draped over his lap, the television on. CNN. One thing you could always count on, even in the middle of a Bears game on Thanksgiving with all the grandkids around, was her dad asking if they could put on the news. "Just to hear what's happening! What's wrong with that?" But he's not watching this time, just staring out, blankly.

She notices his hand shaking. "Pop?"

The day nurse seated across from him puts down her book and stands up. "Look who's here!"

He barely turns, no longer hearing so well in his right ear. His daughter goes in and smiles to the nurse, a large black woman from St. Lucia, whom they hired to be with him pretty much full time.

1

When he finally catches sight of her, her father's face lights up in a happy smile. "Hey, pumpkin."

"I told you I was coming, Pop." She bends down beside him and gives him a hug and a kiss on the cheek.

"I've been waiting for you," he says.

"You have?"

"Of course. What else is there to do here?"

Her eyes are drawn to the shelf next to his bed, to the things she put there on her last visit, a month ago.

The Northern Illinois Bar Association Man of the Year plaque that was on the wall in his office. The photo of him and her mom at the Great Wall in China. A shot of the thirty-eight-foot Hatteras he kept in Jupiter, Florida, which they had now put up for sale. Photos of the grandkids, her own boys, Luke and Jared, among them.

Mementos of a full and happy life.

"Greg said he'd be by a little later." Her husband. "He had some business to attend to." Business cleaning up a few issues related to the old house in Highland Park and some lingering matters connected to her mother's estate.

Her father looks up. "Business? Here?"

"Just some things, Pop . . . Not to worry yourself. We'll take care of them."

He just nods compliantly. "Okay." Even a year ago he would have put on his glasses and insisted on reviewing every document, every bill of sale.

She runs her hand affectionately through his still-thick hair. "So, ninety-two, huh . . . ? Still looking pretty dashing, Dad."

"For an old guy, not so bad." He shrugs with a bony grin. "But I'm not doing any marathons."

"Well, there's always next year, right?" She squeezes his arm. "So how *is* he doing?" she asks the nurse. "Behaving, I hope?"

"Oh, he always behaves." She laughs. "But the fact is he's not saying much these days, since his wife passed. He naps a lot. We take walks around the ward. He has some friends he likes to see.

Mostly he just sits like he is now. Watches the TV. He likes the news, of course. And baseball . . ."

"The truth is, he never said very much," the daughter admits, "unless it was about business. Or his Cubs. He loves his Cubs. For someone who didn't even know what baseball was when he came to this country. A hundred and seven years and counting, right, Pop?"

"I'm not giving up," he says with a grin.

"No, I bet you're not. Hey, you want to go for a walk with *me*?" She bends down next to him and takes his tremoring hand. "I'll tell you about Luke. He just got into Northwestern. Where you went, Pop. He's a smart kid. And he wrestles. Just like you did . . ."

A look of concern comes over her father's face. "Tell him to watch out for those farm boys from Michigan State. They're big. And they cheat . . ." he says. "You know they're . . ."

He makes a sound as if he wants to add something. Something important. But then he just nods and sits back, staring out. His eyes grow dim.

She brushes his cheek with her hand. "What are you always thinking about, Pop? I wish so much for once you could let me in."

"He's probably not thinking about very much, since . . ." the nurse says, not wanting to mention his wife. "I'm not sure he's following much of anything anymore."

"I can follow," he snaps back. "I can follow just fine." He turns to his daughter. "It's just that . . . I do forget things now from time to time. Where's Mom?" He glances around, as if expecting to see her in her chair. "Why isn't she here?"

"Mom's gone, Pop," the daughter says. "She died. Remember?"

"Oh, yeah, she died." He nods, continuing to just stare out. "Sometimes I get confused."

"He was always such a vibrant man," the daughter opines to the nurse, "though he always carried this kind of sadness with him we never fully understood. We always thought it had to do with losing his entire family back in Poland during the war. He never knew what

3

happened to them. We tried to trace them once, just to find out. They have records. But he never wanted to know. Right, Pop?"

Her father just nods, his left hand continuing to shake.

"Look, I have something to show you." From her tote, she takes out a plastic bag. Some things he likes. The *Economist* magazine. A few new pictures of the grandkids. A bar of Ghirardelli chocolate. "We found something . . . Cleaning out the house. We were going through a few of Mom's old things she had buried away. Up in the attic." She takes a cigar box out of the bag. "Look what we found . . ."

She opens the box. There are some old photos inside. One of her father and mother during WWII, receiving a medal from two high-ranking military men. An old passport and military papers. A small, creased, black-and-white photo of a pretty blond woman in a rowboat, the front rim of her white cap turned up. The opening page of a Mozart concerto torn in half, then taped back together. A polished white chess piece. A rook.

For a second, her father's eyes show some light.

"And then this . . ." She brings out a velvet pouch and takes something out from it.

It's a medal. A bronze cross with an eagle on it, attached to a blue and red ribbon. The pouch has some dust on it; it's clearly been tucked away in the box for a long time. She puts it in his palm. "It's not just any medal, Dad. It's the Distinguished Service Cross."

The old man stares at it for a second and then turns away. It's clear he's not happy to see it.

"They only give this for the most extreme acts of bravery. The boys looked it up. You would never talk about what it was like for you during the war. Back in Poland. Only that you were in the . . ."

She stops. Whenever the topic turned to the horrors of "the camps," her father would turn away or leave the room. For years he would never even wear short sleeves, and never showed anyone his number.

"Look . . ." She hands him the photo of him with the military officers. "We never ever saw this growing up. How is this possible? You were a hero."

"I wasn't a hero." He shakes his head. "You just don't know."

"Then tell me," the daughter says. "We've wanted to know for so long. Please."

He opens his mouth as if about to say something, finally, but then just shakes his head and stares off into space again.

"If you didn't do something important, then why did they give you that medal?" she asks. She shows him the photo of the pretty woman in the boat. "And who is this? Was she part of your family back there? In Poland?"

"No, not family . . ."

This time, her father takes up the torn music sheet and stares at it. There's a distant glimmer in his eyes. Maybe a smile, something buried back in time that has come alive again unexpectedly.

"A lot of them are like that," the nurse says. "They don't want to remember back then. They just keep it inside them forever until—"

"Dolly . . ." the father finally mutters.

"Dolly . . . ?" His daughter touches his arm.

"It was short for Doleczki. It meant dimples." The faintest smile comes across his face. "She played so beautifully back then."

"Who, Dad? Please, tell me who she is. And how you earned this." She wraps the medal in his palm. "There's no reason to keep it inside anymore."

Her father lets out a breath that feels as if it's been held inside him for a lifetime. He finally looks at his daughter. "You really want to know?"

"I do." She sits beside him. "We all do, Pop."

He nods. "Then maybe it *is* time." He looks at the photograph again. Memories walled in as in a tomb covered over by the sands of years and years. "Yes, I have a story. But if you want to know it all, it doesn't begin with her." He puts the photograph down. "It begins with two men. In a forest. In Poland."

"Two men . . ." his daughter says, trying to coax him on. "What were they doing?"

"They were running." The old man looks out, but this time his eyes are alive with memory. "Running for their lives . . ."

PART ONE

ONE

The barking of the dogs was closing in on them, not far behind now.

The two men clawed through the dense Polish forest at night, clinging to the banks of the Vistula, only miles from Slovakia. Their withered bodies cried out from exhaustion, on the edge of giving out. The clothing they wore was tattered and filthy; their ill-fitting clogs, useless in the thick woods, had long been tossed aside, and they stank, more like hunted animals than men.

But now the chase was finally over.

"Sie sind hier!" they heard the shouts in German behind them. *This way!*

For three days and nights they had buried themselves in the wood-piles outside the camp's perimeter wire. Camouflaging their scents from the dogs with a mixture of tobacco and kerosene. Hearing the guards' bootsteps go past, only inches away from being discovered and dragged back to the kind of death no man could easily contemplate, even in there.

Then, the third night, they clawed their way out under the cover of darkness. They traveled only at night, stealing whatever scraps of food they could find on the farms they came upon. Turnips. Raw potatoes. Squash. Which they gnawed at like starving animals. Whatever it was, it was better than the rancid swill they'd been kept barely alive on these past two years. They threw up, their bodies unaccustomed to

9

anything solid. Yesterday, Alfred had turned his ankle and now tried to carry on with a disabling limp.

But someone had spotted them. Only a couple of hundred yards behind, they heard the dogs, the shouts in German, growing louder.

"*Hier entlang!*" Over here!

"Alfred, come on, quick!" the younger one exhorted his friend. "We have to keep going."

"I can't. I can't." Suddenly the limping man tripped and tumbled down the embankment, his feet bloody and raw. He just sat there on the edge of exhaustion. "I'm done." They heard the shouts again, this time even closer. "What's the use? It's over." The resignation in his voice confirmed what they both knew in their hearts: that it was lost. That they were beaten. They had come all this way but now had only minutes before their pursuers would be upon them.

"Alfred, we have to keep moving," his friend urged him on. He ran down the slope and tried to lift his fellow escapee, who even in his weakened condition felt like a dead weight.

"Rudolf, I can't. It's no use." The injured man just sat there, spent. "You go on. *Here*—" He handed his friend the pouch he'd been carrying. The proof they needed to get out. Columns of names. Dates. Maps. Incontrovertible proof of the unspeakable crimes the world needed to see. "Go! I'll tell them I left you hours ago. You'll have some time."

"No." Rudolf lifted him up. "Did you not vow not to die back there in that hell, just to let yourself die here . . . ?"

He saw it in his friend's eyes. What he'd seen in hundreds of other sets of eyes back at the camp, when they'd given up for good. A thousand.

Sometimes death is just simpler than continuing to fight.

Alfred lay there, breathing heavily, almost smiling. "Now go."

From the woods, only yards away, they heard a click. The sound of a rifle being cocked.

They froze.

It's over, they both realized at once. They'd been found. Their hearts leaped up with fear.

Out of the darkness, two men stepped forward. Both dressed in civilian garb, with rifles, their faces gritty and smeared with soot. It was clear they weren't soldiers. Maybe just local farmers. Maybe the very ones who had turned them in.

"*Resistance?*" Rudolf asked, a last ember of hope flickering in his eyes.

For a second, the two said nothing. One merely cocked his gun. Then the larger one, bearded, in a rumpled hunting cap, nodded.

"Then help us, please!" Rudolf pleaded in Polish. "We're from the camp."

"*The camp?*" The man looked at their striped uniforms without understanding.

"Look!" Rudolf held out his arms. He showed them the numbers burned into them. "Auschwitz."

The barking of the dogs was almost on them now. Only meters away. The man in the cap glanced toward the sound and nodded. "Take your friend. Follow me."

TWO

This was the first time he'd been asked to sit in with such esteemed company, and Captain Peter Strauss hoped, after what he had to propose, it wouldn't be the last.

It was a drizzly Monday eve, and the mood around the table inside the Oval Office of the White House was as somber as the leaden skies outside. News of the two escapees, Rudolf Vrba and Alfred Wetzler, had reached President Roosevelt's inner circle within days of them making it across the Polish border to Slovakia.

As one of Bill Donovan's youngest, but chief, OSS operations officers and a Jew himself, Strauss knew that suspicions of Nazi extermination camps—not just forced labor camps—went as far back as 1942, when reports filtered out from European Jewish groups of some 100,000 Jews forced from the ghettos in Warsaw and Lodz and likely killed. But the firsthand accounts from the two Auschwitz escapees, strengthened by actual documents they brought with them from the camp's administrative offices listing names, numbers, and the factory-like process of mass liquidation, gave credence to everyone's worst fears.

Around the oval table, Roosevelt; his secretary of war, Henry Stimson; Treasury Secretary Robert Morgenthau; William Donovan, his chief spymaster and head of the Office of Strategic Services; and Donovan's aide, Captain Peter Strauss, pored over the grim report

12

and pondered just what it meant. Even more troubling were the escapees' claims that the death camp was rapidly expanding and that the pace of the exterminations, by mass gassing, had increased. Thousands upon thousands were being systematically wiped out each week.

"And this is only one of many such places of death," Morgenthau, a Jew as well, and whose prominent New York banking family had seen that the escapees' firsthand accounts got into the president's hands, uttered grimly. "Reports suggest there are dozens more. Entire families are being sent to the gas chambers as soon as they arrive. Towns."

"And our options are what, gentlemen?" A disheartened FDR looked around the table. A third, bloody year at war, worry of the upcoming invasion, the decision to run for a fourth term, and the advance of his crippling disease had all taken their toll on him but did not diminish the fight in his voice. "We can't just sit back and allow these unconscionable acts to continue."

"The Jewish Congress and the World Refugee Board are imploring us to bomb the camp," the treasury secretary advised him. "We cannot simply sit on our hands any longer."

"Which will accomplish what, exactly?" Henry Stimson, who had served in the administrations of two presidents prior to FDR and who had come out of public retirement to run the country's war effort, asked. "Except to kill a lot of innocent prisoners ourselves. Our bombers can barely make it all the way there and back with a full payload. We'd suffer considerable losses. And we all know we need every one of those aircraft for what's coming up."

It was May 1944, and word had leaked even to Strauss's level of the final preparations under way for the forthcoming invasion of Europe.

"Then at least we can disrupt their plans and bomb the railway tracks," Morgenthau pleaded, desperate to convince the president to take action. "The prisoners are brought there on sealed trains. That would at least slow down the pace of the exterminations."

"Bombers flying all over Europe at night . . . Making precision strikes on rail tracks? And as you say, there are many such camps?"

13

Stimson registered his skepticism. "I believe the best thing we can do for these poor people, Mr. President, is to get to them and liberate them as swiftly as possible. Not by sponsoring any ill-conceived raids. That's my view."

The president drew in a breath and took off his wire glasses, the deep channels around his eyes reflecting the pallid cast of a conflicted man. Many of his closest friends were Jews and had urged action. His administration had brought more Jews into the government than any before it. And, as a humane and compassionate being, always seeking to give hope and rise to the common man, he was more re-pelled by the report of the atrocities he'd just read through than by any that had crossed his desk in the war, even more than the tragic losses of American lives on the beaches in the Pacific or the loss of troops at sea on their way to England.

Yet as a realist, Roosevelt knew his secretary of war was right. Too much lay ahead, and all of it far too important. Plus, the anti-Jewish lobby was still a strong one in the country, and reports of soldiers lost predominantly trying to save Jewish lives would not go well as he sought to gain a fourth term. "Bob, I know how hard this is for you." He put his hand on the treasury secretary's shoulder. "It's hard for all of us, to be sure. Which brings us to the reason we are all here tonight, gentlemen. Our special project. What's it called, 'Catfish'?" He turned toward the head of the OSS, Colonel Donovan. "Tell me, Bill, do we have any real hope that this project is still alive?"

"Catfish" was the name known only to a very few for the under-cover operation Strauss was in charge of to smuggle a particular in-dividual out of Europe. A Polish Jew, whom FDR's people claimed was vital to the war effort.

As far back as 1942, it had been discovered that bearers of certain Latin American identity papers were awarded special treatment in Warsaw. For several months, hundreds of Polish and Dutch Jews were issued counterfeit papers from Paraguay and El Salvador to gain exit from Europe. Many had made their way to northern France, where they were interned at a detention center in the village of Vittel, while their cases were gone over by skeptical German officials. As doubtful as the Nazis were about the origin of these papers, they could not afford to upset these neutral Latin American countries, whose authoritarian rulers were, in fact, sympathetic to their cause. How these particular refugees were able to acquire these papers, purchased secretly through anti-Nazi emissaries in the Paraguayan and Salvadoran embassies in Bern, as well as their dubious provenance, was always clouded. What also remained unclear was how contacts friendly to the United States had been able to get them into the hands of the very subject and his family (aka "Catfish") they were attempting to smuggle out. For a while, the prospects looked hopeful. Twice, transport out of Europe had been arranged, via Holland and France. Yet each time the Germans blocked their exit. Then, just three months ago, an informer from Warsaw had blown the papers' suspect origins wide open, and now the fates of all the Vittel Jews, including the one they so desperately wanted, were completely up in the air.

"I'm afraid we've hit a snag, Mr. President," Donovan said. "We don't know for certain if he's even there."

"Or if he is, if he's even still alive . . ." Secretary of War Stimson added. "Our intelligence on the matter has all gone dark."

The emissaries who had passed along the documents had been arrested and were now in Nazi jails.

"So I'm told we still need this man. At all costs." The president turned to his secretary of war. "Is this still true?"

"Like no other." Stimson nodded. "We were close in Rotterdam. There was even transport booked. *Now . . .*" He shook his head somberly, then took his pen and pointed to a tiny spot on the map of Europe that was on a stand next to the conference table.

A place called Oswiecim. In Poland.

"*Oswiecim?*" Roosevelt put back on his glasses.

"Oswiecim is the Polish name for Auschwitz, Mr. President," the secretary of war said. "Which, in light of the report we've all just read, is why we're here."

"I see." The president nodded. "So now he's one of five million faceless Jews, forced out of their homes against their will, without papers or identity?"

"And to what fate, we do not know . . ." Secretary of the Treasury Morgenthau shook his head gravely.

"It's all our fates that are in the balance, gentlemen." Roosevelt pushed his wheelchair back from the table. "So you're here to tell me we've done everything we can to find this man and get him out. And now it's lost. *We've* lost."

He went around the table. For a moment, no one replied.

"Perhaps not completely lost, Mr. President." The OSS chief leaned forward. "My colleague Captain Strauss has looked at the situation closely. And he believes there might be one last way . . ."

"A last way?" The tired president's gaze fell on the young aide.

"Yes, Mr. President."

The captain appeared around thirty, slightly balding already, and a graduate of Columbia Law School. A smart cookie, Roosevelt had been told. "All right, son, you've got my attention," the president said.

Strauss cleared his throat and glanced one more time at his boss. He opened his folder.

"Go on." Donovan nodded to him. "Tell him your plan."

THREE

"Papa, Papa, wake up! They're here!"

The shrill of whistles knifed through the frigid morning air. Dr. Alfred Mendl awoke in his narrow bunk, his arm wrapped around his wife, Marte, protecting her from the January cold. Their daughter, Lucy, stood over them, both nervous and excited. She'd been at the blanket-covered window of the cramped room that was fit at most for four, but which they now shared with fourteen others. This was no place for a girl to pass her twenty-second birthday, as she had just the night before. Huddled on lice-infested mattresses, sleeping amid their haphazard suitcases and meager belongings, everyone slowly stirred out of their blankets and greatcoats with the anticipation that something clearly was up.

"Papa, look now!"

On the landing outside, the French *milice* were going room to room, banging on doors with their batons. "Get up! Out of bed, you lazy Jews. All those holding foreign passports, take your things and come down. You're leaving!"

Alfred's heart leaped. After eight hard months, was this finally the time?

He jumped out of bed, still dressed in his rumpled tweed pants and woolen undershirt, all that kept him warm. They had all slept in their warmest clothes most every night for months now, washing them

17

whenever they could. He nearly tripped over the family stretched out on the floor next to them. They rotated the sleeping arrangements a month at a time.

"Everyone holding foreign passports packed and out!" a black-clad policeman threw open the door and instructed them.

"Marte, get up! Throw everything together. Maybe today is the day!" he said to his wife with a feeling of hopefulness. Hope that had been dashed many times over the past year.

Everyone in the room was murmuring, slowly coming to life. Light barely crept through the blanket-covered sills. Vittel was a detention camp in the northeast corner of France, actually four six-story hotels that formed a ring around a large courtyard, not exactly "four stars," so the joke went, as it was all surrounded by three rows of barbed wire manned by German patrols. Thousands were held there—political prisoners, citizens of neutral or enemy countries whom the Germans were hoping to exchange—although the Jews, mostly of Polish and Dutch descent, whose fate was being decided by Berlin, were kept together on the same ward. The French policeman who entered their room stepped between the rustling bodies, prodding people along with his stick. "Didn't you hear me? All of you, up, packed. Quick, quick! Why are you dallying? You're shipping out."

Those who were slow to move, he nudged sharply with his stick and kicked open their suitcases that were strewn on the floor.

"Where are we going?" people questioned in various languages and accents: Polish, Yiddish, and awkward French, everyone scurrying to get their things together.

"You'll see. Just get yourself moving. That's my only job. And take your papers. You'll find out downstairs."

"Take our papers!" Alfred looked at Marte and Lucy with a lift in his heart. *Could this finally be their time?* He and his family had waited so long there. Eight harsh months, after making their way with the forged identity papers gotten into his hands by the emissary from the Paraguayan embassy in Warsaw. First to the Swiss border through Slovakia and Austria, where they were turned away; then by train through occupied France to Holland, all the while under the protection of the Paraguayan embassy in Warsaw as a foreign national on a teaching assignment at the university in Lvov. Once, they literally got as far as the pier in Rotterdam where they were to board a Swedish cargo ship, the *Prinz Eugen,* to Stockholm, transport papers in hand, only to be turned back again as their papers needed to be authenticated. Literally in limbo, they were sent here to Vittel, while Jewish organizations in Switzerland and the United States' and British governments argued their cases and pressured the Paraguayan and Salvadoran governments to honor their documents. Since then, they had been kept here in a kind of diplomatic hell. Always promised that the matter was being looked into. One more day, just another day, while the German foreign office and Latin American embassies worked it out. Alfred and his family had even taught themselves Spanish, to make their case all the more convincing. Of course they knew their documents were not worth the paper they were printed on. Alfred was Polish, had been born in Warsaw, and had taught physics at the university in Lvov after years in Prague and Gottingen with some of the best minds in the atomic field. At least until he was stripped of his position a year ago and his diplomas were trashed and burned. Marte was from Prague, now overrun by the Nazis, but had been a Polish citizen for years. They all knew that the only thing that had kept them from being shipped off somewhere and never heard from again was these papers, suspect as they were, that had been arranged by he knew not who with the promise that they would get the family out and to America, where he would be greeted warmly by Szilard and Fermi, his old colleagues. Still, whatever they had suffered these past months was far better than what they would have faced back home. Months ago he'd heard the university in Lvov had been cleared out just like those in Warsaw and Krakow. The last of his colleagues shot, kicked in the streets, or shipped off somewhere with their families, never heard from again.

Bring your papers, the policeman said now. Was this a good sign or a bad one? Alfred didn't know. But everyone around him was springing to life, pulsing with both nerves and anticipation. Maybe it had all been cleared up at last. Maybe they were finally leaving.

A day hadn't passed where he hadn't dreamed of presenting his work to people who pursued good and not these Nazis.

"Darling, come on, quick!" He helped his wife fill up her suitcase. Marte was frail these days. She'd caught a cold in November, and it seemed to have never left her chest. She looked like she'd aged ten years since they'd begun their journey.

They'd had to leave everything behind. Their fine china. Their collection of antique pharmacy jars. All the awards that had been given to him. Anything of value other than a few photographs and, of course, his work. They stuffed whatever they had taken into their small bags. When the time came to leave, it had to be in a day.

"Lucy, quick!" Alfred assembled his papers and threw them into his leather briefcase along with the few books he'd been able to bring along. He could lose his clothing, his academic diplomas, the photographs of his parents on the Vistula in Warsaw, the personal effects dearest to him. Even his best shoes. But his work—his work must remain. His formulas and research. Everything depended on getting them out. One day that would become clear. He hastily bundled it all together in his case and fastened the lock. "Marte, Lucy, we must go."

A few in the crowded room remained behind and wished those who were leaving well, like prisoners saying goodbye to a fellow inmate who'd been pardoned. "See you in a better life," they said, as if they knew their fates would not be as rosy. A strange familiarity had built up among people whose lives had been thrown together for months in such close quarters.

"God be with you! Goodbye!"

Alfred, Marte, and Lucy made their way outside, melding into the river of people heading along the outside corridors and down to the courtyard. Parents held onto their children; sons and daughters helped the elderly as they slowly went down the stairs, so as not to be trampled in the rush. On the ground, they were herded into the large yard, shivering from the January chill, murmuring, wondering to their neighbors what was going to happen next. Above them, a crowd of those left behind pressed against the banisters, looking on.

20

"Papa, what's going to happen to us?" Lucy asked, eyeing the German guards with their submachine guns.

Alfred looked around. "I don't know."

There were Germans—there always were—but not so many as one would think if something bad was going to happen to them. They all huddled together in the cold. Merchants, teachers, accountants, rabbis. In long woolen coats and homburgs and fedoras.

Whistles sounded. An officious-looking captain in the local French militia, a German officer following behind, stepped in front of the throng and ordered everyone to line up with their papers. The German was in a gray wool officer's coat with the markings of the secret intelligence division, the Abwehr, which worried Alfred.

He and his family grabbed their suitcases and joined the queue.

The French officer went down the line, family by family, inspecting their papers closely and checking their faces. Some he instructed to remain where they were; others he waved to the side of the yard. Armed guards stood everywhere. And dogs, barking loudly and pulling on their leashes, scaring the young children and some of the parents too.

"It will be a joy to be rid of this place," Marte said. "Wherever we end up."

"It will," Alfred said, though he was sensing something in the mood of the soldiers that didn't seem right. They had their caps low and their hands on their weapons. There was no levity. No fraternizing.

Those who didn't speak French were directed to the side without knowing what was going on. One family, Hungarian, Alfred suspected, shouted loudly in their native tongue as a French militiaman tried to move them and then kicked open a suitcase, filled with religious articles, which the old man and his wife scampered vainly to pick up. Another man, clearly a rabbi with a long white beard, kept showing his papers to the *milice* captain in frustration. The French officer finally flung them back at him, the old man and his wife bending to pick them off the ground as eagerly as if they were thousand-zloty notes.

21

No, Alfred thought, it didn't seem right at all.

The captain and his German overseer made their way down the line. The soldiers and the guards gradually began to use more force to restrain everyone.

"Don't worry, these have been checked many times," Alfred assured Marte and Lucy. "They will definitely pass."

But a worrisome feeling rose up in him as each interaction seemed to be met only by frustration and anger, and then people were brusquely shuffled into the growing throng ringed by heavily armed guards.

Outside the walls they heard a train hiss to a stop.

"See, they are taking us somewhere." Alfred tried to sound optimistic to his family.

At last the French officer made his way up to them. "*Papers,*" he requested impassively. Alfred handed him the travel documents showing that he and his family were under the protection of the Paraguayan government and had merely been residents in Poland these past seven years.

"We have been waiting a long time to get home," Alfred said in French to the officer, whose shifting black eyes never really looked at him, just back and forth, from the documents to their faces, as had been done many times these past eight months without incident. The SS officer stood behind him, hands clasped behind his back, with a stonelike look that made Alfred feel uneasy.

"Have you enjoyed your stay here in France, señorita?" the *milice* captain asked Lucy in passable Spanish.

"*Sí,* sir," she replied, nervously enough so that Alfred could hear it in her voice. Who wouldn't be? "But I am ready to finally get home."

"I'm sure you are," the captain said. Then he stepped in front of Alfred. "It says you are a professor?"

"Yes. Electromagnetic physics."

"And where did you acquire these papers, monsieur?"

"What? Where did we acquire them . . . ?" Alfred stammered back, his insides knotting with fear. "These were issued by the Paraguayan embassy in Warsaw. I assure you they are valid. Look, there, you can see . . ." He went to show the officer the official seal and signatures.

22

"I'm afraid these papers are forgeries," the *milice* captain declared.

"I beg your pardon?"

"They are worthless. They are as bad as your Spanish, I'm afraid, mademoiselle. *All of you . . .* " He raised his voice so that the entire crowd could hear. "You are no longer under the protection of the Paraguayan and El Salvadoran governments. It is determined that these visas and passports are not valid. You are prisoners of the French government now, who have no recourse, given your situation, but to turn you over to the German authorities."

There was an audible gasp from the crowd. Some wailed, *"My God, no!"* Others simply looked to the person next to them and muttered, "What did he say . . . ? That these are not valid?"

To Alfred's horror, the French officer began to tear his documents into shreds. All that had kept them alive these past ten months, their only route to freedom, scattering from his hands like ashes onto Alfred's shoes.

"You three, over there," the officer pushed them brusquely, "with the rest." Then he moved down the line without another word. "Next."

"What have you done?" Alfred bent to scoop the shredded documents off the ground. He pulled at the arm of the officer. "Those papers are perfectly valid. They have been inspected many times. Look, look . . ." He pointed to the torn signature page. "We are Paraguayan citizens, looking to return home. We demand transit!"

"You *demand* transit?" The SS officer following the *milice* captain finally spoke. "Be assured, transit is arranged."

Two guards edged their way in and pushed them with their guns from the line. "Take your bags. Over there!" They pointed toward the throng of other Latin American passport holders who were now being penned in by guards, a deepening hopelessness beginning to envelop them.

People began to shout out cries of outrage and objection, holding up their documents, eight months of waiting, hoping, being kept in pens, their dreams of freedom suddenly dashed. The French officer announced in several languages that those holding these travel papers had five minutes to gather their belongings and board transportation that had been arranged outside the camp grounds.

"Where are you taking us?" a terrified woman yelled. For months, rumors of dark places where no one was ever heard from again had spread through the detention camp like an outbreak of typhus.

"To the beach," one of French militia laughed. "To the South of France. Where else? Isn't that where you are looking to go?"

"We have an express train for you. Do not worry," another chortled with the same sarcasm. "You Latin American aristocrats will be traveling first class."

Pandemonium spread like wildfire. Some just refused to accept their fate. The old rabbi in the white beard and his wife sat down on their luggage, refusing to budge. Others screamed back in anger at the black-clad guards, who, now that the true purpose of what they were doing had come out and the crowd had grown unruly, began to close in, herding them like sheep toward the front gate, brandishing their weapons.

"Stay together," Alfred instructed Marte and Lucy, tightly clutching their bags. They were separated for a moment by people charging to the front, cursing and showing their discredited papers in fits of rage. The crowd began to surge. The guards closed in, using their rifle shafts like cattle prods. The white-bearded rabbi and his wife still refused to move; a German guard had now taken over and was screaming at them like they were deaf. *"Aussen."* Out. "Get up! Now." Fights began to break out. Some faces were bloodied, struck by rifle shafts. A few old-timers fell to the ground, and the crowd moved over them despite desperate pleas and shrieks from those who stopped to help.

But family by family, there was no choice but to go. Worried, everyone grabbed their things. The *milice* herded them with their sticks and rifles in the direction of the front gate. Some prayed, others whimpered, but all, except the rabbi and his wife, went. Guards infiltrated the crowd, kicking along luggage. "Is this yours? Take it, or it stays!" Moving them like cattle through Vittel's makeshift wire gate, dogs barking, pulling on their leashes, amid outraged shouts everywhere, wails, cries, everyone giving themselves over to their worst fears.

"Papa, what's happening?" Lucy said, afraid.

"Come on, stay close," Alfred said, clutching his and Marte's valise along with his briefcase. "Maybe it will just be another detention center like this. We've lived through worse." He tried to appear as positive as he could, though he knew in his heart it would not be. Now they had no papers. And Marte's health was growing worse. They moved through the front gate, the first time in eight months they were beyond the wire.

A cargo train waited for them on the tracks. At first, people assumed it was not for them. More for cattle or horses. Then everyone was startled by the sudden rattle of the doors being flung open. The French guards remained behind. The soldiers along the tracks were now German, which sent terror into everyone's heart.

"Here are your fancy carriages, Jews," one of them cackled. "Please, let me help you." He cracked a man in the head with his rifle stock. "Everyone up and in."

There was resistance at first, people objecting, fighting back. This was transport fit for swine, not people. Then there were two short bursts of machine gun fire from behind them and everyone turned. The white-bearded rabbi and his poor wife were now lying on the ground in a pool of blood next to their luggage.

"Oh my God, they're going to massacre us!" a woman screamed.

Everyone headed for the trains. One by one they hurried in, pushing the old and young, dragging their belongings with them. If it couldn't be carried, or if someone stopped to load another article first, their bags were torn from them and tossed aside, clothing and pictures and toiletries spilling over the platform.

"No, those are my possessions!" a woman yelled.

"Get in. Get in. You won't need them." A guard pushed her inside.

"There are no seats in here," someone said. Alfred helped Marte and Lucy up and someone pushed him up from behind. When they all thought the car was filled, they pushed more in. In minutes, you could barely breathe.

"There's no room! There's no more room! Please . . ." a woman wailed. "We'll suffocate in here."

25

They filled it even more.

"Please, I don't want to go!" a man shouted over the wailing.

"C'mon, do you want to end up like them?" another urged him onward, glancing back to the rabbi and his wife in the courtyard.

"My daughter, my daughter. *Sophie . . . !*" a woman cried. A young girl, forced by the crowd into another car, cried out from afar, "Mama!"

The guards kept loading and packing people in with whatever they could carry, until the train car grew tighter and more crowded than Alfred could ever have imagined.

Then the door was slammed shut.

There was only darkness at first. The only light from outside angled through narrow slits in the side door. There were a few whimpers in the pitch black, but then everyone just became silent. The kind of silence when no one has any idea what will happen next. There was barely room to move, to even adjust your arms, to breathe. The car smelled, the odor of eighty people jammed together in a space that should hold half that, many of whom hadn't bathed in weeks.

They stayed that way, listening to the shouts and cries from outside, until they heard a whistle and with a jerk the train began to move. Now people were whimpering, sobbing, praying. They stayed upright by leaning against each other in the dark. In a corner were two jugs, one filled with water—but hardly enough, given the number of them in the car. The other empty. Alfred realized what it was for.

"Where are they taking us, Alfred?" Marte asked under her breath as the railcars picked up speed.

"I don't know." He sought out her and Lucy's hands and clasped them tightly in his. "But at least we are together."

FOUR

Gruppen führer Colonel Martin Franke stepped out on the tracks outside the detention center as the train pulled away. It was over. The Jews were all packed up and gone. The deception had come out and now there was no more recourse for them. All he'd had to do was dangle the bait long enough and he knew someone would grab it. These Jews would fight for a half-eaten piece of tripe off the ground even though it meant giving up one of their own. He watched as the last railcar chugged off to who knew where. Where they were heading, no passport or visa in the world would do them good anymore.

"Captain." He nodded to the French police officer, whose men were now cleaning up all the mess in the courtyard, including the two or three stubborn ones who lay behind in pools of their own blood who they'd had to make a show of. "A job well done, Captain." Now not a trace of those who had just boarded the train would even exist.

"Permit me, Colonel . . ." The French officer bent down and picked up someone's scattered ID papers from the ground. "But were they . . . ?"

"Were they what?" Franke looked at him. "Speak up."

"Were they, in fact, forged? The passports. Were they counterfeit?"

Franke took the boot-smeared document from him. The Jew's own kinsmen had probably stomped all over it in their haste to board.

"What does it matter anyway?" The officer shrugged. "They were never going anywhere from the start."

"I'm sorry, Colonel . . . ?"

"See that the rest of the documents are all accounted for. For our records," Franke said without answering his question.

"Yes, Herr Gruppen führer." The captain saluted and then went away.

Franke pulled his heavy, gray officer's coat closed against the cold. He'd traveled two days from Warsaw, and where was he? Not in Paris; not in some warm, crowded café with a bottle of old médoc and nuzzling at the tits of some loose French barmaid on his lap. No. But packing up a bunch of immaterial, frightened Jews in a prison in the middle of a fucking forest. There wasn't a day that went by when he didn't miss his old post. A year ago, he was part of the German attaché in Lisbon, a plum assignment, spending the war attending parties at the roof bar of the Mundial and sharpening his diplomatic skills. With any luck, he would have been chief attaché within a year, and from there, however the war resolved, there would be influence to trade: Bribes. Exit visas for sale. Artwork stolen from the walls of palaces and stuffed away.

But his secretary, Lena, a piece of ass who couldn't type for shit but who'd been screwing half the mission, proved to be part of a British spy network and fled to London with the names of half the Abwehr network in Lisbon and a notebook full of contact codes. Exposed half the contacts in Europe and Britain. Disgraced, Franke was transferred to Warsaw. G section. Sabotage, false documents, covert contacts with certain minority groups. There the only food was boiled, and the only fish came out of the fucking sewer. Not to mention the cold. It was the kind of cold that you never fully got out of your bones. It made Lisbon seem like the South of France. Then to top it off, his wife, whose family owned a thriving metal factory in Stuttgart which kept him in fancy linens and tins of caviar—his own family could barely afford to put meat on the table—wrote to say that she was leaving him.

Still, better the cold than a cyanide pill, Franke resolved. Now he was serving the war effort by twisting arms and running informants to root out resistance fighters on the Polish frontier or stubborn Jews still hiding out in the Aryan sector. Completely beneath his skills, of course, but it *had* been his network of informants that had unearthed the traitorous *chargé d'affaires* from the Paraguayan embassy in Warsaw who was the source of those illegal forgeries. Franke had always been a man who would do whatever it took, whatever means, to accomplish what was necessary. He had been a detective back in Essen, and not some flashy ass-kisser who went straight for the headlines but one who turned over every page, got on his knees to find every shred of evidence, and a man like that was always poised to sniff out the one opportunity that would land him back on his feet. Otherwise, he would spend the rest of the war in this useless, forgotten city, or, if things went badly, as he was beginning to sense, until they sent him out to the front lines in the East to be shot, likely by his own men, while exhorting them to stand fast against the advancing Russian horde. These days, Franke craved only one thing, and that was the chance to prove his worth to his superiors in Berlin again.

But today had been a good one. His network had unearthed the informer in Warsaw who had given his kinsfolk up. The trail went from the ghettos of Warsaw to the embassies of Paraguay and El Salvador. Two hundred forty Jews. Only a drop in the bucket, given the big picture, of course, but 240 Jews who had come to arouse the interest of the United States and British governments and whom Berlin desperately needed certain proof of if it was to challenge the sovereignty of two neutral Latin American friends and resolve this thorny situation. He'd surely get a commendation from Berlin, maybe a nod from Canaris, admitting they had been hasty in their treatment of him in Lisbon. Or even the Reichsmarschall himself. They'd all have to take notice.

Because a man like Franke, who had been brought up in the iron smelting factories of Essen, knew it wasn't so complicated. All that it required was to follow the scent and not be afraid to dirty your hands. That was the problem with these Abwehr stuffed shirts. They were too busy going to cocktail parties and flirting with dignitaries' wives to know an informer from a bartender. But Franke was a person who was willing to risk everything for what had to be done.

Still, for now, he lamented, it was back to Warsaw, and the winter that still had two more months. Another success like this and they would have to offer him his old position. Perhaps Geneva this time, he sometimes allowed himself to dream.

Maybe even Paris.

The last plume of smoke had faded as the train went around a curve. His work here was complete. Franke took out the left-behind identity paper that the captain had handed him. The photo page of a visa that had fallen to the platform. A pretty little thing, for a Jew. Maybe twelve, with pigtails and a happy smile. He read the name: Elena Zeitman. *Zeitman.* No matter, Franke thought. He folded it neatly and placed it in his pocket. He did not know the precise location she was being sent. Some labor camp in Poland, he'd heard. But he did know, looking after the train, that whatever fate awaited her, no visa or passport in the world would be of help to her now.

FIVE

At his desk at OSS headquarters in Washington, D.C., Peter Strauss read the cable from the War Refugee Board attaché in Bern, Switzerland, with a sense of deflation.

It concerned various civilians being held at the Vittel detention camp in northeastern France who were seeking transport out of Europe under the protection of certain Latin American passports.

Passports he had a keen interest in. And had helped arrange.
The cable read:

> It is my misfortune to report that diplomatic protection for these applicants has been permanently denied. Documents ruled falsely obtained. All bearers rounded up and placed on a sealed train. Destination: labor camp in southern Poland. We believe it to be in a town named Oswiecim.

Strauss reread the cable as his stomach fell. It had been a year. A year of carefully setting this up, of getting the documents into the hands of the one man they sought, then routing him and his family out of Poland and through occupied territory. Secretly arranging transport. A year of petitioning the government of Paraguay to resist German diplomatic pressure and to stand behind them.

A year that was now lost.

All bearers rounded up and placed on a sealed train. Destination: labor camp in southern Poland.

Strauss put the cable down. Operation Catfish was finished.

As the son of a cantor, who could still recite the prayers and Torah as well as he could his own name, the hollowness in Strauss's gut felt even deeper. His father's brother was still in Vienna; they had no idea what fate had befallen him, or his entire family. In a way, Strauss had put all his faith and belief in a positive outcome for this war into the hope that this mission would succeed.

And now both had crumbled.

"Any reply, sir?" The young lieutenant who had delivered the communiqué was still standing there.

"No." Strauss shrugged glumly. "No reply." He took off his wire-rim glasses and started to wipe the lenses clean.

"So then it's over? Two hundred and forty of them . . ." the aide inquired. That was as much as the lieutenant knew. "I'm sorry, sir."

"Two hundred and forty lives . . ." Strauss nodded. "All worth saving, no doubt. But only one that was vital."

SIX

They heard the hiss of steam and the jolt of the brakes and after three agonizing days of pressed-together, foul-smelling confinement, the train finally came to a stop. "Where are we?" people asked in the dark. It was night. "Can anyone see?"

For a while they just stood there, hearing shouts in German outside. Dogs barking.

Someone said, "I've heard they let the dogs attack people right off the train. They just take their pick."

"Shut up," a woman replied harshly. "You're scaring the children."

Suddenly they heard the rattle of locks being opened and the doors of the train car were flung wide. Cold air rushed in, along with glaring lights.

"*Rauss, rauss*. Everyone out! Get out! *Schnellen*. Faster." Gray-clad soldiers carrying sticks rushed up to the train and started pulling people down from the cars. "Quick! Now! Assemble on the platform with your things."

Fear leaping up in their blood, Alfred, Marte, and Lucy stepped down from the packed car, pulling shut their jackets against the biting cold and shielding their eyes from the sharp glare. During the endless trip at least four in their car had died. An old woman who was sick; another, a pregnant one, just fell and gave up. Two were infants. There was a moment or two when Alfred wasn't sure if Marte

33

would make it; in the cramped quarters, the rattle in her chest seemed to grow even worse. There was little to eat except what people had brought along and were willing to share. And the thirst . . . Their throats were parched. There was only one water break per day. "You remember on our honeymoon in Italy?" Alfred had tried to cheer Marte up on the journey. "How mad you were at me?"

"Because you bought us third-class tickets." She had nodded, her voice no stronger than a whisper.

"It was all I could afford. I didn't have a teaching position yet," he had explained to Lucy, as the cars rocked back and forth. "In retrospect, doesn't seem quite so bad now, does it?" he had said to Marte with a laugh.

"Your father always knows how to turn a failed experiment into a life lesson," Marte had joked to Lucy.

Then she had let her head fall against him and coughed. It made the time go by.

On the platform now, there was shouting everywhere, dogs barking. Lights being flashed. In the background, Alfred could see guards with submachine guns. Black-clad guards were blowing shrill whistles and herding everyone around.

"This way! Over here. Leave your things where they are! They'll be taken care of."

These past months, Alfred had grown to detest the French guards at Vittel, but now the French were no longer around, and the sense quickly set in that what they knew before would seem like a fond memory compared to what they faced now.

"Stay together," he said, helping Marte amid the surging crowd. "At least we're off that godforsaken train. *Look* . . . " He pointed upward to letters forming an arch high above the gate.

"What does it say, Papa?" Lucy asked. It was in German.

"*Work will set you free.* See, you have to get strong again, Marte. If we work here, we will be safe. You'll see."

She coughed and nodded and, jostled by the bustling throng, reached down for her bag.

"*Here* . . . " Alfred took it from her. "Let me help you."

As the cars cleared, everyone huddled together for a time, mothers holding their children's hands, people comforting the elderly, not sure what was next. They'd all heard the rumors of these dark and terrible places where no one was ever heard from again. Suddenly, to their amazement, the sounds of music started up. An orchestra playing. *How could that be?* It was Schubert. Alfred was certain. He'd heard it played in Prague at the Rudolfinum Hall.

"Schubert's Violin Concerto in D Major," someone confirmed.

"See, they even have an orchestra here." Alfred put his arm around Marte. "What do you think, Lucy?" He tried to sound upbeat. "It can't be so bad."

"This way! This way!" Black-clad guards with SS markings elbowed through the crowd. "Women and their children form over here. All men, even fathers"—one pointed the other direction—"over there. Don't worry, it's just for processing. You'll all be reunited soon."

"We should try and stay together," Alfred said, picking up both their suitcases and squeezing his briefcase under his arm.

"You there!" A large guard in a black SS cap jostled him. "You women and children to the left. You over here."

"Meine frau ist nicht gut." Alfred appealed to him in German. "She's sick. She needs care."

"Don't worry, she'll be well taken care of here. You'll see her soon. Everyone will be happy. Just leave all your belongings."

A large pile of luggage and satchels had formed on the platform, like that of a tour group awaiting transportation.

"But how will we find them?" a woman in a fur wrap asked. "How will anyone know whose is whose?"

"Don't worry, it will all be worked out." The German officer smiled politely. "Now, just go, quick, there, double time . . . You two as well . . ."

Amid the people crisscrossing, the dogs barking, and officers herding everyone around, Alfred noticed a handful of people in blue and gray candy-striped uniforms and tiny caps weaving through the crowd, taking people's abandoned luggage and rucksacks and throwing them onto a rapidly growing pile. Hunched like downtrodden workers and rail thin, they avoided direct eye contact with the new arrivals as they went about their jobs, though one's gaze seemed to land on Alfred's. His gaunt, dark features, shaved head, and sunken eyes with a kind of soullessness in them seemed to tell a different story about what life was like here.

"Women and children must go here! *Schnellen!* Quick!" a German barked, grabbing Marte and Lucy by the arms and dragging them away. In a second they had been separated from Alfred, pushed on by the throng.

"*Marte!*" Alfred lunged after them. "*Lucy!*"

"*Alfred!*" his wife answered him, his name drowning into the din of shouting and wails as she desperately tried to grasp hold of him.

"*Papa!*" Lucy cried out. "I'm over here!"

Alfred dropped his cases and tried to make his way to them, fear lighting up in him as they were being pushed away. "Please, I need to get to my wife and daughter. I—"

"Don't worry, they'll be fine. You'll see them soon," an SS officer interceded. He pointed to the other direction. "You, over there."

"I'm sure I will see you both soon," Alfred called after them. "Be strong. I will find a way to contact you."

"I love you, Alfred!" Marte called out. Through the dark sea of the crowd, he managed to catch a last, plea-filled glance, and in her surrendering eyes he saw a kind of finality he had never seen before.

He waved, giving them both a hopeful smile though his heart was suddenly overrun with sadness and terror and the feeling that he might never see them again. "I love you both, too."

And then they were gone.

All around, on the platform, many were making their last, tearful goodbyes and futile pleas. "Be safe!" "I will see you soon." "Watch over our son," they would tell one another. "Don't worry, I will." The guards told the men to leave their valises and all belongings. Alfred clutched his briefcase. One of the candy-striped prisoners brushed into him and went to take it from him.

"No." Alfred grasped onto it tighter. "These are my books. My formulas."

"Don't resist," the prisoner said under his breath. "They'll shoot you."

"No, I won't let them go," Alfred said, tightening his arms around it.

"Don't worry, you won't be needing any formulas here, old man." A German officer came up with a grin of amusement. "There's only one formula here, and you'll learn it fast, I promise."

"I'm a physicist. This is all my research. My life's work, Herr Obersturmführer," Alfred said, observing his rank.

"This is now your work," the officer said, and motioned to the prisoners hurling their belongings onto a pile. The officer tried to take the case from Alfred's hands. "Do it well and maybe you'll last. Your German is quite good." He pointed to a line. "Go over there."

"Please . . ." Alfred resisted even further. "No."

In a flash, the German's politeness morphed into something completely different. "Did you not hear me, I said, let go, Jew!" He reached in his holster and pulled out a Luger. "Or would you rather your stay here be short-lived?"

"Give it here. Please," the prisoner begged, with what looked like a dire warning in his eyes.

Alfred could see the rage and anger stiffen in the German officer's eyes and neck, knowing that if he resisted even seconds longer he would be dropped right here on the tracks, the way the old rabbi and his wife had been shot back in Vittel. He had to stay alive, if only for Marte and Lucy's sake. He had to see them again.

Reluctantly, he let go.

"Now get over there." The German pushed him toward the line of younger men assembling. "Your German will come in handy." He blew his whistle and moved on to someone else.

Alfred watched as the prisoner took his leather case and flung it onto the mountain of bags and belongings that was growing by the minute. In horror, he saw the clasp become undone, and pages and pages of his work—equations, formulas, research for papers he had written for *Academic Scientifica* and the *Zeitschrift für Physik,* the toil of twenty years—slowly slide out of the case and scatter like debris over the mounting pile of bags, rucksacks, children's toys and dolls, until they disappeared—every page, like bodies hurled indifferently into a mass grave and then covered over by the next.

If only they knew what that was . . .

He was handed a uniform and told to march to a processing building and change his clothes. Over the ubiquitous wailing on the platform and the desperate last goodbyes and shouts of "I love you!" and "Stay strong," Alfred thought he heard his name. He spun around, his heart springing up with hope. *"Marte!"*

But it was likely only another person shouting for someone else. He searched the crowd for one last look at his girls, but they were gone. Then he was pushed along in the throng. *Twenty-eight years . . .* he said to himself. In all that time, they rarely spent a day apart. She had typed every one of his papers and listened to hundreds of his talks in advance, correcting his syntax and cadence. She made him cakes and meat pies, and every Thursday he came home with flowers from the market on King Stanisław Street on his walk back from the university. A panic rose up in him that he would never see her again. Neither of them. That they would all die in this place. He prayed they would be all right. Up ahead, he saw the line he was in being separated into two new ones. He sensed that in one he would live and in the other he would die. But it was too late for fear now, or for prayers.

Looking back and watching his papers scatter like dead leaves on that pile of bags and people's belongings, the small part of him that was still even capable of fear or hope felt nothing.

It had already died.

SEVEN

A black Opel pulled up to the curb at the Lisbon airport, and Peter Strauss climbed into the backseat, ducking out of the rain.

He was not wearing his officer's cap, nor, beneath his raincoat, his army captain's uniform. Only a sport jacket with flannel trousers, rumpled from the two-hour flight in from London. With his valise and leather briefcase, he might have been any businessman arriving who was trying to profit from the war, selling steel or food or buying Portuguese tungsten, as Lisbon was one of the last open and thriving centers of commerce in Europe during the war.

"Captain Strauss," the Swiss-born driver who worked with the War Refugee Committee greeted him, taking his bags. "I know you've had a long trip. Would you like to stop off at the hotel and freshen up?"

"Thanks," Strauss replied. He'd caught a diplomatic night flight to London, then spent two days absorbed with secret phone calls and cables in order to set up the meeting he was here to be part of. "But I'd just as soon get going if it's all the same."

"Very good." The driver put Strauss's bag in the front and climbed in behind the wheel. "Everyone's waiting. Have you ever been to Estoril?"

In about forty minutes, they reached the coast and arrived at the posh seaside resort, home to the glamorous casino where the displaced royalty of Europe wagered for exit visas in evening attire, mingling

39

with British and German spies. The car came to a stop in front of a tile-roofed, two-story home facing the sea behind a high iron gate and a stucco outer wall: 114 Rua do Mare. The villa could have belonged to any well-heeled Portuguese family seeking seclusion and a pleasing view of the sea, but, in fact, it was the summer retreat of the Catholic archbishop. The high walls and remote location, far away from the spy nests in Lisbon and before the summer crowds, made it the ideal location for the men Strauss had flown to meet.

The front gate opened and the Opel came to a stop in the courtyard. A large, Florentine-styled fountain stood in the center. Someone came out to meet him, a short, neatly tailored man with a goatee who introduced himself as Ricardo Oliva, from the International Refugee Committee, and escorted Strauss down a vaulted loggia into the main house. In a large room dominated by a huge stone fireplace and a candled chandelier, a small crowd was waiting for him. The first to greet him was the archbishop's adjunct, a balding man of about fifty in a black frock and crucifix, who introduced himself as Monsignor Correa.

"Thank you for arranging this," Strauss said, shaking the clergyman's hand. "And please convey my government's thanks to His Eminence for offering the privacy of his home."

"Privacy is the only weapon we have today," the monsignor said, nodding, "but soon, it is our hope that such vile business be seen by the world and out in the light of day. In fact, there are some things more pressing than political or religious neutrality. Even in the midst of war."

"That is our hope too," Strauss said to him.

He went around the room and met various representatives from the refugee groups from Bern and Stockholm, two bearded Orthodox rabbis who spoke no English and whom Strauss greeted with the traditional Hebrew *"Shalom, rebi,"* and finally Alexander Katzner of the Jewish World Congress, whose efforts in trying to smuggle Jews out of occupied territory was well known back home. They all seemed to meet Strauss with great anticipation.

40

"We are glad you're here." Katzner greeted him warmly. "It is time that the world see what we've known has been going on for some time."

"Your president must now see," one of the refugee committee representatives said, "what we've been facing. And then act."

"Please, please . . . Leave our guest to get his bearings. Would you care for something to eat, Captain?" Monsignor Correa took Strauss by the elbow. "I know it's been a long trip."

Strauss thanked him but politely declined. "I'm eager to get going, if it's all the same."

"By all means. I understand. This way, then . . ." The monsignor opened an adjacent double door and led Strauss into a spacious, formal dining room. "They are waiting for you in here."

Seated at the long, wooden table with two large, gold candelabras in the center were Rudolf Vrba and Alfred Wetzler.

The two men were dark and thin, dressed in suits that seemed way too baggy, and remained seated as everyone came in the room. They had been out of the camp for only a few weeks and their hair was only beginning to grow in. Wetzler, whom Strauss recognized from photographs, had a small mustache. His Czech compatriot, Vrba, was smoking, seemingly nervously, and remained seated. A Czech member of the War Refugee Committee acted as translator.

First, Strauss shook their hands and congratulated them on their brave escape. "You both showed remarkable courage. All the world owes you a great debt." A cup of black coffee was put in front of him with a piece of hard sugar.

The Czech translated and the two men nodded, mildly enthusiastic.

"This is their report," Katzner, of the Jewish World Congress, said, pushing a thick sheaf of papers in front of Strauss. "But I think you are already familiar with the important details. For a long time it's been no secret what's been going on. What everyone here wants to know is, what is the delay with a response? This is not war the Nazis are waging against us. It's murder."

"I'm a military man, not a diplomat," Strauss said, "but I want to assure you that even the president has been made aware."

"You are a Jew yourself, are you not?" a Swede from the refugee board inquired of him.

Strauss nodded. "Yes."

"So you must see this clearer than anyone. Thousands upon thousands are dying every day. How does your government not act?"

"The U.S. government is interested in all lives threatened under the Nazi regime," Strauss said, though the words sat like an undigested piece of meat in his gut and had a hollow ring. It was clear the people here looked on Strauss's visit as a sign that the kind of military response they were all pleading for would soon follow. That the United States, home to the most Jews in the world outside of Europe, would send in an air strike against the camps or bomb the train tracks leading in. That his visit brought long-sought hope at last from the Allies.

But that wasn't why he was here.

Nodding almost apologetically, Strauss turned to Vrba and Wetzler. He reached in his briefcase and took out a folder. "There is a photograph I'd like to show you both." The Czech translated his words. Strauss took out an eight-by-ten photograph and slid it across the table. First to Rudolf Vrba, who took a sideways glance at it. "Do you recognize this man?"

As the Czech translated, the escapee looked at Strauss without giving any recognizable sign.

"At the camp," Strauss explained further. "Have you seen him? Is he there?"

Vrba slowly picked up the photograph of Alfred Mendl.

Vrba had short dark hair, a flat nose, and sharp, low eyebrows. His mouth had an upward curve on one side, giving him an almost impish quality. While Strauss waited, he took a long look. Finally Vrba looked back at him.

"Sorry." He shook his head, speaking in halting English.

Strauss felt a stab of disappointment. This was his last hope. Many people's last hope. A year's work hung in the balance. He passed the photo over to Wetzler. He had more of a studious face, with a high forehead and bushy eyebrows. He studied the photograph for a long time, but then slid it back across the table with kind of an indifferent shrug.

"Please," Strauss urged him. "Look at it again. It's important."

Wetzler glanced at it again almost perfunctorily and then reached onto the table for a Portuguese cigarette. As he did so, his sleeve bunched up and Strauss's eyes were drawn to the bluish numbers written into the underside of the escapee's wrist. Wetzler lit the cigarette and took a drag. Then he spoke for a long time in Czech, never once taking his eyes off Strauss.

"Mr. Wetzler wants to know . . ." the Czech finally translated, "what has this man done that deserves your attention above all others? Hundreds of innocent people die every day. Women, children. As soon as they get off the trains they are stripped of the possessions and gassed. They are all good people . . ." Wetzler spoke quickly, and the translator did his best to keep up. "They all lead worthwhile lives. Who is *this* man, that you travel all this way and need to know if he is there?"

The escapee slid the photograph back across the table, as if awaiting a reply.

"There is no answer," Strauss said, meeting the man's eyes. "There is only urgency. Though I understand your plea. And I will take it back with me to the highest levels of my government. You have my promise."

The escapee sniffed, flicking an ash into the ashtray. His eyes darted toward his friend, Vrba, as if there were a kind of silent agreement between them. Waiting a moment, Strauss went to place the photo of Mendl back in his briefcase.

Then Rudolf Vrba suddenly said in heavily accented English, but with a begrudging nod: "He is there. Your man. Of course, that was two months ago. Hundreds die every day. So who knows for sure . . . ?"

Strauss felt a surge of optimism run through him. *He is there.* These were the very words he had traveled across the ocean to hear. "How can you be sure?" he asked the Czech. "There must have been thousands of faces there. And he must look different now. Everything has changed." Recollection was one thing, but Strauss needed confirmation. Something firm.

Vrba shrugged. "He was some kind of professor, is it not right? At least that was what people called him."

"Yes." Strauss nodded, his blood galloping now. "He was."

"And besides, there is always LR seven . . ."

"*LR seven* . . . ?" Strauss looked back in confusion. He jotted the number down on a pad. "What is that?"

"Lower right molar. I studied dentistry back home. They brought him to me once. For an abscess." His impish mouth curved into a smile. "In the camp, I never looked at faces too closely. But I never forget a tooth."

EIGHT

That night, Strauss sat at the bar at the Hotel Sao Mamede, on a dark side street, a world away from the noise and festive life of the casino. Even farther from the Pallácio Estoril Hotel and its bustling, wood-paneled bar where German and British spies mingled over cognac and where everyone who stepped in was sure to end up on someone's list.

There was only one other couple, drinking Aperol and nuzzling in a quiet corner.

Here no one would notice him. No desk clerk would look through his messages. Strauss read over the cable he had just sent back to Washington, D.C.

It was to a telex number established solely to get his message into Colonel Donovan's hands unobserved. Mostly, it described the mundane details of his trip. Clients seen, orders pending. An application to the Department of Minerals. All fake, of course. Made up.

It was only the message's last line that carried any meaning.

"You're not going to help us, are you?" Alexander Katzner appealed to him after Vrba and Wetzler's admission, the real purpose of Strauss's visit now made clear.

No. I cannot.

Strauss had studied Torah until his teens. His father's family still had relatives in Europe. He thought of the numbers he'd seen etched into Wetzler's wrist. If they would send in planes to bomb the fucking sites, he would man the first plane himself.

The barman came up to him.

"Scotch," Strauss ordered. "Whatever's best." He wasn't normally a drinker, but tonight, thinking of what Donovan's reaction would be, a drink seemed the right thing.

Hundreds of innocent people die every day, Wetzler said to him. *What has this man done that he deserves your attention above all others?*

"How do you not feel it yourself?" one of the war refugee officials looked in Strauss's eyes. "As a Jew?"

Yes, he felt it. How it ached him that he could not answer.

It just wasn't why he was here.

The barman brought his scotch. Strauss downed it in a gulp. He felt his heart light up. He smiled, imagining his boss's response, three thousand miles away, when he received the news.

He ordered one more.

An abscess . . . Strauss had to laugh and shook his head. At least now they knew where he was. In a place more hell than living. Now all they had to do was get him out.

Fishing looks promising here, he had ended the cable. *Get your pole ready. Catfish is in the pond.*

NINE

Roosevelt stared at Strauss, who set his papers on the table. "We're talking about this man that's in Auschwitz, Captain . . . You said there was another way?"

"Yes." Strauss glanced at his boss, Donovan. The OSS chief nodded for him to go on. "If we can't buy him out, or can no longer barter for him," the captain cleared his throat, "then I suggest we simply take him."

At first no one said a thing.

"Take him . . . ?" Treasury Secretary Morgenthau looked at him as if he hadn't heard correctly. "You mean just go in there? Into a death camp guarded by a thousand Germans. In the middle of occupied Poland?"

Strauss felt the dubious reaction. This was absolutely the biggest stage he had ever played on. *And maybe the last*, the thought occurred to him. He looked back at the treasury secretary, one of the president's closest confidants, a man he knew he would need to convince, and nodded firmly. "Yes, that's what I'm suggesting, sir."

Strauss turned toward Henry Stimson as the air in the room grew thick with skepticism. "You say you need this man, don't you, Mr. Secretary?"

FDR's secretary of war nodded grudgingly. "He was a professor. In Lvov. Electromagnetic physics. He's one of only two people in the

47

world who has this precise expertise. Without him," he turned to the president, "I'm afraid our people out West feel we would fall further behind."

It was the first time Strauss had heard that phrase, "out West," but it was clear it was something big. Word had filtered out within the intelligence network that they were close to delivering a weapon of decisive magnitude.

"You say he's one of two . . . ?" Roosevelt kept his gaze on Stimson.

"Yes. But according to General Groves," the OSS chief cut in, "the only one *not* currently working for the Germans in *their* own uranium experiments," Donovan clarified.

"I see." Secret scientific experiments on nuclear fission to produce a chain reaction capable of creating a weapon a thousand times more powerful than the world had ever seen were racing forward on both sides of the Atlantic, in the United States, at Los Alamos, New Mexico—"out West"—headed up by physicist Robert Oppenheimer and his military overseer, General Leslie Groves. In this room, only Roosevelt and his secretary of war knew the real stakes of this race and that the outcome of the war would likely go to the winner.

"So in that case," Captain Strauss looked around the table, "that's precisely what I propose we do."

"You mean a raid?" Now it was the president's turn to question him. "Into Nazi territory? Just send in a squad. Disable the guards. Find him and whisk him out?"

"No, Mr. President," the OSS captain explained. He opened a folder and took out a map, a rendering of the camp Vrba and Wetzler had drawn themselves. "A raid would be impossible. The camp is heavily guarded. Plus, there are additional detachments of troops nearby. It can't be done by force, at least not that quickly. There are thousands of prisoners in there. I'm told they are identified by numbers, not even names. I saw this, in Lisbon." He held out his arm. "Numbers burned into the prisoners' wrists."

Roosevelt winced in disgust, then turned to Donovan. "Then what is your plan?"

"One man." The OSS chief took Vrba's map. "We drop him in at night nearby. We link him up with local partisans, whom we've already made contact with. We can sneak him into the camp. Then he has seventy-two hours to find his mark. And get them both out."

"*A single man?* It would be like finding a needle in a haystack in that place," Henry Stimson declared. "*If* he's even still alive."

"Yes. I agree." Donovan nodded soberly. "That is a big 'if.' The odds would not be good. But the stakes of not having this man, as I understand it, are not good either."

"*One man . . .* " Morgenthau said out loud what they were all thinking. "Who would even undertake this mission? You read what atrocities are going on in there. If he's caught, or can't get out, it's suicide. And he *will* be caught, Colonel Donovan, be sure of that. And then what?" He turned to FDR. "It'll jeopardize all our larger negotiations at this time. Eichmann himself is set to barter for thousands of Jewish lives. And you can't send in a trained operative. He'll stick out in there like a sore thumb. In minutes. He'll have to speak the language, look the part . . ."

"We think we have someone," Peter Strauss interrupted, opening another file. He passed around a photo.

It was of a man with dark, Semitic features. In his twenties. A gaunt, narrow face, dark eyes.

"He's not an operative. He's an intelligence lieutenant here in D.C.," Strauss said. "Currently decoding German and Polish cables. His name is Blum. Nathan."

"He's Jewish?" Morgenthau asked, picking the photo up and staring closely at it.

"Yes."

Stimson looked at the OSS captain with incredulity. "You're going to sneak a desk-bound translator into a labor camp in enemy territory on one of the most vital undercover missions of the war? Are you mad?" The war secretary's disdain for what he took to be the recklessness of many of the OSS's ventures was well known in the intelligence community.

"He's not just a translator. He came here from Warsaw in 1941," Strauss explained. "He snuck out of the Krakow ghetto and risked his life to carry a revered religious document to safety in Sweden. He spent a year at Northwestern, where he was the school's lightweight boxing champion, then he enlisted. He's fluent in four languages, including Polish and German."

"And you think he'll do this?" Roosevelt looked at the photo and then handed it back to Strauss. "Go back to the very place he risked his life to escape from? On a wild-goose chase to find this one man?"

"We think there's a good chance he will," Colonel Donovan cut in. "He's already asked to do something more."

"Oh, this definitely classifies as more." Stimson snorted derisively.

"Plus, there's one other thing . . ."

"And that is . . . ?" Roosevelt's war-heavy eyes fell on him.

"His entire family was killed by the Germans six months after he was here." Donovan looked the president in the eyes. "According to those who know him, he feels he left them there to die."

TEN

Nathan Blum sat at his desk, one of a row of twelve, in the basement of the C building at OSS headquarters in Washington, D.C. A stack of cables, some in Polish, others in Russian and Ukrainian, often in code, from partisans in occupied Poland and Ukraine had come in. As a Grade C junior analyst, it was Blum's job to translate them from the original and then pass them on, sorted by priority, to the appropriate personnel in his department, which was known inside the building as UE-5, or Underground Activities in Europe, the "5" for Poland, and was devoted to contact and coordination with insurgent activities there.

That morning a series of photographs had arrived in the sealed pouch from London. They were of several large pieces of debris that had been picked up by the Polish resistance from the Bug River near the town of Siemiatycze in eastern Poland. Two weeks prior, they had intercepted cables detailing how two key German scientists from the secret missile laboratory at Peenemünde were headed to that area of Poland, where apparently the Nazis had set up some kind of secret testing facility. Now Blum had a sense why. Two days ago, partisans near Siemiatycze had reported a flash in the early morning sky, which then spiraled back to earth—clearly the failed test launch of some kind of secret missile. Combining the reports, Blum was certain these photos weren't of just any debris. This was the real thing, he felt for sure, likely a test flight of the Nazis' rumored guided weapon, the V-2, which they would be able to launch from the mainland against a defenseless England. The actual debris pieces were now in the hands of the Polish underground, awaiting transport to another location where they could be transported to England and gone over by experts, an action known as Operation Most, which meant "bridge" in Polish.

The images Blum was staring at could turn out to be one of the biggest intelligence breakthroughs of the war.

Though he was barely twenty-three, and the OSS's principal day-to-day liason with the AK, the Armia Krajowa—the Polish resistance group that was actively engaged in a war of sabotage and assassination behind enemy lines, pretty much making life on the Nazis' collapsing Russian front a bloody hell—Blum had spent the last year in this musty basement, aching to do more. Only three years earlier he had been a student at the university in his hometown of Krakow studying economics while continuing to practice Liszt and Chopin on the piano to please his mother, though he much preferred the more contemporary music of Fats Waller and the American jazz artists who had taken the continent by storm. He was a decent player, though never in the same league as his younger sister, Leisa, was on the clarinet; everyone said she would one day play with the national orchestra. His father owned the finest hat store in Krakow, on Florianska Street, with a small factory upstairs. They sold homburgs, Borsalinos, fedoras, even the smaller tweed Alpine hats so popular with the Austrians and Germans these days. Even rabbinical hats. Hats had no country, his father always said. Before the Nazis came, they lived not in the Jewish Quarter but in a spacious apartment on Grodzka Street near the Mariacki Cathedral. His father's customers were businessmen, government officials, professors, rabbis, even members of exiled royal families. They had music in their life, and art, and friends from all segments of Polish society. They spoke Polish, not Yiddish. They didn't even keep kosher.

His mother always told the story of her visiting Aunt Rosa, who complained, "I know it doesn't matter to you, but couldn't you at least put out a different knife for buttering the bread and cutting the meat?"

To which his mother replied, "But don't you know, good aunt, the meat is fried in butter to begin with?"

Their poor aunt went pale.

That was all before 1941, of course, when all Jewish businesses were forced to close and Jews of all commitment were relocated to the ghetto.

While at the university, Blum joined the free political youth movement there. He even helped publish an antifascist newsletter, *He-Haluc HaLohem, The Fighting Pioneer*. Then, in October, Jews were told they could no longer study there. His father's store was looted and marked with a big yellow star, and they were all given armbands and patches which they were forced to wear. Then they were made to close, after sixty years in business. For two generations they had sold hats to the finest gentlemen in Poland. In the ghetto, they had to move into a cramped, run-down apartment on Jozefinska Street with their cousins, the Herzlichs, twelve of them sharing four small rooms. Blum became what was known as a ferret inside the walls, taking out mail regularly and passing along family messages, even money for safekeeping, bringing in food and needed medicine, and even guns. His friend from the university, Jakob Epstein, grew up in that area and showed Blum all the underground sewers and tunnels, the doors between buildings no one knew, secret hiding places if they were chased, even the chasms deep underneath the synagogue and the passageways over the rooftops, until he knew them as well as any local thief. To be captured smuggling something in meant certain death as well as harsh repercussions for his family. Blum's main asset was his innocent face and trusting way about him, masking an inner resolve.

Once, to avoid capture, he had to hide underneath the chassis of a German troop truck at the very moment a raid was under way and then roll out and duck behind trash cans as the truck pulled away, troops clinging to the side. Another time he was stopped outside the gate with packets of money and letters sewn into his rucksack and he produced a forged pass that said he was a worker at Struhl, a German sugar factory in the outside sector. "You look a little young to be a worker." The guard regarded him skeptically. "I'm not the manager," Blum replied, never betraying his fear, "only the floor sweeper." They let him pass. And once he was shot at as he fled across a rooftop; fortunately his arm was merely grazed, a reminder of how real the danger was, though his mother treated it as if it was a mortal wound.

In the spring of 1943, the ghetto was closed for good and the treatment of Jews and his family worsened. A sense of uncertainty prevailed, rumors of executions in Lodz and Warsaw. Mass deportations to places unknown, where no one was ever heard from again. A perpetual sadness became etched into his father's face. Everything his own father and he had built was now lost. All the government customers he'd had over the years, relationships with some of the wealthiest families in Krakow, who now wouldn't even return his letters. One day Blum's friend Epstein was pulled from his apartment and taken away to Gestapo headquarters in the Dom Slaski. No one ever heard from him again. Blum's mother pleaded for him to stop; it was only a matter of time for him, Nathan, to be caught. Soon after, Rabbi Morgenstern came to his father. Krakow's main synagogue had an important Talmud dating back to the twelfth century, with a commentary written by a student of the venerable Maimonides himself. The holy tract had to survive at all costs, the elders of the temple agreed. And who was the best prepared to smuggle it out and deliver it for safekeeping into the right hands?

Blum.

He didn't want to leave, to abandon his parents and his sister, who had always been his closest friend. Rumors of mass deportations spread like wildfire through the ghetto. Who would watch out for his family? Who was better able to take care of them? Some of his friends spoke of remaining in the ghetto and putting up a fight.

But his father insisted that this Talmud was a treasure as great as in any synagogue in Europe. And what hope was there to remain here, except for Nathan to end up like his friend, Jakob, taken by the Gestapo. No doubt dead. It will happen one day for sure, he insisted to Blum. "Then where will your mother be?" Or to be taken off in one of the mass deportations. Then what had he gained by staying? "At least this way there is hope." The underground had a way of getting Blum north. First, on a milk truck; then up the Vistula on a barge to the port city of Gdynia; and then across the Baltic to Sweden on a freighter. It was a great honor, his father said, to be chosen for this. In the end his father's pressure wore Blum down. Against his wishes, he agreed. It took a month, but Blum delivered the tract that was bound and wrapped like a sausage into the hands of a Jewish refugee agency in Stockholm. His mother's side had a cousin who lived in Chicago who put up the money for his transit to the United States, and so Blum, barely twenty, without speaking a word of English, but with a year and a half of avoiding the Germans, made the journey across the Atlantic.

English came quickly, watching the cinema, taught by his cousins; he had a skill for languages. The following year he was accepted by Northwestern University, where he went for a year and picked up his old subjects. Then news arrived that in retaliation for the shooting of a Gestapo officer, the Germans came into the ghetto and marched everyone from Blum's family's building into the square, his father, mother, and sister among them, and shot them. His cousins the Herzlichs as well. Forty for one, they called it. Forty lives, worthless Jewish ones, for every German. The smuggled-out letter that reached them spoke of his father's bloody body hung up with several of the other men for days, unburied, putrefying in the public square, as a reminder to anyone else who harbored the same idea. Isidor Blum had been a gentle man whose only love in life, besides his family, was helping to choose the perfect hat for each head, Germans and Austrians among them. And poor Leisa, whom everyone said would one day play with the Polish National Orchestra. She didn't even know about politics. All she knew was Mozart, and her scales. Blum was inconsolable at the thought of her. He would miss her most of all.

All he could think of was that if he had remained there, he would never have let them go outside. He would have seen the trucks pull up and found a way: the narrow passage out of their old building he had used after curfew a hundred times: through the basement, to the alley that led to the shirt factory next door and then out onto Lwowska Street. Or onto the roof, if the Germans were already in the building, and across to 10 Herzl, then down the fire stairs to the alley. If he was there, he would have warned them never to go out into that square. He had seen firsthand how the Germans dealt with retaliation.

After the news, life at the university no longer meant anything to him. He was in a strange place, studying subjects that meant nothing to him, in a new tongue. Everyone he loved was gone. After Pearl Harbor, all the students were signing up anyway, so Blum did too, hoping to be the first to march back into Poland, to proudly rid his country of the hated *szkopy*, German swine. But because of his language skills, he was placed in intelligence. It was a great honor, he was told again. This is the best way to serve.

A year later, he was still there.

There was an outfit that was being assembled: young soldiers, mostly Jews of German descent, who were being trained in intelligence at Fort Ritchie in western Maryland, who would go ashore as part of the invasion (which everyone knew was coming) and aid in the interrogation of German prisoners and establish contact with local partisans. Blum had already put in for a transfer with his superior officer. Here he was just sitting in a basement, using skills he had mastered as a child. Stamping and translating papers and transferring them upstairs. There at least he could put his life on the line for his family. The feeling had never stopped haunting him for a day: that he was the one who had left, while all those he loved had remained behind and died. He ached to do something that really mattered before the war came to an end. Otherwise he would see the images of his dead family in his mind's eye for the rest of his life. He asked and pushed until he made himself a nuisance. He was told his file was being looked at. He should know any day.

But that morning . . . He put the photos of the debris in from London in a manila envelope marked URGENT and sent it up channels. *Attention: Captain Greer.* Inwardly, it gave him pride that Polish combatants were the ones who had put their lives on the line to find it.

He was sure the right people would be going over them "with a fine-tooth comb," as they said here, within a day. Then he took out the rest of the day's incoming cables. From Pilava. Lodz. Troop movements sighted on the Ukrainian frontier. A bridge over the Bug River blown, blocking the German retreat routes. Warsaw in flames. It had taken a while but the Poles were finally fighting.

His mind went to his parents the day they had sent him off on his new journey.

"I don't want to leave," he had said to his father. "You need me to remain here with you. Who else will watch over you?"

"God will watch over us," his father, who wasn't religious, said. "God always protects the righteous, right?" He winked like he was letting Blum in on an inside joke. "Especially," he said, "if he is wearing the proper hat."

His father removed his hat, a prized homburg that his own father had worn, and placed it on Nathan's head, brushing the felt and tilting the angle slightly, just right. His father always said you could judge a man's character more by his choice of hat than by any other aspect.

"He hasn't deserted us yet, Nathan." He patted his son's shoulders. "Now let's go. To the rebi, shall we? Before curfew." He stopped and looked at Nathan for a long time.

"What?"

"When I see you next you may finally have yourself a beard," his father said, his eyes misting slightly. "But you will never be more of a man to me than you are today."

They hugged, and Blum knew for certain as he felt his father's arms around him that he would never see any of them again.

"*Blum* . . . "

His thoughts rushed back. The duty officer, a big, broad-shouldered redhead named Sloan, who had played football at the University of Virginia, stepped up to his desk.

Blum stood up. "Sir."

"Take a break. You're wanted over at the Main Hall."

"Main Hall . . . ?" That's where all the bigwigs worked. Blum had been there only once, the day he arrived, to the administrative offices to receive his assignment and sign the confidentiality papers. He felt a surge in his blood. "Personnel . . . ?" he asked, certain that his transfer to Fort Ritchie had finally come through.

"Not quite." The duty officer chuckled knowingly. "The Big Man wants to see you upstairs."

"The Big Man . . . ?" Blum looked back as if the duty officer must be joking. *"Me?"*

"Look smart, Lieutenant." The big redhead nodded and tossed him his cap. "Colonel Donovan."

ELEVEN

A female JG led Blum, cap in hand, past rows of secretaries and chattering telexes, into a suite of carpeted offices on the third floor.

"Wait here." The female duty officer knocked on the door of the corner office and put her head in. "Lieutenant Blum is here, sir."

A voice said, "Have him come in, please."

Not fully believing, Blum stepped into the large, red-carpeted office with a substantial oak desk flanked by an American and an Allied command flag and a photograph of President Roosevelt on the wall.

Colonel William Donovan, whom Blum had only even seen a couple of times on visits to the pen and whose hand he had shaken once as the Big Man passed his desk, stood up from behind it. He was of medium height, large-chested, with a strong Irish nose, a solid chin like a prizefighter, and narrow, deep-set eyes. Everyone knew he had won the Congressional Medal of Honor for acts of valor in the previous war, acts that had earned him the nickname "Wild Bill." At the long conference table, another officer stood up as well. He was shorter, thin, with dark hair that was slightly receding already, though he had a young face with thin lips.

Blum had no idea how the person responsible for the U.S. intelligence network for all the war even knew who he was.

"Lieutenant Blum, is that right . . . ?" The white-haired Donovan came from around his desk.

"*Sir.*" Blum stepped up hesitantly, pushing back the urge to glance behind him in case there was another officer with the same name standing there.

"Lieutenant Nathan Blum, assigned to the Fourth Division, UE-5 . . . ?" the OSS chief rattled off, seeing Blum's indecision. "I have asked the right officer up here, haven't I?"

"Yes, sir. That is me."

"Then relax, Lieutenant. Why don't you take a seat over here." Donovan motioned to the long conference table where the captain stood on the other side. "Please . . ." Colonel Donovan said, indicating a chair near the head. Then he pulled out his own chair at the head of the table and sat. "Cup of coffee?"

His legs feeling slightly rubbery, Blum took a seat. "Please."

"How do you like it, Lieutenant?" the Big Man asked. A secretary came in with a tray and put it down at the far end of the long table.

"Black, please, sir."

"Me too. Since I was a kid. There are many things that can get an old Irishman into trouble, but, in my book, coffee, and as much as you can drink it, isn't one of them . . ."

Blum, who had been shot at before he was twenty and who had made his way past checkpoints after curfew with Germans who wouldn't blink to execute him on the spot, had never felt his heart beat as rapidly as it did now as the man responsible for America's vast intelligence network addressed him face-to-face. His eyes took in the office's impressive surroundings.

"You can relax, Lieutenant. All reports are that you're doing a first-class job down there. This is Captain Strauss." He nodded to the thin, dark-featured officer. "He's been handling some operations for me. I see a request in your file for a transfer, to that new outfit they're putting together up at Fort Ritchie, boys of European Jewish descent . . ."

"Yes, sir," Blum replied. He still felt a slight hesitation when addressing someone of stature and education in his new tongue. "I'm happy with what I do here, sir. It's just that . . . that I feel I can best serve—"

60

"No need to explain, son," the colonel interrupted him. "That's a good outfit they're putting together up there, and I have no doubt you'd be a real asset."

"Thank you, sir." The secretary poured the coffee.

"It's just that Captain Strauss and I are putting something together too. I've spoken with your superior officers and they tell me you've been quite open with your desire to do something . . . how shall we say it . . . ? Something more."

"Yes, sir. That is correct," Blum answered, his heart picking up a beat in anticipation.

"You already *are* doing something, son. My people tell me you're one of the most capable translators we have here. That's already important work," he nodded, "and it all helps the war effort. In fact, I've read through some of the communiqués you've passed on."

"That's very kind of you, sir." Inwardly, Blum felt a surge of pride. "Wild Bill" Donovan actually knew of him.

"Yes, the captain here was just briefing me . . . About your family. Back in Poland."

Blum glanced at the other officer, who had so far remained silent. He assumed that what had motivated him to enlist was in his file. "Yes, they were killed in my hometown of Krakow," he said in as matter-of-fact a tone as he could manage. "A Gestapo officer was shot in the ghetto and so they took everyone in my family's building outside and executed them in retribution, right in the square. 'Forty to one,' they called it."

"Yes." Colonel Donovan nodded somberly. "I'm afraid I know all that. My condolences," he added. "My father died young too. Though of natural causes. That's quite a burden for anyone to carry. A man of your age . . ." He took a sip of coffee.

"My sister too," Blum said. "She played the clarinet. She was very good. Everyone said one day she would play for the Polish National Orchestra. But that was all a while back. A different world. Anyway, thank you, sir."

Donovan put down his cup and looked at Blum. Almost looked *through* him, Blum felt, as if he was studying him with those hard, deep-set Irish eyes. Even more—measuring him in some way. The impressive surroundings, the enormous desk and long table, the brass in the room, the official flags, all made Blum feel almost small.

"I see you made your way here, to America, completely on your own," the colonel said.

"Yes, sir," Blum confirmed. He was starting to get the sense that this was not about his transfer at all. "But with help. The Armia Krajowa helped me to Gdynia. Up north . . ."

"The Ar-nia Krajora . . . ?" Donovan questioned, mangling the Polish like some rawboned Texan cowboy trying to speak Spanish Blum recalled from a film.

"It means the Home Army. The Polish underground. From there a Swedish diplomat arranged for transit to Stockholm. I have a cousin in Chicago, and he arranged for me to—"

"I'm quite familiar with the AK, Lieutenant," the OSS chief let him know.

"Of course, sir," Blum said.

"So why *you* . . . ?" Donovan pushed back in his chair, his khaki uniform jacket decorated with several ribbons for rank and valor. "There must have been a million young men as yourself with an urge to get out of Dodge."

"Get out of Dodge, sir . . . ?" Blum looked at him. "I'm sorry, I'm not sure I—"

"Just an expression, son. It means get out of town. Fast. It's from a Western."

"I like Westerns as well. I'll have to see that one." Blum saw the Big Man was still awaiting his answer. "I was asked to deliver an important package to safety. An historic text. The Talmud from our temple. It's a collection of laws and interpretations, from the Torah . . ." This time Donovan merely smiled, glancing toward Strauss, indicating he knew what the Talmud was as well. "It was written in the twelfth century by a famous rabbi. But for the record, sir, I did not ask to."

"Didn't ask to *what*, son?" the OSS chief said back.

"I didn't ask to leave. I wanted to stay and do what I could there. And take care of my family."

"It was suicide to stay there, son, given the chance to get out. You know that now, don't you?"

"Yes, I know that." Blum glanced toward the quiet captain, Strauss, wondering if he might be Jewish too. "But in any event, that would not have changed my mind. It was my family, sir. I'm sure you understand."

"Of course. I understand perfectly. Nonetheless, you have to have a strong nerve, aren't I right? Your file says you were a pretty good ferret back in your days there. In Krakow. That takes a load of courage. Do you have a strong nerve, son?"

Blum shrugged, feeling the colonel's eyes fixed on him. Still, it wasn't something you said about yourself. "There have been many times in my life, sir, since the Nazis came, where to survive, I've had to do what was necessary."

"Yes, I think I understand what you mean." Donovan nodded. "Each of us has to give of ourselves in some way. Ways we never imagined. That put you to the test." Everyone knew the Big Man had single-handedly held off a German machine gun position while wounded several times, saving his entire unit. He flipped through Blum's file for another moment, then placed it back on the table. "So we're prepared to give you that chance, son, what you've been asking for, if you're up for it . . ."

"The chance for what, sir?" Blum looked back at him, sure that somewhere he had missed their meaning.

"To do something more. Isn't that what you asked for, Lieutenant?" The OSS chief took one more sip of coffee, then put down the cup. "As you said, to do what is necessary."

TWELVE

They refilled their cups as Captain Strauss, whom Blum was now certain was a Jew himself, likely of German descent, mapped out why they had called him there.

The captain began a little vaguely. "As you know, Lieutenant, Poland is an extremely unforgiving place now . . . to be a Jew. And then to ask someone, someone who has been able to get himself out, at no small risk to himself, and then start to build a new life . . . to consider, at great personal sacrifice for his new country . . . perhaps even the world . . ." Strauss cleared his throat and looked at Blum. "There would, of course, be no negative consequences should you feel that what we're about to ask of you is too much."

Both Donovan and Strauss had their eyes fixed on Blum. There was an extended silence in the room.

"You want me . . . to go *back*?" Blum said, as it finally became clear to him just what they were asking.

"Not just go back . . ." the captain said. He got up with his file and came around the table, pulling up the chair next to Blum. "We want you to locate someone there for us. In Poland. And bring him back out for us."

"Out of *Poland*?" Blum continued to stare, not quite believing. "You know how difficult that would be."

The captain nodded. "I'm afraid what we're proposing is even a bit trickier than that, Lieutenant . . ." He took a breath and opened his file. "No doubt you've heard of the labor camps over there?"

"Of course, but please forgive me, Captain, these are labor camps in name only. Word is, people are shipped there and never heard from ever again. Families, entire towns. In fact, these are death camps," Blum stated. "I think we both know that."

The captain didn't reply, but in his knowing nod and Donovan's continued steady stare, it became clear to Blum precisely what they wanted. "You want to send me back to Poland. To one of those . . . *camps*?" he asked.

"To a place called Auschwitz." Colonel Donovan took the lead. "I believe Oswiecim is the town's actual name. You've heard of it?"

Maybe not by that specific name, Blum nodded in the way when something terribly grave and unutterable is better left unsaid. But the whispers from Jewish enclaves all through Europe were rampant with what was happening in places like that—places so dark, so filled with evil and death, it stretched the mind to even believe they could be true. "Yes. I've heard."

"We need someone who's familiar with this area and who speaks the language. And who would . . ." Strauss looked at him. "Fit in."

"Fit in . . . ?" Blum repeated, still not sure what they were asking of him.

"What we're proposing, Lieutenant," the man known as "Wild Bill" Donovan leaned forward and set his deep-set eyes on Blum, "is to sneak you into there, inside the camp, I'm saying, and for you to bring someone back out."

"Into the camp?" Blum stared back in consternation. "*Who . . . ?*"

"A fair question." Captain Strauss took over for his boss. "But I'm afraid we just can't share that with you right now." He removed a map from his file, a blown-up rendering of the area surrounding the camp. "We can drop you in by plane. At night. *Here.*" He pointed to a spot. "It's about twenty kilometers from the camp. Have you ever jumped, Nathan? I didn't see it in your file."

"From a plane? No." Blum shook his head. "Only in training."

"No matter. We'll take you through it. You'll only have to do it once. On the ground, we can rendezvous with the local resistance. We know how to set this up. We can get you inside. As part of a daily work crew. That's the easy part. Apparently local workmen enter and leave the grounds routinely."

"You are certain of this?" Blum pressed. They made it sound as if it was like taking a trip on the Chicago rail line: First you take the L to Lake Street, then you switch to the Southside line, to Garfield, and then . . .

"As you might imagine . . ." Donovan leaned forward with the hint of a wry smile, "getting someone *into* a place like Auschwitz is not generally the issue."

"Yes, of course," Blum said, betraying that same smile. "And you can get me out? With this person? And then back?" His mind raced through how very risky this would be. Just getting into Poland itself would not be easy. This deep, behind enemy lines. The jump alone terrified him. And then what if he was unable to meet up with the local resistance? He'd be stranded there. Alone. Or if he was unable to find this man—even if he was able to get inside the camp. Or if the Germans saw through him. It would be certain death.

"Yes." Strauss nodded with conviction. "I believe we can."

"But once inside, you'd have to know you'll be completely on your own," Colonel Donovan said. "We'll construct your laborer's clothing to reverse into a camp uniform. We don't know for sure exactly where this person is inside the camp. To be frank, we don't know for sure that he's even still alive. He's fifty-seven, and not in the best of health. It's probably more like seventy-seven there. And from what we've heard . . ." the Big Man tapped his meaty index finger on the table and his mouth twisted into a frown, "it's not exactly a walk in the park in there."

"Yes, I've heard the rumors," Blum agreed. "May I smoke?"

"Please," Colonel Donovan said, and reached for an ashtray and pushed it toward him. Blum took out a pack of Luckys, tapped the top, and lit one up.

From his file, Strauss removed a crude, hand-drawn map and slid it across. "This is the camp." There was a double perimeter of wire, with several guard towers. Dozens of what appeared to be prisoners' quarters, called "blocks," all numbered. A women's camp was marked nearby. Blum's eyes were drawn to a small rectangular building that went by the sinister name *Crematorium*.

"We know he was there a month ago. We know how to get you in and out. What we need is for you to find him in there. We have an escape route that we're confident will work. We also have the names of several people on the inside, fellow prisoners, even guards, who you may be able to rely on. The thing is, you'll only have seventy-two hours, and no way to be in touch. The rescue plane will land precisely where it drops you, and only once. It can only remain on the ground for a few minutes, and then it will leave. You will have to be there."

Blum looked at them. "And if I'm not . . . ?"

"If you're not, then I'm afraid you're completely on your own." Colonel Donovan knitted his fingers together. "In a very hostile place. You miss that plane, there's no return ticket, son."

"Seventy-two hours . . ." Blum ran the prospects through his head. None made the outcome particularly rosy. "And if I find him, are you sure he will even come with me?"

"In truth, Lieutenant," Strauss sat back in his chair, "we're not completely sure of anything, on the inside. We don't know what health he is currently in. We don't even know for certain if he's even still alive."

"Yet you are willing to risk all this? To send me there?"

Strauss looked to Donovan. "Yes. We are."

"And you won't even tell me who this man is? Or why he is so important?"

"I'm afraid we can't," Colonel Donovan said. "Not right now. Right now, we can only show you a photograph. And obviously you'll have his name."

Blum tapped an ash on the edge of the ashtray. "I'd be risking my life for this one man," he said, looking at both their faces, "and you can't even tell me what he does?"

The captain nodded. "I'm afraid that's the case, Lieutenant. Yes."

Blum looked back at the map, taking it all in. He did speak the language and look the part. He would, as Strauss said, "fit in." And he

67

had escaped before. But what if he couldn't find the man? Or get himself out? He'd be stranded. His family was dead now. Many of his friends were likely dead as well. He had nothing left there. "How do you know all this?" Blum looked back up at them. "The layout. How to get in. This rendezvous you can set up with the local resistance."

Strauss pulled out two more photos from the file. "I was in Portugal a week ago. I met with these two men, who, one month ago, were able to escape from Auschwitz. The first to do so.

"Rudolf Vrba . . ." The captain placed a photo on the table. "And Alfred Wetzler. They're Czech. They told me everything. The layout of the camp. The routine there. The surrounding area. Prisoners inside who might prove helpful. Certain guards who can be bought. This map is theirs. It's accurate up to one month ago. It will work, Nathan. They've even agreed to assist on this mission."

Blum ran his eyes back over the map: the double perimeter of wire, the marked guard towers. They came to rest on the rectangular building. "And what did your two escapees tell you about what happens here?"

He pointed to the place marked *Crematorium*.

Strauss didn't answer at first. He eyed his boss. Then he nodded, kind of circumspectly. "Are you certain you want to know?"

"You are asking me to risk my life, to go back to a place I was blessed to get away from, to find a single person who you won't even tell me what he does. What is the expression here . . . ?" He looked at Donovan. "A needle in a haystack? So, yes, what happens here?" Blum placed his finger on the building again. "I think it is fair to know what I might face, if I go, should all these detailed preparations of yours not fully come together."

"I didn't mean as a part of this mission, Lieutenant," Strauss glanced at Donovan and said. "I meant," he cleared his throat, "as a Jew. People are gassed there." He moistened his lips. "In large numbers. Thousands. Tens of thousands. More. Then their bodies are burned. These are ovens." The captain pointed to the building on the map Nathan had asked about. "Though what I've now told you is in the strictest confidence and cannot be repeated, either to someone in uniform," he looked at Blum with the utmost seriousness in his eyes, "or not."

A hollowness rose up in Blum's gut. *Ovens.* He sat back, the color draining out of his face, nausea knotting inside him. *Gassed.* He drew in a deep breath through his nostrils, and let what Strauss had said out. *Thousands. Tens of thousands. More.* They'd all heard of such horrors. Killings on such an unprecedented scale. Still, everyone prayed it was only a rumor. Now he saw that it was all true. And he saw something else behind the gritted jaw and single-minded cast of the OSS captain's face. Sorrow. Pain. Etched into the fixed resolve in his eyes.

"*Bisse yid?*" Blum inquired, speaking in Yiddish. *Are you Jewish?*

Strauss paused only a moment. Then he nodded. "Yes."

"And this man . . ." Blum placed his index finger on the map of the camp. "This will not help any of them, these people who are already in here . . . ?"

"Not a single one, sadly." The captain shook his head, enough for Nathan to see that he had already asked that same question of himself.

Blum nodded, in the way a close relative might when told of grave family news, sinking back into his chair. "People being gassed . . . This man, who you won't tell me a thing about . . . Only seventy-two hours to find him . . . Otherwise, no chance of coming back . . ." He turned to Donovan. "If you don't mind me saying so, Colonel, you certainly know how to drive a hard bargain."

"Yes." The OSS chief chuckled back. "And that's not all, I'm afraid. We'll need your answer quickly."

"How quickly?" Blum put out his cigarette.

"Tomorrow." Donovan stood up.

"*Tomorrow* . . . ?" Blum's eyes widened in surprise.

The Big Man stood up, put his hand on Blum's shoulder, and smiled again. "I believe you're the one, Lieutenant, who expressed the interest in doing something more."

"Yes." Blum stood up too.

"You're doing a fine job, son," the colonel said, "for your new country. I'm sure that reassignment you put in to the Ritchie boys will be coming through at any time, if that's how you'd like it to go." He put out his hand. "You can only imagine how much we feel depends on this mission."

"Thank you, sir," Blum replied. The Big Man's hand was firm and rough. "But I do have one question, if I may."

"Of course. Go ahead." His hand was still wrapped in Donovan's.

"This man . . . If I get him out. Will it save lives or cost them, in the end?"

"In the end . . ." The Boss nodded, the dark side and shadows of the war etched in his deep-set eyes. "The answer is both, I'm afraid."

Blum nodded and took his cap from the table and took a step toward the door. "Thank you, sir." Then he stopped, hesitating a moment, feeling something rising up in him, courage or foolishness, he would decide later, and turned back. "Just one more thing . . ."

Donovan was already back behind his desk and had picked up a report. Strauss, reassembling his file, looked up. "Of course."

"You still haven't told me how you plan on getting me out."

THIRTEEN

That night, after most of the base had gone to bed, Blum smoked a cigarette on the back stairs of the officers' barracks near K Street. Thunder rattled in the far-off skies.

If his meeting in the A building earlier had been to confirm his transfer to Fort Ritchie, Blum might have celebrated by catching a film; a new one, *To Have and Have Not*, with Bogart and Bacall, based on the Hemingway book, was playing on the base. Or there was this girl he had taken out a couple of times, the cousin of a neighbor back in Chicago who worked in the cosmetics department at Woodward & Lothrop, the big department store chain there. She was pretty and laughed easily, which always reminded him of his sister. And, as opposed to many of the officers in his unit, she seemed not to mind his European accent.

Instead, he just stayed in his barracks. He felt in a similar way to how he'd felt the night he set out from Krakow, when he sensed in his heart he was saying goodbye to his family for the last time. That a choice had been put in front of him for which he had no logic or means to properly evaluate, but still, one he knew he must take.

Will it save lives or cost them, in the end?

Both, Colonel Donovan had said.

The night was warm. It reminded him of many such nights back home, humidity so thick you could spread it on bread with jam when there was no butter, his mother used to say.

So how was he to choose? *Will it save lives or cost them?* What other calculus was there for deciding? It is what his father would have asked the colonel. He could almost hear his measured voice, pipe in hand, posing the question.

Or Rabbi Leitner, his instructor? There was something from the *Mishnah* he recalled, one of those countless tenets of Jewish law that had been drummed into him in dark-lit rooms as a boy, while his thoughts drifted out the window to things he found much more fun: playing football with friends in Krasinski Park, or the Sabbath goose his mother might have waiting for him later. With barley soup and *kreplach,* and a *kompot* of stewed apples and prunes.

Pidyon shvuyim was how it was phrased in Hebrew.

To redeem a captive.

Taking a drag from his Lucky, Blum recalled the old rabbi once asking, his voice echoing in a corner of the empty synagogue, whether paying a ransom for the freedom of a man held hostage *in the end* would cost or save lives. Or just maybe, he explained, only bring additional hardship and suffering. "What is good cannot be fully known in the short term, do you understand that, Nathan?" The rabbi had come around the desk. Surely a life would be saved, he admitted. Yes. "But then would others then be taken and held in ransom the same way? Would funds that were meant for improvement of the temple be spent toward this ransom, and thus, let it fall into decline? Of course, if it was your son, or your brother," the rabbi had shrugged, "the answer is not so clear."

To Blum, if he did what Strauss and Donovan had asked of him, it was not so much that he would be "buying" back a life as putting *his* up in its place, in the same way a ransom would be offered. In effect, Blum would be the ransom. Sitting there, he smiled, as he could see the old rabbi pensively stroking his gray beard, muttering how else could you determine whether or not to pay for a captive's life unless you know this answer? *Will it save lives or cost them, in the end?* Taking out of the equation whose life in fact it was that was held—a brother or a complete stranger. That was the only answer or reply.

Blum thought back to how since he was seventeen and the Nazis had first marched into Krakow, no answer was ever easy.

He reminded himself that his parents and his sister had forfeited their lives so that he could be here now. There were many others who could easily have been picked to go instead of him. There was Perlman, Blum recalled, or Pincas Schreive. They were just as skilled as Blum was at avoiding the Germans. *Why did they not choose them?* Blum's mind brought back the glimmer of hope in his father's eyes amid the sadness of their final goodbye. Hope dimmed, because they both felt a sense of the different fates that awaited them, like diverging branches of the same tree.

And now to go back, Blum reflected, on a mission that was clearly more suicide than hope. For some man, only a name and a face, whose value might never be known to him. It made his decision to leave Krakow—*It was a great honor,* his father had insisted—stand for nothing if he ended up forfeiting his life in the same place they had given up their lives for him to leave.

So how else could he decide? He had looked into the colonel's somber eyes hoping to find the answer. *You can see how vital we think this is* . . . His look was just like his father's that last time. But then, *We don't know for sure that he's even still alive.*

The odds against the mission's success were long. He saw that clearly in Strauss's and Donovan's sober faces. Beneath the need and the strategic importance of this man, the two of them clearly knew precisely what they were sending Blum on.

He reached into his wallet and removed the small photograph he had of him and Leisa, she, fourteen, sitting on the sill of the open window at their family's country house in Masuria. He, still barely able to shave.

She said, *I have a gift for you.*

They had sat on the fire balcony of their cramped apartment on Jozefinska Street, their legs dangling over the edge.

"I don't want you to go," she told him.

He swung his feet. "Neither do I."

"Then why . . . ?" she pleaded. "Tell Papa you changed your mind."

When he was six and she was three, his father had made him promise to always watch out for his sister, in school, at the park. Once, when she was an infant, his father even playfully held her aloft above their fourth-floor window, saying "I'll throw her out. Unless you promise to look after her."

"I promise. I promise," Blum yelled, unaware there was a shelf beneath her and Leisa was never in any danger.

"I have to go," he replied. "The temple is depending on it. You'll be all right. I told my friend Chaim to watch out for you if something happens."

"Weissman? He's an ass." Leisa turned up her nose.

True, Chaim was pompous and boastful. But he knew the paths and alleyways out of danger as well as anyone in the ghetto, and he always seemed to find a way to ask about Leisa.

"Nonetheless, if things get bad and he comes for you, you must go with him." Blum looked squarely at her. "Even if Mother and Father don't. This is important, Leisa. You must promise me."

She just looked at the street below, spotting a vendor pushing a lorry of vegetables four stories beneath them.

"I need you to promise me," he said again.

"All right, I promise," she finally agreed.

Blum looked closely at her.

"You have my word. I do."

Blum smiled. "Good."

A bit of time passed before she looked at him. "You think we'll ever see each other again?"

"Absolutely," he replied. "I'll stake my life on it."

"We'll see. I'm not so much worried about us, Nathan—Father always gets by—as I am about you. America is such a different place. And you don't speak a word of English."

"That's not true. I can say 'Put 'em up!' " he said in the kind of slow, Western drawl he'd heard in films and cocked his finger like a gun.

"Nathan, don't tease me. Anyway, I have something for you. Wait here." She crawled inside and came back out a minute or two later with a piece of sheet music. It was Mozart's Clarinet Concerto in A Major. One of her favorites. What she played at the conservatory's recitals last year. She took the opening page and tore it from the binder.

"Leisa, don't!"

Then she folded it in half, lengthwise, and neatly split the page in two.

"See . . ." She folded up one side into a small square. "You'll keep this half and I'll keep mine. When we see each other again, we'll put them back together. Like this." She unfolded hers and joined them again, the bars and passages once more fitting perfectly together. "That's our pact, okay? It's like a ticket. You won't lose it, will you?"

"They'll have to kill me to take it off me." He grinned.

"Well, I prefer you don't let that happen." His sister looked at him, her dark eyes wide and bruised with an unknown foreboding. "But the same for me." She threw her arms around his neck. "I'm going to miss you, Nathan."

"I'll miss you too, Doleczki."

She wouldn't let him go.

"Whatever you do, Leisa, you continue to play. That's who you are. Never let them take that from you."

"I won't," she said, her body trembling with fear.

"And remember, when the shit hits the fan . . ."

"Yes, Chaim." She nodded, her head buried against him. "If you say I must."

Outside the barracks, Blum opened the folded sheet music he had kept with him these past three years. "*Wolfgang Ama—*" his side read at the top. "*Concerto ein—*"

Then the opening bars.

He closed his eyes and imagined that Leisa was clutching hers when the bullets came. At least, he knew in her heart she was.

A couple of enlisted men hurried past and he stood up. The two saluted. "Sir."

Blum saluted them back.

I'm sure that reassignment you put in to the Ritchie boys will be coming through at any time, Donovan had said, *if that's how you'd like it to go.*

He remembered at his bar mitzvah in Krakow, he had spoken of *aliyah.* Like all Jews, he had made a promise to go to the Holy Land one day. A promise most would never keep. So maybe in a way this would be his *aliyah.* To honor his parents and their deaths. His heritage. Not to Jerusalem, to the Holy Land, but to a camp in the woods of southern Poland where terrible things took place.

His promised land.

To find this one man.

With no return ticket.

He folded Leisa's music sheet back into a square and placed it inside his wallet, next to the small photo of her he kept there. Crushing his cigarette out, he picked up his cap and went to go in. He stopped a second. Thinking of her, which he tried not to do much these days, had brought a tear.

Months after he'd found out her fate, he'd also gotten word: Chaim Weissman had died in a fall off a rooftop onto Limanowa Street while fleeing the Germans the very morning Blum's family was murdered.

When that troop truck pulled up in front of their building, the Germans ordering everyone to get outside, *"Schnell!"* she probably waited, just like Blum had made her promise. Hid in the stairwell, hoping. Maybe until the moment they barged in and dragged her, screaming, down the stairs.

He'll be here, he'll be here, she probably told herself. *Nathan promised.*

Even as they were lined up against the wall and the bullets came.

FOURTEEN

Before his work shift the following morning, Blum went back to the Main Hall and asked for Captain Strauss's office, which turned out to be a small, poorly lit cubby on the third floor at the end of a long hallway. He stood in front of it for a few seconds, put his cap in his hand, and then knocked on the door.

The captain looked up from maps and reports and seemed pleased to see him. "Lieutenant."

Strauss's office was a world away from his boss's. The only light was a bright lamp on the metal desk, other than what came through a shuttered window. One wall of shelves was stacked with heavy books and binders. A map of Poland and another of Europe were tacked to the other wall. On the desk, Blum saw two framed pictures. A pretty dark-haired woman, likely the captain's wife, and two young kids, and another of an older couple, the man dressed in a dark suit with a short beard, his wife in a white dress and hat.

Strauss pushed back from the desk, waiting.

All Blum said was, "So when do I have to leave?"

The captain edged into a smile. He stood up and put out his hand. "Day after tomorrow. At least, for Britain. The actual mission date is set for the end of May. That gives us two weeks there to prepare. Familiarization with the local terrain and the camp. What you can expect inside. You'll need to lose a few more pounds. Shouldn't be so hard, on what they feed us these days."

Blum grinned.

"The Boss will be pleased. Damn pleased." Strauss sat on the edge of his desk. "He'll want to congratulate you himself, of course. He's up on the Hill today. Do you mind, can you let me see your wrists."

"My wrists . . . ?" Blum held them out.

Strauss nodded, turning the left one over. "You don't happen to have a problem with needles, do you?"

"Needles . . ." Nathan shook his head. "No. Why?"

"Not to worry. We'll explain it all later. I know this is all coming at you pretty quickly. Anyone here who ought to know?"

"*Here* . . . ? You mean in the States? Just a friend, perhaps. No one special. Maybe my cousin and his wife back in Chicago. They brought me over."

"Let's just be sure we keep the real reason behind your trip to ourselves. How about we just simply tell them that you're being deployed? Everyone's being shipped over there these days. No need to mention anything more."

"I understand."

"Oh, and then there's this . . ." Strauss reached across his desk and opened a file. He took out a photograph. "I suppose, no reason not to show you this now."

It was of a man, middle aged, in his fifties maybe. A heavy but pleasant face, sagging cheeks, wire glasses, graying hair, combed over from the side.

"Here's your man," the captain said. "Though he may not look exactly the same now."

Blum ran his eyes over the photograph.

"Don't worry, before we're done you'll have every wrinkle on his face committed to memory."

"What's his name?" Blum asked. He looked kindly yet, at the same time, the eyes were serious, wise. There was a mole on the side of his nose. Who was he, Blum wondered, and what did he know, to make him, above all others, worth Blum risking his life to save?

"His name is Mendl. One 'e.' Alfred. He's a professor. From Lvov. I'm afraid that's about all I can tell you now."

"Mendl . . ." Blum muttered out loud. "What is his area of specialty?"

"Electromagnetic physics. Something very heady like that. Know much about it?"

"I know an apple falls to the earth if you drop it."

Strauss grinned. "That's about my limit too. But a lot of very smart people here who do, say that what Mendl knows is indispensable. And that it's worth whatever we can do to bring him here. I think you should know, Nathan—I hope it's all right that I call you that, we're pretty much going to be tied at the hip for the next two weeks—that this mission, long as the odds might seem, goes all the way up to the top. And not just in this building, if you know what I mean. All I can say is, what you've agreed to do, you're doing your country a great service."

Blum nodded, feeling a surge of pride. "Thank you, sir."

"What you asked me yesterday . . ." Strauss sat back down and looked at him. "If I was a Jew. Actually, my father is a cantor." He turned around the photo on his desk of the man in the dark suit with his wife. "His congregation is in Brooklyn. Temple Beth Shalom. Everyone always asks him *why* . . . ? Why are we not doing more to help? So many horrible things coming out about what's happening over in Europe. I tell him that we are, but I know, in my heart, that's no answer. Shortening the damn war best we can, driving the Nazis from power, that's the only answer. And this . . . what you're helping us do, if we're successful, though I can't fully explain the details of what's at stake, will help more than anything either of us will ever do. Do you mind . . . ?" Strauss reached across the desk and took back the photo of Mendl with kind of a rueful smile. "It's my only one right now. Don't worry, you'll know every pore on that face by the time you go. So I'll inform your superior officer. I assume there's someone there who can step in for you?"

"Mojowitsky," Blum offered. "He's in EU-4. He's quite strong."

"Good, then . . ." The OSS captain nodded and then stood up.

Blum stood up too.

"If you don't mind," the captain took off his glasses, "I'm curious about something . . . ?"

"What is that?"

"I guess we've both thought out the risks of what you're doing. I can only imagine, Colonel Donovan and I, we weren't that good of salesmen . . ."

"You want to know why I would agree to go?"

"Yes. Keeping in mind, of course, I'd sign up myself in an instant if I was what they were looking for."

Blum gave him a thin smile. His eyes lifted to the metal shelves on the wall. Amid the files and thick binders, he saw a couple of leatherbound books in Hebrew. Strauss was the son of a cantor. "I see a Talmud. Do you happen to have a *Mishnah* up there as well?"

The *Mishnah Sanhedrin* was the earliest written credos of Jewish law from the Torah, something a cantor's son might have been read from in his very first lessons.

"Somewhere." The captain shrugged. "Perhaps."

"Chapter four, verse five." Blum stood up. "I don't have any better way to explain it."

"Chapter four, verse five . . . I'll see if I can find one then. Anything else?"

"No, sir." Strauss saluted him; Blum returned it. "Actually, there is one last thing . . ." Blum said, turning in the doorway. "I do have a fear of something."

"I hope it's not small spaces," the captain said. "Things are liable to get pretty tight in there once we drop you in."

"No." Blum shook his head and smiled. "Heights."

After the lieutenant left, Strauss sat as his desk a long while. He felt buoyant. Catfish was back in the game! He picked up the phone to get word to Donovan—the Boss would be ecstatic too—but then he thought better of it and put the receiver back down. He stood up and checked the shelves for what Blum had mentioned. It was at the bottom of a stack. He didn't even know why he had it. Certainly not because of any religious feeling on his part these days. He'd been to temple only on Yom Kippur for the past three years. To please his father, perhaps, who had given the holy books to Strauss before he left for duty and who was disappointed that his son, after law school and in the service, had pulled away from the faith.

One day you'll come back, he told him. *You will.*

The *Mishnah Sanhedrin.*

Strauss pulled the book out and sat back down, paging through the blue, leatherbound copy until he found it: chapter four, verse five.

It was on the story of Adam. Some nameless scholar, Strauss had no idea whom, had written his commentary of the text, highlighted in red.

Then, starting to read the passage Blum mentioned, he let himself smile.

He knew exactly what came next; it was one of the first things ever drummed into him in religious school. He thought of Blum, the family he had left behind. All dead now. But whom he felt responsible for. It was a brave thing he was doing. But not so brave, when you'd lost everything. Everything but this one thing. All that he had left. And all that mattered.

God's speed, Strauss muttered to himself. *To all of us.*

Then he read the next passage, though he already knew the words by heart:

> It was for this reason that man was first created as one person, to teach you that anyone who destroys a life is considered by Scripture to have destroyed an entire world; and any who saves a life is as if he saved an entire world.

PART TWO

FIFTEEN

In Block Thirty-Six, the barracks he shared two to a bed with 250 others, Alfred marked that he had been in the camp three months now. The biting Polish winter had finally given way to a late, muddy thaw.

They'd taken his books, his papers, everything, on his first day of arrival. They probably had all ended up in smoke like ordinary kitchen trash. *If they only had some idea* . . . Still, it gave him the slightest measure of satisfaction that it was a far better result than if these monsters had been able to use his work for their own ends.

Word was, even while he was in Vittel, that the Germans were making advances toward creating a fissionable isotope. He knew that work on this was taking place at a laboratory in Haigerloch on the Eyach River, using heavy water from Norway. But enriching uranium was only the first step of a long process. Then they needed to extract plutonium from the uranium and then separate the fissionable isotope, known as U-235, from its heavier cousin, U-238, which he'd heard that Fermi had successfully isolated at his cyclotron in Chicago. And to do this there were several untested methods. You could bombard the isotopes with electromagnetic waves. Lawrence had shown that an electrically charged atom traveling through a magnetic field moves in a circle whose radius is determined by its mass. Lighter U-235 atoms

85

would follow a narrower arc than the heavier U-238s. But to separate the quantities needed, it could take years.

Then there was thermal diffusion, circulating uranium hexafluoride between cool water jackets and high-pressurized steam.

But the best path Alfred's research had shown was through gaseous diffusion, which meant they could separate the needed isotopes by pumping uranium gas against a porous barrier, with the lighter molecules passing through more rapidly than the heavier ones. The rate of effusion of a gas is inversely proportional to the square root of its nuclear mass. Sooner or later they would all run into the problem. The Germans, the Americans, and the Brits. Though he had gotten word that after his escape to London from occupied Denmark Bohr was now in the United States, so maybe the Allies had combined their efforts. And there were only two men in the world who had been working on this kind of research. The other, Bergstrom, he'd heard, was with the Nazis now. For Bergstrom, it had always been about the work—no matter who funded it. And staying alive. Alfred had also heard the Americans were making progress too.

He knew now, as he jotted down some formulas in what remained of the thinning light, that he should have gotten out long ago. Everyone had pushed him to. "Make your way to Copenhagen," Bohr had urged. "You can work with me. It will be safer for Marte and Lucy." But Lvov was their home; Marte had family there. They had built their life there. For two years it had been safe, protected by the Russians under the nonaggression pact. But once the Russians fled, travel across Europe became impossible. One day, men in brown shirts and swastikas, boys really, barged into his office and told him he was no longer a professor. Just a Bolshevik yid. They ripped his books down from the shelves and trashed his papers—thank God he always kept his truly important work at home—and hurled him down the stairs. Right in front of Mrs. Zelworwicz, who had worked in the lab with him for eleven years. Alfred was lucky. Many of his colleagues were dragged out into the square and shot. Soon all Jews were forced to move into the ghetto. Rumors were everywhere about mass deportations to camps.

Then, two months later, an emissary from the Paraguayan embassy in Warsaw managed to find him and explained in a café on Varianska Street, *We have a way.*

He had thought of making a new life for himself in America with Marte and Lucy. Maybe taking a teaching position. At the University of Chicago with Fermi, or in California, reuniting with Bethe and Lawrence. Maybe even Bohr. All Nobel winners. As a scientist, he had never been on their scale, of course, when it came to the theoretical side. But as a researcher, his work had value too. *Now look . . .* Alfred stared gloomily around the barracks. People dragging themselves back to their bunks, exhausted, like soulless ghosts. The one or two who had something to barter for cigarettes were greedily inhaling them. Two had died today alone on his work detail. One from a club to the head, dropped where he stood; the other, simply from exhaustion, just gave up, and was shot.

Yes, he had waited too long.

Marte was dead. He knew that in his heart, as sure as he could bring her beautiful image to his eyes. She'd grown ill while at Vittel, and it had only worsened on the train. These animals didn't even waste soup on sick ones like that. The only reason he had been directed to the left and permitted to remain alive was that he spoke German as well as a *Volksherren,* a prized commodity in here.

And Lucy . . . his beautiful, gentle Lucy. She was likely gone as well. He'd married late in life, and his daughter was an unexpected treasure to him, like uncovering the atomic theory and the principle of origin at one time. Early on, he'd gotten word through a barrack mate's wife that she'd contracted typhus, which was as good as a death sentence in here. Alfred's own strength had started to wane as well. *And why not?* What purpose was there to staying strong and remaining alive? Every day hundreds went missing. Entire barracks. The guards said they'd just been transferred to some other work facility. The nearby work camp at Monowitz. "They're happy there," they would say. But everyone knew. The stench emanating from the flat-topped building near the gate was damning enough, and the dark plume of smoke that came from neighboring Birkenau, just to the west, and hung over the camp was an everyday reminder. Himmelstrasse. "The road to heaven," it was called. And each of them would walk it soon enough.

The road to death, it was better named.

A month or two ago, Alfred had begun to put together parts of his work by jotting them down on whatever scraps of paper he could find. He went through the hundreds of progressions again in his head, ten years of research, starting with the basic assumptions: The rate at which gases diffuse is inversely proportional to the square root of their densities—Graham's Law; the various methods to separate the needed isotope U-235 from its much more abundant cousin, U-238. All jotted on the backs of food labels stolen from the kitchen or roll call lists crumpled and left in the snow. Rewriting the endless progressions of formulas and equations. He scribbled out rough sketches of the isotope as it passed through its various radioactive stages; his vision for the kind of membranes they would need to pass through; even his own thoughts on the triggering possibilities for the actual "device," which was what they called it, in its most theoretical form: a device that would theoretically harness the gargantuan explosive energy created by the chain reactions from the separation of the isotope. He had first discussed this possibility with Szilard at a conference in Manchester in '35. He rewrote much of his own early research in his head. Speeches to the *Academic Scientifica*; classes he'd given. His work with Otto Hahn and Lise Meitner at the Kaiser Wilhelm Institute in Berlin. Ten years of research, whatever he could recall, all kept in the coffers of his brain. At the least, it kept him sane. He wrote it down and stuffed the papers in a coffee tin that he hid in the flooring underneath his bunk, covering it when either SS guards or their malevolent Ukrainian *kapo,* Vacek, came inside.

Everyone around him must have surely thought him a pathetic sight— the old professor, muttering to himself in his far-off world, scribbling down his endless equations and proofs. *And to what end?* they would snicker. It was all just nonsense that soon would die along with him here.

But it wasn't nonsense. Not a single number. It all meant something. And it had to be saved. Life here was governed by a futile, mindless regimen: just get through the day, sleep, and then start another. Avoid eye contact with the guards and try to survive. *"Schnellen."* Double time. Faster.

But thought had to continue, did it not? That was a principle of existence. Even if it was simply to declare that his life still meant something. Or that in the midst of this hell there was still hope; or amid the chaos, order. So each afternoon he threw himself onto his bunk, his feet raw and swollen from his ill-fitting wooden clogs, and, turning away from his bunkmate, wrote down whatever he could recall. Because he knew that in the right hands, this "nonsense" meant everything. They would pay a ransom for it. But each new day he felt his own will growing weaker. Because of his age and his language facility, he was assigned easier jobs. But he didn't know how much longer he could survive. One day he knew he would be the one who simply looked into the face of the gun and gave up.

"Professor . . ." Ostrow, an ex-bookkeeper from Slovakia and the bunk's most skilled forager, kneeled down and interrupted his work. "Care for a little treat for your afternoon repast tomorrow? Our chef has gone to great personal risk to procure this rare delicacy."

The Slovak showed him a rind of crusty cheese in a grimy napkin, probably stolen out of the German mess garbage, as prized in here as a tin of caviar.

"Give it to Francois over there or Walter," Alfred said. Either looked like any day could be their last. "Besides, I have nothing to trade."

"Nothing to trade? You joke, of course," the forager said for anyone around to hear. "Two of your formulas and they're yours. An entire equation, I'll get you a beefsteak."

A few of their neighbors chuckled.

"E equals mc squared," Alfred said to the forager. "How's that? And, please, make mine medium rare."

There were a few more laughs. It was good to laugh in here, even if he was the butt of it, for whatever the reason.

Suddenly things were interrupted by the shrill of whistles being blown. Guards stormed into the block, sticks clanging loudly on the walls and doors. "Everyone out! *Out*, filth! *Schnell.*"

Every heart came to a sudden stop. Every whistle, anything that was unexpected when it came to the Germans, everyone felt the dread that their time had finally come and it was over for them.

Hauptscharführer Scharf stepped into the block accompanied by two other guards, and Vacek, their soulless *kapo,* trailing behind. Scharf was one of the more brutal of the SS guards. He acted as if his only reward in getting through the war in this miserable camp was the infliction of as much pain and misery on the prisoners as he could. Alfred had personally seen him execute at least twenty or thirty himself, for nothing more than letting a shovel fall from their hands after ten hours' hard labor and barely a drop of water, or when he had shouted, *"Schnell! Schnell!"* and a prisoner tripped or fell behind. Vacek was a petty criminal from Smolensk who, here, turned into a dreaded menace. He had an efficient, one-two method to bludgeon prisoners to death: a blow to the back of the legs to drop a person to their knees and then one to the back of the head to finish them off. Alfred could not believe that a Jew, no matter how low, could act that way toward another. They were all going to die in here at some point, even the *kapos.* What price was it worth to prolong it by inflicting misery on others?

"Aussen! Aussen!" the Germans barked, *out, out,* banging their sticks against the walls and wooden bunks. *"Schnell!"* Alfred stuffed his writings back under the floor beneath his bunk and replaced the floorboard. He fell into the line outside. "Faster, faster, you lice-ridden maggots." The guards jabbed their sticks into their ribs. *"Run!* That means you, old man. Now!"

Though it was April, there was still a chill in the air at night, and everyone looked at each other with concern, huddling to keep warm. Any change of routine was always a cause for alarm. They awaited the dreaded word to march. They all knew where. It was only a matter of time anyway, and everyone knew at some point theirs would be up.

"Line up!" the guards barked, jabbing at them with their sticks. Everyone formed a line.

"So how is that steak tasting now?" Alfred leaned close and said to

Ostrow, who had fallen in next to him. The ferret had ground the stolen cheese into bits under his pants and let the crumbs fall through his pant legs to the ground, grinding them into the dirt with his clogs.

"Perhaps a little tough, Professor, to be completely honest," he replied with a complicit grin.

After a couple of minutes it became clear that this wasn't the end, only an inspection. Nonetheless, if the guards found something, it was still a cause for alarm. Outside they could hear the guards tearing up the bunks, upending their flimsy, flea-infested mattresses and knocking their sticks against the floorboards looking for hiding spaces.

"Maybe the chef talked," Ostrow leaned over and sniffed to Alfred.

"I think not," Alfred said. "I don't think it's food they're looking for."

Vacek jabbed him in the back with his stick. *"Quiet!"*

After a few moments there was shouting from inside the block and then Scharf's agitated voice. Everyone's stomachs fell. The sergeant came out holding up a makeshift blade that had been fashioned from the top of a food tin. The prisoners only used it to slice the scraps of stolen bread or cheese that came to them.

"And may I ask whose is this?" the sergeant major asked, holding up the blade. His accusing gaze went down the line. With his furnace-like eyes, flat nose, and thick lips, the bastard even looked like a butcher. Everyone stood frozen. No one uttered a sound. It was common to punish an entire block for one prisoner's offense. One thing you didn't want to do was rankle Scharf when he was on a rampage.

"Speak up!" Vacek, the *kapo,* commanded, weaving in and out of the lines. He put a hand to his ear. "Cat got your tongue? Did I hear anyone?" He toyed with them like children, which only made their hatred of him worse. He stopped behind Ullie, a baker from Warsaw, one of Alfred's friends. "Anything to say, baker?" Vacek uttered, close to Ullie's ear.

The baker shut his eyes. The blade was his. He knew it was the end for him.

"Nothing?" Vacek took his stick and drove it into the back of Ullie's legs, dropping him to his knees.

91

"It's only for food, Herr Hauptscharführer," Ullie pleaded, owning up to the offense. His eyes shook with terror. "Nothing more. I swear."

Someone had ratted him out.

"Just for food, did I hear right . . . ?" Scharf nodded agreeably. But everyone knew it was just an act. "Well, that's okay then. Right, Vacek? I mean, if it's just for food . . . Only, I find an actual knife works far better for cutting food." His tone was clearly mocking. He circled around Ullie. "Don't you agree that a knife works better, baker?"

"Yes, sir. It does, of course." It was a joke. A mirthless one. Spoons were all they were allowed for the thin ladle of soup of overcooked, rotted potatoes and, if you were lucky, a sliver of grisly meat at the bottom.

"Don't you agree, Herr Vacek?"

"I do, sir." The Ukrainian nodded, his eyes lighting up with the obsequious lust he had for pleasing his ruthless bosses.

"Please, sir . . ." Ullie bowed his head, but knew what was in store for him. His eyes futilely found those of a few friends, as if saying his last goodbyes.

"Herr Hauptscharführer!" Another guard ran out of the barracks, holding a large tin in his hand, which, Alfred knew, contained his writings. His stomach fell. Scharf shook his head and grinned, not even questioning whose they were, and stepped over to Alfred.

"And what do we have here, Professor?" The SS killer glared. "Still with your silly fantasies? Didn't we teach you to give them up?" He took out a fistful of papers and crumpled them into a ball. "For a professor, you don't seem to learn very well. Herr Vacek, do you have a match?"

"Of course," the Ukrainian said, and handed one to him.

"They're simply writings, Herr Hauptscharführer," Alfred begged. "Nothing. They mean nothing to anyone but me."

"Who you were means nothing in here now!" the sergeant major shouted. He lit the match and glared at Alfred with a cold smile as the papers were caught up in flame. He dropped them to the ground, the edges curling and crisping. "Do you not understand? Forget who you were. You are just a worker now. A fucking number. You stay alive at my whim. Do you understand that?"

"Yes, Herr Hauptscharführer."

"I'm not sure you do. But I will remind you. *Watch!*"

He took out his Luger and put it to the back of Ullie's head. "Did you think we had forgotten why we came, baker?" Ullie hung his head, knowing what was in store. "Next time anyone wants to hide weapons, think about this!" Scharf pulled on the trigger. Ullie shut his eyes and let out a whimper.

The gun did not fire.

Scharf spat out a curse and squeezed the trigger again. Again, nothing. "Fucking shit!" He pressed it to Ullie's head and kept on squeezing. *Click, click, click.* Each time the gun jammed. His eyes were lit with rage. "Corporal," he said to one of the other guards, "hand me your weapon."

The Rottenführer moved toward him, unbuckling his holster. Then, from the direction of the main guardhouse, Scharf's name was shouted.

The sergeant major turned around.

"Captain Nieholtz," the guard replied. "He requests your presence in the guard room. Immediately."

The muscles on Scharf's neck, like a cord about to snap, were visible for all to see. In frustration, he kicked the kneeling baker onto his side. "Why waste the fucking bullet? Get back in line, you filthy rot. Your time is coming soon enough anyway."

He stormed off, Vacek swinging his truncheon and chuckling with an amused smirk. "Next time, baker! I'd do you myself, but if ever there was a man who deserved the reprieve, you're him." He walked away as well.

Shaking, Ullie rolled over, his complexion white as the moon. He'd shat all over himself.

"Back among the living, comrade." One by one, people helped him back up.

Alfred stared at the smoldering scraps of his work, now turned to ash on the ground. He went toward it—maybe there was one or two of them he could salvage. Then he just stopped.

What purpose was there now? Scharf should have just ended it here for both of them with one to the head. New ovens were being built every day. People no longer even came into the camp; they were just sent off the trains over to Birkenau and disappeared. A hundred thousand Hungarians, he had been told, in just the past week alone. They were all going to die here too.

Poor Ullie, would it have been such a bad way to go? One to the head. He looked at the smoldering remains of his work, crisping at the edges.

Ten years.

What was the sense, could anyone explain it to him, of delaying it any further?

SIXTEEN

In the camp, the work never ended. The train tracks were being extended, right up to the gates of neighboring Birkenau, where the real killing was being done now. Two shifts, both day and night. Just three kilometers away there was an IG Farben chemical plant that was under construction. The joke was that it saved the Nazis the transportation costs of bringing the deadly gases in.

Every day, the work teams lined up after the morning meal. Construction workers, electricians, painters, diggers with hoes and spades. Lines endlessly straightened and counted, rolls called over and over. All marched out to twelve-hour work days to a procession of rousing music played by the orchestra. Then back at night, exhausted and battered, wheeling the dead in carts, to the same lifting tunes.

Still, there was downtime too. Before the work details assembled; in the minutes after roll call or after a meal. Or, during the day, if you were put on one of the night shifts. And getting yourself checked into the infirmary for a day or two was like a vacation.

Alfred's latest job, with respect to his age, was cleaning the officers' bicycles of mud every day. Endlessly polishing and polishing, scraping the tires of mud. The week after Scharf's inspection, while replacing a punctured tire, he was instructed by Obersturmführer Meitner to escort a sick prisoner to the infirmary. There he came upon a small crowd watching two prisoners playing chess.

One was a middle-aged man with somber eyes and a serious expression who was said to be the camp champion. The other a boy, not a day more than sixteen, it would seem. They played with stones carved into rough shapes of pieces on a makeshift cardboard board. The Germans permitted this. Just as they allowed, even demanded, that the orchestra play as the trains of new inmates came in and when the work details marched out to their jobs. The music imparted a small feeling of everyday normalcy and even culture to the camp against the backdrop of death and madness. The level of chess that was played was said to be high, and now and then, even the SS guards would rest their sticks and weapons and watch the matches for a while. Even Dr. Mengele, it was said, took an interest on occasion. It was almost like the gladiators of ancient Rome; the longer you continued to win, the greater the chances were that you were kept alive.

After dropping off his patient, Alfred folded into the crowd observing the match. He hadn't played much since his university days, but it was still intriguing. There was complete silence. SS officers and the lowly prisoners who routinely lived in fear of them each standing around and commenting amid their own ranks, completely absorbed. By the time Alfred came on it, today's match was in mid-game. After each move, the older player removed his wire glasses and kneaded his doughy face, nerves showing. Conversely, his young opponent had an effortless air about him. A beginner could see the kid had the advantage. Even the Germans were muttering and nodding among themselves in admiration of how neatly the younger one was disposing of the other.

"Are you sure you want to continue this fight?" The boy sat back and put his hands behind his head.

"That kind of boastfulness has brought down players far better than you," his opponent scowled back, declining the invitation.

"Because bishop to king's knight four puts your rook in a real jam," the youth pointed out to him.

"I'm not a fool," the champion replied.

"No doubt. So then by moving my pawn to queen's bishop five, should you choose to save the rook ... I'm sure you'll also see ..."

Even Alfred saw that the boy's next move gave him complete control of the middle board. The outcome was inevitable.

The older player kneaded his jowl a few more moments, delaying his fate, then quietly nodded with a defeated sigh, offering his hand.

"We have a new champ!" The crowd cheered. "Young King Wolciek!" another crowned him. Even the Germans talked among themselves, impressed, two of them exchanging a few bills, clearly having wagered on the outcome. Then the guard who had lost the bet turned on the crowd. "Fun's over, shits. That's it. Get your asses back to work. Did you hear me?" He raised his stick at a few loiterers, no longer in a good mood. *"Now!"*

Now the Germans could return to the real business at hand of killing each one of them.

As the crowd dispersed, Alfred noticed an attractive blond woman in a printed dress and cardigan who had seemed to clap with appreciation at the conclusion of the match. The SS officers seemed to greet and address her politely. As the crowd cleared, she went back inside the infirmary.

"Pretty, eh?" The prisoner next to him nudged Alfred. He was a Frenchman with a red triangle on his uniform, signifying a political prisoner.

Alfred replied in French. "Who is she? A nurse perhaps? I haven't seen her before."

"Don't know." The Frenchman shrugged. "But quite the chess fan, it's clear. I've seen her watching before. Brains and beauty, a nice combination, right?"

"Yes, a nice combination," Alfred said. His thoughts immediately went to his own daughter, Lucy, and it made him sad.

"That kid's something, huh?" The prisoner continued to chat on their way back to the barracks. "He's beaten everyone he's played here. Apparently, he's got a photographic memory. Claims he can remember every game he's ever played."

"Is that so?"

"I was once in a barracks with him. He didn't know a soul there, except one, a cousin from Lodz or somewhere. Someone put him up to a memory test. He said he would do it for fifty zloty each. We asked where he possibly had two thousand zloty to cover if he lost, and the brat replied cockily, Why did it matter? He wouldn't lose. So we all went in on it. We gave him our names and our birth towns too, just to make it more difficult. Maybe thirty of us there." The Frenchman stopped in front of a barrack. "This is my block. Twenty-two."

"And . . . ?" Alfred urged him to finish.

The Frenchman shrugged. "The kid recited back every one correctly. Every damn one. Someone got mad and accused him and his cousin of setting the whole thing up, so he went one better. One by one, he recited the town where each of us said he was from. Remarkable, huh . . . ?"

"Yes, but I've known a lot of young men and women with minds like that. The secret is to put their skill to some kind of practical use."

"And what do you do then, if you don't mind me asking?" the prisoner inquired. "Teach, I suppose?"

"Currently I'm in transportation, sadly." Alfred showed him the bicycle tire.

"Yes, we've all found new occupations here, haven't we?" The Frenchman laughed. "I was mayor of my town."

"So what's his name?" Alfred asked, removing his glasses and wiping the afternoon sun off his brow.

"Wolciek, I believe," the Frenchman replied, heading inside his barrack. "Leo. Watch him again if it all works out."

They both knew precisely what "all works out" meant.

"Just watch your money. It could cost you fifty zloty."

SEVENTEEN

A week later, Alfred happened upon the boy playing again, this time against an opponent named Markov, an Estonian, whom everyone said had been a local champion there. Leo used the King's Indian Defense and, to the delight of the crowd, dispatched the more experienced man in just twenty moves.

Even Markov applauded the boy's ability.

Alfred also noticed the attractive blond woman there again, leaning against a railing on the steps of the infirmary, quite absorbed in the game. But as soon as it was over, to the polite bows of the German guards, she went back into the infirmary. She must be a nurse. Or even a new doctor there.

As the crowd split up, Alfred made his way over to the winner, whose pockets were stuffed full of well-earned treats and cigarettes. "May I have a word with you, Pan Wolciek?"*

"*With me?* Do I know you, sir?" the boy questioned. It was natural to be suspicious here. Everyone, even those in a striped uniform, would either want something from someone they thought could protect them a bit longer or could possibly even be a spy.

"Well, I was called Herr Doktor Mendl while at the universities of

*Pan/Pani is the Polish equivalent of Mr./Mrs.

Gottingen and Lvov," Alfred introduced himself. "But in here, I suppose, simply Alfred would be fine."

"And I was simply Leo while back in Lodz." The boy grinned. "But in here I've become King Leo."

"Well, it's a pleasure to meet you by any name, young man." He was clean-faced, tow-headed with blue, sparkling eyes. "Word is, you have quite the memory skills. You certainly know your chess."

"I'm pleased if it keeps me around here an extra day . . . Back in Lodz, I was junior champion before we were forced inside the ghetto and then most of the competition dried up. Chess just didn't seem so important then. What about you, Professor, do you play?"

"Not since my university days," Alfred admitted. "And as you can see, that's been quite a while."

"Well, in here we are all pretty much the same age," Leo smiled philosophically, "since you never know when any day may be your last. Anyway, it's been a pleasure, Herr Doktor, but if you don't mind, I'm afraid I have to—"

"Are you as good at math and science as you are this game?" Alfred confronted him. "We used to say, brains without application is like beauty without kindness. It's all a waste."

The boy shrugged. "I'm afraid much of my formal education was put aside when we were forced to move inside the ghetto. Still," he grinned, slyly, "I suppose I could give you a quick demonstration, if you're so curious."

"I'd be honored."

The boy had light features, blond hair if it was allowed to grow out, a narrow face with alert eyes, and clearly a wit as sharp as his chess with a kind of cocksureness to match. "Can you provide me the date of your birth, Herr Professor?"

"As I've said, I'm an old man. Maybe too old to play this game with you. But it's October 7, if you must know. Fourteen years before the turn of the century."

"That's 1886, correct?" Leo replied quickly. He made a flourish with his arms and bowed. *"See?"*

"My, that *is* quite amazing," Alfred said with mock praise.

"Oh, you expected more? All right, then . . . So October 7, 1886. That is what you said, correct . . . ?"

"Sadly." Alfred agreed.

"Then let me see . . ." The boy closed his eyes, put two fingers to his forehead, silently moving his lips as if in the midst of calculating. Then he opened his eyes and said, "Congratulations, Professor, you are a very special man to have been born on the Sabbath."

Alfred's eyes went wide.

"I can also calculate that it is only one in seven who can make that claim." Leo grinned teasingly.

"The first trick was quite good enough," Alfred said, undeniably impressed.

The boy was right! Alfred's mother always joked that it was a wonder he hadn't decided to become a rabbi and not a scientist, since he was virtually born at *schul*. For the lad to have gone through that many years and iterations, over five decades, and then having to factor in leap years as well . . . "That is quite amazing. If you don't mind me asking, how did you manage it? And, without a pencil and paper, so quickly?"

"I devised a formula. It involves numerical properties for each day of the week as well as for each century. In any given year, the dates 4/4, 6/6, 8/8, 10/10, and 12/12 tend to fall on the same day. Then you have to factor in leap years, of course. In your case, fourteen of them. So I can compute any day in my head. So how is that for 'application,' Professor?" the boy asked, gloating a bit.

"I would say it's quite strong," Alfred nodded grudgingly, "if you aspire to be a calendar."

"And what is it you aspire to, old man? In the time you have left here."

"How about try this . . . ?" There was an exercise Alfred assigned to only his very top students as a means to calculate numerical primality. "I'll give you a number. Memorize it."

Leo stared at him and shrugged, seemingly ripe for the challenge. "Should be no problem."

"It's long: 9,007,199,254,740,991. Now repeat it back to me."

"That's it?" Leo shrugged. He gave the numbers back to Alfred in rapid order. "What's the trick to that?"

"Now express that same number as a power of two," Alfred instructed him.

"*Hmmm* . . . as a power of two . . ." Leo bunched his lips in thought. "That isn't easy." He took in a breath, as if accepting the challenge, his brow wrinkling and his gaze tunneling. He put a hand to his chin. "How much time do I have . . . ?"

"A lad like you . . ." Alfred smiled. "I don't know, two, three minutes . . . How much do you need?"

"Two or three minutes should be fine . . ." The boy started in, appearing to go through many abstract calculations in his head, muttering numbers to himself, shifting his index finger back and forth, like a musical metronome. Time passed. "Of two, you say," he asked again, looking a bit frustrated. Ultimately he just looked back at Alfred, shaking his head, and shrugged. "I told you my formal education was interrupted by the war. It's not that I can't figure what you asked, it's just . . . I would need maybe some paper and a little more time. I'm quite sure I could get it though."

"I'm sure you could." Alfred patted him on the shoulder. "No matter, it's not so easy." The guards were now ordering everyone to get back to their jobs. "Can we talk again, perhaps? I have some things I'd like to discuss with you."

"You need me to teach you some chess, Professor? You said it's been years. That might take a while."

"Maybe it's I who would like to teach *you* something," Alfred responded.

"And that would be . . . ?"

"Electromagnetic physics."

"*Electromagnetic physics* . . . " Leo rolled his eyes. "Oh, that *is* useful indeed, Professor. That, and a note from Reichsführer Himmler himself might just keep you alive in here another day."

"Don't be so smug. Its applications are vital. So can we speak again? How about tomorrow?" Alfred pressed. He could see the guards had lost their good humor. The sticks had come out and they started prodding everyone along.

"I'm afraid that the chess takes up most of whatever time that is free here," Leo said with an apologetic shrug. He started to back away. "But I enjoyed talking with you, Professor. And oh, just to be clear . . . On that other matter . . ." He raised his index finger in the air as if a thought had just come back to him. "I believe the answer you're looking for is two to the fifty-third. Isn't that right?"

"*Excuse me?*" Alfred muttered, taken by surprise.

"Your number, Professor. It's two to the fifty-third power, is it not?" Leo grinned coyly. "That *is* what you wanted to know, right?"

Alfred's jaw parted, as if a weight was attached to it. He had given the boy only two or three minutes . . . Even his most advanced students would have needed at least an hour and a notebook full of paper to calculate that out. "Yes, that is correct." His mouth was as dry as cotton. "Well, almost, that is . . ."

"Yes, you're right!" Leo agreed. "Stupid of me. It's actually two to the fifty-third *minus one*," he corrected himself with a victorious gleam in his eye.

Alfred blinked. "Yes, minus one." He cleared his throat and nodded back, knowing the color had drained from his face.

"So yes, let's talk again, Professor, by all means." Leo backed away and waved, grinning.

Alfred just stood there, between shock and astonishment. A small smile crept onto his face. "And what is *your* birth date?" he called after him. "If you don't mind."

"*Mine?*" Leo said. "Why, January 22, Herr Professor. And to be clear, that would be twenty-eight years *after* the century."

"Yes, after, of course . . ." Alfred followed him as the boy melded into the crowd. Over the years, he had encountered many great young minds. Some had gone on to have brilliant careers. Others just faded into the professions of the law, business, or civil service. But this one . . . *Yes,* the Frenchman was right. Astonishing. No other word for it.

And he was just sixteen.

EIGHTEEN

A few days later, a corporal named Langer entered Leo's block as Leo rested after his twelve-hour work detail. Despite his age, Leo was assigned to the motor transport team because his first night off the train he had said that his cousin had been a mechanic back in Lodz, which was true, so they threw him on it, and he'd had to learn on the fly as fast as he could.

"Prisoner Wolciek." Langer stopped at his bunk.

"Rottenführer!" Leo leaped out of bed. His heart nearly jumped out of his chest.

"Put on your cap. You are to come with me."

"Come where, Rottenführer, sir . . . ?" Leo questioned, pushing back a stab of worry. To be asked for by one's name was never a good sign, and never seemed to end with a positive outcome.

"Just get your ass up, you little shit, and don't ask questions." The corporal cracked his stick against the wooden boards of the bunk. "Come with me. *Schnell!*"

A tremor of nerves wound through Leo's gut, though he put on his clogs and grabbed his cap without delay, doing his best not to show it. *Had he done something? Was this it?* Maybe they didn't like the manner in which he had flaunted his skills at chess, or the games of memory he played, which could be interpreted as elevating himself above the other prisoners and flew in the face of everything the Nazis

104

tried to ground into you—that you were nothing. His barrack mates all looked on with bowed but sympathetic faces as Leo was taken out the door. At the same time, all breathed sighs of relief that it wasn't them the Rottenführer had come for.

"So where are we going, sir?" Leo asked outside with rising concern. Langer was a brutal pig who had never shown a moment's hesitation about clubbing an innocent prisoner senseless at the drop of a hat. Just yesterday Leo had watched him take a shovel and send someone reeling into a ditch and then piss on the dead man while laughing to his fellow guards about a story he had just heard about one of the cooks, as if the dead man had not been a living, breathing person just thirty seconds before.

"Just walk," the SS guard growled, prodding Leo ahead with his stick in the direction of the front gate.

Leo's heart began to patter. *Where was Langer taking him?* They continued on past the rows of blocks, nothing ahead of them but bad places. The black wall that prisoners were thrown up against and shot. Or the flat-roofed crematorium from where the odor of death and the gray plume of smoke perpetually emanated. Maybe he would be given a job there, the thought occurred to him. Tossing dead, disfigured bodies into the ovens or cleaning out the ash afterward, picking through skulls and bones. He'd heard of such horrors taking place in there. And such jobs. The prisoners even had to live there.

Or maybe this was indeed it. His own private Himmelstrasse. If so, he would face it bravely, Leo sturdied himself. It was bound to happen soon enough. He just wished he hadn't studied so much for his next match.

As he marched, the winding turns of the long journey that had brought him here came back to him. His father had had a small but successful law practice in Lodz and took pride in accompanying his young prodigy to chess tournaments. Once Leo even played in a competition in Warsaw. But his father was run over by a streetcar and killed when Leo was just eleven. He and his mother and younger sister moved in with her brother. When the Nazis came and things got bad, they were forced to move inside the ghetto. Leo's promising chess career came to an end. A friend of his uncle offered to take Leo and two others south, through Slovakia to Hungary, where the pro-Nazi government had not yet given up its Jews. All agreed it would be safer for him there. They left in a large commercial truck filled with industrial parts and valves, and everything seemed to be going along as planned until they stopped at a vegetable stand only thirty kilometers from the Slovak border. The coast appeared clear, and Leo hopped out and ran back the thirty meters or so to buy some dates and plums with the little cash he had. At that moment, a German troop truck happened to drive by, and the stand owner, seeing what was ahead, grabbed the young boy's arm. "Quick, son, over here," he said, drawing Leo behind the stand. The Germans inspected the truck and discovered the two young passengers hidden in the back, clearly Jews. Over his uncle's friend's pleas, they marched them all into a field, Leo peeking out from behind a stack of crates to watch, and machine-gunned them all, the children too. Then the Germans came over to the stand and chewed on peaches and figs, commenting to the stand owner how delicious they were, all the while with Leo huddled and his heart racing only a few feet away.

After the Germans left, the stand owner gave Leo some fruit and a jacket, and for two weeks, he lived in the fields as he continued south toward his destination. One morning he awoke to find two black-clad local police standing over him. He was put in a room at a border checkpoint and then sent by truck to a wired-in camp named Majdanek, near Lublin. It was cold there, the conditions bleak and harsh. The guards treated them with a brutality Leo could never have imagined human beings would treat one another. Fortune had it that a distant cousin happened to be in the same bunk, and he taught Leo how to survive: work hard, do not stand out, do not make eye contact. Do everything double time. Leo grew so weak and thin, they stuffed newspaper into his cheeks to puff them out and make him appear healthier and able to work, so as not to be selected by the guards. And he started playing chess again. Eight months ago, his was part of several barracks that were crammed into a sealed train and transferred to Auschwitz. The prisoners were herded off the train and onto a long line. A call went out that they needed one hundred able workers. Leo's cousin pushed him in front and whispered for them to volunteer, even though Leo was as scrawny as they came and only fifteen. "Stay by me," his cousin muttered. "Whatever you do, get on that line." In the jostling, others pushed their way forward, separating them. An SS officer was counting off the volunteers, one by one. Leo was number ninety-eight. His cousin was three places behind. Those who missed the cut were herded the other way; they were told they would be deloused and take showers. All were dead, Leo had heard, barely an hour later, including his cousin. Of the thousand or so on his transport, Leo's work group was the only hundred to survive.

And now as they approached the black wall, Leo thought maybe his charmed journey had come to an end. He remembered his cousin's calm but knowing farewell look as Leo was marched off on the line of volunteers and he was left behind. He had trained Leo well.

"In here."

To his surprise, Langer directed him into the delousing showers Leo had been put into on his arrival at the camp. It was empty. For a moment, Leo's heart leaped with fear. The guard pushed him under a shower head and turned the water on. *"Wasch dich,"* he barked, pointing to a bar of soap. *"Mach dich sauber."* Scrub yourself completely clean.

Leo stepped in, not quite understanding. But the freezing water actually felt good as the grime came off. All the while, Langer stood not ten feet away, and lit a cigarette. When Leo was done and had stepped back into his clothes, the German nudged him back outside with his truncheon. "Let's go."

To Leo's further surprise, they continued on, past the front gates. Langer exchanged a few mocking jokes with a couple of soldiers standing guard, as if this was a big, important responsibility for the Rottenführer, escorting this skinny prisoner. Leo saw that it angered the SS guard.

"Where are we going, Rottenführer?" Leo asked him again. He had not been out here, the other side of the ramp, since his arrival a year ago.

"Don't ask questions," the SS corporal barked, having lost all patience. "Turn left here. Just march."

Leo was sure the coldhearted bastard had him clean up just to march him out into a field outside the grounds and shoot him into a ditch. And then piss on him, just like Leo had seen before.

So this was it.

But they went on and past the ditch and turned on a road Leo had never been on before. There was a row of three brick homes. They stopped in front of the second one in, with gables and a red roof, stone steps, and a hanging flower basket on the recessed front porch.

"Wait here," the Rottenführer said.

"Where are we?" Leo asked.

"Just look smart, yid." The Nazi jammed his stick into the crook between Leo's legs, making Leo wince. "No prisoner has ever stepped foot in here before. This is Lagerkommandant Ackermann's house."

Ackermann. A chill ran down Leo's spine. The assistant commandant of the entire camp. What had he done that they brought him here? Maybe they wanted to turn him into an informer, Leo surmised. If they did, he would refuse. Even if it meant his death. There was no class of prisoner more reviled than those who it was known brought an earful back to the Nazis. Or maybe they wanted to do some vile experiments on him. Leo looked down at the row of homes, hedges, and transplanted fruit trees in the yards, like some bucolic postcard of normalcy amid all this hell, just across the wire. At the end there was an even larger house. This must be where Kommandant Höss resided. Or maybe the dreaded Mengele himself, whose very sight engendered such fear in everyone. This was where the shits could play their cherished Mozart at night and sing their beloved drinking songs, and pretend that the horrors of what they did during the day were just a dream.

Yes, that's what they were going to do to him, experiments . . .

Langer went up the steps and knocked at the door. A few seconds later, it opened, and he spoke briefly to someone inside. *"Up here. Now!"* he called back to Leo.

Leo climbed up.

"Go." The corporal pushed him to the door. "In."

Warily, Leo stepped inside. His heart beat rapidly, as if speeded up to five times its normal rate by some drug they had already injected. An interior door was open to reveal a small entry foyer, decorated with flowers and portraits, that led to a tasteful family room. A patterned couch. Wooden side tables, photos on them. A polished wood armoire. Sconces with fluted candles on the walls.

Even a piano.

To Leo, everything about the place seemed to speak of normalcy. It reminded him of his uncle's home in Moravia. Not the home of a man who had overseen the deaths of thousands of innocent people.

In the camp, Leo had seen Ackermann several times, darkly handsome and expressionless, looking on at roll call or touring the camp with guests, conversing and gesturing naturally as they passed prisoners being beaten like vermin, as if it were the most common thing in the world.

Another guard came up to him. This one, younger, no cap, dark hair, steely gray eyes. "In. *There!*" He pushed Leo into the family room. "Take off your cap, Jew. Don't touch anything." He gestured toward a sitting table, near the windows that were blocked from the sun by patterned curtains.

On the table, there was a chessboard, the pieces set to play.

In front of it were two chairs.

NINETEEN

Footsteps emanated from deeper inside the house, coming down the stairs. Leo's heart quickened. *Ackermann.* He heard voices, the young guard snapping to attention in the hallway and announcing that the prisoner was in here.

A voice said, "Thank you, Corporal."

But it was not the Lagerkommandant's voice he heard, nor was it he who stepped into the room.

It was the pretty blond woman he had seen in the camp observing some of his matches. She had on a blue print dress, a white sweater over it, and her hair pulled back in a conservative bun, as his mother used to wear it.

He thought she was merely an attendee at the infirmary.

Instead, she was the Lagerkommandant's wife.

"So you are the famous Leo?" she greeted him in proper German. She gave him a smile; there was a hint of kindness in it. But still at a distance. Not exactly warm.

Leo stood there with his cap in his hands, his mouth dry as sandpaper. "I am, ma'am. Not so famous, though, I think."

"I am Frau Ackermann," she said. She took two steps toward him but, of course, made no move to put out her hand. The young guard watched them by the door. "My husband is . . ."

"I know your husband, ma'am," Leo said respectfully.

"Yes, of course. I hoped . . . You may relax. In fact, please, come over here. " She gestured to the chessboard.

Leo stepped over to it. It was hard to ignore the fine, hand-carved pieces in front of him. "May I . . . ?" Leo asked if he could inspect them.

"By all means." She nodded. "Of course."

They were alabaster. As finely polished and smooth as any Leo had ever seen. With exquisite detail. The king carried an imperial staff with a crest on it, and the queen was draped in a long, flowing robe. The castles had the kind of finely carved turrets he had seen only in history books. He picked one up, then thought better of it, and placed it back down. "They're very nice."

"It was my father's," she said. "He liked to play after dinner. With his cigar. He was very good, actually. He could beat most anyone he played. Please, I want you to sit down."

"Sit . . . ?" He looked at her, not quite understanding. He could see that she seemed as awkward and unsure as him. A prisoner. A Jew, no less, in the Lagerkommandant's house. Langer said, *No one has stepped foot here before.* "Me, madame?"

"You are the camp champion, are you not?"

He shrugged indifferently. "I suppose. Yes."

"Then sit, yes. For many years, after my brothers left home, my father had only me to play with." She gestured him toward a chair. "I asked you here to play."

"*Play . . . ?*" Leo looked her, unsure how to respond. "Ma'am."

"Yes. Isn't that what this board is for, Herr Wolciek? To play against me."

He sat. Probably a good thing, as his legs suddenly felt numb and lifeless and almost gave way under him. His heart hammered inside. Play—with *her*. The Lagerkommandant's wife. In their home. *How could he even tell anyone about this?*

Who could ever imagine?

"May I . . . ?" she asked, inquiring if she could play white. She gave him the slightest of smiles. "After all, you are camp champion. I have watched you."

"Yes, ma'am. I have seen you there, but . . . And of course, white."
Leo put out his hand and pulled up to the table.

She smoothed her dress and took her place on the chair across from
him. "*So . . .*" she said, and met his eyes.

Leo's head was dizzy. "So."

She began. Pawn to queen four. Knight to king's bishop three. Leo
recognized it quickly as the King's Indian Defense. A heady opening.
Not many players these days started that way. Leo thought back to a
famous match between the great Capablanca and an Englishman,
Yates, and tried to recall through his daze how the moves devel-
oped. He was nervous. Petrified to make a wrong move. She played
quickly, confidently. His heart beat through his chest. He had to keep
his wits together just to keep up.

The young guard stood and watched them impassively at the
door.

"This is good," she said, pleased to see how Leo countered her advance. "My father used to say, if you can outwit the King's Indian,
you will have no difficulty outwitting the vast majority of people in
life. Do you agree, Herr Wolciek?"

"I do not know, ma'am."

"Yes, I'm sure you're a bit nervous to agree to anything. Please
relax. It's just chess. It is just the two of us. Well, three." She eyed the
young guard with the tiniest of smiles.

"Yes, ma'am." Leo was too afraid to say anything else.

A housemaid stepped into the room.

"Coffee?" Frau Ackermann asked. "Maybe a cake? Or some fruit?"

Coffee? Fruit? A cake? Leo was sure she could see the lump travel
down his throat. These were delicacies here, available only in the
imagination of someone keen on torturing himself. Or maybe paid for
by only the largest of bribes. And then, only scraps, stolen from the
kitchen trash. Whatever the Germans left behind.

Leo licked his lips but still shook his head. He was too unsettled to
even speak. He just moved his piece. Bishop to queen four. "Later
then, Hedda," Frau Ackermann said to the maid. "You may leave the
basket."

"Yes, Frau Ackermann," the housemaid said, and left. She had seemed as nervous as Leo.

They continued on. He watched her thinking out his moves, a finger pressed to her lips, and then quickly replying. It was clear her father had taught her well. She saw through a few of his early ruses, meant to lure her into an unfavorable exchange. And when she did spot his intent, she met his eyes with the faintest of pleased smiles.

"I am happy to have already lasted this long with a player of your skill."

Queen to king's bishop five. Leo cleared his throat and barely got the word out of his throat. "Check."

"I see." She was beautiful. Even in the modest way she covered herself up. Early thirties, he thought. Her eyes were almond-shaped and a soft blue. When she thought she sometimes bit her lower lip, which had a soft covering of red lipstick on it. When Leo looked at her, he glanced at her only for a split second, and when she looked at him, he quickly averted his gaze.

In truth, he had never been alone with a woman before.

"Let's see now . . ." She advanced a pawn, blocking her king from the danger.

They continued deeper into the game. A dilemma began to develop for him. How was he expected to play this? This was the Lagerkommandant's wife. She held the power of life and death over him. Like any of the guards, if she snapped her fingers, she could just have him sent and killed. Should he let her win? Clearly she knew what she was doing, so it would take only a single careless move and would not be so hard. If this were her husband, or any one of the guards, he could see them disposing of any Jew with the audacity to insult one of them. Even a perceived insult. And this was the camp boss's wife? His head went into a spin, and everything he knew about the game seemed to spiral away as if caught up in a swirling wind. He decided to give her a test. He moved up his bishop to attack her queen but left it open to her rook.

"Herr Wolciek," she said, pausing after his move. "Your bishop . . . ?"

Their eyes met. For the first time really. Leo's heart was galloping

113

three times its normal rate. He was afraid she would hear it above the silence, pounding like mad in his chest. He was afraid she would detect what was going through his head.

"But of course you saw that," she said, letting him off the hook. Her eyes narrowed just a bit, both apologetic and in their own way, reproving, as if to say, *Not again. Please.*

"Thank you, ma'am."

The rest of the game they did not converse. They just played; the time between her moves grew longer. Once or twice, Leo let his eyes linger on the tempting shape of her dress. He could not help imagining what she looked like underneath. He let his mind wander, to her undergarments—he had never seen a woman's undergarments, save his mother's. The fluid curve beneath her sweater as she leaned to move. Her breasts . . .

"Herr Wolciek . . . I believe it is your move."

"Sorry, ma'am." He cleared his throat. Rook to queen five. With a blush.

They were set up for a multipiece exchange, which Leo saw would not be to his advantage. Nonetheless, he decided to take the plunge. It would leave him down a rook. They moved the five moves of the exchange in rapid succession. It left his castled king weakly protected. When she saw her position at the end of the exchange, she looked at him again, her eyes suspect, glistening a little, not quite sure.

"I should never have taken the bait," Leo admitted with a shrug. "I fear there is not much point in letting this continue on."

He could see, she didn't know whether to be pleased or angry with him.

"You play very well, Frau Ackermann." Leo turned over his king. "Your father has taught you well."

"Thank you. Perhaps we will play again." She met his eyes. "If you are lucky."

Lucky. The word ran through him. Leo knew precisely what she meant. And it was nothing to do with the chess. "I hope that will be the case," he said.

"And maybe the next time I will beat you for real," she said with a tone of admonishment. Her sharp eyes contained the hint of a sage smile.

"Please get the Rottenführer," she called to the young guard. "Our guest is set to leave. But you will take these, of course." She wrapped two sugar cakes and an apple in a napkin. "With my compliments. Here they will only go to my husband's waistline."

"Thank you, Frau Ackermann." Leo stood up and took the offering. The hair on his arms raised as their hands slightly touched.

"May I?" Leo asked. He pointed warily toward a large plum. It had a private significance to him. He had not even seen one since that fateful day at the fruit stand.

"Of course. See he gets back safely, Corporal," she said to Langer, who had come in from the outside. "And *with* my gifts, if you please."

"Of course, Frau Ackermann." Leo could see Langer gritting his teeth with held-in anger at having to escort Leo back to the block with his cache of treasures.

She got up.

"And next time," she looked back at Leo, the slightest smile in her eyes, "you will have to earn your treats, Herr Wolciek. Not be given them. Do you understand?"

"Yes." Leo bowed his head and smiled back. "I do understand."

Next time . . . Leo said to himself on the walk back to camp. Those words were about the happiest he had heard since he first arrived in this godforsaken place.

The place didn't look quite as bad as he came back to it. Even with Langer prodding him.

He had someone watching out for him now.

TWENTY

She sent for him again the following week. And then again, a few days after that.

The next week as well.

Each time Rottenführer Langer came around to the block to escort Leo late in the afternoon while her husband was still at work. And each time they stopped at the shower and he had Leo scrub himself clean. Though with each new visit the guard seemed to grow more and more displeased with the task.

And each time he marched Leo past the black wall and through the front gate, past the train ramp where he had arrived that first night, to the row of brick houses whose flowers were now starting to bloom. By the third visit the guards at the front gate merely shook their heads in amusement and rolled their eyes at Langer as he and Leo went by. And each time the same young SS private watched by the parlor door while Leo and the Lagerkommandant's wife played their game. And no longer did Leo let her win unchallenged.

And each time he returned to camp he carried back with him a napkin wrapped with treats: cakes, fruit, even chocolates, worth a hundred cigarettes in there. Prizes he willingly shared with his block mates, some of whom laughed at him for his well-placed protectress. *The Queen of Mercy,* they named her, for as long as Leo remained under her protection, maybe his good fortune would spill over onto them. He was their Scheherazade. Just keep her amused, they all begged. "The longer you play, we will all be safe."

Others scowled that Leo was no better than the lowest form of collaborator. How could he spend time sucking up to such filth? She was as guilty as any of them. "She shares the bed of the very bastard who makes sure the daily death quotas are met!"

"I am perfectly happy doing what I have to do," Leo defended himself, "if it buys me one more day here. And you should as well, Drabik, if you had any brains in your head."

Their second match, Leo played much more relaxed. Frau Ackermann tried a more conventional opening, which Leo easily handled. In truth, he could have put her away within twenty moves, but he enjoyed the time he spent there—in the spell of a beautiful woman, and the fact that no Jew had ever had this privilege. He didn't want it to end so quickly. So he prolonged things by swapping a few pieces that made it a fight for territory in the end game, which he easily won.

Each new match, Frau Ackermann grew more relaxed as well. She actually dropped the formal "Herr" and called him by his given name now and then, and between moves, she even asked where he was from and how he learned to play. She volunteered that she was from Bremen, in the North, where all the big breweries were. "You like beer, Leo?" she asked. He felt sure she was toying with him a bit. "You're probably not old enough. You've probably never had a good beer."

"I've had beer," Leo said, trying to make himself seem older than he was. In fact, it had only been once, a few sips, on his father's last birthday before he was killed when Leo was eleven.

She had beautiful, large eyes, and when pleased, like when Leo complimented her on a move, or when she saw what he was up to and countered smartly, they were quick to brighten into a sage smile. And yet he saw that there was a sadness to her as well. Like a caged bird that had grown accustomed to her captivity but dreamed of something beyond. Or someone living a life other than what she had envisioned. He imagined that in a different setting, she could be charming and witty and smart, and in his mind he saw her, at a party, with a glass of champagne in her hand, in a free-flowing, red dress. Yet here, by his fourth visit, he began to get the sense that this was the one thing she looked forward to most. That freed her from the horror she was party to here. His fifth game, it was a warm, summery day and she no longer wore her sweater. Her collar was open another button and fell tantalizingly over her breast so that between moves, Leo's mind roamed to what was underneath, the tiniest hint of cleavage showing through. Maybe once she even caught Leo leaning forward just a bit to stare at it.

"It is your move, Herr Wolciek," she said with a slightly reproving smile.

"Yes. Of course." He cleared his throat. "Sorry."

He was embarrassed at the sudden stiffness he felt in his pants. Both under the chess table and in his bunk at night. She was the wife of the Lagerkommandant. To her, he could be only a lowly Jew who would not live long. His only value was that he amused her. For all he knew, she had the maid wipe down the very pieces he touched with a cloth after he left.

Yet, that fifth match, he saw that she was happy to see him. She must have studied up for she played white and tried a new opening. A variation of the Sicilian Defense. It was the kind of passive opening that easily led to a long middle game and went against his standard Ruy Lopez, and Leo resisted a quick exchange of pawns and knights that would have resolved things sooner.

At some point she asked him where he was from.

"Lodz," he said, looking up. "It's in the center of Poland. We have beer there too." He smiled and looked down.

"Polish beer, you say? Never heard of it. How could there be such a thing?" They played on a few more moves. "And your father . . . What does he do?" Leo looked up at her. "If you do not mind me asking."

"He was a lawyer, Frau Ackermann. He represented people in small business transactions."

"And he is . . . ?" She hesitated, so that he assumed she either meant dead or even worse, *was he here?*

"No, he died, madame, before the war." Leo moved up his rook to put pressure on her knight. Then he added, "Luckily, I think."

Her eyes met his this time. It was the first time he had injected his position and fate into their game, and he was angry at himself because he felt it suddenly separate them. She retreated her knight and the game wound on. Leo glanced at the young guard. He was no more than twenty-two or -three. A private only, but surely this was a plum assignment to guard the wife of the assistant camp commander. Still, one that kept him away from all the "fun and games" going on next door. The way he looked at Leo—narrow, impassive, staring right through him—Leo couldn't help but wonder just how many of his buddies on the other side of the fence this young private had killed. Emptied his Luger into the back of someone's head as they kneeled and waited. Or clubbed them senseless with a blow to the head. Or clamped the "shower" door tight and chuckled to his pals at the gagging and cries for mercy coming from within. Maybe put down a few reichsmarks on how long they would last in there. Three minutes? Five? *Eight?*

Maybe she saw this in Leo's eyes.

"Private, can you please call in Hedda?" she asked. The maid.

"Of course, Frau Ackermann." The young private clicked his heels and left.

She picked up her queen and went to play—to king's knight six, Leo assumed, uselessly attacking his queen—when she held onto it without placing it down and waited for him to meet her eyes.

"I know what you must think—what anyone would naturally think, of course. But I am not the monster you may imagine, Leo. I studied economics at the university in Leipzig. When I met Kurt, he was studying for his law degree. He was very dashing," she said. "Driven. For a young girl, it was . . ."

It was *what?* Leo wondered what she was about to say. *Impressive? Irresistible?* He looked up and her gaze seemed to lock on his even more strongly now, more resolutely, and this time Leo did not pull his away.

"Just because I am here, because I am with . . ." She paused again, short of saying his name. *Him.* "It doesn't mean that I endorse . . ."

Endorse *what* . . . ? The hell that was happening day and night that her husband was overseeing just across the gate? Not for the first time Leo saw what looked to be sadness in her eyes. Something vulnerable inside her, from deep inside her heart, coming forth. The look seemed to say *I don't know how long I can save you, Leo. You understand, not forever . . .*

But all he said back was "Yes, Frau Ackermann." Though he met her eyes as if to say he understood. Then his gaze shifted back to the piece she still held in her hand. "Your queen, ma'am . . ."

"Yes, my queen, of course." She placed it down on the very spot Leo was sure she would. "Check."

At that very moment Hedda, the housemaid, came in. "Can you prepare some fruit and cakes for us, Hedda, please?"

"Right away, Frau Ackermann."

"And please make sure that—"

No sooner had the words left her mouth than the sound of boots was heard coming up the front steps.

"Who is that?" She turned, nerves spreading on her face.

The front door opened. Leo's heart came to a complete stop.

It was the Lagerkommandant himself, coming back to his home.

He turned to face them in the sitting room and took off his hat—dark hair, smoothed back, eyes to match, a jawline as rigid as stone.

"*Kurt* . . . " Frau Ackermann stood up, nervously smoothing out her dress.

"Greta." He smiled back—his tone neither warm nor off-putting.

Then his gaze fell on Leo. Like a heavy weight plummeting deep into the sea. That same smile, but this time, a chill in it, unbending, cold as the wind rattling an open door in winter. Leo felt it remain on him for what seemed an eternity, almost draining the light out of the room. "I see you have a visitor."

Leo lowered his eyes.

"We were just finishing . . ." Greta said. "We're in the midst of a competitive game."

"Then by all means . . ." he said, his eyes still fastened on Leo, seeming to indicate *play on*.

Leo felt too frozen to even lift a piece. He didn't know whether to stand up in the presence of the camp commandant, in his own parlor, no less, and with his wife. Or drop to his knees. But his heart would not move a beat. So he just stayed. His throat like sandpaper.

"Whenever you're done, of course, darling . . ." the commandant said, opening the top button of his uniform. Then he continued on into the house, his boots sounding heavily on the wood floor. "Hedda . . . !"

"I am sorry," Frau Ackermann said, still standing, the color still gone from her face. "I didn't expect him until later. I'm afraid we will have to continue this another time." Her face was flushed and when she looked at Leo, he saw a combination of apology and nerves.

"Of course, Frau Ackermann." Leo stood up too. He went to reset the pieces. He was sure that this was it. That he would never be invited to play again.

"Please, don't." Frau Ackermann reached out to stop him, touching his arm. "Next week, we will pick up from where we are."

TWENTY-ONE

The angular, lanky man in the plaid outdoors jacket and brown fedora went up to the dusty Ford sedan that had made the ninety-minute trip up from Sante Fe.

A man with thinning white hair, rounded shoulders, a high forehead, and almost sad, deep-set eyes stepped out from the back seat.

"Bohr." Robert Oppenheimer went up and put his arms around the celebrated Danish physicist, welcoming him to the most heavily guarded scientific facility in the world, where dozens of the world's foremost physicists, chemists, and mathematicians were sequestered on a research effort known only to a very few as the Manhattan Project.

"Robert." The Dane warmly clasped the American's hand. Even at fifty-eight, Niels Bohr was still among the most respected theoretical physicists in the world, one of the originators of the quantum theory, and before the war, his Copenhagen Conferences had brought nearly all of the world's leading physicists to his doorstep at the university there.

"I trust this trip was a little easier than the jaunt over to London?" Oppenheimer grinned, patting the Dane on the shoulder.

During the war, Bohr and his family had chosen to remain in his native Denmark, sure that the Nazis dared not threaten one of the world's most venerable scientists, recipient of the 1922 Nobel Prize.

122

Still, he resisted every effort to cooperate with his captors. Then in September, barely three months ago, he was tipped off that because of his mother's Jewish background, he was about to be arrested the very next day and deported to one of the camps, an arrest that would have likely been a death sentence for a man of his age. That very night, he and his wife, with only a single suitcase between them, crossed the Oresund by moonlight to neutral Sweden in a tiny boat, weaving between mines and German patrol boats. Two months later, with a parachute strapped on his back and literally passing out due to lack of oxygen, the world's most celebrated physicist was secretly shuttled to the U.K. in the empty bomb bay of a British bomber, carrying the mail pouch between London and Stockholm. After such an escape, the winding ride in a Ford sedan up to the top-secret enclave in the Sangre de Cristo Mountains must have seemed like a trip to the shore.

"Immeasurably, it would be fair to say," the Dane replied affably.

"Well, we're glad you've come," said Oppenheimer. "I think you'll find some old friends who are awaiting you."

An hour later, over lunch in his cottage, Oppenheimer, Richard Feynman, Hans Bethe, and the great Enrico Fermi sat by the fire and brought the Danish scientist up to date on their advances. Bohr had always been concerned about the consequences for humanity of creating such an instrument of destruction, and as he ate his steak listening to his fellow physicists, he suppressed both a theoretician's thrill at the progress they had made and a feeling of impending worry at the same time. On matters that, only a few years back, were merely the musings of physicists over a cognac at scientific conferences.

The biggest obstacle they now faced was the separation of U-235 from its weightier and much more prevalent cousin, U-238, and in quantities sufficient to produce a series of suitable chain reactions.

And, as the clock was ticking, most important in the little time they had left.

They were eager to question Bohr about where he thought Heisenberg was in this process working for the Nazis.

They had narrowed it down to three possible methods of separation, which they mapped out for Bohr, sketching on napkins and table-cloths. Electromagnetic bombardment, thermal diffusion, and gaseous diffusion. All were laboriously time-consuming and required enormous outlays of funds. Massive cyclotrons were under construction, vast diffusion tanks in Oak Ridge, Tennessee—one a series of fifty-eight connected buildings, over forty-two acres, all capable of separating and then separating again the lighter, gasified isotope 238 in thousands of stages. Bohr was awed. It was the largest scientific apparatus ever conceived and built by man. And the most expensive.

Yet it all was trial and error, Oppenheimer bemoaned. At times, since none of this had ever been done, it was much like the blind leading the blind. The materials for these separation chambers had to be incredibly resistant and airtight. Any leak or erosion could cause them to be shut down. New compounds were being constructed. And it was all in a race against the clock, as they feared the Germans were ahead of them.

And to the winner went the war.

"This gaseous diffusion process . . ." Oppenheimer said, lighting his pipe after rhubarb pie. "We are beginning to think that that one is the way."

To Bohr, it all spoke of a world of unimaginable and unforeseen consequences. And now Teller was talking about activating plutonium and creating even deadlier bombs. And what of the Russians? They were on it too. Did we share what we knew with them, our supposed allies? And if not, what of the world then when they finally got their hands on the same powers, as they would eventually?

"Gaseous diffusion?" Bohr said, nodding.

Oppenheimer took a bite of his pipe. "Yes. But it's a crap shoot. The quantities are slim. And Bergstrom, as you recall, who knows this process, is now in bed with Heisenberg."

"Yes, Bergstrom . . ." Bohr nodded after a long pause. He complimented the pie; such delicacies he had not been able to procure in Europe for some time. Then, "I may know of someone," he said between bites. "On this gaseous diffusion process. A Pole. A Jew, in fact. He once worked in Berlin with Meitner and Hahn, you may recall," he said to Bethe, "on this very thing. Kind of a narrow specialty for such a sharp mind, if you ask me."

They all waited. There was too much room for error. They needed someone to shortcut this process.

"The only problem . . ." Bohr said, taking another bite of pie, with a disappointed shrug back at Oppenheimer. "I'm not sure he ever made it out of Europe."

TWENTY-TWO

"Leo . . ." Alfred spotted the young man again in the yard after the afternoon roll call.

"Professor. Good to see you are well," the boy replied. "Have you thought up any new brainteasers for me?"

"Not yet, but have you thought at all about what I asked you?"

"You mean your physics project? I'm afraid I've been a bit occupied."

"Playing chess with your new admirer, I suspect. We've all heard. Perhaps the rigors of something truly important are just too serious for you right now, as opposed to a mere game."

"Chess is no more a 'game' than what you do, Professor. And that admirer may just keep my block mates and me alive in this hole a bit longer. But just for argument's sake, what was it you have in mind? To teach me electromagnetic physics, I think you said. To what end?"

"Not teach. Let's talk somewhere for a moment. Just hear me out. I'll explain."

"All right. I guess a few minutes can't hurt. Lead the way, Professor."

They went back to Alfred's block. Everyone was in their bunks stretched out from their day's work, awaiting the evening meal. They wove through the block to where there was a small sick bay section in the rear. Six beds, so those who had a fever or dysentery wouldn't infect the rest. And the latrine.

"Please sit down, Leo."

"Your office, Professor?" Leo leaned back against an empty bunk. "Impressive."

"Please, what I have to say is no joke, son. And though I can't tell you why just yet, I promise, it's more important than anything you have ever imagined. What I am proposing to do is to go over my work with you. Equations, formulas, proofs. You don't have to learn it. I just want you to listen to me and to commit it to memory."

"To memory . . . ?"

"Yes. To keep it all locked away in that exquisite mind of yours. Will you do that, Leo? I am old and starting to lose my strength. You can see, my bones are starting to come through. Who knows how much time I have left?"

"Who knows how much any of us have?"

"But you, son . . . you are young. You have a chance to make it out of here. And if you do, what I will teach you will be more valuable than all the chess games ever played. You have to trust me on that. But it will not be easy. It will take a lot of time and concentration, going over things. I promise, even for you. Elaborate proofs and progressions. Things you've never heard of and may not understand how they all fit together. But it's vital. Are you up for it?"

"*Physics* . . . ?" Leo turned up his nose like he had asked what was for dinner and been told turnips.

Alfred nodded. "And math. And much of it very complicated."

"So I can do *what* one day, if I manage to survive . . . ? *Teach* this?"

"Physics is a lot more than just formulas and equations, son. It has real-world applications. Things people want to know very badly. For now, and for the future as well."

"I don't know *what* my future holds." Leo shrugged. "But right now, chess seems like a better guarantor of it than this."

"I need you, young man. In some way, the world needs you. Are you game?"

"The world? You make it sound like what you have there can win us the war. All right." Leo took off his cap. "Let's say I take the bait. Go ahead. Try me, Professor. Lesson One. As long as we're already here."

A smile crept onto Alfred's lips. He sat down on the cot across from Leo. "You're going to hear a lot about atoms, boy. And various gases. Things called isotopes."

"Isotopes . . . ?"

"You're familiar with the molecular structure of mass?"

Leo shrugged. "I studied the elements chart in chemistry. Back in school."

"That's a start. Well, atoms of the same element can have different numbers of neutrons. The different possible versions of each element are called *isotopes*. For example, the most common isotope of hydrogen has no neutrons at all. There's also a hydrogen isotope called deuterium with one neutron, and another, tritium, that has two . . ."

"Deuterium . . . ? Tritium . . . ?" Leo blinked at him hazily. "Must I know all of these in order to save humanity?"

"Don't worry about that now. And please don't mock me, son. So let's start with something basic. Graham's Law. It was formulated by a Scottish chemist in the last century. It states that the rate of effusion of a gas is inversely proportional to the square root of either its mass or its density."

"*Effusion?* And just what does that mean, old man?" Leo rolled his eyes.

"Not 'old man.' If we're going to do this, you can start by addressing me as Professor. Or even Alfred, if you prefer. I'm going to teach you things well beyond what you know or can imagine. So this will be like any class in school. There's an instructor and a student. And it starts with respect. Respect for those who know more than you. Do you understand?"

For a moment, Alfred was certain the boy had already tired of him, and would just take his cap and walk out. Go back to the game that was clearly more fun, and had gotten him cakes and chocolates and all the adulation.

But to Alfred's surprise, he remained, his eyes shifting from bored and then reproved, to apologetic, and finally even to interested, filled with some contrition at the same time. "I'm sorry, Professor. I didn't mean to be rude. Please continue."

Inside, Alfred smiled. Strip away the brashness, forgivable in such a precocious lad, and inside that perfect brain was an inexhaustible basin ready and waiting and an unquenchable curiosity to fill it with whatever knowledge there was.

"Good. Now to your question, boy, effusion is the rate of transference of a gas through a probe or, better yet, a membrane. Graham's Law postulates that if the molecular weight of one gas is two times that of another, it will diffuse through a porous layer, or even an opening the size of a pinhole, at the rate of the other times the square of two. It is the key postulate in the separation of isotopes—which have the same molecular structure yet different atomic weights."

"Separating isotopes . . . Porous layers . . . Why do you need to teach me all this?" Leo shrugged, clearly already a bit bored.

"For now, just let this all soak into your head, lad. Look—" Alfred took out a piece of chalk. He had a tin sheet, a scrap of metal left from the motor shed. "All that matters now is how it's expressed as a formula." Alfred scratched out:

$$\text{Rate}_{\text{diffusion}} \propto \frac{1}{\sqrt{\text{density}}}$$

He asked, "Do you have it?"

Leo stared at it, repeating it to himself. "I think so."

"Therefore the *inverse* of this equation is . . ." Alfred erased it with his sleeve and wrote out a new formula, "that the *density* of a gas is directly proportional to its molecular mass."

$$\text{Rate}_{\text{effusion}} \propto \frac{1}{\sqrt{\text{density}}} \propto \frac{1}{\sqrt{\text{MM}}}$$

129

"Are you with me, son?" Alfred saw the boy's eyes glaze.

Leo nodded, a little fuzzily. "I guess."

"All right, then give it back to me, please. Just as I have written."

Leo shrugged. "The rate at which a gas diffuses is inversely proportional to the square root of its densities."

"Good. Now, here, write it out as a formula." Alfred handed him the chalk and tin and covered up what he had done. "Exactly as I gave it to you."

Leo hesitated for a moment, blew out his cheeks, then wrote it,

$$\text{Rate}_{diffusion} \propto \frac{1}{\sqrt{\text{density}}}$$

just as Alfred had conveyed.

"Excellent. Now how about the inverse of that? For density?"

Leo thought on it a second. "The *density* of a gas is inversely proportional to its molecular mass."

"No. Not inversely. The opposite of that. It's *directly* proportional," Alfred corrected him.

"Excuse me, Professor . . . ?" Leo scrunched his eyes.

"The density of a gas is *directly* proportional to its mass. It's the exact inverse of the first equation I gave you. You see—"

"All right. Sorry. I think I've got it now." Leo wrote out the formula,

$$\text{Rate}_{effusion} \propto \frac{1}{\sqrt{\text{density}}} \propto \frac{1}{\sqrt{\text{MM}}}$$

this time correctly. "*Directly* proportional. Then this would be the symbol—he drew it with a stylish flourish:

$$\propto$$

"Very good. Now, in gaseous diffusion, we're dealing with the identical principle, except we are working with two radioactive isotopes. Uranium-235, which is a fissile property. *Fissile* meaning it can be split and is capable of creating what we refer to as a 'chain reaction,' if separated from its more plentiful, but *not* fissile, cousin, U-238."

"*Two thirty-five? Two thirty-eight?* Sorry, but my head is starting to feel like it's fissile, Professor."

"Don't try and understand it all now. You know of uranium, right?"

"Yes. Its symbol is U. And I think it has the highest molecular weight of any element."

"Second highest. But no matter, plutonium is only newly isolated and probably wasn't even on the element chart when you would have studied this. Uranium-235 occurs in a 0.139-to-one ratio in natural uranium ore. Meaning that only 7 percent of all uranium is U-235. The rest is 238. It's quite rare. The trick, then, is to separate this rare, highly charged isotope, which has the same properties but a different molecular weight than its more common relative, U-238. To do that, or at least to do that in the kinds of quantities you would be seeking, you need not only a diffusing membrane but the only compound of uranium sufficiently volatile to engender this, uranium hexafluoride, UF-6, which is completely solid at room temperature but sublimes once it approaches—"

"*Sublimes?*" Leo's eyes started to glaze over again. "I'm afraid you're beginning to lose me, Professor."

"*Here* . . . " Alfred took the tin again and scribbled a far more complex equation. "Just memorize this . . ."

$$\frac{\text{Rate}_1}{\text{Rate}_2} = \sqrt{\frac{M_2}{M_1}} = \sqrt{\frac{352.041206}{349.034348}}$$

"Which is equal to, I think . . ." Alfred closed his eyes and went through a series of calculations in his head. "One point oh oh four two nine eight or something . . . Where—and this is important, Leo—RATE One is the rate of effusion of U-235 and RATE Two is the effusion of . . . ?" He looked to Leo to finish.

"U-238," Leo replied, after a moment of thought.

"Correct! And M*1* is the molecular mass of U-235 and M*2* the molecular mass of U-238. The slight difference in weights explains the 0.4 percent difference in the average velocities of their neutrons." He looked at his student. "So how does that sit?"

"To be honest, it sits a bit fuzzily, Professor."

"Keep at it. I know this might as well all be Greek to you right now . . ."

"No, Greek I actually studied in school . . ." Leo rolled his eyes.

"Look, you don't have to understand it all now. But what's important is that you have a basic grasp and commit the equations . . ." he drew a double line beneath the equation, "into that stellar brain of yours. So, look at it again. Let it sink in."

Leo ran his eyes over the equation again, then closed them.

"Do you have it?"

"RATE small 1 over RATE small 2 is equal to the square root of M small 1 over M small 2 . . . Must I read you back all the numbers, Professor? I'm pretty sure I can . . . One point, zero, zero, four . . ."

"That's not necessary. Anyone with a third-level math degree can calculate that out."

"Then, where Rsmall1 is the rate of effusion of . . . UF6-235, and Rsmall2 is the effusion for UF6-238, and M*1* . . ." Leo pressed a finger to his forehead, "the molecular mass of U-235, and Msmall2, the mass for 238. And so on, and so on, and so on . . ."

"*Bravo!*" Alfred said, leaning forward and squeezing the boy's knee. He coughed up a bit of phlegm.

"One question, Professor, if you don't mind . . . ?"

"Of course. Go ahead."

"I still don't understand why you need to separate this U-235 from 238? And you said before 'in sufficient quantities . . .' Sufficient quantities for what?"

"Let's not get ahead of ourselves." Alfred cast him a patient smile. "All that is to come, my boy. To come."

"So that's it? That's what you needed me to memorize? The physics that will save humanity?"

"That's Lesson One," Alfred replied. "It's enough for today."

"Lesson One . . ." Leo cocked his head a little warily. "*One* of . . . ?"

"*Hundreds,* my boy." Alfred slapped him on the shoulder. "Hundreds. However, I must warn you, tomorrow it actually starts to get a little complicated."

TWENTY-THREE

Weeks went by. They met whenever they were able, for a few minutes at a time after roll calls in the mornings, before meals, most every day.

Other than Tuesdays, when Leo was usually summoned to play chess with the Lagerkommandant Ackermann's wife.

Which bristled Alfred. "Why do you choose to play a game when we have serious work to get done?"

"Because that *game,* as you call it, may one day be the difference in saving my life. And yours too, I should remind you. I tell her all the time that I share the treats she gives me with my uncle, the Professor. She promises to watch out for us."

"Watch out for us . . . I think you just like to go because you are sixteen and you can stare at a woman's tits. I may be old, but not so old that I can't remember the pleasure in that."

"That as well, I suppose." Leo blushed, with just a little shame. "Still, she is nice to me. And, I believe, she is not her husband when it comes to what goes on in here. I think she is genuinely reviled by what she sees him do. That's why she helps with the sick at the infirmary."

"You think that's so, huh? She shares all this with you?"

"She does. While we play."

"I think that playing this game with you is how she puts her guilty conscience to rest," Alfred said. "In a way, you are her absolution."

"Ah, I see you are Dr. Freud now, too, as well as Dr. Mendl." Leo sniffed with a roll of his eyes.

"In this case, boy, studying the atom is as good as studying the mind. In the end, she is the Lagerkommandant's wife. And you are just a Jew." He turned over Leo's arm. "With that number on your wrist. She'll watch out for you until your time is up. Then she won't give you a thought."

"We'll see." Leo shrugged. "In the meantime, the cakes and chocolates she gives me are nice."

"Yes, well, you're right, we'll see . . ." Alfred coughed, bringing up a little phlegm, and wiped his mouth with his hand. "Anyway, let's get back to work." The cough had worsened, growing a bit more hacking with each day, and his bones and ribs were starting to show through even more. "Sorry that all you get to look at here is me."

"Yes, the view is decidedly less appealing. Here, let me put a blanket over you, old man. Sorry, excuse me," he grinned. "I meant, Professor, of course." It was one of the thin, grimy pieces of burlap that did nothing to protect you from the cold.

These past weeks, Alfred had begun to grow fond of the boy. And he thought Leo felt the same about him. You learned on your first day in this place it wasn't wise to have feelings for another prisoner or to even invest in a person's history. You never knew how the next day might unfold.

"It's nothing," Alfred said. But he wrapped the cloth around himself nonetheless and, for a moment, it stopped the chill. "Thank you, boy."

As Alfred warned, the work grew harder and more complex each day. Now he was taking Leo through something called *Bessel functions*— complex, mind-stretching equations that were almost like going through an entire chess game in his head. A dozen games, Leo felt, each requiring the concentration of playing against a master, though Alfred rattled off the detailed numbers and values without a moment's hesitation, as familiar to him as was his own birth date or house address.

"Remember, we are dealing with highly charged materials here," he explained, "that are in flux from state to state and, in the case of diffusion, through a confined space, in this case, cylinders. So we must introduce the general neutron diffusion equation for such a state." He scribbled on the back of a torn-down health notice:

$$\frac{\partial N}{\partial l} = \frac{v_{ment}}{\lambda_f}(v-1)N + \frac{\lambda_f v_{ment}}{3}(\nabla^2 N)$$

"Okay . . ." Leo stared at it, a little numb. "I see."

"You have to know it, Leo. Know it cold. That is a must."

"I'm trying, Alfred."

"Then try harder. You must focus more. The goal here"—Alfred coughed into his rag—"is to apply the neutron population within a cylinder. The spatial part of the neutron density, characterized as N, will be a function of the cylindrical coordinates (p, o, z), and is assumed to be separable and expressed as . . ." He leafed through the scraps of paper he kept from yesterday's session:

$$N_{p\phi z}(\rho, \phi, z) = N_\rho(\rho)N_\phi(\phi)N_z(z)$$

Leo looked at him blankly.

"Are you with me, son?"

The boy puffed out his cheeks and blew out a long blast of air. "You're going too fast, Alfred. I'm not sure."

"*Not sure?* I thought we went over this yesterday."

"I know, but it's not like chess. I don't fully understand why it's important."

"Right now, it's important because I say it's important. So let's do it over again. What is the coordinate o in the equation, if you don't mind?" Alfred asked him.

"O . . . ?"

"Yes, small o. Where is your head, boy? We've been through this several times. It's the angle between the cylinder's width and radius. And p?"

"*P* . . . ? *P* must be its height then?" Leo answered tentatively.

"Yes. Height. Dimension. I thought you were smart, Leo. I thought you could grasp this. You must concentrate, this is the easy part. Otherwise there is too much to learn."

"Can we take a break, Professor? My head's about to explode. And what is the purpose of all this, anyway? Did you invent it or something? This precious, gaseous diffusion process? We just keep going over and over the same boring things!"

"Because you must learn it, boy. Like you know your own name! Do you hear me?"

"Yes, I hear you!" Leo leaped up from the cot. "*I hear you. I hear you* . . ." His head was bursting with all these numbers. A feeling of total frustration and pointlessness swept over him. "Maybe we should just call it a day."

Alfred looked at him, knowing he had pushed too far. He let the boy calm a moment. Then, "No, I didn't invent it," he said. He put down the sheet. "In fact, the Brits are developing it as well at the same time. And I've heard researchers at Columbia University in New York are on the same track as well."

"Then let *them* learn it," Leo said testily.

"That would be easy, wouldn't it?" Alfred nodded, sitting back. "All *I've* done," he said, "is simply to carry the data to a further state. *Here* . . . " He took the back of a poster on the spread of typhus that had been put in the block and drew out a rough, hand-sketched drawing. A kind of an interconnected system of tubes with long cylinders feeding into smaller tubes, through a network of coils and pumps. "If the uranium gas, hexachloride 6, which is extremely caustic, is pumped against a porous barrier of some kind, the lighter molecules of the gas, containing the enriched U-235, would pass through the cylinders more rapidly than the heavier U-238. Right?"

Leo nodded. That much he *had* learned.

"Which is exactly what this formula represents. You must have this down cold, Leo. No matter how dull or complicated it may seem. This is the heart of what you need to know."

"'Need to know' *why* . . . ? Who gives a fart about this stupid dif-fusion process anyway? Or is it *ef*-fusion?" Leo snatched the drawing from the cot, crumpled it into a ball, and flung it into the corner. "Do you know what I saw today . . . ? I watched as six men were pulled from my line at work and ordered to lie down. Then told to '*Get up!*' And then, '*Lie down*' again. Snap, snap, double time. And then, '*Up* again! *Then down! Faster!* Faster!' And then to '*Run in place!*' and then '*Squat!* Squat ten times!' And then to '*Get up again! Quick. And then lie down. On the double! Schnell! Schnell!* Faster.' Until, one by one, they all just stopped in complete exhaustion, totally out of breath, and were finished off with clubs while they attempted just to suck oxygen into their lungs. The last one, red in the face, barely able to lift his legs, the guards laughing at him as if he were a marionette on a vaudeville stage. Until they beat him dead as well. So tell me, what did Graham's Law do for them?"

Alfred just looked at him.

"And did you hear? Two nights ago, everyone in Block Forty-Six was marched into the night and never came back. Did all these cylin-ders and diffusion equations save *them*? Soon it will be us. You're a fool, Alfred, to think the Germans will ever let any of us leave. Any of us! You know that as well as me. We're all going to die in here. You *and* I. So what does it matter, in the end, if it's small *p* or large *P* . . . U-235 or 238? My head is bursting, Alfred. Every day we do this. Over and over. And *why* . . . ? You force these things in my brain and you won't even tell me why?"

Alfred nodded. He sat back against the wall and let out an under-standing breath. "It matters a lot, my boy. You're right, I probably will die in here. But *you* . . . The war has turned, Leo. You hear it from the new people coming in. The German Army is in tatters in the East. The Allies are set to invade. You can see it in the guards' eyes. They are growing concerned. One day you may well get out of here, and I will give you the names of people to ask for. Respected people. Because what I am showing you on these torn slivers of paper and on the backs of these filthy food labels is worth more than all the gold the Germans take out of our teeth. A thousand times more."

"I know. You keep saying that, Alfred. But *why* . . . ?"

The professor bent down and picked up the crumpled diagram Leo had thrown against the wall and smoothed it out on the cot. "Right now, in laboratories in Britain and in the United States, even in Germany, the most accomplished scientists, ones who make me seem as dull as an oxen, are going over the very same things . . ."

"So then what do they need you for?" Leo pressed. "And all these equations you're jamming into my head?"

"Ultimately, they don't." Alfred shrugged. "Except that I know this one thing, and know it very well. And that is how to assemble a sufficiently large mass of uranium to capture and use the secondary neutrons before they escape through the surface of the material. And though this may not seem like much to you, Leo, because there's no chessboard to mull over or pieces to move, be assured that whoever understands this process, understands it *first* . . . it is *they* who will win the war. And all the guns and tanks and planes in the sky won't be able to stop them."

"This *effusion* process . . . ?" Leo squinted back at him. "Or *dif*-fusion, whichever?"

"Diffusion." Alfred nodded with a smile.

"You keep using the words 'sufficient quantities,' Alfred. Quantities sufficient for what?"

This time Alfred just looked at him, with an elder's gravity that it was time to explain difficult things to a boy who would now become a man. "You asked me once, what is the purpose of separating U-235 from U-238 . . . ?"

"I can see now, it's clearly some form of harnessing energy," Leo said. "Maybe some kind of powering device? An engine. For a tank, perhaps? Or a ship?"

"Yes, but much, much larger than that, I'm afraid. And with a far more devastating effect."

"You're talking a bomb?" Leo's eyes grew wide.

Alfred sank his back against the wall and smiled with a kind of resignation. "A small part of one, yes. But a larger and far more destructive bomb than the world has ever seen. More like a thousand bombs, Leo. In one."

"A thousand bombs . . ." Leo looked at the flattened-out drawing again. "And all from this? This diffusion process?"

Alfred shrugged guiltily. "My friend Bohr postulated that the bombardment of a small amount of the pure isotope U-235 with slow neutron particles of atoms was sufficient to start a chain reaction great enough to blow up his laboratory, his building, and everything in the surrounding countryside for miles. *If* you can separate the isotope, Leo . . . And in sufficient quantities." He nodded. "There's your answer, boy."

Leo sat back down. He saw the pallor on the old man's face and his eyes grew solemn. "I'm sorry. I'm sorry I crumpled your drawing, Professor . . ."

"That's okay. Happens, from time to time. Among colleagues. Look, I know this is difficult. I know your head is loaded with things I haven't fully explained. I know you'd rather be playing chess in whatever time is free here. Indisputably, I know your new opponent is a lot more captivating than me to look at."

Leo grinned, a hint of guilt in his blush once more. "So who is it you want me to get this information to? All you've crammed in my head. If I make it out."

"Scientists." Alfred shrugged. "Famous ones. They will want to see this. Maybe in Britain. Or even America."

"America?" Leo's eyes grew wide. "That *is* a dream, Professor."

"Yes. It's a dream. But, trust me, it's no dream that they will want you when they hear what it is you know. They will need you. They will."

They both sat for a while, staring at the diagram. Leo seemed to be taking it all in. A bomb. *The size of a thousands bombs. In one. Larger and far more devastating than the world had ever seen.* The kind of knowledge that turns a boy into a man.

Then Leo looked back up at Alfred and said, without a blink in his eye: "Neutron density for coordinates, small *p*, small *o*, small *zed*, equals the neutron small *p* times small *p*, times the neutron small *o* times small *o*, times the neutron small *zed* times small *zed* . . . where *p* equals a cylinder's radius, *o* equals the angle between the diameter and the radius, and *zed* equals the cylinder's height."

"Perfect." Alfred's eyes lit up. He clapped lightly.

"See, I am smart," Leo said.

"Yes, you are." Alfred coughed again, his whole body rattling.

"You're sick. I should take you to the infirmary."

"It's just a cold. And if you don't get better in there in two or three days, you know where the send you . . . up the chimney."

"And if you don't get better out here, who will deliver your theories and equations?" Leo asked.

"You have a point there," Alfred conceded.

They sat for a while, the boy's head swimming with what Alfred had told him. Then he said, "We'll both get out." He met Alfred's eyes. "You'll see. You'll take your formulas and drawings to America."

"Now, that *is* a dream." Alfred smiled back fondly.

"Someone told me that there's one thing they don't get to take from you in here . . . and that's your dreams."

"Yes, I believe that as well." Alfred nodded.

Leo looked at him with certainty. "We will. You'll see." Then he handed Alfred back the drawing. "We still have time. Teach me more."

TWENTY-FOUR

He woke up in the night, shivering in sweat. He couldn't remember exactly where he was or why he was in this scratchy bed gown. Only that his head was dizzy and reeling; his belly cramped. He called out, in the darkness: *"Marte!"* It was a warm night, yet he was shivering like it was January, not May. *"Marte, where are you?"*

"Shut up, old man!" the person in the bunk next to him growled.

Who is that? Alfred had a sense of someone staring over him.

"Shit, he's got the fever," his bunkmate said.

"I'm so cold," Alfred said, teeth chattering. "Help me," he called to anyone who would hear. "Oh God," he shot up, "my stomach . . ."

They rushed a bucket to him from the latrine and he let it all out, retching his insides over the side of the bunk.

"The Professor's sick. We have to get him out of here," he heard someone say.

No, please. You can't. Not yet.

Instinctively, he still knew that letting them take him to the infirmary would only result in his death. He heard a commotion—voices, cursing, people gathered around.

"I'm sorry," he muttered. "Where's Marte?"

"Your wife's dead, old man," he heard someone tell him.

Yes, that's right. She's dead. Lucy too. Both dead.

142

"Wrap him in a blanket and keep him in the back," a voice said. Ostrow the forager. "In the morning we'll take him to the infirmary."

"If he makes it to morning," someone wagered.

"Hang in there, old man." Ullie, the baker.

He felt himself lifted in the air. Almost, as if he could see what was happening below. Three people carried him, mummified, to the rear of the block where the sick were kept.

Maybe this was best. Maybe it was time to just give up. Marte would be waiting for him with his tea and almond biscuits and the afternoon paper.

"Professor, you're going to be all right. Just hang in there," someone exhorted.

"Christ, he's burning up!"

"He's got it bad," he heard another voice say.

"Get him some water." A minute later, he felt a thin stream of warm liquid moisten his parched lips.

"Thank you."

In a flash of lucidity, he came out of the delirium for a moment and realized what it was he had. As a man of science, he knew what it meant. *It was like a death sentence in here.* The disease hadn't yet reached his bowels. That was good. Still, it was fifty-fifty. At best. But in here, where no one gave a shit whether you lived or died, who could know?

He couldn't die. Not yet.

There was still more work to do.

The voices died down. He lay there, bundled up, chattering like when he was a boy and went skating with his father on a frozen lake in the mountains and fell through a thin patch of ice and his father had to fish him out. It all seemed so real to him. The pond. His father's grasp. In his life, he had never felt so cold.

Then someone else's face crept into his mind.

The boy.

We need more time, Alfred said to himself, though it was likely out loud, and anyone who heard would just think him delirious.

It's too soon.

143

First thing is that you mustn't give yourself over to the fever, he told himself. *You must keep your wits.*

Your brain.

Fighting the urge to drift off, the oddest thing came into his mind. His friend Polanyi's principle of chain reactions. A chemist, of all things. What was it now? "One center of a chemical reaction produces thousands of product molecules, which occasionally have a favorable encounter with a reactant and instead of forming only one new center, form two or even more, each of which is in turn capable of engendering a new reaction chain . . ."

An expression of it being *1; 2; 4; 8; 16; 32; 64; 128; 256; 512 . . .*

He lay there shivering but calculating it out. *1,024; 2,048; 4,096; 8,192; 16,384; 32,768; 65,536; 131,072 . . .*

How much farther can you extend it?

262,144; 524,288; 1,048,576; 2,097,152; 4,194,304 . . . 8,388,608. 16,777,216.

Inside, he smiled.

You can't die yet, Alfred. There's still more for him to learn.

You haven't discussed the Displacement Principle yet. Or your views on the composition of the diffuser membrane.

To his amazement, a universe of numbers and equations, spheres and mathematical proofs danced out of the darkness, swirling, reaching toward him.

Not yet. Please. It's too soon, he told himself. *You can't. There's still much more to learn.*

But, Marte, you should see this! he said in wonderment. The sky was lit with numbers and equations. *I'll be there soon.* He stopped fighting. A heaviness was making him close his eyes.

It's too soon, he repeated. *But it's all so beautiful!*

TWENTY-FIVE

MAY 20

NEWMARKET RACE COURSE, SUFFOLK, ENGLAND

The whir of propellers and the heavy drone of bombers taking off to drop their loads over the continent was a constant backdrop here. In the past two days, they had been battering the coast of France and pounding factories in the German homeland night and day.

"Softening up the defenses," Strauss said. "For the big one." The forthcoming invasion. Everyone knew it was coming.

"When?" Blum asked.

The OSS captain shrugged. "Who knows? Soon."

Nathan had been in England for ten days. He and Strauss were being housed at this historic race course, once the site of two of the country's Classics, seventy miles from London, now a bustling RAF base, home to the 75th squadron of Wellington and Stirling bombers. Assigned to them were two British MI-6ers, Majors Kendry and Riggs, and a Colonel Radjekowski, from the Armia Krajowa, the Polish Home Army based in London, who was to set up the contacts with the local resistance.

On a strict diet, Blum had already lost eight pounds. His face, narrow to start with, now had the protruding cheekbones and sharp, gaunt jaw of someone living on a once-a-day diet meant only to keep you alive. Every night he inspected himself in the mirror in his quarters tucked away from the main barracks and saw his eyes grow dark and a bit more sunken.

They taught him to jump. From practice ramps. Taught by an RAF sergeant major. The big one was yet to come.

They worked on his gun skills, shooting at targets twenty yards away with a Colt 1911. Brushed up on his Polish, mostly slang and idioms, which had been dormant the past three years. Went over his identity. Mirek, his name was. A carpenter from the town of Gizycko in the lake country of Masuria. As a boy, Blum had shown a knack for woodworking. Such skills always have a place and value in the camp, Strauss said. And they pored over the maps. Over and over them. Endlessly. Maps of the surrounding area. The drop point, in a field near the Vistula, about twenty kilometers from the camp. The extraction location, a quarter mile to the southeast. "Though not to worry too much on this, the partisans will get you there." The endless memorization of local roads in case it was necessary. The little hamlet of Rajsko that was nearby. A safe house he could call on there should things go awry.

"You mention the words *ciasto wisniowe*," Radjekowski, the Polish intelligence officer, said.

"Cherry pie?"

"Short notice . . ." The officer shrugged apologetically.

"No matter." Kendry, the Brit major with a pencil-thin mustache, tapped out his pipe. "Not to worry. If things do go awry on the ground, you're probably dead anyway."

Blum smiled flatly. Kendry was a man he didn't much care for. "I will try and improve on that, sir."

More maps. Maps of the camp itself, hand drawn by Vrba and Wetzler. Nathan went over them until his eyes ached. Every structure was committed to memory. The train tracks leading in. The front gate. The prisoners' barracks, called blocks. The infirmary. The double perimeter of electrified wire. And the rectangular flat-roofed building he had asked about with Strauss and Colonel Donovan.

The crematorium.

Maps of the surrounding area outside the camp.

"This is particularly important." Strauss kept driving this one point home. "You must have this area one hundred percent committed to memory."

The IG Farben factory, which was under construction. The new train tracks almost leading to neighboring Birkenau. The surrounding woods and river. They went over and over these until Nathan had it all burned into his head as well as he did the neighborhood he grew up in back in Krakow.

They gave him the file on Alfred Mendl, his man. Photos and photos. At scientific conferences, at the university where he taught. His kindly face, graying hair pulled over to the side, high forehead, round, doughy jaw. The mole on the left side of his nose.

"He may not look like this now, so that mole will be your confirmation, Nathan. Look for it. Memorize every pore."

So he did, including every detail they had amassed on Mendl. Where he was born: Warsaw. Where he studied: the universities of Warsaw, Gottingen, and the Kaiser Wilhelm Institute in Berlin. His mentors: the famous Bohr, Otto Hahn, and Lise Meitner. His particular area of expertise: electromagnetic physics. The gaseous diffusion process. *Whatever the hell that was.* Mendl's wife and daughter, Marte and Lucy, who were shipped to Auschwitz with him and were very likely dead. They still wouldn't divulge the real reason why they needed him so badly. Why they were sending Nathan in.

"In case you're captured" was how Strauss explained it with merely a shrug. Blum saw the true meaning behind it.

Captured and *tortured*, he meant.

Back in his quarters, at night, Blum smoked and continued to read through Mendl's file. Why him above all others? There were stray cats all over the base, foraging, and one of them hung around Blum's quarters. A calico with wide, gray eyes. It reminded Blum of the cat they'd had on Grodzka Street. Leisa's cat. The one they couldn't bring with them to the ghetto. *What was his name?* Blum tried to recall.

Ah, yes, Schubert, of course.

Blum fed it crumbs of bread and let it lick the cream from uneaten desserts off his fingers. It brought back a life that seemed such a distant memory now. He preferred to remain by himself at night, going over his maps and files.

"You see this man?" Blum showed the photo of Mendl to the cat, who had jumped up on his open window ledge. The calico meowed for some milk and arched his back. "I am expected to find him, in a camp of thousands. Maybe a hundred thousand. Crazy, is it not? I suspect even you must agree. And if I can't . . . locate him, I may end up like you," Blum said, scratching his back. He pulled off a bit of a tart. "Stuck there forever. Except no one is going to give me bits of cream and pastries . . ." He let the cat lick his fingers.

"Since we're at a race course, I suspect no one would bet too heavily on my success." The cat meowed. "Ah, I see even you agree, Schubert, my friend."

Day Five, they finally showed him his uniform. Sewn by tailors specifically assigned to MI-6, it was a laborers' outfit, loose fitting, with thin pants that reversed to a zebra-striped burlap tunic and pants. Every detail on it had been gone over with the escapees, Vrba and Wetzler. It came with a pair of tight-fitting wooden clogs that Blum had to squeeze his feet into.

"A bit snug, I see?" Kendry bit on his pipe.

"They'll be fine."

"Probably a better fit than most in there, I suspect. You'll have proper boots for the jump, of course, but you'll have to ditch them before you go inside the camp."

A few days after that they met in a small meeting room on the base where the mission commanders generally briefed the pilots. Strauss stepped to the blackboard, a rough map of the camp and the surrounding area drawn on it. "I know you've been waiting to hear with a bit more detail how we're planning to get you back," he said with a smile.

"A passing interest, yes." Blum smiled too.

Even Kendry chuckled behind him.

"We're told that camp labor is being used to help finish the new railroad tracks to Birkenau." Strauss pointed to the blackboard. "Which is nothing but a death factory right next door. We have it that Hungarian Jews are being transported there and liquidated upon their arrival. By the thousands. Gassed."

"Thousands . . ." The number hit Blum like a blow to the head, and he muttered under his breath. *"Pieprzy."* Fuck.

"Every day. According to our sources, the work to finish these tracks goes on day and night. There seems to be quite a rush, it appears"— Strauss sniffed—"to ramp up the killings. What you've got to do is get yourself assigned to that particular work detail on the third night you are there. Vrba and Wetzler insist this is not a difficult task. The guard who generally oversees this assignment, an Oberführer Rauch, is known to be open to a bribe. In fact, they claim this is an everyday occurrence in the camp for all sorts of things. In the case of the night detail, apparently there are some who actually desire this particular work detail as it gets you a second meal."

"*Bribe?* Bribe him with what?" Blum questioned.

"More on that later . . . In the meantime, what is important is that on this particular night, at zero thirty hours, local partisans, who the colonel here assures me are quite ready and capable, will organize an attack on the work detail from the nearby woods. *Here.*" Strauss tapped his pointer against the blackboard. "This is why it's so important that you have the surrounding terrain committed to memory. You—and Mendl, of course, we're counting on—will run from the attack not toward the woods but toward the river. *Here . . .*" Strauss pointed. "It's vital that amid the commotion you and Mendl make your way there, Nathan. You'll be met and taken to the landing site. The plane will be set to land precisely at zero one thirty hours. The guards should be occupied for at least a few minutes, till reinforcements arrive, and it would seem logical that anyone looking to escape would run in the direction of the woods, where the partisans will be firing from, and not toward the river. In any case, the ambush will give you cover. Do you have all that?"

Blum nodded. "Yes. I believe so."

"Of course, should you somehow be unable to find Mendl, or

in the event he's dead or in no condition to escape"—Strauss shrugged—"then it will just be you."

"I understand."

"So that's the plan. We'll go over everything several more times." Strauss sat on the edge of the table. "I'm sure you have questions . . ."

"Just one to start. I'm betting my life on the belief that the local Armia Krajowa will attack," Blum said.

"They will," Radjekowski, the Polish colonel, said. "You can be sure of it."

"And"—Blum turned back to Strauss with a smile—"that this particular guard can be bribed."

"Yes." Strauss tapped the pointer twice against the map. "That is the case. *So* . . . "

A stiff silence settled over the room.

Blum felt it was time to ask the question. "So when do I go?"

Strauss glanced toward the Brits, receiving a last, confirming nod from the Polish resistance officer. "The twenty-third. It's a full moon. Highest visibility. We'll be needing it to spot the landing sight. You'll be making the trip in one of the RAF's brand-new Mosquito bombers. Lightweight, high speed. It's able to fly well above the German radar. Oswiecim's about a thousand miles one way, direct, but you'll be flying over to Gothenberg, Sweden, then south, across the Baltic. The Mosquito cruises at about three hundred miles per hour. Given the detour, it should take around four hours or so. We'll do our best to occupy the Luftwaffe with some diversionary bombing runs." He looked at Blum, in the way a trial lawyer might look at the end of his closing argument when there was no more to say. "All clear?"

"So the twenty-third then . . ." Blum nodded. A stab of nerves edged through him.

"Yes." Strauss put down his pointer. "Two days."

TWENTY-SIX

The following day was Sunday, and Blum was given the morning off though he was up at dawn, his nerves unsettled. He leafed through the files one more time—the map of the camp, Mendl—even though everything was already firmly etched in his brain.

At noon, Schubert came around his bunkhouse, the cat's food options clearly diminished elsewhere. Blum was putting a few crumbs on the sill when he heard a knock on the door.

It was Strauss. "Sorry to bother you, Nathan," he said. He had an expression Blum couldn't quite read. Sober. Unsettled. He was with Kendry, the quiet Brit. Blum didn't trust him. "Mind if we sit?'

"Please . . ." Blum said, clearing his clothes and files off the other bed. Kendry chose to lean against the window and took out his pipe.

"So . . ." Strauss gave him a lukewarm smile. "Tomorrow night it is . . ." He looked at the files and pictures on the other bed. "You're all set?"

"I think so, sir."

"Got everything down?"

"Like I was from there." Blum gave him a smile.

"Yes." Strauss smiled too. "Of course, there's a few more details we have to get settled. You'll be pleased to know we've gotten the final thumbs-up from the people on the ground. They're expecting you.

And the weather looks spot on." He took off his cap. "There is, though, just one more thing . . ."

"What is that, sir?"

The Brit took a step forward and took a puff on his pipe. "We're concerned about one aspect, Lieutenant, that wasn't part of the training."

"What is that?" Nathan sat there, looking at them.

"The question, Lieutenant . . . can you kill?"

"Can I kill?" Blum looked back at them, unsure. He'd faced being shot at. Several times. But even in the ghetto he'd never had to kill someone. "I'm a soldier," he said. "Of course I can kill. If I have to."

"I'm afraid that's just not quite good enough, Nathan." Strauss stood up. "With all that's on the line, with everything that's at stake, there may well be a time on this mission when you will have to. When your life, and everything else that's involved, will depend on it. And you won't be able to decide there if you can or you can't."

"Then I will. You can count on it," Blum declared firmly, looking at the two of them.

"So then we'd like you to prove it," Kendry said. He unbuttoned his side holster and took out his Browning.

Blum regarded them in some confusion. "How?"

"I see you've made a friend," the Brit said, smiling to Schubert on the sill. He held out his finger and the animal sidled over to him, arching his back, brushing against him.

"Yes, I think I told you about him," Blum said. "He—"

The Brit looked back at him.

Suddenly it became clear to Blum just what they were asking. "You can't be serious?" he said, shaking his head. The Brit's gaze hadn't budged. "He's just an innocent cat. He's my friend."

"From here on out, you have no more friends," the major replied. "And there's no such thing anymore as guilt or innocence. Only people standing between you and what you have to get done. So, in fact, I'm perfectly serious . . ." He cocked the pistol and held it out for Blum. "We both are. Show us."

Blum's jaw parted, then he turned toward Strauss. The OSS captain offered him no relief. He merely shrugged. "Unfortunately, Nathan, we can't quite run with this uncertainty. There's simply too much on the line."

Blum stared, disbelieving, at the gun. He could not accept what they were asking of him. "There is a difference," he said. Schubert jumped from the sill to the bed. The Nazis were murderers. They killed innocent people, his parents and sister. Many of his friends. He'd talked his way past German guards and checkpoints with needed medicine in his pockets. He crossed Poland with a holy tract of the Talmud in his luggage; was snuck onto a Swedish freighter, when being discovered would have meant immediate death. *But this* . . . There was a line. This was on the other side of it. The cat jumped onto the floor and brushed up against the bed.

This made him just like them.

Strauss said, "You think this is any worse than what you will likely face when you land?"

Kendry continued to hold out the gun.

Blum's gut felt as if a knife was tearing through it. It was as if whatever value he held dear, any remembrance of the life he once had, his parents and his sister, anything that separated him from the soulless goons who murdered them was being shredded for good.

You're the one who wanted to do more . . .

"He's innocent, I know, Nathan. But there may be others who are innocent who may threaten this mission. If you can't," Strauss stood there, waiting, "I'm afraid we cannot trust you to go."

Schubert made his way along the floor. *Run. Now. Please . . .* Blum begged inside. The cat stopped at the door and looked up at Blum, likely expecting an affectionate pet or some food maybe, and meowed.

Blum took the pistol. "Forgive me," he said, and stepped up to him.

He put the gun down and squeezed the trigger. There was a loud retort. The pistol jerked back in his hand. The cat fell over on his side. Blum stood there looking at it, as something hollow and shameful knotted in his gut, knowing something in him had now changed and gone over to the other side.

"*Here.*" He handed the Browning back to Kendry.

Strauss came over and put a hand on Blum's shoulder. "Nathan, I'm sorry. I know what that took. Still, we had to be sure."

Blum nodded. "I understand."

"And trust me . . . " Kendry placed the gun back in his holster. "This won't be the worst thing you'll be forced to do on this mission."

TWENTY-SEVEN

The day he was set to go, Blum was asked to take a call at the communication headquarters.

Strauss set him in a private room, with a radio receiver and a telephone handset.

He figured it was Donovan to wish him luck, or maybe a member of his new family, in Chicago, but when the caller got on, through the scratchy static and hissing, he recognized the famous voice from his speeches and "fireside" chats.

It was the president of the United States.

"Am I speaking with Lieutenant Blum?" FDR asked.

"Yes, sir." Almost by reflex, Blum stood up, although the great man was an ocean away. "Mr. President . . ." His throat grew dry.

"I wanted you to know that I am fully aware of your mission, Lieutenant. And I called to wish you all good luck."

"Thank you sir," Blum said, swallowing. "I'm honored you were even told of it."

"Told of it." The president chortled. "I damn well ordered it, Lieutenant."

A wave of pride washed through Blum. He looked at Strauss, the blood rushing into his face.

"I know the risks," the president said, "and what you are giving up to do this. We owe you a debt, young man. But do not fail us. You have no idea how much depends on the success of what you do."

"I won't," Blum said, his chest expanding. "Sir."

"Good. Then all I can do is to wish you all God's speed and that His watchful eyes will be over you. I've been assured on many levels that we have chosen the right man."

"I'm humbled, sir," Blum said again.

"Then I await the news of your safe and successful return." The president signed off. "Good luck, young man."

Blum heard a beep and the receiver showed that the line had disconnected. Still, Blum filled his chest and uttered, "Thank you, sir."

Before he left he was given three last things.

The first was cash. Five hundred pounds sterling. "You'll need something to bribe the guard with. It'll be sewn into the lining on your tunic." Strauss showed him. "Along with something else."

He had a small blue pouch with him, which he tossed to Blum. Blum opened it, and his eyes went wide.

It contained a diamond.

Quite a large one. Larger than anything he had ever seen, even on the fingers of the fancy wives who would accompany their rich husbands into his father's shop. *Eight karats,* Blum estimated.

"Ten, I can see you wondering," Strauss said. "Nearly perfect quality. Worth a tidy sum. In case you get into trouble," the captain winked at him, "and you have to buy your way out. It's better than cash or gold in the camp and far more transportable. You know where to hide it, don't you? In a pinch . . . ?" Strauss gave him kind of a crooked smile.

"Oh. Yes. I see." Blum said, blushing slightly.

"Use it wisely. And by all means, try not to forget it's there."

"No, I won't. Of course not." Blum cleared this throat.

"In the meantime, I'll just hold onto it, if you don't mind . . ." Strauss put out his hand. "For safekeeping, until you leave. Oh, and something else . . ." He dug into his pocket. "Not exactly sure how to broach this one with you. You're going into a nightmarish place. Even

I'm not sure myself just what you'll run into in there. Especially, in the chance something goes wrong . . ." He opened his hand, and there were two reddish capsules in a plastic case.

Blum looked at them closely, then back at Strauss, the meaning clear. "I see."

"Instantaneous, practically painless, I'm told. Have to admit, though"—he smiled sympathetically—"haven't tested them myself. They'll be sewn into the top of your tunic. I guess the idea is, even if your hands are tied, you can just, you know . . ." Strauss put his jaw close to his shoulder. "Bite. I leave it up to you. The official line is, we won't be coming to your aid and the less known, of course, the better . . ."

"Of course." Blum nodded, swallowing.

"And between us"—Strauss snapped the container closed and placed it back in his uniform pocket—"it might just be the best alternative, if you're captured, if you know what I mean."

"Yes, I understand," Blum said.

Strauss shrugged. "I guess there's not much more to add . . ."

Blum smiled and met his eyes.

"Other than . . ." Strauss put his hand on Blum's shoulder. "*Mazel tov*, Lieutenant Blum. Colonel Donovan and I have nothing but one hundred percent respect for what you are undertaking . . ."

"*A sheynem dank.*" Blum grinned and replied. *Thank you very much.*

"Yes, *a sheynem dank.*" The captain smiled. "Certainly haven't heard those words in a while."

The two men shook hands.

There was a knock on the door. "Ah, almost forgot . . ." Strauss said. "One last thing." A short, squat Brit in a civil defense uniform carrying a small metal kit came in.

"Captain." Then he looked at Blum. "*Leftenant . . .*"

The man put down his kit and took out an electric shearer.

"Say goodbye to your hair for a while," Strauss said.

Blum sat as the man put a sheet around his shoulders. Blum asked, "You were a barber before the war?"

157

"Not quite, sir," the Brit said, turning on the shearer.

He shaved Blum's head. The dark hair fell at Blum's feet. Afterward, Blum looked at himself in the mirror. The sunken eyes and protruding cheeks seemed even more pronounced. He looked indeed like what he would be in a day: a prisoner. His heart swelled with the depth of the responsibility they were placing on him. A Pole. Someone with no standing. Who had escaped from the world of darkness only three years before.

Strauss shrugged. "That leaves one last thing . . ."

He nodded, and the Brit went back into his kit and came out with a tattoo needle. He plugged it in and dipped it in a bluish ink. "I did *this* before the war, sir," he said to Blum. Strauss passed the man a six-digit number. The instrument began to vibrate.

"Sir," the man said to Blum, "would you mind giving me your left arm?"

TWENTY-EIGHT

Colonel Martin Franke sat at his desk at German intelligence head-quarters in Warsaw on Szucha Street. His aide, Lieutenant Verstoeder, put his morning *kaffee* on his desk. Not the watered-down gruel the Poles drank with sugar and cream to hide the taste. German coffee. Hearty. Black. Brought in from Dallmayr's in Munich. He paged through the overnight cables that had come in over the intelligence wires. Some had been intercepted from coded transmissions; others from directly over the radio. From the BBC. Those that piqued his interest Franke kept in what he called the "A" box by his desk. The others just went in the "B" box to be filed. True intelligence wasn't just a round of drinks at the bar in Estoril or wagering at the casino. That was Rule One. It demanded thoroughness. And follow-through. Follow-through, but instinct too. A good nose.

A good nose was worth all the drinks in Lisbon.

Still, Rule Two. Everything was filed.

The past four months since Vittel had only made Franke's desire to reclaim his prior standing even stronger. The war was not going well. Any fool could see that. The Red Army was advancing; it was almost in Poland now. There was fighting as close as Lvov. Even the Poles were starting to rise up and make a nuisance of themselves. And everyone knew the Allied invasion was imminent; Normandy or Calais? It was only a matter of where.

In Warsaw, the ghetto had been burned and razed. The last Jews, other than those who had taken refuge in the Aryan sector, were either dead or shipped out to places they would not return from. His current job was to root out those still in hiding or with forged papers. And round up suspected Polish collaborators, toss them into the basement of Pawiak Prison, and basically let some Gestapo strongarm pummel their faces raw until they talked. Or didn't, in the rare case. Either way have them shipped out to the Katlan Forest, lined up against a tree and shot.

The woods there were so thick with blood, the joke was going around, this spring, the grass was growing in red.

Still, Franke knew, it was all basically police work. Stuff for the *Ordnungspolizei,* perhaps. Not intelligence.

He had received merely a letter from SS Brigadeführer Schellenberg, his new overseer from Berlin, congratulating him for his "helpful role" in rooting out those phony passport holders in Vittel.

Helpful role? Two hundred forty Jews he had given them.

While the war was being lost by fools, he was being left behind.

Over his *kaffee,* Franke leafed through the day's stack of cables and intelligence messages. Mostly phrases meaningful only to whoever they were intended for: "Lila's shoes have arrived. Pick them up any time." "Oskar wants you to know, the cello lesson is set for next week at the same time." "Jani can't wait to see you again. But this time, she asks you bring the red hat instead of the blue." Everything meant something, of course. Part of Franke's job now was to pick out any that might have a particular connection to the partisan network, whose members were starting to make pests of themselves on the front and in Warsaw, and then track them down.

Like this one perhaps . . . Franke reread one from last night that had caught his attention.

It was the kind of message that to most might well go unnoticed. It came in just before the BBC's *Evening with the Philharmonic.* It mentioned a truffle hunter on his way to Poland. It read, "They are growing very well this season amid the birchwood trees."

Birchwood trees?

160

"What are truffles?" his aide, Verstoeder, asked, as he went to collate the A and B piles.

"They are like mushrooms. Only far more expensive," Franke said. "They grow in the roots of trees. But in Italy," he remarked curiously, "not in Poland. That's what strikes me of interest here. And in the fall. They use pigs to find them."

"Pigs?"

Franke nodded. "Pigs and dogs." The kind of message that to most might go unnoticed.

"So who is this truffle hunter?" Verstoeder asked. "And why is he coming to Poland?"

"In springtime . . ." Franke clarified.

"Yes, in the spring."

"A good question." Franke sipped the last of his coffee. "And another would be, who is the pig?"

The thought of truffles made Franke's stomach growl yearningly, for it had been a long time since anything had found its way into it other than potatoes, cabbage, and sausage. But it was a game of scents, the colonel knew, and this one he could smell as clearly as if he held one of the little buggers in his hand.

"Keep or file?" the lieutenant inquired, deciding in which box to put the cable.

"Keep, I think. At least, for now." There would be more to come, he suspected, about this truffle hunter.

He had a nose for things like this. And this one made it itch.

Franke placed the cable in the box marked A.

TWENTY-NINE

In the belly of the de Havilland Mosquito, flying fifteen thousand feet over Poland, Blum pushed back his nerves.

He looked at his forearm. It still smarted from the number etched into it in blue ink. A22327. Rudolf Vrba's number. So if needed, it matched up against a number that was real. It hardly mattered anyway, Blum knew. If he was caught, he would be interrogated and shot straightaway as a spy. All the numbers in the world wouldn't save him.

Or any diamond.

The plane rattled up and down. Occasionally antiaircraft flak could be heard in the sky. The Allies planned a bombing raid over Dresden to divert enemy aircraft and artillery, but still it was terrifying, knowing what lay ahead, the plane lurching up and down. He held onto the jump strap to settle himself.

He thought about the conversation he had had earlier with President Roosevelt. How much was riding on this; the faith they had in him. His blood still surged with pride. That a Pole, a Jew from the Krakow ghetto, should be speaking across an ocean with the most powerful man in the world. If only his father and mother could have known. They would never believe it. And Leisa. She would have rolled her eyes and told him, "Don't get such a swelled head. In a minute you could be shot down. Or land on the back of a Nazi troop truck. And then what of your conversation?"

Blum smiled, reminding himself why he was there, trying to settle his nerves. The plane lurched, hitting turbulence. It shook so hard for a second Blum felt like the screws holding the fuselage together were about to come apart. He looked at his watch. Only another few minutes. *Then . . .*

Then the jump. His stomach shifted uneasily, thinking of it.

"Get ready!" the copilot called back from the cockpit. "We're dropping to six thousand feet."

Blum gave the thumbs-up sign, but inside his nerves were in a riot. If there was any light in this godforsaken place, he knew his face would appear like a white sheet.

"We're jumping at twelve hundred feet! Six minutes."

"I'm set," Blum said, though there wasn't a cell in his body that didn't stiffen at the thought. He went through the contingency plan. What if the resistance wasn't there to meet him on the ground? He'd have to make his way to the village of Rajsko, eight kilometers to the east. To the safe house. He went over the password again: *ciasto wisniowe.* Cherry pie.

He had maps. A compass. Money. A Colt 1911 holstered to his belt. The chute had been checked and rechecked. *Five seconds,* he reminded himself. His count before pulling the cord. He tried to block out of his mind, what if he botched it and fell? What then? *Do not fail us, Lieutenant.*

"Two minutes!" The copilot scrambled back into the fuselage. "Let's get over to the hatch."

Blum's stomach tightened.

He checked his pack and made his way over, clipped himself to the jump line. He tightened his helmet strap.

"We'll be back for you in seventy-two hours," the airman said. "Aught one thirty hours. There's a cleared field just off the main road. Three kilometers east of the drop site."

Blum nodded. He'd gone over and over it. He had it in the map of his mind. But it wouldn't matter; the partisans would take him there.

"Remember, we'll stay on the ground for only two minutes. That's all. Then we hightail it out of there, as fast as we can. You'd best be there."

"I understand."

"And whatever it is you're bloody well doing down there"—he gave Blum a slap on the shoulder—"All good luck!"

"Thanks."

"Hang on tight now . . ." The airman pulled open the outside hatch. Cold air rushed in.

"Look, down there!" The airman pointed into the darkness.

Straight ahead of them was an array of lights on the ground in the shape of an X. "That's your mark. The wind is good. We're under twelve hundred feet. Shouldn't be too hard. Done this before, I assume?"

Blum shook his head. "Only in training. Off blocks."

"Off blocks?" The airman rolled his eyes. "Well, it's just the same." He gave Blum's helmet strap a tug. "Just take a deep breath and go on my mark. You'll be down before you know it." The plane lurched like a horse trying to throw him off. Blum had to hold onto the rail to keep from falling out.

Count of five, Blum reminded himself. *Then pull*. His chest was hammering inside him.

"Set, now. We're almost there." Cold wind battered him in the face.

"Remember . . ." The airman put his hand on Blum's back. "Seventy-two hours." He looked back to get his bearings, holding onto Blum's strap. "Now, go!"

Blum's heart leaped into the sky, but his feet, frozen in place, remained locked to the plane. He saw the lit-up X approaching below them. They were almost directly over it.

"Go, I said! Now! *Hit it!*" the airman shouted.

He took Blum by the shoulder straps and basically hurled him out into the night. Blum closed his eyes and let out a yell. It was freezing, pitch-dark; he felt himself falling faster than he imagined he would. "*One, two . . .* " He heard the roar of the plane pulling away, banking upward. Wind smacked him in the face, jostling him around. "*Three . . . Four!*"

Five!

He held his breath and yanked the cord. To his relief, it was like the elevator he was riding in jolted to an abrupt stop. For a second it felt like he had slipped through his chute and was plummeting on his own. Fear shot through him.

Then he opened his eyes.

He was okay. Floating. Everything completely dark. His heart settled back to a normal pace. He had overshot his mark by a ways. He wasn't going to be landing near the X, but still not too far away.

A bolt of worry jolted him: What if the resistance had given him up? What if there weren't friends but a truckload of German troops waiting for him on the ground? He saw the darkened tops of trees, coming up fast. This would be it then.

Hold on . . .

He floated to the ground, faster than he'd anticipated, hitting the field with an exhalation of air and nerves, and rolled. His pack almost knocked the breath out of him.

There wasn't a light anywhere around.

The first thing he did was take out his Colt. The brush there was thick, and it was perfectly silent, dark. He gathered his chute together. He'd expected people to be rushing up to him but so far there was no sign of anyone, not even voices. He spotted a wood to the left—the south, according to the compass on his wrist. He balled up the chute and headed over to the cover. He got down and dug a hole in the brush. Fortunately the rains had been generous and the spring soil was moist. He stuffed the chute in it and covered it up, spreading a blanket of leaves and brush around it.

His heart was pounding.

For the first time, it dawned on him that he was back in Poland.

It was silent. Blum had no idea who was waiting for him. Resistance, or German soldiers? He peered out from the woods. No one. This wasn't what he was expecting. Just what had he gotten himself into? he asked himself. What if no one comes? He'd be alone here. In occupied territory. He'd—

Behind him, he heard a twig crack. Blum's blood snapped to attention. Someone was near . . . He stood as still as he was able, sweat inching down his temple. He raised his gun and placed his finger on the trigger. He was about to find out very soon, he thought, what he was capable of. Then he heard a clicking noise. This time, only a tree or two away. He knew there were friends around, but there could be enemies too.

He heard the clicking noise again. This time he recognized what it was.

The sound of a gun being cocked. *Whose?*

Blum wrapped his finger around the trigger.

He heard a man's whisper. In Polish, thank God. *"Lubisz trufle . . . ?"* the voice said. *You like truffles . . . ?*

"Tak," Blum whispered back. *Yes.* "But not nearly as much as beets."

"Well, you've come a long way then . . ." Two people stepped out of the darkness. "For beets."

A man and a young woman. The man in a hunter's jacket and a hat. Carrying a rifle. The young woman in a knit sweater and cap with blond pigtails. Holding a Blyskawica submachine gun.

"Witaj w domu, przyjacielu," the partisan said with a wide grin. He patted Blum heartily on the shoulder. *Welcome home, friend.*

THIRTY

They got in the farm truck, heading on the side roads, some not even paved, traveling without their lights on. "What happens now?" Blum asked.

"Now? Now you spend the night," the driver in the hunter's jacket said. "At least, what's left of it. In Brzezinka. Fifteen kilometers north. In the morning, we will get you onto a work detail into the camp."

"What's your name?"

"Josef," the driver said. "My niece is Anja."

The girl, no more than twenty, and pretty, in her men's garb, seemed to be smiling a bit at him.

"What's so funny?" Blum asked Josef.

"My niece, she thinks you don't look much like a commando. We were expecting someone, how do you say, a bit more . . ." He shrugged. "A bit more like a commando."

"You can tell your niece she doesn't look much like a soldier herself," Blum said, not that his Polish needed any translation.

In the back, Anja giggled.

"Just know, if we hit trouble, you'll be glad you have her," Josef said. "She's killed more Germans than men twice her age. Pretty on the outside, but ice in her blood."

"Anyway, I'm not a commando," Blum explained. "And if I did look like one, I wouldn't exactly blend in inside the camp."

"A fair point," Josef acknowledged.

The truck bounced over an open field, then onto a dark, dirt road. At some point Josef stopped and Anja jumped out of the back to open a gate and then close it behind them once they'd passed through. They put on the headlights.

"You're sure you know what you're in for in there?" Josef glanced at him. "Where you're headed."

"I don't know." Blum shrugged. "We'll see."

"Tomorrow we're having pierogi and sauerkraut. You're welcome to stay. We'll have you back here in three days." He looked at Blum and grinned. "Who's the wiser . . . ?"

"That would be an enormous waste of petrol," Blum said. "And a lot of planning." He showed the man how under his jacket his tunic reversed to the prisoner's stripes.

"Planning is cheap"—Josef shrugged—"but petrol . . ." He cut back through a larger bush and onto the paved road. "You're right, can't waste that. Anyway, you're lucky, my wife can't cook a lick," he said with a wink.

Anja laughed from the back. "He's right. Her dumplings are hard as bricks. If you drop one on the floor, it'll leave a dent."

"Yes, I admit that's true." Josef laughed. "But—*shit!*" He looked up ahead. "Hold on." Literally in the middle of nowhere, they came upon the railroad tracks, two guards, German, with a troop car blocking the road. "Whatever the fuck are they doing here?"

Blum noticed the eagle with a swastika underneath on their uniforms.

"Einsatzgruppen . . ." Josef looked back at Anja. "Bad folk. Here for the Jews." He slowed and pulled up a bottle of vodka from the floor. "Just pretend you're drunk. And cover the weapons. We've just come from your cousin's birthday party in Wilczkowice. If they ask us to get out"—he glanced at Blum and signaled toward his gun— "you know what to do."

Blum nodded. His heart had started to race. He pulled down his cap over his eyes.

In the back, Anja threw the weapons under a blanket, but Blum heard her cock the action on her hidden pistol. "If they make a move," she said under her breath, "it'll be the last thing they ever do."

"Don't be so rash, niece," Josef cautioned. "We have our guest to protect here. Dead Germans cause trouble."

Josef pulled the truck to a stop. One of the guards jumped down from their vehicle and stepped up to the truck. A sergeant, Blum saw. But he also saw the two SS lightning rods on his collar.

"Evening, Untersharführer," Josef said. He held out a half-empty bottle of potato vodka. "I know it's a little early, maybe, but compliments of the Luschki family birthday celebration . . ."

"Keep your booze. Where are you heading this time of night?" the guard questioned them in German. "Have you never heard of a curfew?"

"Across. To Brzezinka. And I know it's late, Sergeant. We were at my cousin's. In Wilczkowice I assure you, the booze was flowing. Would have slept it off there, but it's my job to make the bread in the morning. First thing. So I—"

"You're a baker?" The German looked around the cab, eyeing them all with a hint of suspicion.

"If I'm not at the oven by five, no one in the village has breakfast." He shrugged. "And I don't make any friends."

"And who is this?" The guard shined a light on Blum. "Let me guess, the butcher?"

"Mirek, sir," Blum replied good-naturedly. "Actually, I'm a plumber. I told my cousin here it was way too late to drive all the way back home. But my sister, you see her back there, is in school"—he nodded to Anja—"and she can't miss another day, or the nuns get . . . well, you know how they get . . . Plus, I took responsibility for her, and—"

"And *what* . . . ?" The German shined a light in the back on Anja. "It's the middle of the fucking night. Bakers and plumbers are exempt from curfew?"

"Of course not," Josef said. "But, in truth, it's rarely enforced out here in the woods . . ."

"So what else do you have in there?" The German flashed his light inside the cab. A bead of sweat ran down the back of Blum's neck. His hand drifted to his gun.

"Nothing, sir. Only flour."

"Flour? Still," he peered around. "Maybe I'll just take a look."

Suddenly they heard the sound of a train approaching. Not a whistle, but a rumble, and a sharp light coming from down the tracks. The German still in the troop car jumped out and waved. *"Sergeant!"*

The sergeant flicked off his light. "Wait here."

The two guards went to the checkpoint and stood there. In a minute or two the train rattled by. One of them put up a hand and waved to a guard atop the lead car. Blum had never seen a train like it. It was dark and boarded up, what looked like barbed strung wire over the blacked-out windows. It had about ten cattle cars, heading east. He knew where. It wasn't exactly the first-class carriage to Warsaw.

"Oswiecim." Josef grunted with a shake of his head and spat out the window. He crossed himself.

Blum's blood simmered with anger. He could only imagine the horror inside. On their way to who knows what fate? *People are gassed there . . . Thousands,* Strauss had said. Sitting there, his free hand balled into a fist. He wondered how many of those who were inside would even be alive when he snuck in tomorrow.

"Far more direct, by the way"—Josef nudged him—"if you'd like me to flag it down for you and catch a ride."

"Thanks," Blum said, smiling back. "I'm fine here."

In a minute, the train passed. One of the guards climbed back into the empty troop truck. The sergeant came back over to them.

Blum's hand retreated back inside his pocket for his Colt.

"You're lucky, baker," the German said. "It's late, and we're in good spirits. Just know, if I catch you out and about again, you won't be smiling next time."

"I understand, Herr Unterscharführer. Thank you," Josef said. "And here . . ." He offered him the bread and cheese.

"Keep your bread," the guard grunted. "The bottle, though . . ." He beckoned with his fingers. *"Here . . . "*

Josef handed him the vodka.

The German took it and headed back to his troop car.

Blum finally removed his hand from his pocket. He let out a long breath.

"Hope it kills them in their fucking sleep," Josef muttered, putting the truck back in gear. "Sorry, Anja. Next time we see him, we shoot first, then give him the vodka."

They watched the sergeant show his loot to the other German in the half-truck.

Then they waved them through.

THIRTY-ONE

Martin Franke sipped his *kaffee*. Another coded dispatch had been intercepted during the night.

This one from Britain. Over the BBC radio. It was one of twelve messages that were read off before the weekly concert, *Famous Orchestral Marches*.

"For cousin Josef. You'll be happy to know the truffle hunter is en route."

Franke knew, it could have been destined for anyone in Europe, but he had read the similar cable just two days before.

There he is again, Franke noted. *Truffle hunter.*

Separately, a report had crossed his desk that very same morning that a plane had been heard during the night. Low, over the forests near the small town of Wilczkowice, near Rajsko, some three hundred kilometers from Warsaw. *Rajsko.* He'd never heard of the place. A local farmer had spotted someone parachuting in. Probably making contact with the resistance, Franke suspected. Or more likely an arms drop. Or planning some sort of sabotage in the area. That was happening frequently now. *But to send someone in for it . . .*

Franke's nose itched. *"Verstoeder!"* he called.

"Herr Colonel?"

"Bring me those dispatches from the other day. Our truffle hunter friend."

172

"Yes, Colonel."

In a minute the young lieutenant came back in with a file full of papers.

"What is in Rajsko?" Franke asked him.

"*Rajsko?* Not much, I believe." The junior officer went over to a large wall map of Poland. "It's in the middle of nowhere. Only a large birchwood forest. But I am told there is a work camp nearby. Where Jews are being held. Auschwitz. The Polish name is Oswiecim, Herr Colonel."

Auschwitz . . . Franke knew of it, of course. The Jews of Vittel had been sent there. Along with half the Jewish population of Warsaw. No one knew much about what went on in a place like that. The SS kept tight control. Other than that no one ever came back from there. That much was certain.

"What has struck your interest, Colonel?" the aide inquired.

"*Birchwood* . . . " Franke said aloud, this time in English. "Quick, find me their last transmission."

Verstoeder dug back into the thick file. "Tuesday, I believe, was it not?"

"Quickly, Lieutenant, *today*!"

"Here it is, Herr Colonel."

Franke ripped the document from his hand. He ran his finger down the text until he came to the very spot he was looking for: *They are growing very well this season amid the birchwood trees.*

That's what had struck his interest.

Someone parachuting in . . . Franke rubbed his chin in speculation. *Into a fucking birchwood forest. Near Oswiecim. The truffle hunter* . . . He got up and went to the map himself. *Why would anyone be heading there? In the middle of fucking nowhere.*

Nothing around but a birchwood forest and a labor camp.

Auschwitz. He kept on saying to himself.

"Ring me command," he instructed the lieutenant. "General Graebner. Now."

"Right away." The junior officer ran out.

Franke let the pieces come together in his head. However loosely, one by one, they were all beginning to fit. If his hunch was wrong, what would it matter anyway? He was condemned to spend the war in this useless position.

But if he was right . . . There could be many reasons for it: An escape. Reconnaissance. Or even to bomb the camp.

If he was right, this might be just the opportunity he'd been waiting for.

Truffle hunter . . . *What does a truffle hunter do?* he asked himself, staring at the map.

He digs.

But digs into what?

The phone rang. Franke went back to his desk. He took a moment to compose his thoughts, then cleared his throat and picked up the receiver.

"General Graebner . . ."

He felt certain that the Allies had sent someone in to sneak inside Auschwitz.

THIRTY-TWO

At eight that morning, Blum sipped his coffee in the main square in the village of Brzezinka. He and Josef had managed to catch a couple of hours' sleep at the resistance fighter's cabin in the woods outside town. As Anja had said, the bread the man's wife offered him around the fire would have broken a tooth if he tried to chew it, it was so hard.

The square was bustling. Blum counted ten German soldiers and a procurement officer organizing labor details, ordering people around. *"You*, here!" He pointed to one. *"Carpenter, you say. Over there!"* Prospective laborers huddled by several trucks pulled up to take them to various work sites. The IG Farben plant needed bricklayers and electricians. Birkenau needed carpenters and heavy laborers. Most of the work Vrba and Wetzler had described was performed by slave labor from the camps. Ten- to twelve-hour shifts without a break, prisoners pushed to the limits of their strength and stamina. Anyone who dropped, from utter exhaustion, from the unquenchable thirst, was shot on the spot.

But certain technical skills were needed for various projects: skilled carpenters, able plumbers, and mechanics. Masons. Strong workers who could do the job of ten undernourished prisoners. From all accounts, there was a vast amount of expansion going on—"ramping up the pace of the killing," Strauss had called it. Barracks under construction at neighboring Birkenau, the rail tracks extended to its gate.

175

The infirmary at Auschwitz, where various medical experiments were being conducted. The Germans paid a meager wage, and the contractors took most of it. But any wage was good if it could buy a loaf of bread or an undernourished capon in the midst of war.

"Come," Josef said to Blum. "I spoke to one of the local contractors. Get in that line over there. It's going to the main camp."

About twenty workers were in line to board a rattletrap farm truck.

Josef went up to the stocky man in a thin flannel coat and flat tweed cap who seemed to be in charge. "This is my friend I was telling you about. He's around for a couple of days. He's very handy with a hammer."

"What sort of work do you do? Roofing? Spackling? They need people in the main camp."

"Yes," Blum said.

"Well . . ." The foreman gave Blum, who didn't exactly have the build or hands of a carpenter, the once-over, and not without a little skepticism. "If Josef vouches . . . I can offer you ten zloty a day."

"Ten?"

"All right, twelve, once I see what you can do. Okay?"

Blum nodded.

"Climb aboard then," the foreman said.

Blum hoisted himself into the truck. It was already mostly full. He found an open spot next to a man in overalls and a pipe, carrying his own tools.

A soldier came over and counted the people in the back of the truck. *"Eins, zwei, drei . . ."* Blum bent over to tie his shoe. "You there, up!" He counted again.

There were eighteen in his truck. They moved on to count another.

"Good luck, my friend!" Josef smacked the side of the truck. "Till Thursday night . . ." Though beneath his breath he was likely muttering, "God watch over you. I doubt we will ever see you again."

"Thursday." Blum waved.

The truck started up. A German private hopped in the front cab next to the driver. The officer got into a gray half-track with five or six soldiers in it and fell in behind.

176

Blum caught sight of Josef smoking, watching them leave. He pulled down his cap. When he looked back again, the partisan was gone.

The truck was filled with men of all ages. Many were in their forties or fifties, lifelong tradesmen, too old to have fought in the war. Quickly, the truck lumbered out of the small town and onto the paved main road, heading south. Blum had left his Colt back at Josef's farm, along with his watch and compass. He had no need for them now. Sewn into his shirt lining though, was enough cash to buy everyone in the truck. He kept his eyes forward as the truck lurched into third gear. He glanced down at his pant legs. His cuffs had rolled and if you focused, you could make out the stripe of the uniform on the other side showing through. Blum's heart clenched tightly.

Without attracting attention, he bent forward and calmly folded the cuffs down. No one saw. No one spoke much; a couple of locals were going on about the late frost this season and how crops were behind. Blum cast his eyes down. The road was uneven and there were only benches in the back to sit on, so everyone was jolted at every bump. The second truck followed close behind, and the half-track of soldiers twenty yards behind them.

Oswiecim, a road sign said. *8 km.*

Blum's heart picked up.

"First time in?" the man in the overalls asked in what Blum took as a Galician accent. He had a thick mustache and deep, hooded eyes under his cap.

"Yes."

"Where're you from?"

"Masuria," Blum answered. "Gizycko. Near Lake Sniardwy." He kept his face forward, wanting to remain as inconspicuous as possible, as he would not be on the truck on its trip home.

"A piece of advice." The workman leaned close. His breath stank of nicotine. "Cover your nose when you get in. The stench can be unbearable."

Blum nodded. "I will. Thanks."

"And whatever you do, don't ask what it is. Doesn't go over well with the Nazis at all."

"I hear you," Blum said with a smile of thanks. He looked down at his hands, and to his dread, saw that his wrist was slightly exposed, showing the first two digits of the number that had been burnt into him. *A2* . . . If noticed, it would instantly give him away.

He glanced at the man across from him, who had closed his eyes a moment and seemed not to have noticed. Blum relaxed. He pulled down his tunic under his light wool jacket, his heart beginning to regain its normal rhythm in his chest.

He'd almost given himself away, twice.

The road went along the rim of a dense forest. And along the Soła River, where he and Mendl would hopefully head to sixty or so hours from now, which continued all the way to the Slovakian border. After about ten minutes the road left the trees and river behind. Blum saw a road sign. *Rajsko.* An arrow pointing east.

Then another for Oswiecim. *3 km.*

To the west.

The truck jerked forward and made a left turn. Now the road picked up the line of the railway tracks. The first thing Blum noticed up ahead was a gray cloud, low above the trees. Hanging like fog over a bay.

Then a putrid smell in the air. What the man next to him had told him. A little like sulfur, Blum thought. Or lead. Only sweeter. Followed by the nauseating sensation in his gut when it became clear to him exactly what it was.

Noticing Blum reacting to the smell, the worker next to him caught his eye and winked with a grim chuckle.

Ahead, Blum caught sight of a long brick façade. A pointed tower atop it. Several towers. And wire, stretching for as far as he could see. Double rows of wire, maybe ten feet apart. Barbed and electrified. Signs of *"Verbotten!"* with skulls and crossbones underneath placed at intervals. Clearly a city inside. A city of death. Guard towers every hundred feet with machine gun tripods. The train tracks led right up to the front gate. Everyone around was German now. SS.

The truck stopped outside the gates.

A ripple of nerves wormed through Blum's bowels. He found himself uttering to himself what he remembered of a prayer. The Kel Maleh Rachamin. For the soul of the departed. "*Ayl molay rachamin, shochayn bam'romin* . . . " O God, full of compassion, who dwells on high, shelter him who has gone on, with the cover of wings . . .

That was as much as he knew.

Suddenly there was shouting, voices elevated, in German. An officer came up to the truck, gesturing emphatically for them to continue farther down the road. He was telling the driver of the truck to move. "*Nicht hier! Nicht hier!*" Not here.

Blum's heart stopped. He kept hearing the officer shout "*Birkenau.*" And point in that direction.

Birkenau was only a short way away but it was a completely separate camp, Vrba's map made clear. Mendl was said to be *here*. In Auschwitz 1. The mission fully depended on Blum being here.

If he was diverted to Birkenau the entire day would be lost. The odds were already long that he would be able to find Mendl in the three days he had, let alone *two*, should he have to come back and try again tomorrow.

If he could even get himself on a new crew.

Shit.

Blum overheard the heated discussion among the new officer, the Polish foreman, and the SS work procurer Blum had seen back in Brzezinka. No one else in the truck seemed to care. Work was work, as long as they were paid. They didn't give a damn.

Finally, the foreman got back in and the German waved emphatically toward Birkenau. Blum's heart plummeted. Then he realized the officer was pointing toward the second truck, the one pulled up behind them, which pulled out of line and continued past them toward the new camp. Blum's truck was waved toward Auschwitz. It continued right up to the main gate, which he recalled from Vrba's drawings, then lurched to a stop. The foreman jumped out again and came around and brought down the rear hatch. He waved for everyone to get off. "*Wychodzic.*" Come on, come on! "*To jest to.*" This is it. "Let's go!"

"Everyone forms a line," the SS officer instructed them as they pooled together in front of the gate. "Break out of it, and you'll be shot. No questions asked. Understood?"

Everyone nodded. The work team lined up.

"We hear it every time," Blum's truck mate whispered to him. "But I wouldn't test it if I were you."

"I don't need convincing."

But inside, Blum knew that that was precisely what he was about to do. Test it more than the workman in his wildest dreams could ever imagine. He looked around and tried to get a sense of where the railroad tracks led on to Birkenau. The woods were about sixty yards away. And the river . . .

"Forward!" the officer yelled. They started to march along the tracks up to the gate. A metal sign arched over it: "Arbeit Macht Frei."

Yes, free, Blum said to himself. He muttered the prayer again, for the soul of the departed. As the dead are free. The dead.

For he surely was among them now.

He passed beneath the raised, arced letters into Auschwitz.

THIRTY-THREE

Leo walked up the stone steps of the Lagerkommandant's house again, while Rottenführer Langer took a smoke and remained outside. This being Leo's sixth visit, the guard no longer even followed him up to the door.

It had been six weeks since he and Frau Ackermann first began their matches. In that time Leo could tell that their visits were no longer exclusively about the chess. She had clearly grown fond of him, visibly looked forward to their time together, and even he had to admit, no matter how he tried to pretend to the contrary, he felt the same. She couldn't quite beat him. That had long been established. And she understood that too, though he would let her linger in games he could have ended quickly in order to draw them out and extend their time together.

In these weeks she began to share things with him about her life, her feelings. Her parents, eager for advancement, had pushed her into marriage. She longed for a bit more freedom, even a career, teaching, which she had put on hold. Leo saw for certain she didn't support the horrible things she saw go on there. In the infirmary, people said she tried to ease her patients' suffering as best she could. And then there were the twisted things performed there by the sadistic Mengele. She had uttered his name only once with Leo, and her jaw stiffened and eyes grew baleful with the deepest contempt. Yet Leo saw it was her fate too that she was essentially trapped there, a captive, as confined here and isolated as any of the prisoners.

Once or twice she opened the collar of her dress just enough that he saw the marks she bore. A dark crease along the side of her neck. When she went to move a piece, a bruise on her arm. Her lower lip a little too puffy. Seeing them, if it were possible, he grew to detest the Lagerkommandant even more. He longed to mention these marks to her. To ask why she remained in this place. This marriage. Why she consented to it. She could leave. *She was, in fact, the only one who could leave!* The rest, guards, prisoners, were forced to stay.

But he did not dare bring up these things. He could not threaten the fragile footing they danced on in their games. He was still a lowly prisoner, and if he offended her, she could have him killed with just a snap of her fingers. Yet he could not imagine not seeing her again. Many times he could see into the cage of sadness she seemed to live in. To be with such a monster. Her hopes and desires dashed. Leo wished her to be happy. To be free. And he knew that was a little of what he brought her every Tuesday, even though she was a woman and he barely a man. Freedom. A brief flight from her cage. And he was afraid to close the door on them by overestimating their intimacy. To say the wrong thing and have it come to an end. Afraid also of the Lagerkommandant's wrath should Leo lose her "protection."

"Ah, Herr Wolciek." She smiled, pleased, when she stepped into the parlor and saw him there, her blue eyes brightening.

"Frau Ackermann."

It was May now. Warmer. The flowers were in bloom. She wore her print dress open around the collar with a light white sweater around her shoulders in a way Leo had never seen before.

A thin gold chain was around her neck. For the first time, in all his captivity, he smelled the scent of perfume.

"Where is Private Horschuler?" he asked. The impassive young guard who usually watched over their games.

"He's away on some work detail, I believe. Clearing the woods. All hands on deck these days, I suppose." She looked at him. "Why?"

"No reason, madame." But it pleased him not to have the private looking at him so contemptuously.

"Shall we play?"

She took the white and began with the Ruy Lopez. He countered with a variation of the Brazilian defense. When she leaned forward to move a piece, he caught a glimpse of the strap of her bra underneath. And for an instant her chain danced at the very spot where her breasts came together.

His imagination did the rest.

After seven or eight moves, she picked up a piece and did not put it down, seeming distracted. "We will not be able to play next week," she announced. "I am going home for a few days. To Bremen. To visit my family."

Going home. How the thought appealed to him. "That is nice." He nodded. "If only I . . ." He stopped himself in midsentence. *If only I could do the same. If only I could even know if my family was even alive.*

"I'm sorry." She locked onto his eyes. "That was stupid of me to say. I only wanted you to know. If you didn't hear from me." She moved her bishop forward, making sure it was protected by her knight. "So you wouldn't . . . think I no longer looked forward to our games."

"The Lagerkommandant will be going as well?" Leo asked. He countered her advance by moving up his pawn.

"I'm afraid he will not." She moved up a pawn as well. "Kommandant Hoss will still be in Berlin. So his business keeps him here."

"I see." Inside Leo shuddered. *The business of murdering people.* What burrowed through Leo's mind was what might happen to him when she wasn't here. Wasn't here to watch over him. Was this her way of letting him know? That it was over. That she was powerless to stop the inevitable from happening now.

Then, out of the blue, she said, "You are the only ray of light for me in this godforsaken place." She looked at him. "You know that, don't you?"

He had never stared at her so closely. He had never noticed the tremulousness in the soft blue shade of her eyes.

"That this is the only thing I look forward to here. This time together . . ."

He nodded, his heart slamming off his ribs like a metronome on the highest speed. "Frau, the game," he could only reply, averting his eyes back to the table. He sat there too afraid to take his gaze from the board. Inside, his heart beat with an insistence he had never felt before. He pushed back the embarrassing pressure going on between his legs, praying that his thin uniform wouldn't give him away.

"Yes, of course, the game." She smiled at him.

The match was now barely an afterthought. He was nervous to even pick up a piece, lest their hands casually touch. Desires he had kept to himself, ones he had let loose only in his bunk at night, praying that his Lithuanian bunkmate would not wake, sprang forward. Filling him with longing. He kept his eyes down from hers. He was unsure of what to do.

When he finally looked up she was looking at him.

He set up an exchange of pieces and she accepted. The moves came quickly. Four, five of them, taking off rooks, pawns, and a knight for a bishop. At some point, in the rapid exchanges, their fingers brushed against each other. This time instead of drawing them away, they stayed there.

Their eyes met again. "You know I can't protect you forever, Leo." There wasn't insistence in her voice. More like sadness, and in her gaze as well.

"I know, madame."

"Greta."

He nodded. Swallowed.

"You can say it. Say it, Leo."

He took a breath. The storm in his chest was raging now. It took everything inside him to summon the strength. The strength to say it. The sound barely fell off his tongue and onto his lips like a stone. "Greta."

"See." She smiled.

He did as well. He felt a tingling down his loins. *What was happening . . . ?*

"Hedda!" she called out. For the maid. At the other end of the house.

Half a minute later she appeared at the door. "Frau Ackermann?"

"Would you go to the store please, in town? I believe my husband said he would like some ice cream tonight with his strudel."

"I believe we have some, ma'am. I'll just—"

"Fruit ice cream, Hedda. Any flavor. I'm sure you'll pick the right one."

The maid hesitated at the door and then said, "Yes, ma'am."

The match was over. They didn't make another move. They just waited, minutes it seemed, unending minutes, until they heard the sound of the back door closing.

"You are a virgin, aren't you?" Frau Ackermann asked him.

Leo swallowed, wishing he could tell her differently, every cell in his body ajitter.

"Come on, you can tell me, Leo. Kurt is the only man I've ever been with. It's all right."

He knew this was the most dangerous thing he had ever done. To even answer such a question. If her husband happened to walk in, if she ever disclosed this, he would be dead barely a second after his pistol was out of its holster. "Yes."

She got up. She came across the table and stood in front of him. The fullness of her breasts in front of his eyes, her breaths silent, but in and out. The curve of her hips. She put his hand there. Her eyes were liquid and pained. "I wish I could stop it all, Leo, but I can't . . ."

"I know."

She came over and straddled across him on the seat. The pressure between his legs was now impossible for him to conceal. Slowly, she unbuttoned her dress. One button, two . . . "Here, put your hand here . . ." she said, taking it in hers. Inside her dress. On her bra. "Like that. And here . . ."

She lifted slightly and took his other hand and put it inside her skirt, against her undergarment, where it was all soft and moist. He was locked on her eyes.

185

"You don't want to die a virgin, do you, Leo?"

He swallowed, almost too nervous to even speak. "No."

"You can kiss me." She put her mouth close to his. She laughed. "You know, if he came in now he would kill us both. Are you prepared to die with me, Leo?"

He looked into her beautiful, deep eyes. "Yes."

"Do you know why I am doing this . . . ?"

He didn't reply.

"Because you are good. And because I want to know what that feels like. Just once."

She climbed onto him and looked down in his lap. His striped pants. In his dreams, he never imagined he could have an erection like that. He blushed and tried to cover it up.

"Don't." She took his hand away. "You don't have to." Her smile made it all seem okay. "Trust me, Leo . . ." She put his hands on her hips and gently began to rock. "You'll leave today a much happier man than if you did with just an apple."

THIRTY-FOUR

He was inside the camp.

Blum was placed on a construction team that was building additional barracks inside the main camp. He spotted prisoners everywhere. Thin, eyes sunken, wearing their loose-fitting zebra suits, many ravaged by what appeared to be sores and pestilence, scurrying around like mice, trying to stay one step ahead of their SS guards who constantly shouted at them and prodded them with heavy truncheons. Many looked so sickly and beaten down they wouldn't even survive the day. Not a one made direct eye contact with any of outside crews. In the main staging yard, one prisoner had been hanged on a gallows, his neck crooked, left for everyone to see. A warning to the others, it was clear. As he hammered nails and sanded down the roof beams, Blum smelled the damning, sweet odor coming from the adjacent camp. A thin gray cloud hovered when they arrived and never left. *They're gassing them by the hundreds. Thousands . . .* Strauss had said. And amid all the sickening brutality and hopeless misery these people were suffering, somewhere Blum heard the sound of an orchestra playing.

They all just did their work as ordered and stuck to themselves.

At noon, on a break, the work crew was fed a thin, tasteless gruel from a wooden bowl: a broth of cabbage and potato, accompanied by a piece of hardened bread. A couple of the prisoners who passed by

187

seemed to eye the bowls covetously; clearly next to what they were being fed, this must be a delicacy! Blum would have happily left his half-finished bowl for one to take, but they'd been strictly warned by the officer in charge who had brought them inside to avoid even the slightest contact. The last thing Blum could risk was to be thrown off the work detail. He was here for a purpose, he reminded himself, and so, while it pained him, he simply did his work as best he could and kept to himself, trying not to make himself noticed. He wore his wool cap low over his eyes. The guards pretty much left them alone. He had to wait for just the right moment—at the end of the day, when the work crews were breaking up. It would cost him some time inside, but any earlier, and his disappearance might well be noticed. These Germans seemed to have a determination to count and recount, form a line and keep everyone in it. But even if there was a discrepancy, they would likely never know who was responsible for it, and once he switched uniforms, it would be impossible to find him in a camp of this size without tearing the whole place apart.

While he hammered in the joints, Blum kept his eyes peeled, staring at every face in a striped suit that passed by. He'd rehearsed what he would say, once he spotted Mendl. The shock and incredulity the man would undoubtedly feel. *I've come for you, Professor.* But no one Blum saw fit his looks or was even close to his age. At fifty-seven, from Blum's view, Mendl would be an old man in here. *We don't even know for certain if he's even still alive,* Strauss had admitted. That would be the ultimate joke, Blum thought, helping to steady the roof beams as they hammered the flat roof in place: to come all this way, to have risked his life and possibly never make it back out, and all for a corpse. A dead man. A person who could never have helped them. And looking at the shaven, rail-thin mice scurrying by who seemed more like walking ghosts than men, Blum suspected with concern that that might well be the case.

The sun had moved to the west in the sky. Blum judged it was going on five p.m. They'd only be working for a few minutes more. He had to find the right time to make his move.

In the next few minutes the camp came alive with activity. Where there were hundreds of prisoners before, suddenly the number doubled, tripled. Now it seemed there were thousands of them, returning to the camp through the front gate, hunched over and exhausted, trudging more than walking upright, guards every ten paces or so. A few wore striped uniforms as well, yet they seemed more like guards in that they carried truncheons of their own, some with green or blue triangles on their chests, prodding the pack along with shouts and insults like cattle moving into a pen. The returning prisoners were all lined up in the main yard. Carts, being wheeled and pulled along, were filled with twisted corpses, their skinny limbs and open mouths protruding grotesquely. The ones who didn't make it back that day.

The yard filled. *Kapos* and guards started counting each block. The constant drone of "*eins, zwei, drei* . . . " heard everywhere. Even the cart of dead bodies was counted; prisoners tossed out the dead like blocks of firewood. "Ten, eleven, twelve . . ."

Blum's stomach turned.

The foreman called out for Blum's work team to call it quits on the hour. Ten more minutes. "Take your tools and line up," he alerted them. After, they'd all be loaded back in the truck.

This was it. He had to make his move. He had to summon the courage to do what every instinct for survival inside him cried out was suicide. Yet he knew it was now or never. This was either the bravest thing he'd ever done in his life or surely the stupidest, he reckoned. The most calamitous.

"*Tak, tak.*" He raised his hand to get the foreman's attention.

"What is it?" The foreman came over.

"Toilet, sir." Blum signaled. There was a latrine by one of the blocks that the work crew was allowed to use.

"Go ahead," the foreman said, pointing to his watch. "But hurry."

"I will, sir. Thanks."

The man went back around to the other side of the half-built barrack and Blum set down his hammer. A while back, he had removed his jacket in the afternoon heat, rolled it into a ball, and tossed it in the bottom of one of the supply bins.

189

He made his way over to the latrine. No guards were near. Everyone was distracted by the counting and assembling of the prisoner work teams returning to the yard. Blum stepped inside. He stood for a second at first, his heart beating with more insistence and drumming louder than he had ever felt from what he was about to do. Cross a line he might never again be able to come back from. Amid the putrefying stench of the open hole, he reminded himself why he was there. Why he was doing this for a person he didn't even know and for a country he might not even make it back to. This is your *aliyah,* he reminded himself. Your commitment.

Your penance.

His penance for being the one who had made it out.

You cannot go back now, Nathan.

He ripped off his shirt, pulling the arms inside out, and reversed it to the faded blue and gray burlap stripe on the other side. Then he flung it back over his head and buttoned it to the neck, to hide what was underneath. He kicked off the wooden clogs he'd had on all day that were similar to what they wore in the camp and reversed out his loose-fitting trousers.

He was in a prisoner's suit now. From an inside pocket he took out the cap that was like a thousand he had seen that day and placed it on his head.

Less than sixty hours left to do what he had to do.

Sucking in a breath, his last moment of anything resembling freedom, Blum cracked the outhouse door and peered outside.

Across the yard, the foreman was rounding up his work crew. Two guards passed close by. His heart clenching, Blum pressed the door closed again. He caught his breath. If the wrong person saw him coming out of there, the game was over from the start. He'd be shot on the spot. He composed himself again, wiping off a bead of sweat making its way down his temple, instructing his heart to quiet and his nerves to calm. Inside him, a voice of doubt whispered he could just reverse back into his work outfit and rejoin his crew. He could hide with Josef and meet the plane in two more nights and say he was unable to find Mendl. *Who would be the wiser . . . ?*

No . . . He opened the door and looked out again. This time no one was around. *Go.* He stepped outside and quickly shut the door. He took a look toward the work detail; no one was focused on him, only inventorying the tools and forming the line. He hugged the wall and went around the far side of the latrine, away from them, facing the wire.

He stared at the vast commotion in the yard, prisoners lining up in formations in front of their blocks. *It was suicide.* Thousands of sickly looking prisoners forming lines, raising their hands at the call. *You will never come back.* Guards shouting in their faces like vicious dogs. Like some stomach-turning nightmare out of a Bosch painting of hell. Suicide. *Do not fail us, Roosevelt had said.*

Now.

"Was machst du denn?" A voice barked sharply behind him. *What are you doing?*

Every cell in Blum froze.

He turned. A burly SS corporal was staring directly at him. A heavy rope twisted with several thick knots hung menacingly at his side. "Which block are you from?" the corporal asked.

"Zwansig, sir." Blum cleared his throat, averting his eyes. The report was that the Ukrainian *kapo* who oversaw Block Twenty was as human as there was in this place, meaning he wouldn't crack you in the head with his truncheon merely for the sport of it. There would have to be a reason. Blum's heart began to pound with dread. He was sure the guard would hear it inside his chest.

"Then get the fuck on back, yid! Unless you'd rather I give you a nudge . . ." The German raised his knotted rope. Contempt and a total disregard for humanity oozed from him like an icy, terrifying vapor.

"No, Rottenführer." Blum nodded, contrite. "I mean yes, now. Thank you."

"Get your dirty ass out of here!"

"Yes, sir."

He quickly ran toward the rows of barracks, praying as he did he wouldn't feel the lash from the knotted rope strike him from behind.

He knew just how arbitrary the line between life and death was here. The wrong guard, at the wrong time, one who just killed for the thrill of it or simply just to relieve the boredom, the way others might bet on the flip of a coin . . . And your time was up! Prisoners kept flooding into the large, staging area, guards shouting at them, beating them like angry dogs.

"Line up! Roll call. Now! On the double!"

Blum blended into the throng, melding safely into the vast numbers.

He wove through the crowd until he found a group lining up in front of a barrack.

"*Dwadziescia?*" he asked someone in line in Polish. *Twenty?*

The prisoner never looked at him, just nodded. "*Ja. Dwadziescia.*"

Across the way, Blum spotted the work detail he had been on forming a line and being marched toward the front gate and out of the camp. He watched them filing out, not knowing if, like any of them, he would ever see the outside again.

"Line up! Everyone line up!" the guards yelled.

He muttered a few words of the prayer he had recited earlier: *Ayl molay rachamin, shochayn bam'romin.*

This time it was for himself.

For he was truly in the middle of the nightmare now.

PART THREE

THIRTY-FIVE

Colonel Bill Donovan went down the White House steps and to the black Cadillac waiting for him in the driveway.

Another black sedan pulled up just as he was about to step in. It had a blue flag with a star on the front grille signifying the vehicle of a one-star general. A junior officer in dress khakis jumped out and opened the door for his senior officer who was in the back.

"General," Donovan said, recognizing who it was before climbing into his own car.

The Army officer climbed out and offered his hand. "Bill."

General Leslie Groves was the military's chief overseer of the top-secret weapon program that had every top brain in the country not assigned to code breaking working for it, known as the Manhattan Project. Donovan didn't understand a word of the "science," but what *was* clear was, with the attention it received from FDR and his war secretary, and the rumors of its vast budget and top-secret locations, that if it was successful, whatever they were conjuring up would give the Allies the decisive edge they needed to end the war.

"Got a moment, as long as we bumped into each other . . . ?" Groves asked.

"Of course, General," replied Donovan.

"Can we walk?" Groves said, leading the OSS chief away from the parked sedans and their drivers and onto the South Grounds.

"I suppose this isn't about the game Dutch Leonard pitched last night, is it, Leslie?" the head of the OSS asked.

Groves smiled and shook his head. "No. It's not."

An engineer by training, Leslie Groves was a brilliant thinker with a driving personality. The concepts he was faced with understanding and evaluating, deciding between alternatives and also funding, required a Nobel Prize winner's grasp of science and a chief economist's understanding of finance. He was large, broad shouldered, and tall, with a square, solid jaw.

"That physicist we spoke of a few weeks back . . . Mendl . . . ? I'm told you're mounting an effort to locate him," the general started in.

"I believe we *have* located him," Bill Donovan replied. " In fact, we have someone on it now."

"And at what stage of the operation are you, if that's something you can share with me?"

Donovan looked the general in the eyes and saw how vital the man he sought was. Still, this was a top-secret operation that was under way with only a few on the inside. "What I can share is that he's there now. On site. In two days your man will either be in a transport plane on his way to D.C. or you'll have to do without him for good, I'm afraid."

Groves nodded soberly. He pulled Donovan farther away from the cars. "We're in a race, Bill. A race to hell, some might say, but Oppy assures me this Mendl guy can save us six months. You realize what six months can mean—in the race for the supreme weapon. And in lives."

"All I can say, General, is that I promise we're giving it our best."

"Then that's all I can ask." Groves checked his watch. "I'd better go. The president expects us military types to be on time. Senators and cabinet members can wander in as they please."

"Yes, that's always the case." The OSS chief and the Manhattan Project overseer started to head back. "Before you go, Leslie, I assume you have other research along these lines going on, simultaneously?"

"Along these lines . . . ?"

Donovan stopped. "In this man Mendl's field."

"Gaseous diffusion." Groves stopped too. "It's a process. Separates uranium-238 from its lighter cousin, 235."

Donovan shrugged. "I was never very good at chemistry, Leslie."

"And if I knew I'd have this job I might have paid a bit more attention myself," Groves chuckled back. "But to your question, yes, Bill, we do have other avenues being looked into. At Berkeley . . . and at the University of Minnesota. We're making progress. But like I said, it's a race. The Germans might have things going on as well." They resumed their walk back toward the cars. "Why . . . ?"

"I just wouldn't want to raise any expectations . . ." the OSS man stopped and looked at the general again, "on the prospects of this mission. Like I said, there's a man in the field, and his senior officer, Strauss—I think you met him once—he believes he's a good one and that there's a fighting chance of success. But to be frank, we never assigned much hope to seeing either of them sailing up the Potomac. If you know what I mean."

"Yes, Bill." The head of the Manhattan Project nodded soberly. "I understand perfectly what you mean."

"A shame too, if you ask me . . ." Donovan opened the door to his car. "He seemed like a game young man when I met him."

THIRTY-SIX

The block Blum had wormed his way into held around three hundred prisoners, two or three to a bunk.

After the outside head count he wandered inside next to weary prisoners returning from their days, emitting audible sighs and groans of exhaustion, tossing their emaciated bodies on the thin straw mattresses and nursing their blisters and sores. Blum figured there had to be some time until they could reconcile the head count with those who were newly dead.

The reek of body odor and human excrement made him hold his breath. There was every noise imaginable. Groaning, coughing, scratching, farting; others simply rambling to themselves in a kind of incoherent daze. Back in England, they'd inoculated him as best they could against the kinds of diseases that were rampant in here. Typhus. Dysentery. But the stench alone almost made him retch. And the thought of lice. He finally located a bunk with only a single person on it.

"This free?" he asked the man lying there.

"Zugangi?" The prisoner looked at Blum with bloodshot eyes. Blum thought his accent sounded Lithuanian or Estonian.

"Sorry?"

"Novy . . . ?" the man above him clarified. *Are you new?*

"Yes," Blum answered. "Today."

"New arrivals in the back." The man in the bunk pointed to the rear. "Near the shit hole."

Holding his breath against the smell, Blum kept on going. He saw another bunk with only one in it.

"Up there." Someone pointed from underneath a bunk, directing him.

Near the very back, two prisoners were stretched out on the top bunk. One was a giant, picking at the sores on his feet, which were open and oozing pus. The other was gaunt with a pinched-in face like a ferret, with flitting, suspicious eyes. Neither moved as much as an inch to let him up.

"We've been saving it just for you," said a man in a lower bunk who had on a flat tweed cap and appeared to be a kind of leader within the block. "The previous occupant died of fever just the other day."

"My good luck, then," Blum replied.

"There's a bowl." The man in the cap pointed to one hanging from the bedpost. It was made of filthy and corroded tin, and who knew whose disease-inflicted hands had recently been on it. "If I were you I'd attach it to yourself. No bowl, no food. That's the way it goes here."

"I will. Thanks." Blum pulled on the slats of the wooden bunk and hoisted himself up.

"Over there." The large man grunted inhospitably, indicating the spot closest to the open latrine. Which was basically no more than a separated-off area with a shit hole and a stool.

"Where are you from?" someone called up to him.

"Gizycko. Near Lake Sniardwy," Blum said.

"Masuria, huh? Pretty. How did you manage to hold out so long?"

"I've been hiding on a farm." He was told to stay as vague as possible about his new identity, as someone might be from there or know someone who could expose him. "Damn postal deliverer gave us away."

"Postman? You can't even trust the mail these days. So what can you tell us? From the outside."

"Not so much." Blum didn't want to attract attention or to make himself so well known. *Still . . .* "Only that the war in the East is going badly. The Russians are now in Ukraine."

"Ukraine!" someone exclaimed joyfully.

"And in England the Allies are set to invade."

"Invade? *Where?*" Another sat up.

"The French coast. Calais. Normandy. No one knows, of course. But soon, the BBC says. They say it's the biggest army the world's ever seen."

"Not soon enough for us," someone sighed from the next bed. "Let's face it, the Germans will kill every one of us before they'll let anyone see what is going on here. And if they don't, the Russians surely will. Trust me, I've seen what a pogrom looks like there."

"We're told the trains are all full of Hungarians now," another spoke up. "We hear them, thousands arriving every day and night. But, poof, they don't even bring them into the camp anymore. They just go up in smoke."

"I wouldn't know about that." Blum shrugged. Even though he knew well what Strauss had said, and from Vrba and Wetzler, that it was true. "Listen, maybe one of you can help *me*. I am trying to locate someone. I'm told my uncle is here. His name is Mendl. Alfred. He was a professor. In Lvov. Anyone know of him?"

"*Mendl . . . ?* Don't think so," the man in the tweed cap said. "But no one knows names in here, just faces."

"I knew a Petr Mendl," another spoke up. "But he was from Prague. A fishmonger, not exactly a professor. Anyway, he went up the chimney a long time ago."

"Up the chimney?" Blum said.

He could hear a few chuckles.

"That stench outside, you didn't think that was from the chocolate factory, did you?"

More laughter.

"Or the kitchens . . ." someone said. "But you'll soon see, it surely tastes that way."

"I have a photograph." Blum removed a small, dog-eared picture of Mendl from his waistband. "Pass it around. Maybe one of you will recognize him."

The photo traveled from bunk to bunk. One or two shook their heads, then passed it on. Another just shrugged blankly.

"Looks familiar. But not lately, anyway," one said, handing it to the next.

"Sorry." That one passed the photo to the bunk above him. "There's not many from Lvov here. I try not to look at faces anyway."

"There are thousands and thousands here." The man in the tweed cap shook his head solmenly. "And sadly the cast changes daily."

"I have an important message for him," Blum said. "If anyone knows him."

"We all have important messages," someone laughed. "Unfortunately, none of them get delivered."

"Philosopher." The man in the tweed cap rolled his eyes.

"If I were you I'd forget your uncle," someone advised him. "He's probably dead anyway."

"We all have uncles," another chimed in. "You clearly *are* new here to even care."

"Shut the fuck up," another hissed from down the aisle. "I'm trying to sleep."

"Sorry." The picture came back up to Blum.

He slid it back into the pocket inside his shirt. The giant next to him was already snoring. Blum leaned back against the slats. It was foolish to even think it would happen like that. At the snap of a finger. There were thousands in here, hundreds of thousands, and as the man said, the cast changed every day. A needle in a haystack, Blum reflected. That's what it always was. In a hundred haystacks. A hundred haystacks with a lit match thrown onto them, as the clock was ticking down and there was only a short amount of time. Day One was already gone. Just two more. *No, of course it wouldn't happen just like that,* he admonished himself.

Blum closed his eyes, weariness finally overcoming him.

"You and your uncle must be very close." His other bunkmate, the one with the ferret-like face, remarked. "To carry around a photo-graph of him." His eyes seemed to carry a flutter of suspicion in them. A distrusting smile.

"Yes," Blum replied. The same smile. But inwardly, he realized he'd already been careless in his haste. "He was actually more like a father to me."

"A father . . . I see," the man remarked, shifting his eyes. "So it's Lvov, then," he added after a pause. "I thought you said you were from Masuria?"

A tremor of nerves ran down Blum's spine. There were informers everywhere, he'd been warned. And if it wasn't already enough to have to dodge the Germans for another two days, he now had others to worry about who were even closer at hand.

Yes, very careless.

The man rested his head against the mattress and closed his eyes.

In the distance, Blum heard the sound of music playing, an orchestra. He sat up. "I hear music."

"New arrivals," someone sighed, like it was nothing new.

"The ovens are heating up." Another rolled over. "Someone say a prayer."

A prayer . . . Day One was gone. *Fifty hours* . . . That was all he had left. There's a prayer. Blum glanced over at the ferret, who now seemed asleep. Fifty hours to pull off a miracle.

If, he finally shut his eyes, Mendl was even still alive.

THIRTY-SEVEN

On his way back from chess with Frau Ackermann after she'd returned that week, Leo left Rottenführer Langer at the gate and went into Block 36.

He found the old man on his bunk.

"How are you doing today?" Leo sat down across from him.

"Better." Alfred sat up, forcing a weak smile. "A little more each day."

"Here, I've brought you something. I think you'll be happy." He pulled off a cloth napkin and brought out a steaming mug.

"*Tea?*" Alfred's face lit up. "This must be a dream. From where?"

"From where do you think?" Leo said. "Of course, Langer was poking at me the whole way back in the hope that I would drop it. But he didn't dare do it. Still, I'm afraid it's not as hot as it was when I left."

"No matter." Alfred took a sip and inhaled the perfume-like aroma. "Ah, clove . . . This is heaven."

"I told you she would watch out for us," Leo said proudly. "And for you as well." There was something kind of sorrowful and almost resigned in the boy's eyes that Alfred detected but couldn't read.

"Yes. You were right on that one, my boy."

She *did* watch over him.

He hadn't died.

Indeed, it had been typhus after all, but only a glancing blow. Though Alfred remained in the infirmary for a full week while he regained his strength. *Now, that was a miracle!* Two days in a sweat-filled daze until the fever broke. In his delirium, images of Marte, calling for him; his work and formulas parading before his eyes.

And then this other dream, so very strange, something he couldn't fully make out until he finally regained lucidity: A young woman. Pretty, blonde, by his bed, caring for him. Overseeing the doctors. Instructing them to make sure he got well. "At any cost," she insisted.

At any cost.

Why?

Later he found out they had injected him with the vaccine normally reserved only for the Germans. They gave him antibiotics, transfusions.

Leo grinned. "See, she was an angel for you too."

"Indeed, she was." Alfred nodded. "I give you all thanks. If thanks is what I should feel to find myself back here."

He'd been back for a week now. Allowed to regain his strength, instead of being sent to the gas or being thrown back into the toil, like the rest. Though he was still a bit weakened. A nurse even came once to look in on him. Unprecedented. The most surprised people in the camp were his block mates when he came back after being away. "We almost gave away your bunk." Lazarus, they now called him. Back after a brief respite from the dead. No one had ever done that before.

Leo checked on him every day.

And every day they found a little time to work. Alfred saw that there was still so much to teach him. And now so little time. He took out his chalk and scratched his formulas on his slate tray each day. He put down his tea. "That was wonderful. Now let's get going."

"Alfred, there's no more point in it. We've been through it all."

"No. We haven't covered the dispersal pattern. You know that all atoms in the diffusion process are presumed to be moving at speed (v), but the fundamental problem is—"

"The fundamental problem is to compute the number of atoms that escape through a hole or even a million holes over an elapsed time." Leo picked up Alfred's thought. "Expressed as delta (t). Am I correct?"

"Well, yes, you are," Alfred admitted.

"And then given that the number of atoms contained would be the product of the volume of the diffusion cylinder times the density of atoms p small (n) plus large N over large V where N is the number of atoms in the cylinder and V, of course . . . just give me a second . . . is the volume of the cylinder."

"Yes, all right, go on . . ."

"My pleasure. The number of atoms equals the density of those atoms times the surface area of the cylinder . . . then times the velocity the atoms are traveling times the slant length of the tilt angle." Leo took a breath. "The entire equation expressed as . . ." he took the chalk and tin,

$$N_{cyl} = \rho_N S \langle v \rangle (\Delta t) \cos\theta.$$

"So how was that?" His eyes twinkled with a ray of pride.

"That was good, son. All right, it was excellent, I have to admit. But have I gone over"—Alfred started to write—"that not *all* these atoms will be moving in the correct direction to achieve maximum escape? And that will create the dispersion. So to account for it . . ."

"So to account for it we have to multiply the above formula by the probability of an atom having its velocity so directed. Yes, you went over all of that with me, Alfred. I promise." Leo tapped his forehead. "It's all in here."

"Oh." Alfred nodded, his memory a bit strained. "I remember now. But did I—"

"Did you tell me that by extending this logic out, we can take our two gases for enrichment, U-235 and U-238, despite the difference in atomic weights, and quantify the extent of the enrichment, which is calculated as . . . let me think . . . %(235) = 100 $\{x/x+1\}$, where x is the number of atoms of 235 over the number of atoms of 238? Yes, you went over that with me as well." Leo put his hand on Alfred's arm. "I promise you, it's all safe. I have it all."

"Then bravo." Alfred said. He smiled with satisfaction. "We did it."

Leo nodded. "To what end, I still don't know, but yes, I believe we did."

"So now you're the world's reigning expert on the gaseous diffusion process . . . I offer my congratulations!"

"Second greatest expert," Leo said.

"Well, I fear soon you'll have that distinction all to yourself. And I told you, there are people who, once they know that . . ."

"Yes, Professor, you did. There are people who will need to know this. I will await them all." Leo's smile faded and he returned to the kind of look he had when he came in that Alfred couldn't read.

"Something is troubling you, boy?"

"Not to worry. If everything's okay with you, I'm fine. Drink up . . ."

"All right." Alfred took another sip of tea and closed his eyes dreamily. "I never thought I would ever have this pleasure again. Thank you, son. Now, don't forget the displacement theory."

"How could I possibly? It's as engrained in me as is pawn to king four."

"Then I've done my job. You'll probably want to be rid of me now. Now that there's nothing left to learn."

"You're telling me there's nothing of value left to share in that vast mind of yours, Professor . . . ?"

"You're right, there must be something," Alfred said. "There's *thermal* diffusion . . . Much harder process and far more difficult to achieve the required enrichment levels." He looked at Leo, who shook his head crossly. "Anyway . . ."

Leo put away the chalk and tin. "We'll work up to that then, shall we?"

"Yes. But something *is* wrong. I see it. Don't pretend, boy. You and I are friends."

Leo finally nodded. "She gave me another gift today, along with the tea." He dug into his pants, came out with something, and opened his hand.

It was a chess piece. A fine one, Alfred noted. A rook. Of beautiful white alabaster. Carved with great detail.

Leo set it in Alfred's hand. "I think it means our games have come to an end."

"Yes." Alfred nodded and put his hand on Leo's knee. "That's what it would seem."

"Which then means, of course . . ." Leo smiled, but it was more of a resigned one, with an edge of sadness.

"Which then means you're lucky you know all this stuff I've been teaching you . . ." Alfred bolstered him and winked. "At least, you won't go out with an empty mind."

Leo chuckled. "I don't think either Lubinksy or Markov or who-ever else I've trounced at chess would exactly attest that my mind was empty."

"And what have Lubinsky or Markov ever done to expand the body of knowledge, pray tell . . . ?"

"I took this as well," Leo said. He brought out a creased photo. It was of Frau Ackermann in a rowboat. She wore a white nautical cap, the front rim raised, showing her bright smile and happy eyes. "I saw it amid a stack of photos. When she left for a moment I put it in my tunic. She looks so happy."

Alfred saw it was the very woman who had overseen his care at the hospital. "Yes, she does."

"She won't let me go." Leo looked at him. "Or you. Not so easily. You watch."

"I suggest we do not get ahead of ourselves, Leo. Perhaps it was no more than just her husband putting his foot down. You knew he was no fan of your games. We must continue to have hope. Where there is hope, there is life. And where there is life . . . there is more to learn, isn't that right?" Alfred smiled.

"Well, here's to hope then," Leo said. He lifted the teacup and handed it back to Alfred.

"And here's to more to learn." He raised the cup and took a last sip of tea. "Where our true hope lies. Are we agreed?"

"Why don't we just leave it at hope, shall we?" Leo replied.

THIRTY-EIGHT

WEDNESDAY.

At dawn, the Daimler personnel car with the swastika under the war eagle on its door sped through the Polish countryside, its headlights flashing through the fog.

Colonel Martin Franke sat in the back.

His still-wet-behind-the-ears driver wore the Abwehr insignia on his collar but was just months out of whatever they were putting the new call-ups through these days as training and clearly didn't know his way behind a wheel. It was over three hundred kilometers from Warsaw to Oswiecim, four hours in good weather along the rutted S8, longer in this soup.

"Please, faster, Corporal," Franke said impatiently. "Go around that truck." A supply truck had slowed in front of them.

"Yes, Colonel," the corporal answered, hitting the gas.

Franke had persuaded his superior, General Graebner, to authorize him to go to the camp. The call had gone to Berlin, where the camp commander, SS Colonel Hoss, was in conference with Reichsführer Himmler and Reinhart Heydrich he was told. A Major Ackermann had been left in charge. So Franke knew he had better be right on this; the showdown between Canaris and Himmler for the Führer's favor was not a secret. To embarrass either of them would mean nothing but the Eastern Front for him.

But Franke felt certain, more so each time he went through it, that his instincts were correct. That the camp there had to be the target of whatever was being planned. The cable "*the truffle hunter is en route.*" The local report of the sighting of a plane. The parachuter who'd been spotted. The birchwood forest. The region was thinly populated and there were no known troop activities or items of any strategic interest that would point to anything else.

It made Franke's blood stir. Blood that had long sat dormant. For the past year he'd been underused and pushed aside. *Someone was definitely here.* From where? England, perhaps. And what for? An attack? An escape? An act of sabotage?

Now he just had to find out the who and the why.

If he was successful, Franke could almost taste how all his past shame would finally be put behind him. Himmler himself would be watching now. His wife would take him back, and with it, his position, the comfortable *schloss* in Rottach-Egern.

Everything depended on him rooting out this man.

Three more hours. He glanced at his watch. "It would be good to arrive *today*," he called to the driver, who had now slowed for a herd of goats crossing the road. The Polish roads were all oxen paths. The driver hit the horn loudly.

A hunger churned inside Franke. Someone was clearly here. He just had to find him. This man. Wherever he had come from.

This truffle hunter.

It was a match of wits, Franke said to himself. A chess match.

You think you are alone. You think you are under the net. But you are wrong.

There is my net. My nose that will smell you when I see you.

Now it is just you and me.

THIRTY-NINE

Blum opened his eyes before first light. Zinchenko, their Lithuanian *kapo*, entered the barracks loudly banging on the walls and bunks with his stick. "*Rauss. Rauss!* Rise and shine, my little pets. Another day of wonder and adventure awaits you. Get your asses moving!"

In their bunks, people began to stir slowly. "Is it light yet?"

"Just another two minutes, please, Zinchenko!"

"*Up!* Up now, pigs!" the *kapo* called back without pity. "I try to be nice to you, letting you sleep an extra five minutes, and look what I get."

Blum had woken at least a dozen times during the night. Between the awkward position he was forced to sleep in, tugging for a sliver of the thin, grimy blanket that the three of them had to share and that wouldn't have kept the bed lice warm, the constant snoring, and the fitful worry of what lay ahead for him today, he barely got an hour's sleep.

"Work details in thirty minutes! Roll call in five!" the *kapo* instructed. He was a muscular man with a heavy growth on his face and a flattened hat on his head, separating him from the average prisoner. As well as the red triangle sewn on his chest, signifying him as a common criminal. "Five minutes! Everyone outside!"

Slowly the block came alive. There was no washing up. Several lined up for the latrine and peed or shat in the revolting bucket.

Blum climbed down and found the man in the tweed cap he had spoken to last night, folding his blanket. "I need a job," he said. "Anything you can get me? Something in the camp, if possible. At least for a day or two. I want to find my uncle."

"Talk to *him*." He pointed to a short man with heavy-lidded eyebrows. "He was an attorney in Prague. He's *blockschreiber* here." The block clerk. Wetzler and Vrba had mentioned those. It was their role to assign the work duties.

"Thanks."

Blum went over and found the man through the hurrying crowd. "I'm new." He told the block clerk how he wanted a day to find his uncle.

"What's your name?"

"Mirek."

"Number . . . ?"

Blum showed him his arm. The *blockschreiber* kept note of it in a small black notebook.

"I have just the position." The man chuckled grimly. "Rosten, congratulations!" he called out. "You've been promoted."

"Hallelujah!" someone yelled out from the throng.

"Sanitary brigade," he said to Blum.

"What is that?"

He jotted it in his notebook. "Rosten will show you the rounds."

The job, as Blum was shown, was to carry the buckets of shit and piss from the latrine to the camp's cesspool, located outside the main gate. Not just theirs. Blocks 18 through 32 as well. The main benefit, Blum soon realized, was that he would be able to enter several of the other blocks where there would be people around.

"Just be careful," the *blockschreiber* warned him. "If one spills on public grounds, you'll likely get a bullet in your head. Rosten will be very upset. He'll have to go back to it."

"Then I'll be especially careful in that case," Blum agreed.

"And keep your eyes out. Sometime the guards will jab you with their sticks just for sport. If the bucket spills, you can say your prayers. Guess they figure anyone we give this job to isn't much worth feeding."

"Thanks. So how has Rosten survived at it then?"

"Rosten?" The *blockschreiber* shrugged. "Guess he doesn't eat all that much."

Outside, whistles sounded and people filed out their blocks and lined up for roll call. The morning was damp with a chill in the air for May, enough that everyone stood around hugging themselves in their thin burlap uniforms. Blum was nervous. The roll call was one of the times he could easily be exposed. The SS Blockführer came up. Lieutenant Fischer. Holding a dog-eared stack of papers on a clipboard. "You know the routine," he barked. "Line up. A to Z. Step forward when your name is called." Everyone edged into four long rows. He started in, *"Abramowitz . . . "*

"Here!" a man in the back row shouted.

The guard licked his pencil and checked him off. *"Adamczyk?"*

"Yes. Here."

"Alyneski . . . ?"

Blum huddled amid the crowd in the fourth row. They were going by name. He could get lost in the crowd and not have to shout one out. If they had gone down the rows man by man, and each had to call out his name, his name, Mirek, would not have matched up. That would have been a lot trickier.

"Bach?"

"Here!"

"Balcic . . . "

It took almost twenty minutes to go through the entire block. The staging area was so crammed with prisoners, each in front of their own blocks, each line melded into ones from the block next to it, making it one vast throng, names shouted out from competing Blockführers. The man next to Blum in line leaned over. "New here . . . ?"

Blum nodded. "Yes."

"Anyone taken you through the rounds?"

"Rounds? Not yet."

"So listen up. It'll keep you alive. Fischer," he nodded toward the

213

Blockführer calling out names, "he's one hundred percent by the book. Doesn't look for trouble, won't help you a lick either. That one . . ." He pointed to an SS corporal. Reddish hair, flat nose. "Fuerst. He's got a sick sister at home. He does his job, but sometimes he can be open for business, if you know what I mean."

"You mean a bribe?"

The man shrugged. "If you've got something to trade. But whatever you do, don't get in the way of that asshole . . ." He gestured to a hound-faced guard with thick lips and heavy-lidded eyes. "Dormutter. He's just a lunatic. He's in heaven in here. He can kill whoever he wants. Stay out of his way. I can't describe the things I've seen done."

"I will. Thanks," Blum said.

He took Blum through some of the other guards and *kapos*. The true monsters, the ones who would just kill you for sport. And those who were just doing their jobs. The ones whom Blum could count on and who at all costs he had to avoid.

"We all get the tour once," the man explained. "From now on you're on your own."

Before they broke into their work details, the block lineups merged for a while, people catching a quick word with their neighbors, trading stories of what was new, who was lost in the past day, bartering for cigarettes and scraps of food.

Blum took out his photograph. "I'm looking for my uncle," he said to someone from a neighboring block. "His name is Mendl. Do you know him? He's from Lvov."

"Sorry." The person shook his head. "He's not in here."

Blum went through the crowd and asked someone across the yard. "I'm looking for this man. He's my uncle. His name is Mendl."

Again the person shook his head. "Don't know him. Sorry."

He went from group to group, looking around, inspecting faces in the teeming crowd, keeping an eye out for the guards, grabbing onto anyone who made eye contact with him.

"Do you know this man? Have you seen him? Mendl."

"No," he kept on hearing. "Sorry."

"This is his picture. Look, please."

214

One said, "He looks familiar. But I can't help you. Do you have any extra smokes though? I'm dying."

"He's probably dead." Another shrugged. "Why do you care anyway? We all have uncles here somewhere."

"Sorry."

It could all be too late, Blum feared, watching the thousands seeming more dead than alive just trying to get through the day. Vrba and Wetzler confirmed that he was here, but that was January. Four months ago. The cold could have gotten him. Or typhus. Or a club to the head. Or the gas. He realized this could all be futile. *Do not fail us,* President Roosevelt had urged. But even Roosevelt had no control over the whimsy of life and death here.

There was a chance he might have come all this way just for a corpse.

Breakfast came around. Blum made it back to his block and edged into the line with his metal bowl. He hadn't had a bite of food since the stomach-turning soup he'd had yesterday at lunch. This was far worse. He couldn't tell what it was: cabbage, potato, a ladle full of thin, tasteless swill made from rinds, peels, and boiled grizzle. With a stale chunk of bread. He looked around at his barrack mates huddling outside their block, sucking it all in.

What if I'm unable to find him? Blum asked himself. *What then?*

And what if I'm never able to make it out of here? This would be his life. As long as it lasted.

He sipped from his bowl, wincing at the first rancid taste. Then sipping it again. Sucking it into his mouth. As everyone else was. He would have to work the day too.

The whistles sounded again. "Line up. Line up. Meal's over."

The work details had begun.

FORTY

"*Guten morgen*, Herr Lagerkommandant!" The staff in the commandant's office stood as Ackermann stepped in.

"Good morning. As you were." With a wave, the major proceeded to his desk.

There was a coffee on his desk for him. He sat and scanned the morning reports. The number of prisoners "processed" yesterday: Over twenty-one thousand. *Very nice.* A full 12 percent above the norm. Most had arrived that very day and had gone straight through. He looked at the number expected for today. Another nice one. Two trains. One from Theresienstadt near Prague and one from Hungary. It would be another busy day and night.

He had his daily quotas, but he wanted to exceed them in Kommandant Hoss's absence. He wanted everyone to see he could run the place both efficiently and with appropriate discipline. And who knows, he had begun to think, perhaps his boss was even being promoted on his extended trip to Berlin. Maybe that's why he remained there the extra days. It was important for everyone to see that, in his absence, the place remained in strong hands. That the work was being maintained; the numbers met. What went on here was under the direct eye of Reichsführer Himmler and his inner circle. If promotions were in the offing, he wanted his name at the top of the column too.

Which left him with a particular problem that morning, Ackermann reflected.

Greta.

It was beginning to worry him that his wife had taken such a liking to the chess-playing Jew she'd invited into their house. One or two games, perhaps; that he could understand. But then it must be seen that she showed him no particular favor. Instead of showering the boy with gifts and petitioning Ackermann for his protection. He would have to clear that up for good, he'd decided, on his short walk over this morning. Apparently it had already become banter for the troops. Which was always bad for morale. Hoss had even mentioned it before he left, not in a direct way, of course, but over a schnapps, almost anecdotally. "Greta must be becoming quite the chess player by now . . ." He laughed. But Ackermann knew precisely what Hoss meant. He'd take care of it, he resolved, before his boss's return. "Special Treatment" must become what it always was. An organized purification of the Reich. Not some foolish and misguided favoritism. Greta must see that. He could do it in a snap, of course. Get rid of the whole block. No one would be the wiser. But women could be difficult, of course. That's why the problem was so thorny. He knew she wasn't happy here. It had already been over a month since she'd shown any interest in him.

Yes, he grunted to himself, *it* was getting bad for morale.

His aide, Lieutenant Fromm, stepped in and came up to his desk. "Sorry to bother you, sir. But I have a message for you. From Warsaw."

"Warsaw . . . ?" Ackermann looked up.

"Yes, from a General Graebner there. Of the Abwehr."

"Abwehr . . . ?" Ackermann rounded his eyes. Intelligence. The camp took its orders directly from Berlin. From Reinhart Heydrich and Reichsführer Himmler themselves. "What the fuck could the Abwehr possibly want here?"

His aide said, "Apparently a Colonel Martin Franke will be arriving today." He handed Ackermann the cable. "It seems he has some questions. Concerning security."

"*Security?* Here . . . ?" The Lagerkommandant snorted back a laugh. "He must be joking. A nun's snatch couldn't be any tighter than it is in here."

"Nonetheless, the general has asked that, in Kommandant Hoss's absence, we would show him every courtesy."

"Courtesy, huh?" Ackermann scowled. "Let him come." Just what they needed today, the Abwehr poking their uppity noses around. When there were numbers to be met. "But I'm not showing him around. Get Kimpner to do that." Kimpner was a bean counter in charge of operations. Kitchen. Infirmary. Procurement. "There are other things for me to attend to today."

There were two trains. Another twenty thousand to process. And then this matter with his wife.

But on this he had to find the right way. His pecker was getting edgy. He had to show her that what was bad for morale, and for him, was bad for her too.

Yes, this had all gone far enough, the Lagerkommandant thought.

He passed the cable back to Fromm. "Let me know when he arrives."

FORTY-ONE

Blum carted the buckets of congealed waste across the camp's grounds to the refuse ditch located just outside the wire. He held his breath at the awful smell. He moved past the guards, swiftly but carefully, keeping his eyes down, knowing he could be the target of any of them at their whim. Then he emptied the contents in the ditch, hosed the buckets clean, and brought them back inside.

In each block, even with the majority of prisoners out on work details, there were always a few around. Those that were either infirmed or simply resting, back from the overnight work shifts.

And in each block Blum took out his photograph of Mendl. "I'm looking for my uncle," he would ask. "Have you seen him?"

And in each he received the same, deflating response.

"No. Sorry."

"He's not in here."

An indifferent shrug of the shoulders. "Sorry. There are so many."

He began to think it was fruitless until finally, in Block 31, a man lying in bed took the picture and after a few seconds actually nodded. "I do know him. Mendl. He's a professor, right?"

"Yes," Blum said, lifted.

"From Lvov, I think."

"That's right," Blum confirmed. He grew expansive.

But then the man just shook his head fatalistically. "Haven't seen him in over a month now. I heard he had the fever." He handed Blum back the photograph. "Sorry, I think he's dead."

"*Dead,*" Blum said, falling back to earth. "Are you certain?"

"I know he was taken to the infirmary. Very few end up coming back from there. Ask the chess boy. They were friends. He would know."

"The chess boy . . . ?"

"The camp champion. They play here every couple of weeks. You'll see them. Over by the infirmary. Sorry. I can't be more help."

The chess boy. They play every couple of weeks . . . Blum said to himself. His hope plummeted. He had two days. Less, now. *I think he's dead.* Had he risked everything, come all this way, he thought as he lifted the wretched shit bucket out from under the stall, only for a corpse?

He considered checking at the infirmary. If he'd been sick, someone had to know of him there. But that might also arouse suspicion. This "chess boy . . ." It couldn't be too hard to find him. But he'd already put himself out there, showing the photograph to anyone who would look. Now, to suddenly start asking around for someone else . . . That would definitely make him stand out.

But what other choice did he have?

He lugged his new set of buckets outside the gate. Guards were everywhere. He was especially careful here, to avoid direct eye contact. And not to spill a single drop. Yet these particular buckets were especially heavy and filled to the top. He sensed a guard snickering at him as he hurried by. *Just get past him . . .*

"*Stop!*" someone called out from behind him.

Blum stood there, erect.

"Where do you go so quickly with such fine wares to sell?" a guard said to him mockingly.

Blum closed his eyes for a second and then shuddered when he opened them and saw it was the very guard pointed out to him during roll call this morning. Dormutter. *He's just a lunatic. At all costs, don't provoke him. He's one to avoid.*

The guard had a khaki SS cap tilted over a square face, deep-set sunken eyes, thick lips, and a sneer of superiority in his gaze. "Looks heavy," he said, brandishing a thick club. He stepped up behind Blum.

"It is heavy, sir," Blum replied. "But it's fine." He took a step forward. "If I might just continue to the—"

"I'll tell you when to go, yid," the guard snapped back with ice in his tone.

"Yes, sir." Blum froze.

"What's your name?"

"Mirek," Blum answered, his tongue dry and coarse as sandpaper.

"Yes, they're definitely overloading this poor man!" Dormutter said loudly to his fellow guards nearby in mock concern. From behind, Blum felt a tap from the club on his left arm. The bucket lurched forward. Blum brought it back as best he could to keep it from tipping over.

"*Hmmph,*" Dormutter grunted, from behind him.

Then Blum felt a second tap. On his right arm this time. And this time, the bucket, filled almost to the rim, swung forward too. Remembering what the *blockschreiber* had warned, Blum put every ounce of strength he had into righting it. But it was clear what the guard was trying to do.

"We don't like it when they are careless and let these buckets fill too high. It brings up the possibility that . . ."

Blum felt the club bump into his left arm again. This time harder. Both buckets swung. Petrified, Blum struggled to keep them righted. The handles dug into his fingers. The pails grew heavier.

If one spills on public grounds, you'll likely get a bullet in your head, echoed through Blum's head.

"You can see what a health risk it is, should any happen to drop. Jew shit, all over a public setting. Not so good?"

"No, Sergeant." Blum nodded in agreement. His arms began to feel like they would soon give out.

This time he felt the end of the heavy club jab into his back. The buckets lurched forward. Blum did everything he could to keep them from tipping. Literally commanding them not to spill. Somehow they didn't.

"By health risk, just to be clear . . ." the German said, digging the club into the small of Blum's back. "Of course I meant to you, yid." He jabbed the club into him again.

The buckets dug deeply into Blum's fingers. He knew he couldn't withstand a much harder nudge. Sweat wound down his brow. At any second he expected to feel the weight of the club smack into his skull like a bat on a ball and he would drop, a dead weight, the buckets spilling, and then be finished off.

Blum felt the club nudge him forward again, the buckets jerking, and he took a step. Waste lapped right to the edge and dripped onto the side of the pail, sending panic through Blum.

He could not hold them much longer. If so, he resolved he would not die like his family. Without putting up a fight. A similar man, with a similar hate in his eye, had likely murdered them all. He would turn and empty his buckets all over the guard. Let whatever would happen, happen. He tightened his grip, waited for the final provocation. Waste that had accumulated lapped over the rim's edge.

This could be it.

"I merely wanted to tell you," the SS guard said with a sniff, "that the officers' guardhouse needs to be cleaned out as well."

"The officers' guardhouse," Blum muttered back, dry-mouthed. "Yes, sergeant."

"And consider yourself lucky," Dormutter said, "that we have an important visitor today in camp and that I've just shined my boots. Or otherwise . . ." The German made a kind of clicking noise with his tongue. "I might find some other Jew to lick out the guardhouse latrine. Now go."

"Yes, Sergeant." Blum nodded, picking up his step.

"And remember, the guardhouse. You'll need a pass." He came up again and stuffed a white form into Blum's clenched hand.

"Thank you, sir." A breath of relief blew out Blum's cheeks. He hurried on with his buckets.

"And Mirek . . . You have quite good sense of balance with the pails there," the SS man called after him. "You should consider the high wire in your next life."

He laughed, as did a couple of the other guards in listening range, and turned away, letting Blum go on.

Blum hurried through the gate, his legs almost giving out from under him. He put down the buckets next to the waste ditch and let out a grateful sigh. He wrung out his fingers and then disposed of the waste.

He just wanted out of this place now. It was clear, there was no longer a mission to fulfill. Mendl was likely dead. Now he just had to make it back out himself. He wanted so much to have brought back the man they needed. *Do not fail us. You have no idea how much depends on your success.* But what could he do? Even if Mendl was somehow here, *alive,* it was clear there were so many places and no way to search them all, and not enough time. Three days. That was all they had given him. *A needle in a haystack.* From the very start . . . In a *hundred* haystacks, Blum said to himself. The task was impossible.

He hurried back through the gate and replaced the buckets in Block 31. He still had two more barracks to clean. But he didn't want Dormutter finding him again before he had fulfilled his task. He knew where the guardhouse was. He had memorized every building in the camp on Vrba and Wetzler's map. Part of him said, *Go fuck the Nazi bastard.* With God's help, Blum would only be in here another day. The name "Mirek," if Dormutter looked it up, would mean nothing. There were thousands and thousands here. The SS man would never find him. Just as he had never found Mendl. *Let some other yid lick out their shit.*

Still, he went.

He went because some other yid would only be taunted or even killed to do his job. And he went because he had been lucky at the gate, and to ignore God's grace that had been bestowed on him would make him undeserving.

The officers' guardhouse was through a gate near the clock tower.

"Over there." The guard manning it pointed without even looking at Blum after inspecting his pass.

It was a long, brick building with a peaked, slate roof. On one side, there were a couple of vehicles parked. An empty troop truck with a war cross on the door. And the German version of a Jeep. A guard stepped out, heading past him.

Blum showed him his pass. "Latrine . . . ?"

The SS man pointed around the back. "Back there."

On the other side of the building, there was a bicycle rack, and in front of it, a man, another prisoner, hunched over, scraping the tires of mud. Blum prepared to go around the back as his gaze fell on him.

Blum's heart came to a stop.

The man was clearly older than most here. Hair, white now, no longer gray, and thinned. But still combed over to the side.

Thinner. His cheek bones coming through. A shadow of himself.

Barely even resembling the photo Blum carried on him.

But when he looked up, Blum saw the full, flat nose, the sagging line of the chin that had been burned into his memory. *Can this be?* And then, a tide of joy rising up inside him, the black mole on his left cheek. *That will be your confirmation,* Strauss had said.

Confirmation, Blum said exultantly.

He took a step forward. "Professor Mendl?"

FORTY-TWO

The man looked up.

For Blum, it was like he was seeing a mirage, in the desert. Was it real? Or was it only what he wanted to be real? The old man looked so gaunt and sickly, it was amazing he hadn't already been shipped off to his fate. It was amazing Blum even recognized him.

"Do I know you?" he asked.

"Professor Alfred Mendl? You taught at the University of Lvov? You lectured in electromagnetic physics?"

The old man squinted at Blum as if he was some student he had once had. "Yes."

Elation surged in Blum. *It was him!* Thinner. The color gone from his face. His eyes beaten. Barely a shadow of his former self, physically. Somewhere between a ghost and a man.

But him!

"Don't be alarmed, sir." Blum came a step closer. "And please don't think I'm crazy, what I'm about to say." He looked around to make sure there were no other guards around. "But thank God I've found you. I've been looking for you all over."

"Looking for *me* . . . ?" The professor squinted back uncomprehendingly.

"Yes." Blum nodded. "*You.* Look." He brought out the photograph he had tucked inside his uniform.

Mendl stood up and stared at his own likeness, his eyes growing wide. Then, not quite understanding, he handed it back to Blum. "Why me?"

"Professor, what I'm about to tell you may sound crazy." Blum met the old man's gaze. "But it's not, I promise, and I can prove every word." He spoke low enough that no one could overhear. "But I've snuck inside here. Inside the camp. I've come from Washington, D.C. In the States."

"*Washington . . . ?*" Now the professor did squint back with a look of incredulity. "And you say you've snuck in *here?* Into the camp. Why, possibly . . . ?"

"For you, Professor. To get you out."

"Out of *here . . . ?*" Mendl sniffed, as if he were definitely speaking with a lunatic. "Now you are talking nonsense, whoever you are. Only two people have ever gotten out of here. And no one's ever known how they ended up."

"Wetzler and Vrba," Blum said back. Mendl's eyes raised. "Look . . ." Blum yanked up his sleeve and showed his wrist. "This is Rudolf Vrba's number. A22327. They made it, Professor. They're in England now. They helped me. In order to get inside."

Mendl took Blum's arm and stared, bewildered, at the number, then back at him.

"I realize how this sounds, sir. But I can prove every word."

"Then who the hell are you, having gotten your way inside here? Some kind of commando? You hardly look it. But your Polish is flawless. Yet you say you came from Washington? I'm old, but I'm not a fool, young man."

"My name is Blum. I am Polish. Until three years ago I lived in Krakow. My family was killed by the Nazis, and I escaped to the United States. I enlisted there in the Army. A month ago they contacted me to come back here. For you specifically. To get you out. And take you back to the States."

"*To the States . . .*" Mendl's eyes grew wide. Then he just smiled and shook his head. "Look around, son. Do you not see two rows of electrified wire and all the guards? Do you intend to just call a cab and have it drive up to the front gate? Get out *how*, do you propose?

"We have a way. It's been worked out. They are still working on the train tracks, are they not, outside the camp gates?"

"Day and night. You can smell the ovens over at Birkenau. Twenty-four hours a day. The more trains, the more fuel for the fires."

"Tomorrow night, we volunteer for the work detail there," Blum said under his breath. "There'll be an attack. By Polish partisans."

"*Partisans?* Here?"

"Yes. It's all been arranged. We have a plane. Two days ago it dropped me off. It's to take you back to England and then on to the United States. Whoever you are, sir, I can only say they want you very badly."

"Whoever I am . . . ?" The professor's look grew skeptical. "If this is a ploy of some kind, I assure you I—"

"They tried to get you out before with papers from the Paraguayan embassy. You were contacted by an emissary from the embassy in Bern." Blum rattled off what he knew. "You went to the Swiss border and then on to Rotterdam to board a cargo ship. The *Prinz Eugen*. Is that not right? Then you ended up in France, at the detention center at Vittel . . ."

Mendl's look slowly changed from disbelief to one of astonishment. Gradually, he nodded. And then smiled. He saw now.

"This is no ploy, sir. I promise you." Blum looked him in the eyes. "They wouldn't tell me what it is you did or why they need you. Only that it was vital to get you out. Which is why I'm here. And to give you this . . ."

Blum tore a seam on the inside of his uniform and reached inside. He came out with a folded piece of paper and handed it to Mendl. The old man looked at it, still suspicious at first or, at least, still a bit unsure, and then unfolded it, continuing to eye Blum with a bit of wariness. He took out his wire glasses and put them on.

It was a letter.

An image of the White House at the top.

The professor's eyes stretched wide.

"Professor Mendl . . ." He read softly under his breath in English. "The war effort needs you. I am encouraged to tell you that we are close. On what, due to security, I am unable to say here. But I know you know of which I speak. I am writing to say that you can trust this man, Nathan Blum, with your life. He is my direct emissary. Freedom and the fate of the war require that you come here and share your research. The grateful arms of the United States need you and await you. With all God's speed, Professor. And for the good of mankind."

"My God," Mendl uttered, his jaw slack.

It was signed Franklin Delano Roosevelt, *President of the United States*.

Mendl looked back up at Blum, the color drained from his face. "How did you possibly get this?"

"It was given to me. In England, before I left."

"The heavy water experiments?" Mendl began to put it together. "Are the Americans close? They must be, if they sent you here for me."

"I've heard of this, but I don't know. I was only told to give you that letter. And to get you back."

"The bastards have destroyed all my work." Mendl shook his head forlornly. "Not once, but twice. And besides, you can see I'm hardly in the top of health. I'm way too old to be playing secret agent."

"You must come." Blum insisted. "I've put my life at risk to bring you out. And that's what I'll do. I don't know what it is you know, or why they want *you*, above all others, but many people have put their lives on the line to get me here and to hand you this, Professor. So you must. You must come."

Mendl let out a breath and ran a hand fitfully across his face. "We must put this away now." He folded the letter back up again. "If anyone would see this . . ." He looked around with both foreboding and bewilderment in his gaze, still in shock, stuffing the letter into his waist.

"I have to ask, sir," Blum inquired. "Your family . . . ?"

Mendl shook his head. "They are gone. Soon after we arrived."

"I'm sorry. Mine are gone as well. So then there is nothing to hold you back. I can vouch for the partisans. They are capable and dedicated soldiers. They will do what they are charged to do."

"And then we do just what?" The professor chortled skeptically. "Throw down our shovels and run? Toward the woods. And the Nazis will simply look the other way?"

"No. Not toward the woods. Toward the river," Blum said. "The opposite direction. We'll be met there."

"Met there . . ." The professor laughed cynically. "It's been a while since my track running days, I'm afraid, if you can't already see that. Plus, I've been sick."

"They'll be chaos all around. The attack should occupy the guards. I'll get you there."

"And when is all this to happen?"

"Tomorrow night. At zero thirty hours." Blum said, "I'll be going, whether you're with me or not. Though I'd much prefer it if it was the two of us."

"And you say that there's a plane?"

"It will land about twenty kilometers from here. The partisans will take us."

Mendl closed his eyes for a second and nodded as if deep in thought. "This is where my Marte and Lucy died. A part of me feels it's right that this is where I should die too."

"What's right, to me, is that you make something of their deaths, Professor. As I am trying to of mine. I'm only here another day. That's all the time there is. Whatever it is you know, sir, the Allies seem to desperately need you."

"This is all just so incredible . . ."

"That may be, sir. Nonetheless, you must come."

Two soldiers stepped out of guardhouse, chatting. They came down the wooden steps, spoke for a second, then noticed Blum and Mendl. "*Was gibts hier?*" one questioned. *What's here?*

"Latrine, sir." Blum held out his pass to them. "I was just asking . . ."

"Then get on with it," he snapped. "Let the old man do his work. It's back there. Go on." They went off, resuming their conversation, and climbed into the half-track on the other side of the building. The engine started up.

Blum looked at Mendl. "I need your answer, sir. I should go. It's best I don't draw any attention . . ."

"My answer." The professor still seemed conflicted.

"Yes. There is still work to be done."

"Then, yes! My answer is, yes, I'll come." Mendl put his bony hand on Blum's shoulder and squeezed. "You're right, it is too late for Marte and Lucy. But not for what I know. I'll come with you."

Blum squeezed the professor in return. "I give you my word, sir, I'll get you back. Or die trying."

"There's just one thing . . ."

"What?"

"I won't be coming alone. There is someone who must accompany me."

Blum shook his head. "I'm afraid that's impossible."

"There's a boy. In truth, he's no longer a boy. He's seventeen."

"It's out of the question," Blum insisted. "It will be hard enough to make sure I can protect *you*. But a boy like that . . . This isn't a popularity contest. This is about the war. The government of the United States has gone to extreme lengths to set this up."

"I'm afraid it's not a wish, Panie Blum. It's a condition. For me to come. And he's not just some boy . . ." Mendl hesitated a moment. "He's my nephew. I won't leave him." His gaze was resolute. "Without him, I don't go."

"Nephew . . ." Blum drew in a troubled breath. Three would be more to manage. To take responsibility for. More conspicuous in the escape. What if the boy was hit? What then? Would the professor go or remain with him? He saw it clearly. Mendl would not so easily leave him behind.

"You wouldn't leave your own flesh and blood behind, would you, Panie Blum?"

Blum felt himself soften. What choice did he have? And Mendl's question seemed to hit the right nerve. "This boy, he can keep a secret?"

"I'll make sure of it." Mendl nodded. "He's a remarkable lad. In many ways."

"I don't care how remarkable he is, he still can't breathe a word. Everything depends on it."

"He won't," Mendl promised. "I give you my oath."

Blum saw that it was a risk. He didn't know what someone like Strauss would do, faced with the same decision. But what choice was there? He saw the resolve in the professor's eyes. Without this boy, there was no Mendl. And that was why he was here. "All right. But no one else can know. No one."

"You'll see, he won't be a burden. I give you my word."

"I hope so. All our lives depend on it. Before we go, I want to meet him. Which block are you in?"

"Thirty-six."

"I'm in twenty. And we'll have to get our way onto the work detail."

Mendl nodded. "I know how to get that accomplished. There's a guard, Richter, who generally oversees it. And a *kapo* I know. They are always looking for workers. Or bribes. If I had money."

"I can take care of that part. So I will find you tomorrow. Maybe play sick." Blum put out his hand. "I'll be by your block."

They shook.

"You know, from the day we left Lvov," Mendl looked at him sadly, "Marte and I dreamed of taking our daughter to America. Of course the minute we got on that train we all knew that dream was dead. So maybe it's best, in a way, that they're gone now. Maybe that's how history intended it to be. If either was alive, even by a breath, you know I would never leave them."

Blum nodded. "I know that."

"I wonder whether anyone will ever take note of that fact one day, should we reach there?" the professor mused. "Or in the end, if it even really matters?"

FORTY-THREE

The Abwehr Daimler was waved through the camp's front gate and directed to the administrative offices.

Martin Franke stepped out.

A major in an SS uniform, handsome, with strong, dark features, came down the steps to greet him.

"Herr Colonel . . ." The officer gave Franke a quick *Heil*. "I am Lagerkommandant Ackermann. I am in charge of the camp while Kommandant Hoss is away."

"Major." Franke raised his palm. They shook hands.

"You've come a long way this busy morning for a visit. I'm very sorry the commandant couldn't be here himself to welcome you."

"I'm sorry to have arrived on such short notice. I hope I'm not interrupting your work. But I have a matter of some importance that I believe relates to your camp."

"If the Abwehr feels it is a matter of such urgency . . ." Ackermann smiled, his sarcasm showing through, "then no work is too important to interrupt. Come, it's been a long journey from Warsaw. We shall discuss it over a *kaffee* inside."

They went into the administrative offices. Lieutenant Fromm came in with two coffees, and they sat around the small conference table in front of a map of the camp. "I am sorry that the commandant is not here. Unfortunately, he's been detained an extra day in Berlin, in meetings with Obersturmbannführer Eichmann and Reichsführer Himmler."

"So I understand," Franke replied, noting the SS man's superior tone. While technically Franke had the higher rank, the political battle between the Abwehr and its chain of command through Admiral Canaris and Göring, and the SS, reporting to Himmler himself, all competing for the Führer's ear, was not a secret. This Ackermann, Franke judged, would likely hide behind that protection. Franke was determined to prove him wrong.

"So please, if you don't mind . . . ," Ackermann said with a glance at his watch. "I don't mean to be rude, but there are many things I must attend to."

"I'll get right to it then. I believe that someone may have entered your camp, Major."

"Entered the camp?"

"Someone dropped in by plane, nearby. Either as an advance agent of some kind, perhaps to liberate it for the Allies. Or possibly for some other reason . . ." Franke put down his coffee.

"Some other reason . . . ?" Ackermann leaned back skeptically and crossed his legs.

"Perhaps to locate someone, Major. Someone inside."

"No one can just enter here without being detected." The camp commander looked at Franke with a narrow, skeptical gaze. "And for what . . . ? You have seen the Jews rounded up in Warsaw. You must have some idea what goes on here. Only the biggest fool in the world would make his way in here knowingly."

"Perhaps to take someone back out then." Franke looked at the major's deep-set eyes.

"I'm sure you took notice of the security as you drove in. There is a double row of wire. Electrified. It is patrolled night and day by guards with dogs. Everyone has a number, accounted for daily. Every vehicle in and out is thoroughly searched."

"Yes, Major." Franke opened his briefcase and took out the file he'd prepared. "I did notice the security here. But I'm not sure if you are aware that a low-flying plane was heard two days ago near Wilczkowice, approximately twenty kilometers from the camp, and a parachuter was spotted coming in. Likely to link up with Polish resistance on the ground." He laid out the report of the local farmer's sighting. Ackermann read through it slowly.

It appeared he wasn't aware.

"You are busy, Herr Lagerkommandant. This is the sort of drudgery we in the intelligence corps concern ourselves with. By the way," Franke laid out the next sheet, "you don't happen to have any truffles in the surrounding forests, do you, Major?'

"*Truffles?* Truffles are indigenous to northern Italy. And France," the SS man replied.

"I thought not," Franke said. "But you do have birchwood?"

"Birchwood? Yes, wood is in no shortage." The camp commander looked at him curiously as Franke passed him the intercepted communiqués about the "truffle hunter" and the birchwood forest. He read them and put them down. "But this all proves nothing, of course. This person, even if it is what you say, could be anywhere in the region."

"Is there any other target of strategic importance in the area?"

"There is a prisoner of war camp as part of the overall complex. And the IG Farben facility that is under construction."

"Which you provide the labor for, I believe," Franke said.

Ackermann leafed through the report again and put it down. "Well, if he *is* here, as you suggest, there are no ways out. There are over three hundred thousand prisoners here," the Lagerkommandant said. "In all the camps."

"Yes, and I want every one accounted for," Franke said. "Today."

"*You* want, Colonel?" Ackermann raised a countering eye at him.

"Yes. As per General Graebner in Warsaw and Admiral Canaris in Berlin." Franke pulled out an official order. "And Reichmarshall Göring . . ."

Ackermann took the paper and stared with mounting rage at the signed order from an Abwehr general. "*Lagerkommandant Ackermann, please be aware that on the suspicion of a matter of security I have spoken with my superiors in Berlin and they have instructed you . . . "* He read through the memo without hiding his contempt and then put it down. Canaris, the Abwehr head, was a weakened but still powerful man, known to lock heads with SS Reichsführer Himmler for the Führer's attention.

"Herr Lagerkommandant, we do not want an investigation into something that is potentially harmful to the war effort to be hung up in, how shall we say, a kind of political squabble, while you spend the day attempting to reconfirm with your own superiors what they will likely simply approve anyway. And in the event I am right on this, I cannot conceive you would want this kind of lapse to have taken place while the commandant is in Berlin."

Ackermann's face grew tight. He stared at the order again and slid it back across the table, though Franke could see he would rather have taken it and ripped it up in front of Franke and thrown the pieces on the floor. Then out of nowhere the commandant grew pensive. "You said two days ago . . . ?"

"Yes. On the morning of the twenty-third."

"Yesterday we let in thirty-one laborers into the main camp to assist with construction. Only thirty were counted leaving."

Franke's eyes grew wide. "And you did not follow that up?"

"The guards assumed it was a miscount. It happens from time to time. Not a single prisoner was unaccounted for. And what kind of fool would choose of his own accord to be left behind in this hell-hole, Colonel?"

"Maybe a very daring and well-trained fool, Major. I would like you to bring me the person who organized that work detail."

"That will take some time, of course." There was massive work to be done today, numbers to be met. Two trains were arriving. To be weighed down chasing a folly like this would cost a lot of manpower. Throw everything off. And to what end? There were three hundred thousand prisoners within the wires here. "I'm afraid I will have to discuss this with Kommandant Hoss, Herr Colonel . . ."

"I repeat, Herr Major, I am certain you would not want such a lapse of security to occur while the commandant is away and you are insistent on waging a tug-of-war over who has proper authorization . . . ?"

The SS had little respect for the Abwehr in general, Franke understood. Ackermann likely thought of himself as a man of action, dirtying his hands with the Führer's proper work each day, whatever horror that entailed and was behind the gruesome smell Franke had noticed upon arriving. Ackermann no doubt looked upon Franke as merely some overzealous desk clerk who only got *his* hands soiled going over reports.

Yet Franke could see the assistant commandant knew he was boxed in.

"*Fromm!*" the Lagerkommandant buzzed in his aide. The lieutenant who had served them their coffee ran in.

"Yes, Major. Are you ready for Captain Kimpner now?"

"No. I want you to bring me that jacket that was found this morning. In the equipment locker."

"Yes, Major." The lieutenant looked back, confused. "I'll have it brought up now."

Franke looked at the assistant commandant. "A jacket was found?"

"Just this morning. It could have been from anyone, Colonel. It might have been there days, even weeks . . ."

"Someone is here, Major!" Franke jabbed his finger against the table and his eyes lit up with zeal. "Of that you can be sure. He put his life on the line to get himself in here. And now we are going to find out why."

FORTY-FOUR

Before the evening meal, Alfred wound his way over to Block Forty and found Leo looking over a makeshift chessboard on his bunk.

"Come in the back," he said. "I have something important to show you, son."

"I'm going over some things," the boy said. The old man seemed quite excited.

"Just come. Quick. Now."

"I haven't seen such a spring in your step in some time," Leo commented as they made their way back to the sick area of the block. "What's going on?"

"Your prayers have been answered," Alfred said with a wide smile. "What I am going to tell you remains exclusively between us. You tell no one, not another friend or a bunkmate. Certainly not your new chess partner. Do I have your word on that?"

"*My word?* Of course." Leo saw the spark in Alfred's eyes. "Tell me, what is up?"

Alfred squeezed his arm. "Someone is here to get us out."

"*Here . . . ?*"

"That's right. In the camp."

"And by 'get us out,' I assume you mean . . . ?"

"Get us out of the camp. He has a way to escape."

Leo curled a smile. He put his hand against Alfred's cheek, as if checking his temperature. "Has the typhus hit you again, old man? Because this time you have truly crossed over into the delusional."

Alfred's eyes drilled into Leo. "Do I look sick, Leo?"

"In truth, for the first time in weeks, no." Leo shook his head.

"So then look, I have something to show you." Another prisoner passed by and went to the latrine. "Come over here, and keep your voice low."

"You are certainly going to a lot of precaution. This is some kind of joke, right?"

They went to another corner of the sick area, where, at least for the moment, they found themselves alone. "Listen to me, Leo, someone has snuck into the camp from the outside. Not just from the outside . . . He came from Washington, D.C. In America. For *me*! I know this sounds crazy, and before you think of taking me to the infirmary again . . ." Alfred took out the folded letter from his trousers. "He gave me this. Read it."

Leo reached to take the sheet of paper.

Alfred closed his hand over it again. "First I need your oath once again that this stays entirely between us."

"I already gave that to you, Alfred. As I said, I swear."

"On your family."

"Yes, on my family," Leo swore. "As much as is left of them."

"Then, here . . ." Alfred released his hand.

Leo slowly unfolded the letter, casting a wary eye on his friend, whose mind he thought had completely crossed over the edge. He didn't read English, only a few words he knew from seeing Chaplin films and Westerns at the cinema before the war. However, he fixed on Alfred's name at the top of the letter, *Professor Mendl*. And then above it, his eyes registering the sender in absolute shock, he saw the words *The United States of America* and the image of the White House in Washington, D.C. Where the U.S. president lived.

Leo looked back at him, his throat dry. "How did you get this . . . ?"

"Read on, my boy. And look, look who has signed it!" Alfred said, jabbing his finger.

Leo scanned the short letter and his gaze came to rest on the bold signature with the printed letters underneath.

Franklin D. Roosevelt

President of the United States

The breath grew tight in his chest. "Is this a ruse? If it is, Alfred, I give you credit, but I'm not sure why you would want to—"

"It's no ruse, boy. They've come to get me out. They have a plan. And it just might work." Alfred's eyes were so purposeful and lucid Leo knew for sure that it was no trick. "But there's a catch."

"A catch?"

"Yes." Alfred put his hand on Leo's shoulder. "I need you to come along with me."

"*Me?*"

"You, son." Alfred nodded. "You know it all now. Every formula. Every progression of everything I've done related to diffusion. It's why I've been teaching it to you all this time. God forbid, something goes wrong for me . . ." He took Leo by the shoulders, his eyes brimming with life and renewed purpose, and stared deeply at him. "I need you to be my brain."

FORTY-FIVE

Buoyed with hope, Blum finished up his work detail for the day and went back to his barrack. *He'd found him!* The exhaustion and misery of his fellow block mates could be heard all around him, yet inwardly he was soaring with expansiveness and pride.

He had his man.

His needle amid a hundred haystacks. Now all they had to do was execute their escape tomorrow, still no simple task. It was clear in a second's notice that the professor was in no condition to be dodging bullets. He'd be lucky to even be allowed on the work detail. That was where the bribe came in. And now they had this boy, Mendl's nephew, someone else for Blum to have to watch out for. That added to the risk as well. Still, he saw it was the only way he could get the professor to come. *You wouldn't leave your own flesh and blood behind, would you . . . ?* So it had to be done, regardless of how it turned out.

Tomorrow . . . Blum tried to block out the groans of misery and exhaustion coming from the rest of the barracks. Their task was just to get through their day; but hopefully by tomorrow night, he would be gone. He went through in his mind how the plan would unfold. They had to position themselves on the side closest to the river. At 0030, gunfire would erupt from the woods. Presumably the guards would return fire. In the midst of the chaos, they would move away from the fighting, toward the Sola. A detachment would meet them there. If everything went well, a little over twenty-four hours from now he would know whether he had pulled off the biggest miracle of the war, or just become another forgotten number among the thousands and thousands here whose fates would never be known.

All he had to do was get through the next day.

"So? Did you ever find him?" someone asked Blum from below. It was the man in the tweed cap. "Your uncle?"

"No." Blum said. He'd been careless once; he didn't want to arouse even the slightest suspicion over it. "Everyone was right. He must be dead."

"Well, at least you got the first-class tour of the place on your new job," the man joked good-naturedly. "Don't worry, many of us have had that pleasure. What was it you did before the war?"

"We were milliners," Blum replied. "My father had a shop with a small factory above it."

"*Hats,* huh . . . ?" The man took off his own crumpled cap and inspected it. "Maybe if we ever get out of this hole, I'll be in need of a new one."

"If we manage to get out of this hole, you may never want to take yours off ever again," Blum played along, "for it will surely be lucky. Anyway, if you're ever in Gizycko, be sure and come in. I promise you a good price on a new one."

"Maybe felt, this time," the man said longingly. "With a nice, sturdy brim."

"Yes, beaver," Blum said. "It's by far the best." He thought back to his father, who loved to take Blum through the factory above his shop. Workers, almost exclusively men, shaping and banding over machines. "Crushed and properly shrunk. It's called pouncing. It—"

Suddenly there were shouts and loud banging all around. Guards had come inside the barracks and were cracking their sticks into the walls and bedposts.

"What's going on?" people whispered worriedly. "Can you see?" Any unexpected intrusion filled the ranks with terror.

"You are all in luck," Muller, the Blockführer, announced, walking amid the bunks. "The Red Cross is coming tomorrow and we want you looking your best for them. Time to bathe and clean yourself. Leave all your belongings. You will be coming back shortly. Come on, get up! You'll all feel one hundred percent better in an hour."

Uncertainty swept over them. Mixed with fear. *The Red Cross? They had never been there before. In the children's camp once maybe.* Many of them had been in the camp for years. *Are they lying to us? Was this finally it?*

"You know what that means. They are going to kill us," someone cried out. "Just like Thirty-Four last week. They're all gone!"

"No, that's silly." Muller tried to calm things. "Where did you get such a notion? It's just a bath. You'll be no more dead than I am. And you'll likely smell a whole lot better. And with no lice. That doesn't sound so bad, does it? And your friends in Thirty-Four, they were just transferred. To a different work camp. So, c'mon, up, up, everyone! It's for the Red Cross inspection. Everyone get in line! You know you can trust me."

One by one, people considered their options and slowly climbed out of their bunks. Anxiousness spread among them. Was this a ruse? Were they telling the truth? Was this the dreaded "selection" they'd all witnessed? Guards passed through the rows, knocking on bed-posts, suddenly acting more like concerned caretakers than the ruth-less killers they all knew them to be. "Come on now. Don't be alarmed. No reason to worry here. Let's go!"

The man with the cap Blum had been talking to just sort of tipped it back on his head and muttered philosophically, "Perhaps that hat will have to wait after all."

Worry rippled through Blum. He knew precisely what was happen-ing, where they were being taken. He'd seen Vrba's and Wetzler's re-ports. *But of all the times . . .* He had just found Mendl. One more day and they'd be gone. He jumped down from his bunk. Amid the unease and commotion, he searched for a way out. Maybe through the latrine. There were windows there. Then he saw that their *kapo*, Zinchenko, had made his way back there and in the same calming tone as Muller was reassuring everyone that it was nothing to worry about. "Nonsense, this is not a 'selection.' I'll see you all there. You'll likely be back here before I will," he said, pushing those that had gotten out of their bunks but were making up their minds exactly what to believe toward the front. "Leave any possessions. In an hour you'll be back."

His falsely solicitous tone alone was a dead giveaway of what lay ahead for them.

Blum's mind raced as everyone formed a line, as instructed. Were they so beaten down over time that when their number was finally up, it was easier just to submit than resist? Or the understanding that any resistance was futile anyway and merely delayed the inevitable?

"*Line up! Line up!*" The guards pushed them all forward. One man remained in his bunk and tucked himself into a ball underneath his blanket in a desperate attempt to remain hidden. A guard merely tapped him on the leg and lifted the blanket with his stick. "Have you ever seen anyone so scared of a little bath? C'mon, no stragglers, you as well."

"No, no!" the prisoner shouted. "I don't want a bath. I want to stay here." He clung to the bedpost.

"Get up now, Holecek!" Zinchenko came and pulled up the man off the bed.

"*Please . . . please,*" he begged, clutching the *kapo*'s arms.

"Go on now!" The kapo pushed him into line.

The man in the tweed cap merely folded his blanket neatly and set it on the foot on his bunk.

They know, Blum was certain. They had to know. It was no secret. Still, they were all just going to their fate like sheep.

"We should fight," someone said, lining up.

"With what?" another asked. "Our fists? They have clubs. And guns. And there's always the chance they're right this time. The odds are better than to resist."

"Yes, my friend Rudi got a shower the other day and he came back just fine," another confirmed. "We should just go."

Blockführer Muller barked, "Everyone stay in line and move outside!"

Blum saw there was no option for him but to get into line as well. At the door, an officer was checking off their numbers. Guards were everywhere. Tonight, they'd brought out the whole playing team. There was no point in trying to make a dash for it. And to where? There was nowhere to go. Guards were watching every step, Blum gradually made his way to the front of the line. He pulled up his sleeve. "Mirek. A22327."

"A22327, an old-timer, huh?" The officer looked him in the eye and wrote it down. "Go ahead now. Enjoy your shower."

Outside, they huddled together in anticipation until the entire block had been emptied. Guards went through the barrack to make sure. Blum looked around. There were several helmeted soldiers just watching them, submachine guns drawn. To run would be to be cut down in an instant. The soldiers looked on with impassive stares on their young faces, fingers ready on the triggers.

If there were any doubts before that this was no ordinary trip to clean themselves up for the Red Cross, it now became clear.

A few of them began to whimper.

"Let's go, in a line, toward the front gate!" the officer who had been checking off numbers called.

Toward the place where that awful smell emanated from. His heart beating fiercely, Blum looked into stonelike stares of the guards around them, knowing his life depended on making the right call on whom he could approach. He ran his hand along the inside of his waist seam.

They began to march.

"We're finally going on Himmelstrasse," someone muttered. The road to heaven.

A few muttered prayers, the Shema, and some even wept. Others just kept looking around for a familiar face, saying over and over that it just can't be true. It can't be happening now. "Why us? There are still so many others."

"Our numbers just came up, that's all. Say your prayers, Walter. We all knew it was just a matter of time."

"Why must we die? We can still work."

As Blum filed in, he vowed he would not go along without a fight. As his parents had gone. Lined up against a wall. Probably lied to just the same. Told they were just looking for someone inside. Then mowed down. His father, obedient to the end, probably reassuring his mother and Leisa not to fret, they'd all be back upstairs having tea in a matter of minutes. Blum trudged in step, his gaze darting around. There had to be a way out. There always was. As back in Krakow—a tunnel, a rooftop. There was always something. If you found it.

Then he remembered.

One by one, as he went forward, he fixed on the guard's faces. *Who? One of them had to be the one.*

The one who would spare him.

Under his shirt, he ripped through the seam in his waistband and took hold of the diamond that was embedded there. His heart was pounding.

It was large, like a polished shell in his hand. Ten karats. Blum glanced at it for just a second, just to be sure.

It was worth a bloody fortune.

It's better than cash, Strauss had said. *In case you run into trouble.*

It had better work. Because it was his only chance.

And this, Blum felt the panic start to rise up in his chest, definitely qualified as trouble.

FORTY-SIX

Blum clenched the stone tightly in his fist as he went along.

"Don't slow down! Keep it moving!" The guards pushed them along, people muttering, weeping.

Knowing that his life hung on his next decision, Blum searched up and down the line of guards. They were positioned every ten paces or so, moving the line forward with their clubs and submachine guns. "Come on, keep moving. You'll be happy when you're clean." Most were faces Blum had never seen; he'd only been in the camp for a day. He spotted Dormutter on his left side of the line, the one who had tormented him earlier with the waste buckets. *That would be suicide,* Blum knew. He saw another who had been at the front gate when he'd carried the pails through and to the ditch. And Muller, the Block-führer. What was it Blum had been told this morning? *He just goes about his job. Nothing more, nothing less.*

Not him.

Time was seeping away.

Who, then? He searched the impassive faces. A wrong choice, and he would be shot on the spot right there.

They trudged ahead in two rows, each maybe fifty yards long. Rostow, whose job he had taken this morning, was the row in front of Blum. No celebration now. Two rows behind him was the kind man who had taken him through his "rounds." Even the *block-schreiber,* who had lasted so long here, two rows ahead, his head down.

Nothing could help them now.

As they neared the front gate, they merged with a line of women coming from the women's camp.

Their heads shaved, their haunted faces were white with the same unknowing fear.

"*Why us . . . ?*" a few pleaded to some of the men, sobbing. "We don't want to die."

"Can't you help us?" another begged.

"We can't even help ourselves," a man said back to them. "What can we possibly do for you?"

"Just be strong," the man in the tweed cap, a few rows up from Blum, told them. "What else is there to say?"

Everyone was praying, whimpering, but slowly stepping forward.

Blum looked in the eyes of each of the guards. *Who?*

They were now not far from the brick building with the circular chimneys. That was when, ahead of him, Blum spotted the reddish hair and thick lips of Oberscharführer Fuerst with a Luger at his side. *Fuerst.*

The one who'd been pointed out to him this morning who might be "open to doing business."

It had to be him.

Suddenly a woman with a scarf around her shaved head jumped from the line and cried out loudly, "I won't go!" She broke away, defiantly shaking her head and seemingly heading at a brisk pace back toward the women's camp.

"Get back in line!" a guard ran up to her and shouted.

"No, I'm going back," she said, ignoring his command.

"Get back now! *Now!*" the guard demanded, raising his sub-machine gun.

"Get back! Come on back!" people from both lines called to her. "You'll be—"

Then it seemed to occur to everyone at once, what did it really matter? In minutes they would all suffer the same fate. Only hers would be quicker. The line stopped and they all went quiet, everyone watching her.

"*Stop!*" the guard shouted, red-faced. The woman just kept on going, seemingly ignoring him. "*Now!*"

There was a burst of gunfire. She fell forward, her tattered rag dress suddenly dotted in red. She continued to struggle, crawling, gasping for air, her fingers digging into the dirt. "*Go on!*" people in the line called out to her. "Go." But the guard stood over her and the gun erupted again. Then there was a moment of silence as she just lay there.

"Now, go! *Go!* Don't even look!" Muller waved everyone on.

The merged lines were fast approaching the crematorium gate. Soon it would be too late.

Blum edged his way through the crowd toward where Fuerst was positioned. The Oberscharführer didn't look like a man who was open for business. His SS cap was tilted to the side and he stood there with a stolid demeanor, without so much as blinking his eyes, waving everyone on with his gun. Blum knew, in a moment, if he'd made the wrong choice, it might well be over for him, just as it had been for that woman. But in only minutes they would all file into the flat-roofed building, the door closed behind, and they'd all be dead anyway. There was no other option.

He was now on Fuerst's side of the line, only a few feet from him. He clutched the diamond in his hand. This would be his only chance. He prayed those penetrating, stolid eyes had a mercenary spark behind them. Another step; they all inched forward.

It had to be now.

His heart racing, Blum broke out of the line and flung himself onto the startled German.

"*You!* Get back in line!" Fuerst stepped back and raised his Luger, his eyes flashing with rage.

"Don't shoot! Don't shoot! Please . . ." Blum begged him in German. He whispered, "I have something valuable if you get me out of this line. It's a diamond. Ten karats . . ." He put his fingers an inch apart. "I have it on me. It's yours. Just get me out of this line." Their gazes locked for a moment. "What do you say?"

249

At first, Blum was sure the German was about to squeeze the trigger and end it right there. Whatever "business" might be going through the guard's calculating mind, there were simply too many people around to risk it.

Blum was sure he was done for.

Then the guard took hold of him and blurted out with a scowl of disgust, "You call me *what,* filth? Don't lay your dirty hands on me. Get over here . . ." He pulled Blum out of the line. "And you too, bitch . . ." He grabbed a young woman out as well. "What did you say? Both of you, over here, on your knees!" He pushed them both around the corner of a long, flat building. "The showers are too good for you two!"

As they turned the corner out of sight, Fuerst cocked his Luger, threw Blum against the wall, and shoved it underneath his jaw. The woman began to whimper, sure her end was close at hand. Blum felt the cold steel against his throat and said his goodbyes too.

Then under his breath the guard hissed, "You'd better not be lying or I'll put a bullet through your brain right now. Let me see it, quick! Don't delay a second or they'll be mopping you up where you fall."

Blum knew there was every chance Fuerst would simply take the stone and shoot him regardless. But he'd be dead in minutes as it was, so what choice was there?

"*Here.*" He opened his palm and thrust the diamond in the German's face. Fuerst stared at it, his eyes lighting up. Satisfied, he took the gem from Blum's hand and stuffed it inside his uniform.

Then he spun Blum around and put the Luger to the back of his head.

"*Please . . .* " Blum stood there, his face against the wall, his heart hammering against his ribs. "I gave it to you. Like you asked." He closed his eyes and waited for the darkness to overwhelm him. "We made a deal."

"You bought yourself some time, Jew." The German spat. "But that's all it is, time. Now get the fuck out of here." He pushed Blum along the wall. "If I were you, I'd head into the first block I find before I change my mind."

"Thank you." Blum's blood started pumping again and he nodded.

"I will." Then he looked at the girl. No more than eighteen, he thought. Pretty. White with fear. They both knew what Fuerst was about to do. Blum looked at him. "Her too."

"*Her?* She's as good as dead anyway." The German grunted. "Don't waste your pity. For her, this is quicker anyway."

Terrified, the girl, who didn't speak German but clearly understood what was being said, reached out and grabbed onto Blum's leg. "Please, don't leave me. Don't leave me!" she blurted in Polish.

He had the cash. He could barter for her life too. Any life is as worthy as another, the Midrash said. But that money was needed to bribe the guards tomorrow night. Without it, he had no way to get Mendl out. And that's why he was here. Even now, he knew he had only seconds to get away without anyone seeing what was going on.

"I'm sorry." Blum looked down at her.

"No, don't go! *Please* . . . " She lunged for him in desperation, her wide eyes filled with terror.

"Get away from here now," the German said. "Or you both die."

Blum pulled out of her grasp and started to run, hugging shadows of the long, dark building, taking one last glance behind.

He heard a shot. The woman's sobbing pleas went silent. Then he heard a second one.

The one Fuerst pretended was meant for him.

"Filthy, fucking Jews," the guard grunted loud enough to be heard back in the line, wiping his hands on his uniform.

Blum hurried off in the darkness and turned at the far side of the building. Block 12 was just across the yard. *If I were you,* Fuerst warned him, *I'd get into the first block I see.*

Blum ran across the yard and twisted open the outside door. People were huddled at the one window. "Who are you? What's going on?"

"I need a bunk," Blum said. His heart almost clawed out of his chest. "I was in Twenty. We were being taken to the gas. I was able to bribe a guard . . ." He looked through the window and saw the end of the line of his block mates disappear toward the front gate.

"You can sleep there." Someone pointed to an empty spot.

251

Blum nodded, blowing out a blast of air from his cheeks. "Thank you."

"*Twenty* . . . " someone whispered. "Levy was in twenty, wasn't he? He always wore a tweed cap."

"Yes." Blum nodded. "He was."

"Too bad. He was a good man. He lasted a long time."

Blum climbed onto the bunk, encased in a layer of cold sweat, a part of him holding back the urge to retch, another part on the edge of tears, knowing how lucky he was to be alive.

"Stop shaking," the person next to him said.

"I'm sorry. I can't."

The young woman he had just seen killed came into his mind. He heard her begging him in her last breaths to save her; saw her young and pretty face. *For her, this is quicker.* He'd basically purchased his life with hers, though, truth was, she would have been dead in minutes anyway. Strauss was right: There were things a whole lot worse than a dead cat lying ahead of him.

He lay on his back, eyes wide open, his heart unable to stay still. Both joyful and ashamed.

Shamed that he had bought his life with another's. And that she was now dead.

Joyful that, by doing so, the mission was still alive.

FORTY-SEVEN

Though it was well past mightnight, Peter Strauss was unable to sleep. Just as he hadn't slept more than an hour or two the two previous nights.

Instead, he wrote letters to his wife and kids and then just lay in his bunk, anticipation coursing through him. He took comfort in the early morning drone of the squadron of Wellingtons returning from their nightly runs over Germany. He would count the planes one by one as they went off—thirty of them tonight—rising into the sky at twenty-second intervals and disappearing into the night, pounding the coast of Brittany and the "impregnable" German homeland into rubble and dust. Then, hours later, still awake, he would count them on their return. Imagining, almost like a private wager with himself, that the last one back carried Blum and Mendl, as he prayed that the Mosquito that would leave tomorrow night to pick them up would. Strauss was a thorough man, but these last two nights, he'd given himself over to games.

What else was there, except to drive himself crazy? Each hour crept like an eternity. Imagining details they may have overlooked, things that could go wrong. Each night, an ocean of time for him to navigate until light, and each day, pretending to go about his work, but his mind thinking of nothing else. But what else had his work been for the past year except to plan this one mission? He knew Blum's

253

schedule inside the camp. What would he be doing now? Waking? Having his meal? Finding his way onto a work detail? Did he have access to the others in the camp? *It was one in a million.* Had Vrba's number held up? Had Blum been killed on the whim of some guard, and they would never know?

Was Mendl even still alive?

Their contact, Katja, had radioed back that Blum had landed successfully and then, a day later, that he had entered the camp. So far it all seemed to be going as planned. But they could only plan out so much. Now it was up to Blum. Strauss could do nothing more, but wait. And play these games.

And pray.

Yes, he'd even prayed. For the first time in years. He read over the lines in the *Sanhedrin* that Blum had shown him about any who saves a life is as if he saved the entire world. His father, the cantor, would be proud of him. What would he have called Blum? "A real *Kiddush Hashem*," he would say. A man who acts honorably. Who deserves our admiration.

Strauss smiled. It was true. As much as any man he knew.

But the phrase also carried a second meaning, one far more tragic. It referred to those who had died as martyrs for the faith. They too were *Kiddush Hashem.* And it made Strauss think. What if all the doubters were right? What if Blum didn't make it back? What if it was a suicide mission he had sent him on? Could Strauss live with that? Sending a man off to his death on such an improbable task? Would he one day look at his own son and say, "I never killed a man with my hands, but I sent one, a good one, on a wild chase, and never heard from him again"?

Yet from the moment Blum had turned at the door in Donovan's office that first meeting and asked how they would get him out, Strauss knew he had picked the right man.

Outside, Strauss heard the faraway drone of the first bomber to make it back that night. Zero two thirty hours. He got up from his bunk and stepped out. To the west, he saw the first lights from the Wellington coming in, wings steady, descending smoothly, then touching the tarmac and quickly pulling off the runway as another appeared, not far behind.

And then another.

He'd counted thirty leaving that night, and one by one he felt lifted by their safe return. Soon it was eight, then ten, fifteen, twenty. They kept on coming in.

At last twenty-eight, then twenty-nine . . .

He looked at the sky and waited.

One more.

Ambulances and maintenance workers rushed up to the ones that had landed. Two or three airmen who had been hit were carried off in gurneys. Pilots jumped down from their cockpits.

C'mon, he said to himself, his eyes peeled to the moonlit sky. *Where are you? Make it.*

In his mind, it was the one that carried Blum and Mendl back to England.

One more.

Finally he heard a buzzing. He looked to the west. He saw a wing light that seemed to be wavering, dipping and then rising in the night.

The last of the big, old flying fortresses limping home. It had been hit. It descended lower and lower, dark smoke coming from its left engine. *Make it, you bastard.* Watching while holding his breath, Strauss balled his fists.

Make it.

Finally the bomber touched down. Strauss let out a sigh of relief. A good omen. All back safe and sound. He didn't know who he'd been telling to make it, Blum or the plane.

Tomorrow it would be he running out and embracing Blum and Mendl as they climbed out of the fuselage.

A *Kiddush Hashem.*

Whatever happened, Strauss knew he had picked the right man.

FORTY-EIGHT

THURSDAY.

At first light, the *kapo* came into the block where Blum had spent the night. He banged on the boards. "Everyone outside. Roll call. No delay! Outside, now! On the double!"

Everyone leaped out of their bunks and hustled out, running to take a quick piss or shit, wiping the sleep out of their eyes. The Blockführers were all outside. "Everyone line up by blocks," they ordered. They were told to form rows of four in the main yard. Thousands of prisoners were milling around. The entire camp. No one had any idea what was up.

Blum had a bad feeling inside. *What the hell was going on?*

"Something must be up," the person next to Blum said as they organized themselves into a line. "You rarely see it this way."

A shiver of unease ran down Blum's spine. He'd already cheated death once. He'd found Mendl. All he had to do was hide out in the numbers and make it to tonight, then they'd be out of here. But lining up, seeing the vast array of guards hustling everyone together, *"Schnell! Schnell!"* searching the barracks after they had been emptied, it was clear to him that there was a reason for this kind of attention. No one was being fed or readied for the work groups. Blocks were being counted. Every man. One by one.

If work was being delayed, something *had* to be up. It was almost as if they knew something.

The prisoners all stood there, thirty, forty minutes, until the entire camp was lined up in the vast staging area. Then a dark-featured major in full uniform and boots came up in front of them, clearly the man in charge.

The camp commandant, Blum suspected.

"What the hell is Ackermann doing here?" the man next to Blum wondered out loud. The man was short, with heavy eyebrows and large ears, and spoke in Czech, which Blum knew a smattering of. "And who's that with him? We've got a visitor of some kind."

"I don't know." Blum craned his neck to see.

An important-looking colonel, his gray uniform jacket buttoned to the top, war eagle wings on his chest, walked aside the commandant.

"Intelligence." The word spread down the line like wildfire. It traveled from block to block. "From Warsaw. Some big shot."

"*Intelligence . . . ?*" Blum's neighbor grunted. "What the hell is an intelligence colonel doing here? Looking for something . . ."

Blum's heart began to pick up. Any deviation from the normal routine was a worry, but this lineup, the entire camp, some Abwehr bigwig . . . Today, of all days. Going block to block, stopping in front of each man, the Rapportführer recording the names. Each barrack going through every prisoner both by name and by number.

This wasn't for show. They were clearly looking for someone.

Blum inched up his sleeve and stared at the number burned into his wrist. A22327. Vrba's number, but once it was matched up against whom it rightfully belonged to, the game would be up. They'd be able to trace it back to the block Blum was in now. And the false identity they'd created for him, Mirek from Gizycko, didn't match up against any prisoner in the camp. He listened to the names and numbers being called out, craning, having lost sight of the two officers walking row to row.

"Berger. A33546."

"Pecsher. T11345."

"A transfer. From Theresienstadt," the Czech muttered. "Like me."

Blum's heart began to pulse with worry. Strauss had warned him, this was as big a risk as any he would face inside. There was no way

257

they were able to provide him a valid name and number. The numbers in the documents Vrba and Wetzler had smuggled back with him all belonged to people who were dead now.

The roll call grew closer.

What Blum needed was a name. A name that would match up against someone here and buy him some time.

Each block took about fifteen minutes to go through, the camp commander and his distinguished visitor weaving amid the rows as the names were called out. Time passed—forty minutes, an hour. Then two. Everyone was weary and going back and forth on the balls of their feet. They were on Block Nine now, only three until his. Blum looked around warily.

Occasionally, someone dropped in his tracks from exhaustion.

Suddenly the man next to him leaned over and asked under his breath, "You're the one who came in last night, aren't you?"

Blum's heart stopped cold. He looked straight ahead and didn't answer.

"From Twenty? You're the one who bought himself out?"

Blum hesitated again, nervously watching the role draw closer.

"Abramowitz. A447745."

"Aschkov. T31450."

"Don't worry, you've got nothing to fear from me," the man next to him whispered under his breath.

Blum looked at his wrist again. It would give him away. Mirek wouldn't match up. *What the hell, he'd be caught anyway.* Blum glanced at the Czech and nodded. "Yes."

Had he just signed his own death warrant?

"Well, you're ahead of the game," the man said. "Look over there, Twenty's spot is vacant this morning." Blum craned around. Indeed, all the people he knew whom he had stayed with two nights back were missing. Their space was empty. "Must have been something very special you gave up to get you off the list?"

Blum picked up the intelligence colonel again as he strode, arms behind his back, his gaze focused and narrowed, as they stopped in front of each man in line. They listened to the name and the number.

"Weisz."

"Ferber."

The Rapportführer checking them off on his board, one by one. Staring impassively into each prisoner's face. As if he were looking for someone. For one man. Amid the thousands here. One man who he would know the moment his eyes set on him.

Him.

The closer they came, Blum's blood began to course with fear.

"Krausz. A487193," a prisoner called out. They were up to Block Ten now. Two to go.

"Hochberg. T14657," said a transfer from another camp.

It was almost as if they knew. Knew he was here. Hiding out somewhere. Slowly tracking him down. *But how . . . ?*

The call of names was drawing closer. Blum's heart began to throb. Only one block to go.

"Halberstram. A606134."

"Laska. B257991."

The Rapportführer and the two officers moved on. *"Twelve."* The clerk read off.

Blum's block.

"Twelve! What happened to Eleven?" Blum said to the man beside him.

"There is no Eleven." The man looked back at him curiously.

"No Eleven?" Blum let out a nervous blast of air. *Mirek, it was then. What else?* Now there were just a few more prisoners to go.

The intelligence colonel stopped in front of each man. Blum could see him now, if he leaned slightly forward. He was balding under his cap. The eyes of a patient and methodical man stopping, going face-to-face. A man who would not be deterred. Who would not give up.

"First row . . ." The Rapportführer stood in front of someone.

"Aschensky. A432191," the man called out.

"Kurtzman." The next man said his number and presented his wrist.

A bead of sweat traveled down Blum's neck. He checked his number again, ready to show it. He caught the man next to him glancing over to him.

Was he a spy? All these questions he was asking. Blum had already told him. Would he expose Blum the moment they stood in front of him?

"Gersh. A293447," a prisoner called loudly.

"Bodner. T141234," said the next in line.

For a moment Blum contemplated just dropping in his spot like a few of the others. Maybe be taken to the infirmary. All he needed was to make it through the day.

"You need a name, don't you?" the man next to him whispered, leaning over.

Blum didn't answer. How had this person read his mind? And his fear. There were spies and informers all over this place. It would be worth a king's ransom to root out an imposter like him. Someone who had bargained his way out of death last night. But now last night seemed a lifetime away. Now it was about just getting through this roll call.

"Row Four." The Rapportführer came to the head of Blum's row.

"Livshitz. A366711," the first in line answered.

"Hirsh. 414311," said another.

Blum's heart had climbed in his throat now. Only ten or so until they got to him.

What to do?

"Yes." Blum finally nodded to his neighbor with a glance of desperation, really more of a plea.

"Fisher," the man whispered.

"Fisher . . . ?"

"Use it. You'll be safe. Everyone knows me here. You have my word."

The commandant and the intelligence officer were only a few prisoners away now. Every cell in Blum's body seemed set to burst like an overheated furnace.

"Liebman. A401123."

"Halpern. T27891."

They held out their arms.

The Rapportführer stopped at the man two down from Blum. The commandant's gaze steady and penetrating, then they moved on. The colonel a step behind. Staring at each man with the look of a hunter who could spot his prey the instant he set eyes upon him.

"Koblic," the person next to him announced. "A317785."

"Seven, eight, five . . . ?" The Rapportführer stopped and looked at the man's wrist before he wrote it down.

"*Yes.*"

Then he stepped in front of Blum.

Blum's heart stood as still, as if a single heartbeat would give him away. "Fisher," he said, his mouth dry as sand. "A22327." He raised his sleeve.

"*Fisher . . . ?*" the clerk repeated, looking at the list.

The commandant and the intelligence colonel stepped directly in front of him. Blum was certain the name was a fake, and he was given away. That is, if his own face, which he knew was devoid of color, and the trail of sweat trickling down his neck had not already done so. He avoided the colonel's eyes as he felt the heat from the intelligence officer's gaze fix on him, intense as the focused light in a police interrogation room. Instead he looked at the block clerk and swallowed. "Yes."

It wasn't longer than a second or two that the colonel and the commandant fixed their gazes on him. Yet it felt like an hour. An hour in which he did everything he could just to hold himself together. Like they could see through him right to his core. He half expected them to remove their guns and order him to get onto his knees right there.

"*Next,*" the Rapportführer said, moving on to the short man next to Blum.

"Shetman." The man presented his forearm. "T376145."

The commandant and the intelligence colonel strode past.

Every cell in Blum's body that a moment ago had been coiled as tight as a wire now relaxed, and he let a breath escape from him.

The two officers continued down the line. The call of names grew more distant.

Blum stood there, rigid as a statue until they moved farther away.

Then he heard the Rapportführer announce, "Block Thirteen."

Blum exhaled. He glanced at the man standing next to him, sweat dampening his sides. "How did you know?"

The short man smiled and gestured to the writing on Blum's arm. "Old number, new ink."

Blum looked at it.

"Stick around here long enough, it's the kind of thing you notice. I was a policeman back in Zilina. You're lucky they didn't pick that up."

Blum nodded.

"Plus, everyone who's been in this place a week knows about Block Eleven. Eleven's where they take people. No one ever comes back. It's a place you don't ever want to find yourself."

"Thanks." *Eleven*. This was twice now he'd been spared.

"As you heard, my name's Shetman," the short man said. "Whatever it is you're hiding is safe with me. Though God knows what it is you're doing in this hellhole."

He'd made it through the roll call. At least, until they matched up the names with numbers and saw the discrepancy. Then . . . Now all he had to do was get through the rest of the day. Then the dangerous part began . . .

"So who's Fisher?" Blum leaned to Shetman and asked.

The man shrugged. "Died last night. So fucking many, always takes them a day or two to catch up with the paperwork. It'll be caught, though, you can be sure. They'll trace it back to the block. So it won't give you much time."

Blum followed the colonel and commandant as they made their way onto the next block. They were on to him. Somehow. He was sure. He just didn't know how. Maybe one of the local partisans had turned him in. Maybe Josef himself. That would mean their escape plan was compromised as well. There'd be no way out.

No, he decided, Josef would not turn on him. He'd seen the man's resolve.

Still, the colonel was here for some reason . . .

"Let me know if you need anything else," the short man said. "Sometimes I can get things done in here."

"Thanks. I will." Blum leaned over and shook his hand.

Ten hours more. The block count had taken three.

Ten more hours to keep himself concealed in the vast numbers of the camp and stay out of the Abwehr colonel's way. And he and Mendl would be out of here.

FORTY-NINE

After roll call, everyone wandered back to their blocks for the morning meal and to break into their work details. Blum made his way through the crowd toward where he saw Block Thirty-Six had been assembled. He spotted Mendl amid the throng, slowly heading back toward his barrack. He was with a young man, who looked around sixteen and who Blum presumed was the nephew he spoke about yesterday.

"Are you still ready for later on, Professor?" Blum said, approaching.

Mendl turned, surprise written all over his face, but clearly elated to see Blum. "I'm so glad you're all right." He put his arms around Blum. "We all heard about Twenty. I was sure you were lost. How did you make it out?"

"I was lucky," Blum said. "I found a guard whose greed was greater than his sense of duty."

"Who?"

"Oberscharführer Fuerst."

"The right choice. Bribing the executioner on the way to the gallows . . ." Mendl grinned. "I commend you."

"These past three hours in that roll call haven't exactly been a walk in the park for me either," Blum replied.

"Yes, something is definitely up. Typical Germans. Count, count, count. Anyway, we're both relieved to see you are okay."

"This is the boy you were speaking of?"

"Yes. Leo." The professor put his hand on the boy's shoulder. "Leo, this is the man I was telling you about. So now you know I'm not crazy. And you already have a sense of just how resourceful he is."

"I'm Blum." Blum put out his hand to the lad. He looked barely old enough to shave. "The professor explained the conditions of coming along?"

"You won't need to worry about me," the boy replied.

"I think you'll find that Leo here is quite resourceful as well in a very useful place. Up here . . ." Mendl tapped his forehead. "But I fear something is going on. We haven't had a full roll call like this in weeks. Then today of all days. You noticed the fancy intelligence officer . . . ?"

"I noticed. I noticed as he stared straight into my eyes. I thought I was going to shit. But after tonight, that won't be *our* problem. We're still a go. Nineteen thirty hours."

"The lineup for the overnight work detail is at the gate over by the clock tower," Mendl said, "near where we met yesterday. There's one for the IG Farben factory. Another for the railway tracks into Birkenau, which are almost complete. People always drop out due to sickness or even death. And there are always people looking to fill in for the extra meal. That's where a little money can get us to the front of the line."

"How much do we need?" Blum asked.

Leo shrugged. "I'm pretty sure twenty reichsmarks per head should do the trick. Four or five pounds sterling would do even more."

"I told you, a very agile mind," the professor said. "And quite famous in here. Already the camp chess champion. I told you he won't slow us down."

"Ah, the chess boy," Blum remarked. "Yes, I've heard of you . . ."

"And here in camp for only two days. See, Leo, your fame precedes you. And in another day, if all goes right, you'll be a legend in here!"

"Whatever happens," Blum lowered his voice and turned his back to a passing group of prisoners, "we wait for the partisans to attack and then you stay by me," he instructed the boy. "My task is to bring the professor out at all costs. And that's what I intend to do. If you're not by me, or if you're wounded and can't make it, we can't help you."

"I understand." Leo nodded.

"And that goes for you as well," Blum said to the professor. "If *he* goes down, you leave him behind." Blum looked him in the eyes. "You understand that, don't you, Professor? This is a condition upon going."

"I admit, that won't be easy," Mendl said.

"Well, hopefully you won't have to make the choice."

"You must, Alfred. It's the only way I'll go along myself," Leo urged him.

"Then it works for both of us." Mendl nodded reluctantly.

"I agree," said Leo.

Blum said, "I need your oaths on that. Both of you."

"You have it." They both nodded again.

Music started up from somewhere. The orchestra. It was set up on the other side of the yard behind a row of wire near the infirmary. Their playing was the signal to get ready for the morning work parties. Handel's *Music for the Royal Fireworks*. The Overture.

"Curtain's rising." Mendl looked over at them with sarcasm. "Anyway, I think it's best we go. Do you still have your sanitation job today?'

Blum shrugged. "I suppose it's the best cover I have."

"So we meet near the clock tower? Nineteen thirty hours. Before the night work details?"

Blum nodded. "I'll have the money. And may God watch over us. This time tomorrow, you'll be in England, Professor."

"England . . . ," the old man smiled wistfully, "or the hereafter."

"England, preferably," Leo said.

"This time, I agree with him," said Blum. "So stay out of sight today. And I'll see you both there. Nineteen thirty hours."

Blum waved discreetly and melded into the crowd. Lines had formed in front of the blocks for meals, then to split up into work details. Blum figured, even if his job had already been reassigned, whoever

266

the unfortunate party was who had inherited it would gladly split up the blocks and share. He needed to just stay low and out of sight until it was time to go.

The orchestra changed music. A piece he recognized: Beethoven. The famous Leonore Overture from his opera *Fidelio*; it had always been one of Leisa's favorites.

For the first time, Blum turned and focused on the musicians. There were seven: a trombone, a French horn, a cello, a piccolo, a flute, a bass drum, and a clarinet. He knew the story behind the piece. In the last act, Florestan, the hero, should have died as witness to Pizarro's misdeeds. Yet he lived on, just as the music secretly encouraged all here to live on, not to despair and lose hope but to persevere with strengthened wills.

"Hail to the day, the hour of justice has come . . ." The words came back to Blum. "So help, help the poor ones . . ."

It was Beethoven, hero to the Germans, but whoever had chosen it, it was like a slap in the face to the forces who were in charge.

Blum went closer. The orchestra was set up on a platform near the infirmary on the other side of the wire. No guards around. He fixed on the musician playing the clarinet. A woman. With her shaved head and withered frame, she played as a ghost might play, with a kind of haunting detachment, her head bowed. Yet she seemed to stand apart from all the other performers in her skill.

It was as if there was still some fleeting spark of hope in her that found its way into the music. Even in this darkest of places.

The notes drew him closer, both rousing and familiar, fondly remembering what it was like to hear such beautiful playing. No one stopped him. Most everyone else was in the midst of their meal. Until he stood only a few yards away. Staring up at her. The flow of her fingers on the keys. The precision with which she played. And the feel . . . Such haunting beauty, and . . .

Suddenly everything in him came to a stop.

The woman lifted her head, pale, shaven, as if in a trance, and fixed on him.

Her instrument fell to the floor.

Slowly she stood up, her jaw slack. Life breathed back into her face. Their gazes meeting.

"*Doleczki*," Blum whispered, staring at the face he had pictured in his mind a thousand times.

Her eyes filled with tears. "*Nathan*," she uttered back.

He could not move. His heart stood still. Joy, unbelievable joy flooded every space in him where for these past three years only emptiness had been.

He was staring at his sister.

FIFTY

At first, Blum was too filled with shock and disbelief to even speak, terrified that everything in this moment would shatter and it wouldn't be real. A dream.

But it wasn't a dream. She was standing there. Not ten yards away. She had called out his name. All feeling that had been shut off in him these past three years, that had left him thirsting with grief and guilt, now rose like a basin overflowing with cooling water.

Releasing him.

"Leisa!"

They both ran to the wire and locked fingers—grasping, touching, disbelieving, letting the amazement wash over them like a blanket of inexpressible joy.

"Nathan?" she said, eyes wide. "Am I dreaming?"

"No. You're not," he said. He squeezed her fingers, touched her face through the gap in the wire. "No more than I!"

It was only as he put his hands on her and squeezed that he could truly admit to himself that it was real.

"Leisa, you're alive!" He stared at her with eyes stretched wider than they had ever been in his life, drinking in the incredible sight. She wore a tattered, waistless rag with holes in it. Her head was shaved. She had sores on her face. Yet he had never seen such a beautiful sight. Tears flooded his eyes. "I was told you were dead. That you had all been killed." He grasped onto her hand and squeezed, the tears of joy overflowing now.

"Nathan, what are you doing here? You got away. We were told you were in America. That you were safe! How can you possibly be here?"

"Leisa, I—" He wanted to tell her. *I came back. I'm on a mission. I have a way out. Tonight.* But he couldn't, of course. Not here. There were still guards around them. He glanced toward the infirmary. People were going in and out, both prisoners and orderlies. Anyone might overhear. Suddenly it flashed through him that if his sister was here, against all reason, then maybe there was still a chance that somehow they *all* had made it. That what he'd heard was untrue. "Leisa, is there a chance that Mother and Father are . . ."

"No, Nathan." She shook her head. "They are dead. They were rounded up as part of a retaliation against a German officer who was killed and put against a wall and executed. Right on the street outside our house."

"Yes, that is what I heard. But I heard also you!"

"I only got away because I happened to be giving a lesson to Mr. Opensky's daughter when it took place. When I got back, people wouldn't even let me go to our house to see. I was taken in for a month, friend to friend, until finally the entire ghetto was evacuated and I was sent here."

He held back more tears, his fingers still locked with hers, this time for them. His parents were gentle, civilized people. They loved music, the ballet. They had not an ounce of hate in them, even for their oppressors. So what he'd heard was true. To be left there in the street like homeless dogs. Even worse than criminals.

"I'm sorry, Nathan. There was no way for me to get word out to you."

"Leisa, I thought you were dead." Blum's eyes shone. "My world has been a nightmare for two years since the news."

"And I thought you were safe, Nathan. In America. And yet you are here!" She looked at him again, this time with something verging on anger in her voice. Reproving. "You got out. It was everything Papa wanted for you. How can you possibly be here, Nathan? *How?*"

"Quick, come over here . . ." They moved farther away from the orchestra, which continued to play. "Come close now. Leisa, I can't tell you," he said under his breath and with haste, "but you must believe me, I will only be here until tonight. You are in the women's camp? Is there a way through the wire between them?"

"No, that is impossible." She shook her head. "But what do you mean, 'only until tonight'? Look at you, you're a prisoner. You are trapped here like any of us. What are you talking about, Nathan?"

He glanced around to make certain no one was eavesdropping on them. The staging area had pretty much emptied. Everyone was back at their blocks now. The guards were at their posts as well. They wouldn't have much time. A woman passed nearby, carrying a stack of sheets to the infirmary. "Listen, can you be here later? Just before dark?"

"Here?"

"In the Main Camp. Near the clock tower."

"No. Once we finish, there's no access between the camps. If I'm found there, they would shoot me like anyone else. And anyway, come here for what? What are you doing here, Nathan?" Her eyes shook with incomprehension. "What are you trying to tell me?"

"You're in the orchestra. You must have freedoms. What about to the infirmary then?"

"We have our own infirmary back at the camp."

"Then you must come now."

"*Now . . . ?*" She looked both frightened and perplexed.

"There must be a way through the wire. I will hide you. Leisa, I am only here until tonight. It's our only chance."

"What are you saying, Nathan? I don't understand."

"*Leisa!*" someone whispered sharply. Another woman in the orchestra gestured worriedly at something beyond them.

Blum looked around. A guard was heading their way.

"Leisa, what block are you in? In the women's camp," he said quickly.

"Thirteen. But why?"

He tightened on her fingers through the wire and put his lips close

271

to her face. "Leisa, I can get you out of here! I know it sounds crazy, but you have to trust me. That's why I'm here. I have a way. But it is only for tonight. That's why if you can somehow make it in here, whatever you had to do, I could—"

"*Ssshhh,* Nathan!" Her eyes looked beyond him and tremored with alarm.

The guard came up and jolted Blum between his shoulder blades with the stock of his rifle. With a shout, Blum fell to his knees. "No fraternizing, lovebirds. Get wherever you have to go," he barked at Blum. "And you," he said to Leisa, "back to the music. Or next time it won't be this end of the gun for you to be concerned about, do you understand?"

"Yes." Blum nodded, one hand still locked on his sister's.

"We're done, sir," Leisa said, trembling. "Please, don't shoot. Nathan, we have to go."

"*Leisa* . . . " His heart fell like it had plunged into the sea, weighted down with sadness. *We still haven't arranged . . .*

The guard kicked him in the ribs and Blum fell over. "Did you not hear me? *Go!*" He cocked the rifle and pointed it at Blum. "*Go now!* Or do you want me to shoot both of you here? *Now?*"

"*No. No!*" Leisa begged the guard. "We're going. Nathan, go! Listen to him." Tears of grief and helplessness welled in her eyes too.

Blum put his hand out, feeling her fingers slip away from him, possibly for a last time. He couldn't just let her go. Not after three years. After miraculously finding her again. And now with the means to get her out. But there was no way he could do anything with the guard hovering over him. Except look at her as she helplessly backed away from the wire.

Aching, he pulled himself up to his feet.

"Now, *go!*" the German shouted, jabbing at him with the gun. "Go!"

"Nathan, *please* . . . " Leisa looked at him a last time, begging him. "I have to go back now. I love you. Be safe."

"I will contact you," he said, as he staggered away, knowing the guard couldn't understand. "Wait for my word. Tonight."

The guard pulled back the action of his weapon. "I said enough! This is the last warning!"

Leisa nodded back at him, her eyes flooded and hopeful. She hurried over and rejoined her colleagues on the stand. But Blum knew it was a promise she would never keep.

The woman carrying bedsheets hurried away.

Leisa stepped back up on the stand. The flute player who sat next to her handed her her instrument. She picked up the piece in midpassage and resumed playing. Blum turned once more as he went back across the yard, the guard still behind him, knowing each look he caught of her could well be his last. That he had found her, agonizingly, but only for a few fleeting seconds. And only to lose her once more.

"Lovesick, huh, Jew?" The guard smirked at Blum, nudging him toward the blocks. "Makes me cry."

"Yes," he said, holding back his torment. He couldn't just leave her. He wouldn't, no matter what the mission.

Not again.

He turned and caught sight of her a final time, as the orchestra switched to some happier show tune, and saw the sadness pool in her eyes.

You wouldn't leave your flesh and blood, would you? Mendl had asked of him.

No. He'd already done that once. Never again.

The mission was still everything. Getting Mendl back. The oath he'd made to Strauss. To Roosevelt.

But for Blum, who from across the yard returned Leisa's last, longing look with a nod of promise in his own gaze, the mission had just changed.

PART FOUR

FIFTY-ONE

The iron door to Block Eleven opened and the large man hesitantly stepped in, his cap in his hand. He took an anxious look around, a row of dark cells lining the barrack walls, hearing people huddled inside them, in total darkness, a few desperate moans. Some iron contraptions that looked like chains or harnesses hung from hooks on the walls.

Franke, against the wall, saw the burly man's eyes fall on them uneasily, as if he understood what they were for.

"Come on in." Lagerkommandant Ackermann stood up. "Please, sit down." He pointed to a wooden chair on the other side of the table. "Your name is Macak, correct?"

"Yes, that's me. Macak."

"Pavel, isn't that right? And I'm told people call you The Bear?"

"Because of my cheery disposition, I guess." The bearded man forced a smile. He didn't like Germans much to begin with, only their cash, and now, pulled away from his work line by an armed detail and brought here, to this hellhole, a grim-faced guard at the door and two big-shot officers staring at him, even a man as hardened as he could be forgiven for feeling at bit of unease.

"No doubt." The camp commander grinned. "And you are foreman of one of the construction crews in Brzezinka?"

"That's right."

"And I've been told you have even done work inside the camp here? Even recently?"

"I have." The foreman nodded uneasily, a glance toward Franke, who leaned against the wall. "Wherever the work is, that's where we go. Right now, that seems to be you."

"Even yesterday, if I'm correct," the Lagerkommandant pressed on. "You and your crew helped construct the new barracks by the kitchens, I'm told?"

"If you're happy with it, yes, that was our work." The foreman nodded, forcing a smile.

"And the day before that as well?"

"The job took three days." The foreman shrugged. "We did what was requested."

"The work is fine, Herr Macak. It just seems there was a minor discrepancy in our count between those who were on the truck in Brzezinka and let inside the gate and then those upon leaving at the end of the day. We counted thirty-one in the morning and somehow only thirty left. I'm sure it was simply a mistake."

"*Thirty, huh . . . ?*" The foreman ran a hand across his beard. "I'm quite sure that's what it was. I'm always accurate with my numbers. Besides . . ." A moan emanated from a cell behind them. "This isn't exactly the kind of place one wants to get left behind in, if you know what I mean."

"And why exactly would you say that, Herr Macak?" The Lagerkommandant looked back with a frosty smile.

"No disrespect." The foreman shrugged. "Only—"

"Yes, I was just joking you, Herr Macak. I understand perfectly what you meant. In fact, our initial thoughts went there too. Why would anyone possibly want to be left behind here? Except then we came across this . . ." The commandant got up and removed a tan cloth jacket from a hook on the wall and tossed it onto the foreman's lap. "In a storage bin. Near where you and your team happened to be working. Maybe you remember someone wearing it that day. As I recall, it wasn't exactly warm Tuesday. I could understand someone taking it off, perhaps in the heat of the day. But then finding it at the bottom of a storage bin, under rags and buckets . . . And then coupling it with this matter of this missing person who you say doesn't exist. Number Thirty-One. You know we Germans always need to be precise. So any thoughts on this, Herr Macak? Simply for our records . . ." The Lagerkommandant's eyes remained on him.

The foreman felt the sweat rise up on his neck and kneaded his cap. "Could be anybody's." He shrugged. "I can't quite say." His voice now had a quiver of anxiousness in it.

"Maybe something we could do might jog your memory, what do you think? Perhaps an extended work contract at one of the construction sites around. Steady work is hard to come by these days, is it not?"

"It is," the foreman agreed. "And it would be my honor to have that. But the fact remains, I don't recognize it," the Pole said, trying to hand the jacket back. "Sorry, but if that's all there is"—he glanced at his watch—"I know my crew expects me back and . . ."

"So *we* say there were thirty-one people on your crew . . ." The commandant pulled out a chair directly across from Macak and sat down and stared at him. He held a small horsewhip in his hand. "And you say thirty. But you know what I think?" He jabbed a finger in the air. "I think this jacket belongs to the one who up to now remains unaccounted for. So with all apologies to your work crew . . ." His stare hardened from amiable to icelike, "I'm afraid that is not simply all there is, Herr Macak, and maybe for a long while, until we know precisely who he is."

The foreman let out a breath. He just looked back at the commandant and scratched his beard. Franke could see that the man was someone who knew he had one foot in the soup now and was rolling over in his mind the best path for keeping the rest of him out of the pot.

"Perhaps as you try and think on it, you would consider the possibility of becoming a resident here yourself from now on, Herr Macak? We can arrange that. No problem for us. It is why I arranged for us to meet here. Though I can't fully promise"—the commandant shrugged, his smile fixed—"that your stay here will last long. Do you understand what I'm saying, Herr Macak?"

The foreman inhaled a deep breath. He glanced toward Franke, who had not yet moved or spoken, but whose presence in the room, the gray-suited intelligence officer covered with war eagles, clearly gave him cause for discomfort.

Then he looked back at Ackermann.

"My cousin." The foreman swallowed and picked up the cloth jacket. "He said the guy was visiting. That he was a good worker. I remember he took a break near the end. I didn't keep track of him."

"Describe him," Franke cut in, with a glance toward Ackermann. Validation surged in his blood.

"Medium height. Dark features, kind of thin." Macak shrugged. "Like a lot of people one sees in here. Couldn't work a lathe for shit, that I can tell you."

"And he spoke Polish?" Franke continued, moving over in front of Macak now.

"Yes."

"Like a native? Or perhaps someone who has learned it? Who is from abroad?"

"He pretty much said as little as possible," the foreman said. "But from what I heard, it seemed quite good."

"And so, your cousin?" Ackermann interjected, tapping the horsewhip in his hand. "What is his name?"

Macak drew in a troubled breath.

"I'm asking you, Herr Macak. One way or another we'll find out. If we have to bring your whole fucking work team back in here and put a gun to their knees. So what will be easiest for you, Herr Macak? It would be hard to ply your trade with a bullet in your knee, would it not?"

The foreman looked back at them and swallowed. The stubbornness in his eyes ebbed. He'd tried. Done the best he could. What would anyone expect? He wasn't going to die to save him. There was a war to get through. And he had a wife and two daughters. "Josef," he said, running a hand across his face. "Wrarinski. He's the baker. In Brzezinka."

"*Brzezinka*," Ackermann confirmed.

Macak nodded glumly.

"Pick him up," the intelligence colonel said to Ackermann without hesitation. "Now."

Macak had known Josef for as long as he'd been alive. The baker had prepared the cake for the foreman's own wedding, three tiers with a sweet praline inside and vanilla frosting. He had stayed well into the night, dancing. Every St. Stanislaw's Day, he and Mira brought over muffins and fruitcakes.

But Macak knew he had just signed his cousin's death warrant.

FIFTY-TWO

Blum chewed on a stale crust of bread and sipped the thin gruel in his bowl outside his barrack before the block was split up into their work details.

He could weigh this all day, he knew, but he would not come to a different answer. It would only cost him time. Crucial time. And as vital as it was to do what he was sent there to accomplish, something else rose up inside him now. Something equally important.

Something that would not let him go.

No tragedy is greater than that of a single person who is afraid to do the right thing. *Doesn't the Talmud tell us that?* That to shrink from moral courage, knowing what was right, was the death of light. It became the same as what he saw around him here. *Will it cost or save lives?* Sometimes that was no matter. He realized all he would be putting at risk. The promise he made to Strauss. To President Roosevelt. His mission, with all that was clearly riding on it. Those whose lives depended on its outcome. He was sorry about that.

But it was about *one* life now. A life that meant everything to him.

And saving that one life was akin to saving the world.

He had left her once before, in Krakow—left her to die. Left them all to die.

He had vowed that wouldn't happen again. And now here was his chance to prove it.

The lengthy roll call the camp had stood through had consumed half the morning. It was already after ten. That left only nine hours before he, Mendl, and Leo had to line up under the clock tower for the overnight work detail. Blum knew, four would make it even more difficult to get away unseen. Leisa was never the brave one. He would have to stay by her. And Mendl too. Yet he knew he had to try. A dark cloud hung over the camp every day, but inside Blum, the path was now lit and clear.

Whistles sounded. The morning meal was done. "Line up! Work details!" the *kapos* called. "On the double! Now!"

He spotted Shetman washing out his bowl at the faucet. Blum went up to him. "You said to let you know if I needed something else done in here?"

The little man continued to rinse his bowl. "What is it you need?"

Blum kneeled down beside him. "Is there a way to get into the women's camp?"

Shetman shrugged. "There is always a way. When do you need to go?"

"Today. *Now,*" Blum said back. "In the next couple of hours."

"The next couple of hours . . . ?" Shetman chuckled and rolled his eyes. "Boy, you must have the itch real bad." Forays into the women's camp, situated several hundred yards away, were typically for conjugal purposes.

"It's hard." Shetman shrugged. "And it costs money."

"How much?" Blum reached into the lining of his uniform and peeled off four crisp fifty-pound notes. British pounds.

"But with money, there is always a way." The little man's eyes lit up. "Even in here."

"There's just one more complication . . ."

"Complication . . . ?" Shetman looked at him.

Blum peeled off two more fifty-pound notes. "I need her brought back out."

"Now, that *will* cost you." Shetman met his eyes and smiled. He shook his bowl dry and wrapped the bills into his palm.

"And as long as I'm paying . . ." Blum peeled off another fifty-pound note. "I'll need another men's uniform. A small."

FIFTY-THREE

The woman stepped hesitantly into the Lagerkommandant's office, in a thin burlap dress, her head shaved, a scarf tied around it.

Her nerves showed. Her eyes darted back and forth between the Lagerkommandant and the intelligence colonel, Franke, who sat at the table, seemingly wary even to step foot in the room, into the lion's den, face-to-face with the man who controlled life and death here.

"Don't be afraid." Ackermann beckoned the woman forward. "I promise, we won't bite. Please, sit." He pointed to a chair. "You told the Obersturmführer you had something of importance to share."

The woman stepped closer to his desk and nodded. She could have been forty or sixty; in here, it was hard to tell. "My son," she said nervously, "he's only twenty. He's somewhere in the main camp. I haven't seen him since we arrived."

"And so you shall, my dear, you shall see him," the commandant replied good-naturedly. "And I give you my word, I will watch over him myself. And you as well. Once we hear what you have to say."

"I have your promise then?" She looked at him, distrusting.

Franke saw she would no more trust the Lagerkommandant to pour water on her if she was set on fire and he was holding the pail. No one in here would.

"As an officer, madame. I assure you. Now out with it. Colonel Franke and I have work to attend to. What is it you have to say?"

"This morning I happened to overhear a conversation," she began. "I didn't catch it all, only parts. But what I was told you would find of interest was, there is someone here, inside the camp, who has snuck in. From the outside."

Franke sat up in his chair. They had sent out a team to pick up the baker, but this was even more evidence that his suspicions had been right. "You heard this? You see, he is here!" he said to Ackermann, his blood coursing with electricity. "Now there is no doubt. You are certain of this, madame?" He turned back to the woman. "You saw him?"

"I did."

"And you heard this where, madame?" Ackermann asked her.

"By the orchestra. This morning. I was bringing clean sheets to the infirmary. He claimed he had snuck in. And that he is somehow leaving. Tonight."

"*Tonight?*" Now Franke stood up and faced the woman too.

"Yes. He said he has a way out. But only tonight, he kept saying. I'm sorry, but I think they saw me, so I couldn't hear how."

Franke's blood surged. His suspicions had been correct. A few days ago it was only a puzzle, a puzzle for him to solve, and as the pieces slowly came together, he had put everything on the line. His career. His reputation. He knew from the beginning that this was it! His chance. Now it was only a matter of why. Why was the man here? And how to stop him.

Only until tonight. That didn't give them much time.

"*Who,* madame?" Franke stepped up to the woman. "Who is this man? If you saw him, you must be able to point him out?"

"In this place . . . ?" She shook her head. "I don't know who he is. Or what block he is in. I only overheard him for a moment as I went by."

"Describe him then."

"He was thin, kind of like your height." She pointed to Franke. "Dark features. In a prisoner's uniform. Young looking. He can't be more than twenty-four. I know that doesn't help you much. I tried to follow him as he was led away."

"Led away?

"By a guard. But he blended into the crowd. I've no idea what block he was in. I'm sorry, Lagerkommandant. But I also know something else . . ."

"Tell us, madame," Ackermann pressed.

"You said I could see my son." She looked at him for final confirmation. "That is a promise?"

"Yes, yes." He rolled his hand. "Go on. You will."

Likely in the gas chambers, Franke suspected, if he could trust anything in here.

"I believe he has a sister here." The woman looked at him.

"*A sister* . . . ?" Franke said. His eyes stretched wide.

"Yes. And one more thing . . . She is in the orchestra." The woman nodded. "Her I can point out."

FIFTY-FOUR

"Mirek, this is Levin." Shetman introduced Blum to the head of the camp repair team. "I'm told Pan Mirek here can take a carburetor out of the grave and bring it back to life. As we discussed, he'll be joining you today."

The head of the repairs crew looked at Blum with a complicit nod. According to Shetman, the repairs team had the most unrestricted access between the men's and women's camps, holding passes to freely go back and forth as the situations called for. And the camp's water pump, which was kept in the main camp, was routinely lugged back and forth to the women's camp, in many cases only as a cover for conjugal purposes, and often with the tacit understanding of the guards, whose palms were always well greased to look the other way.

"Good. We can always use a good hand." The repair chief folded a few, crisp bills into his palm.

Blum had given Shetman three hundred and fifty pounds, a vast sum, to get the job done.

"You come along and you don't say a word," the repair chief said. "If any of the guards there are poking around suspiciously, then it's off. Our call. No argument. And no refund either. Those are the terms."

"I understand," Blum agreed. What choice did he have?

"They usually give us about twenty minutes to get the pressure back up"—Levin chuckled, "if you know my meaning. They know what the game is there. We've got some gifts for them. Here's your pass."

Blum stared at the square white paper with hard-to-read script on it.

"Don't worry. It's perfectly valid. So don't sweat over that. Sweat over what you're about to do. We've never brought someone out before."

"Then thanks for doing this."

"Not me." He pointed. "Rozen's going with you. He volunteered."

A man with dark wiry hair and shoulders like wire hangers stepped up. Blum shook his hand.

"It all should work though. If everything falls in line. Which block is she?" the repair chief asked.

Blum said, "Thirteen."

"*Thirteen?*" The repair chief winked at Rozen complicitly. "What is it with the water in Thirteen? We were just there last Thursday."

Shetman handed Blum the uniform he'd requested and patted him on the back. "Good luck."

"*Why?*" Blum asked Rozen as they towed the ramshackle pump toward the front gate.

"Why what?"

"Why are you doing this? Levin said you volunteered." They both knew if they were found out, they'd be shot on the spot. Or strung up on one of those gallows and left there for everyone to see.

Rozen stopped the cart and pulled up his sleeve. "See this number." Blum looked. A11236. "I've been here from the beginning. Since forty-one. No way they're ever going to let people like me make it out. We've seen way too much." He picked up the tow bar again. "They just keep me around because it keeps them in business. So in the meantime I try to do some good."

"Well, whatever the reason, thanks," Blum said.

"Besides, like Levin said, the idea appeals to me." They started up again. "So who is she? Wife? Sweetheart?"

"Sister," Blum said, guiding the pump from behind. It had a cylindrical tin housing that contained the pump and hose feed which was set on an unsteady wooden platform with four wheels and a towing rod.

"*Sister?* So then why do you need her in here?" Rozen looked back, puzzled.

"Is it all right if I tell you tomorrow?" Blum said. By then he wouldn't have to answer the question. They'd be gone.

"You don't have to ever tell me." Rozen shrugged. "It's not my business."

They passed by the kitchens and the administrative building on the other side of the wire. Guards looked them over as they went by. Rozen nodded to a few he recognized. No one gave them a hard time. "I've done business in here a long time. I know most of them at the gates," he said. "I'll do the talking, if that's okay."

"Of course."

"The reason we go now"—he looked up at the clock tower—"ten after, is to make sure by the time we come back, the shifts won't have changed."

At the front gate, they presented their passes to the guards. Blum still felt a knot tighten in his stomach. An SS sergeant with a sub-machine gun slung over his shoulder looked over the pump.

"Emergency over in the women's camp," Rozen told him. "Block Thirteen."

"*Thirteen?* Second time this week." The guard sniffed and shook his head. "What do they do with the water over there?"

"If you'd let us fix the damn pipes for good, we wouldn't have to keep lugging this thing."

"You." He came over to Blum. Blum handed him his pass. "*New* . . . ? Didn't I see you carrying the shit buckets the other day?"

Blum now saw he was one of the guards Dormutter was playing up to yesterday. Blum wasn't sure exactly how to answer.

"He looks young, but he's as sharp a mechanic as we've found," Rozen interjected. "Why waste skills like that in the latrines?"

The guard looked Blum up and down. "Nice promotion." He handed Blum back the pass. "Enjoy the view over there."

They were waved through, and they made their way along the

perimeter of the brick wall, following the road. The rattly cart needed help getting over the scrub and bumps on the path. The women's camp was only a couple of hundred yards down the path, but dragging this apparatus made the trip seem endless. The closer they got to Birkenau, the stench in the air grew even worse. It was like he and Rozen were heading straight for the gray, low-hanging cloud that always hung over it.

A troop carrier passed them by, filled with soldiers. Farther west, Blum noticed the train tracks that were being built, and past them the line of pines and maples where Josef's partisan detail would attack from tonight. These woods were the only spot of green Blum had seen since he had been here. He made a mental reference to Vrba's map. It was accurate enough, he saw, thinking of what lay ahead. He sucked in an anxious breath. *Later.*

"The women's gate is right up here. This is where it starts to get dicey," Rozen warned. "Block Thirteen, you say? Does she know you're coming?"

"No. It was only today that she even learned I'm here."

"You're taking a big chance then, if you don't mind me saying. You know this can only happen once."

"I understand." *Once is all I have,* Blum said inwardly.

He hadn't heard the orchestra playing anywhere in camp for several hours now, as most of the population was out at work. He assumed that meant they were now on break. Or sleeping. It was just after two p.m. Ahead, Blum saw a small brick building at a road with two SS standing guard.

Rozen looked back with a serious cast on his face. "Here we are."

A brick wall ran the length of the perimeter of the women's camp with the occasional guard tower manned with machine guns.

"Ah, Scharführer!" Rozen nodded familiarly to a guard as they wobbled up to the gate.

"Back so soon?" The guard rolled his eyes.

"Trust me, it's no holiday for me either, dragging this contraption over. You'd make my life a lot easier if they had their own here."

"I'll be sure and take that up next time I speak with the Führer," the guard snorted with a sarcastic grin. "Where to today? Thirteen? Again?" he remarked, as Rozen showed their passes. Blum was sure there was a bill sandwiched between them.

"So what is it there?" The guard stepped up to Blum and gave him the once-over. "Frau?"

Blum glanced at Rozen, unsure how to answer. The repair chief gave him a quick nod.

"Yes. My wife."

"Then I hope the old pump works, if you know what I mean." He chuckled complicitly. "See you in twenty," he said to Rozen with a wink, "if I'm still here."

They hurried through, the guard checking his palm as he went back to his post and tucking something in his uniform.

They were in.

FIFTY-FIVE

The women's barracks were similar to the men's—long, two-storied structures, windows on top, with trenches along the sides. Some even had small gardens planted in front with wildflowers growing. There were several dour-looking female guards in brown SS uniforms with pistols strapped to their belts. And male guards too. As they passed, several prisoners made advances at them. "Come over here, lover boys. We need a hose too! Where are you going?"

"Thirteen."

"How come Thirteen gets all the action? What's Thirteen got that we don't? Look!"

"The water's off, that's all," Rozen replied, lugging the pump along the row of barracks.

"Ours is off as well!" a woman called. "Bring that big pump of yours over here." A few of them laughed openly.

"I'll see you on the way back."

They mostly had shaved heads and wore shapeless rags over their skin and bones, and rarely even saw a man other than the guards, from whom they suffered the same brutality as did the male prisoners.

"Thirteen's over there," Rozen said, pointing to a long barrack identical to the others. "You'll open the housing. I'll hook up the pump. You've got twenty minutes. Less, since we have to give the appearance that we're doing some real work. And you can't go inside the barrack. That's verboten. And remember, we take her only if no one's around. And on my say-so. Otherwise I pack the ship up and leave you both here."

"I hear you." Blum's heart began to race in expectation. He looked around. They had their own Blockführers and clerks to watch out for here as well. Not just the guards. A couple of women were tending the garden on the side.

"*Ladies* . . . back again," Rozen announced. "We'll get this thing running yet." He towed the pump along the side of the barrack, so it was mostly out of view. Blum opened the pump housing. A thick rubber hose was wound up around a wooden coil, which he pulled out and gave to Rozen, who flicked the motor on and led it over to the outdoor spigot. He kneeled down and twisted open the tap. A trickle of brackish water ran out. Probably as much as they had had on a good day, Blum presumed, as in the men's camp. Rozen took a wrench and bent down and removed the faucet head, and hooked up the rubber pump nozzle to the pipe going, "*Maestro, please* . . . !" and gave the signal back to Blum, who began to raise and lower the pump handle, forcing the pressure forward.

Then he looked back at Blum and gave him a complicit nod. Which meant *get going*! "I'll take over now."

Blum nodded. He went over to the two women in the garden in front of the barrack, saying quickly in Polish, "Please, Pani, do either of you know Leisa Blum here in Thirteen?"

One shook her head and said, "Greco." *I'm Greek. I don't understand.*

The other shrugged. "*Blum?* No," shaking her head too. "I don't know names here."

"She's in the orchestra. She plays clarinet."

"Ah, *clarinet,* yes!" Her face lit up. "I know her."

"Can you find her for me? Quick, please!"

"But I don't know if she's here."

She went inside the barrack. Blum went back over to the pump and kneeled by the faucet, pretending to check the pressure, as Rozen moved the handle up and down. On the far side of the yard, he saw a heavyset female guard bludgeoning a helpless woman seemingly without mercy; the woman screamed and raised her hands in defense. But soon she stopped moving. The female guard kicked the inert body several times to make sure she was dead and then rolled her over with her foot. Horrible as it was, Blum kept checking the block. Five minutes had passed. What if Leisa wasn't there? What if he had to go back empty-handed, knowing he could have saved her but had failed?

He'd think about this moment for the rest of his life.

Finally, the woman who'd gone off came back, her arms apart, and shaking her head in disappointment. "Sorry, she's not here. But I sent someone . . ."

What if someone had seen them talking earlier? What if the orchestra was rehearsing somewhere? What if a thousand things? Blum thought in a rush of panic. He looked at Rozen. Ten minutes now. *Where was she?*

Suddenly the Oberaufseherin, the block wardress, just as the men had their *blockschreiber*, came out of the barrack in a huff, barking to Rozen, "What's this? I didn't send for you."

"Well, someone did, madame." Rozen coolly threw his hands up. "You can see there's a problem. Anyway, the pressure looks like it's starting to come back."

That seemed to calm her, and she went back into her office, yelling, "Next time, it must come from me!" But time was ticking away. There was only so long they could stay.

Finally, Blum saw another woman coming from a neighboring block all excited, and a few yards behind her, Leisa. *Thank God!* Leisa stopped as soon she saw him, clearly in shock, twenty yards away. Blum waved her over to the side of the barrack down from the pump, like two lovers who were going there to have some moments alone. "Nathan, what are you doing here?" she uttered in disbelief. "I was practicing. I—"

"*Hush.*" He pulled her farther along the barrack to make sure they were completely alone. "Leisa, just listen," he said under his breath. "I told you I have a way out of here. But it must be tonight. And you must come with me to the men's camp. Now."

"To the *men's* camp?" Her eyes flooded with terror. "Now? *How,* Nathan?"

"Inside the pump. Come close," he instructed, "make it look as if we are lovers. It will work, Leisa. You can fit. Rozen goes back and forth all the time. But there's no time to think on it. It must be now. You can't even go back and get anything. You can't even say goodbye. You just have to trust me. And come."

"*Now . . . ?*" She shook her head fearfully. "I can't, Nathan."

"Why?"

"I don't know. I just can't. It's too quick. I have friends . . ."

"You must. Otherwise you will die in here, Leisa. With your friends. Have I ever let you down?"

"No. Never," she said. But he could see how conflicted she was.

"And I won't now. Look, I know you're scared. I'm scared too. I know this all seems out of a dream, seeing me here like this. But I'm on a mission, Leisa. To get someone out of the camp. A scientist. And we have a way to get out. A plane is coming tonight. Nearby. To take us out of here. To England."

"A plane . . . ? *England . . .* " Blum saw her face come alive, but as she looked to make sure no guards were around, the color drained from it. Trepidation came into her eyes. "Nathan, I can't. I want to, but I'm just not ready, I—"

"Leisa, listen to me. You must!" He took her by the shoulders. "If only for the sake of our parents. You know that they would want this for you. For us. We have to try."

Blum gauged the time. Maybe fifteen minutes had gone by. At the most, they had maybe five more. Five minutes to convince his sister to give up everything she knew to be true for the past years and place her faith in him. A shadow from her past, suddenly come alive. And putting herself at grave risk. He glanced back at the pump. Rozen would soon be getting anxious. Blum took her by the arms. "Now that I've found you, I won't leave without you, Leisa. No matter what else is at stake. I won't leave you behind. Not ever again."

Through the conflict in her eyes he could see deep into her heart. The fear alive in there. Her trust in him, which he knew was without

296

limits. She was just frozen, behind these wires. This place had taken everything from her. Her will. Her ability to act. Her hope. Yet a flicker of it still burned deep inside her. Blum could see it. Like a light down a long dark corridor in her conflicted eyes. He cupped his hands on her cheeks and said to her again, "This is me talking. You have to trust me, Dolly. Come!"

At first her eyes shook with indecision. Then suddenly she nodded. "All right, I will. I'll come, Nathan." She kept nodding. "I do trust you. I'll come."

Ebullient, Blum took her by the hands. "I knew you would."

"I just need to get my—"

"No." Blum shook his head. "There's no time. It has to be now."

"My clarinet . . . I just can't leave it."

"Not even your instrument, Leisa. Nothing. We have already lost a lot of time. It must be now."

She swallowed with a sense of resolve, nodding, and he wiped a last tear off her cheek. "Okay, then . . . Let's go."

"We're going to make it," he said, putting a hand to her face. "I promise. Okay, Doleczki?"

She sucked in a breath for courage and smiled. "Yes."

He led her by the shoulders back toward the pump wagon. He nodded to Rozen, who was still at the handle.

She's set.

"Okay, pressure's back up!" the repairman announced. Then he went back to the spigot and switched out the pump hose for the faucet, making a big scene of it. "Come see . . ." Two or three women went and kneeled down and turned the spigot on. Water came out, perhaps a shade more than before. But just as brackish. "Go ahead, drink up," he said. "We're all done."

A couple filled their cups while Blum guided Leisa onto the pump platform and she squeezed herself inside the metal housing. Just enough room in there for her to wedge herself in. Rozen then brought the hose back over and coiled it around the wooden spool, Leisa crouching inside. The more it wrapped around, the more completely it hid her. When the hose was wound back in, Blum shut the housing door, closing her in. "I know it's dark in there," he said through a vent. "But you'll be safe. I promise. Just stay calm."

"All right, Nathan." Her voice came back meekly. Her knew how terrified she had to be, huddled up in there. His little sister was never the one who threw herself off rocks into a lake at their summer cottage or, in the ghetto, dodged between buildings after curfew.

Rozen glanced back at Blum. *"Ready?"*

Blum nodded. "Yes."

"So let's go." The repairman looked around and didn't notice anyone who seemed focused on them. Just a routine repair, prepared to return home. Rozen in front, they wheeled the pump back out into the main yard. "Bye, ladies." He waved. "Till next time."

"Next time, Rozen, you should stay for one yourself," one called.

"I will." He waved to her. "Promise."

They towed the pump—which was heavier now, with Leisa inside— through the main yard of the women's camp and then back to the outside gate. Blum's legs grew rubbery as they wheeled it up, the same guard checking the passes again and looking over the pump, eyeing Blum with sort of a derisive laugh. "Back so soon. You Jews certainly don't last very long."

"You said twenty minutes, Unterscharführer." Rozen watched the sergeant circle the pump. "I'm sure if he had the time, my friend here could have gone on for hours."

All it would take, Blum knew, would be one perfunctory look inside, in the course of just doing their jobs, and they were all dead. He saw himself hanged on the gallows like the other prisoners he had seen, or dropped with a bullet to the head where he stood. Leisa too, which made his worry even stronger.

Just be still, Leisa . . . Do not move, he willed her inside.

"You look a little pale. All a bit too much for you?" The guard chortled at Blum.

"It's just that I hadn't seen my wife in a long time."

"And you may not again. Best to look at each time as your last. Okay, go on." The sergeant finally waved them through. They pushed

298

forward, trying not to make it look like there was an added weight inside. They were almost at the path. Suddenly a second guard came out of the gatehouse, announcing, "I'm off. I'm wanted at the guardhouse over at the main camp. I'll escort them back."

Blum's heart went into free fall. He shot a worried glance to Rozen, up in front. The repairman's look mirrored his own, and read, *Just be steady and don't panic.* And hope that Leisa holds together. There was nothing else they could do.

"Come on, yids. On the double." The guard grabbed his rifle. "I don't have all day."

Blum's gut knotted tight with dread. They pushed on, over the scrubby terrain, the couple of hundred yards between the two camps. With Leisa inside, the cart was even less maneuverable. Its wobbly wheels bobbed up and down over the ruts and gullies. Blum imagined she must be going out of her mind inside. She had to have heard it all. Knowing her death, all their deaths, was so near.

"Nice afternoon, is it not, Herr Scharführer?" Rozen asked him, more to let Leisa know that they had company in case she said something.

The guard was in no mood. "Just keep your mind on what you're doing. I don't have all day."

A few yards behind them, he lit a cigarette and smoked. He waved to a few cohorts riding by on the road. Blum kept the wheels steady with every bit of strength he had. If they broke an axle over a rock or a buried root, it would be a quick end for all of them.

At last they made it back to the men's gate. Luck was with them. The same set of guards were manning it as when they left.

"Look what I've brought you." The guard who had escorted them back chortled, flicking out his cigarette. "Two stinking sacks of shit. Ready for the dung heap. They're all yours now."

"Emergency over . . . ?" the sergeant who knew Rozen rolled his eyes and smirked. "I'm sure the women there are probably all taking baths with all their fresh, new water."

"Pass," the second guard ordered Rozen, holding out his hand. "Let me see." This one was clearly new, and seemed to take his duties a bit more conscientiously than his senior partner. He had narrow blue eyes, blond hair under his cap, and a short, flat nose.

Rozen handed his to him.

"And yours . . ." he barked at Blum officiously.

Blum handed him the small white paper.

He looked it over, checked it even down to the date, it seemed, taking the whole thing very seriously.

"At times they use the men's water pump over in the women's camp." The sergeant seemed to explain the ropes to him. "Happens all the time, does it not, Rozen?" he said with a complicit wink.

"It does, sir. All the time."

"Now and then," the senior guard laughed, "even the Jews have to dip their little peckers into the soup, right?"

"And what a hot soup it was," Rozen said conspiratorially with a glance to Blum.

The blond-headed corporal, his SS uniform new and pressed, stepped around the pump. He looked at the cart's wobbly wheels and the rickety wooden platform and then, to Blum's horror, tapped on the metal housing with the tip of his gun. There was a hollow sound. "What's in there?"

"The pump, sir," Rozen said.

"*The pump* . . . " The guard tapped on the housing again. "Open it. Let me see."

Blum froze.

The sergeant rolled his eyes at Rozen with kind of a helpless sigh, as if grousing, *New man here. Just oblige him. He has to do his job.* But Blum knew what would happen if they opened it and found Leisa inside.

"It's just the pump, Corporal," Rozen said again.

The new guard stared back at him. He looked at the door. "Then open it."

Panic wormed its way through Blum's bowels. He couldn't open it. If he opened that door, they were all dead. Leisa would be barely able to hold together inside. *Stay very still,* he commanded her silently. She had to have heard everything that was happening. Blum glanced at Rozen. There was nothing they could say. The guard tapped the door again. "Now."

"Whatever you say . . ." Rozen shrugged, a cospiratorial glance toward Blum, and stepped around the pump. "But if you fucking Germans would just allow us to fix the damn pipes there once and for all, we wouldn't have to fucking lug this contraption over all the time."

"What did you say?" The guard's eyes stretched wide in disbelief.

"Nothing." Rozen stood upright, awaiting the rain of blows that was about to follow. "I just—"

"*Fucking* Germans . . . ?" The corporal took his rifle and butted it into Rozen's jaw. The prisoner went down. His mouth filled up with blood, a tooth coming out onto the ground. "Fucking *Jews*!" he glowered, his face red with rage. He kicked Rozen in the ribs and groin, as the repairman tried to cover himself up. "Filthy pieces of shit!" he screamed, and kicked him over and over. He took his gun and pulled back the bolt, and put it to Rozen's head.

Blum's blood stirred in riot. He desperately wanted to interfere. Rozen might easily be shot or beaten to death. *But do what?* Whatever he could do would be suicidal for him, and for Leisa too, inside.

Rozen covered up his head, awaiting the end.

"Corporal . . ." The sergeant put a hand on his colleague's arm. "I know him. He's been around here from the start. He'll get his soon enough . . ."

The younger guard tensed on the trigger, trained on Rozen, his eyes ablaze.

"But maybe not today. What do you say there? You'll have your shot," the older guard said. "But I agree, *fucking Germans* . . ." He went up and kicked Rozen sharply in the ribs. The repairman let out a gasp, clutching his side. The sergeant kicked him again. "Let me hear you say a word like that again and my new corporal here can do all he wants, do you understand? And with my blessing."

Curled in a ball, Rozen spat blood out of his mouth and nodded gratefully. "I do, sir. I'm sorry."

"Now get your asses out of here. Are we okay, Corporal?" he said to the younger guard, who still had his gun pointed at Rozen's head.

"Mark your days, Jew." The younger one finally lowered the gun. He gave Rozen one last kick to the ribs. The repairman rolled over and groaned. "Now get the fuck going and count your luck. *Now!*"

"Yes, sir." Rozen picked himself up to his knees and the corporal kicked him in the rear and sent him sprawling forward, his face in the dirt. Blum ran around and helped him to his feet, and picked up the towing rod. "Thank you, sirs. Both of you." Blum pulled the pump, at the same time assisting Rozen, who was doubled over, coughing up bloody spit, staggering alongside him. Blum looked back and saw the sergeant slap the new guard on the shoulder with an understanding grin.

They'd made it through.

"God, that was lucky. Are you all right?" Blum said under his breath, as soon as they were out of earshot. A few prisoners and even SS men who were nearby turned to watch.

Rozen coughed and nodded. Then he winked at Blum with a victorious smile. "A few kicks to the ribs are a lot better than a bullet to the head if he'd opened the door. And *luck* . . . ?" He snorted. "The only luck is that I've greased that bastard's palm so many times, the thought of spending the rest of the war without it was obviously too much for him."

Blum looked in the canny prisoner's eyes and lit up into a smile as well.

"And who needs fucking teeth in here anyway?" Rozen spat out a little more blood. "All they ever feed you is soup."

They wheeled the pump back to the repair shed. No one was around. Seeing the coast was clear, Blum opened the door to the housing and whispered inside, "Leisa, you can come out now. It's safe."

They let out the hose a bit and she crawled out, white, afraid. Elated, she threw her arms around Blum, afraid to let go. She gave Rozen a grateful hug as well.

"Here." Blum handed her the uniform Shetman had provided him. "Put this on, quick. Over there."

She went around the side of a truck, took off her dress, and slipped into the small striped uniform.

It was a little large and hung off her shoulders; it just made her look like skin and bones. Blum handed her his own cap. With her shaved head and smooth skin, she looked like a boy of fourteen or fifteen. But that was enough.

"*Here* . . . " Rozen took a little dirt from the ground, rubbed his hands together, and applied it to Leisa's cheeks and under her eyes. It maybe made her look a year or two older. "Now at least you look fit for work. Welcome to the men's camp." He winked conspiratorially, then rubbed his side. "Whatever it is you are here to do."

Blum shook the man's hand. "Thank you."

He never thought he could feel so happy to be back in this hellhole. *Only four hours left to go.*

FIFTY-SIX

"Kurt . . . " Greta Ackermann turned in surprise as her husband un-expectedly stepped into the bedroom.

It was just three, and she was in the midst of changing to go to the infirmary. He rarely showed up at home this time of the after-noon. She had just finished brushing out her hair and had picked out a modest dress. "I didn't hear you come up the stairs. Have you had lunch?"

"I'm not hungry," he said, and came around her in the mirror as she was set to slip the dress over her undergarments. "Here, let me help you with that."

"I could have Hedda put something out for you. I think there's still some chicken left in the refrigerator . . ."

"I've had my lunch," he said, keeping his eyes on her. He wrapped his arms around her from behind. "Mmmm, you smell nice. It's been awhile."

"Not now. Kurt, please . . ." She tried to pull herself away. "I was just heading over to the infirmary for an hour or two. I said I would assist the nurses in the—"

"What a shame to waste how you smell on those disease-ridden yids," he said, not letting her go. He sank his face in her neck beneath her hair. "They'll be dead in a short while anyway. Or maybe you have a date with your young Jew boyfriend . . . You would dress up for him, wouldn't you? You would open a button or two and give him a free glance. Don't think I don't know . . . ."

"Know *what*, Kurt . . . ? You're talking idiocy." She tried to reach for her dress. "He's just a boy. Besides, it's Thursday. Our matches are Tuesdays. And anyway, you asked me not to play with him anymore, so I've put our game on hold."

"That's good." Inside, he brightened. That solved one issue. Now on to the next. He removed his hat and tossed it onto the bed. He unbuttoned the top buttons on his jacket. "It's been a long time. You haven't fucked me since the night of the Von Hoellens' party. It's been months."

"Yes, and you were drunk that night, as I recall. Anyway, Kurt, please, I need to go. They're expecting me." She tried to twist out of his grasp.

He tightened around her from behind, one arm underneath her breast, the other on her shoulder, and pulled her into him.

"Kurt, please . . . Go back to the office if that's what you're here for. It's not the time for this now."

"Not now, not anytime, it seems." He licked the back of her ear and tightened his hold on her. He whispered in an even voice, "You'd do it for him, wouldn't you? The little yid chess player. You'd get all primped up and fuck him, right? But not me. Your husband."

"What are you talking about, Kurt? I— And you're hurting me . . . Please, let me go." She tried to wrestle away, but he gripped her even more firmly. He wouldn't let her go. She loathed him when he got like this, single-minded, bullying. Usually when he was drunk. She felt him behind her, getting hard and ready. He was right—she hadn't let him inside her in months. She could barely tolerate the random brush of him against her in bed. At their meals, she listened to the numbing details of his days: numbers in, numbers out; work completed. She went to his officers' parties and watched as he and his cronies got drunk and sang their stupid songs, all the while pretending to smile. She listened to his incessant chattering about the sacrifices for his career; his ambition and true worth; his goal to replace Hoss, who would soon be pegged for a bigger job; to use this pit of hell he was responsible for to elevate their future. All the while loathing the sound of his voice, the very touch of him against her, regretting with whatever shame she could still summon her youthful decision to have allowed herself to be swept away, to have married him. And the trap she now found herself caught in. Always scared, as he turned to her in bed, what if she became pregnant? What if she carried his child? What then?

"Kurt, no." She would rather a reptile ran its tongue along her neck. She pushed him away. *"Please . . . "*

"Not no—*yes,*" he replied. His tone seemed to carry a warning in it. "Today, you do not push me away. Today, it is not no, Greta. It is yes."

"I'm not one of your prisoners here, Kurt." She glared at him behind her in the mirror. "You do not order me around or tell me what to do."

"But in fact you *are* my prisoner, Greta. You are my wife. And I do. I do order you." He ran his fingertips along her arm. "There's no way that can be undone."

She spun around in his arms and her eyes had fire in them too. "Then the answer is yes, Kurt."

"*Yes . . . ?*" He smiled; he seemed pleased to have finally persuaded her.

"Yes, I would rather a little Jew fuck me than you."

"You little slut!" He raised his arm as blood rushed into his face and hit her with the back of his hand.

Greta let out a gasp. She stumbled onto the bed. She touched her lip. Blood oozed down her chin. "You are a bastard, Kurt!"

"Not today, did I hear it right . . . ?" He struck her again and she fell. "Oh, yes, today." He kneeled over her, wedging his knees between her thighs, unbuckling his trousers. She tried to wrestle away, slapping at him, fending him off, but he pinned her, one hand under her chin, which sucked the air from her, as the other pulled down her girdle and he pushed his dick close. She glared back at him, tears

306

forming in her eyes as he declared triumphantly, "Today, Greta, *I* get to fuck you."

Later, after he had put his hand over her mouth to cover her screams while he forced her legs up and pushed himself deep inside her; after he had ripped her bra and left his dreaded ooze all over her thighs and sheets; after he left her whimpering and drying her tears, Kurt rolled off the bed and laughed, a wrathful, loveless laugh between his sated breaths.

"See," he said, a mocking gleam in his eye. "I can still be a man to you in a way no one else can."

"You are a bastard to me, Kurt. You are the devil."

"Please, you give me far too much credit, Greta. I am still only Lagerkommandant. But anyway, I have a busy day and night still in front of me. Two trains. One from the West. Prague, I think. The other from Hungary." He stood up and buckled up his trousers. "And then there's the matter of our intelligence ferret from Warsaw . . . *Sniff, sniff.*" He scrunched up his nose like a weasel. "He believes someone has entered the camp from the outside. And who knows, he may be right. In any case, we will have him soon. In the meantime, all it's doing is slowing our numbers for the day." He picked up his jacket and brushed the wrinkles out. "And those numbers are our future, Greta . . . You know that, right?"

She did not answer. She just stared vacantly out the window. The view was not of wires and low-hanging smoke but of the forest, far in the distance. Something pleasing, green.

Far away from here.

"Anyway, we'll have him soon. His little truffle hunter." Kurt put his arms through his jacket and tucked the lapels close. "And on that other matter, darling, I really wouldn't get too sweet on him, if I were you." He buttoned his jacket.

"What other matter, Kurt," Greta said distractedly. "Who?"

"Your little chess boy. It would be quite a waste, you know. Of your attention. Special arrangements are being speeded up."

"Special arrangements . . . ?"

"Don't be naïve, darling. You know precisely what we do here as well as I. What is it called, that little clock that times your moves in chess?"

"The game clock, Kurt," she answered.

"Yes, the game clock. Well, you'd better turn it on, my dear. Tick, tick, tick, tick, tick . . . Because you don't have much time left."

She sat up, worry building inside her. She knew Kurt, and she didn't like how he sounded now. There was something in his mocking tone that sounded as if some decision had already been made. "I've already stopped playing with him, Kurt. Just as you asked. You said you would look out for him." She pulled her dress over her breasts.

"I believe I said for as long as I could . . ." He looked in the mirror and smoothed out his jacket. "But now I'm afraid the matter is out of my hands."

"You promised, Kurt." Greta stood up. "You can still save a single Jew in this hellhole. You're just doing this to hurt me."

"I'm afraid my hands are tied." He shrugged and turned back. "It's all straight from Berlin. Right from the top. Tick, tock. The clock is speeded up. Right, my dear . . . ?"

She stared, revulsion rising up in her like sweat bubbling through her skin. "Who the hell are you, Kurt?"

"Who am *I* . . . ?" His question carried a slight smile.

"What have you become? Something I don't recognize. We used to dream of how our life would unfold. You thought you would practice law. What kind of animal are you now?"

"The same kind of animal that is all around us, Greta. You look at it every day, you just don't see it. Are you blind? Yes, a big night tonight . . ." He put a hand on her cheek and smiled. "And you know how I like to welcome our new guests."

Kurt looked back at himself in the mirror and seemed pleased. He picked up his cap and put it on his head, and tilted it at just the right angle. "Now onto the matter of our little intelligence friend and his truffle hunter . . . Turns out, the little weasel has a sister in here. In the orchestra, of all things. But not to worry, dear, we're about to sort all that out." He bent down and placed a kiss on her cheek, dry as sandpaper. "Have a nice afternoon, my love." He went to the door. "Oh, and darling?"

She looked up at him, an ache throbbing in her belly like she was carrying a child she knew was dead.

"Say hello to the good doctor for me when you're at the infirmary, would you? We should have them for dinner soon, don't you agree?"

FIFTY-SEVEN

Blum took Leisa back to his block and hid her in the area reserved for those who were ill, near the rear.

"Lie down here," he whispered, putting her onto a cot. He handed her a thin blanket. "Keep this over you." It was getting late. The work details would be filing back soon. "You'll be safe back here. No one will know."

Only one other prisoner was stretched out on a cot, his mouth open, looking more dead than alive.

"Nathan, I can't believe you're actually here." Leisa placed her hands on his face, her eyes gushing in wonderment. "That I'm actually touching you."

"And I can't believe that after everything, you're actually alive! For so long, I was sure that—"

"Don't speak that now." She put a finger to his lips.

"I can't help it. To me, it's like you've risen from the dead. That I have my sister back. Do you remember the name I called you when we were kids?"

"Of course. Doleczki," she said. "Dimples. But I'm afraid you can barely see them now. And you were Myszka. Because you were always like a little mouse. For your agility at getting yourself in an out of trouble."

Blum laughed. "Yes, Myszka . . . I can hear Mother calling me that.

310

Whisking me out of the kitchen. 'Away, Myszka, shoo, shoo, or I'll call the big cat on you.'" His eyes lit up as he brought back the fond memory. Then he looked away. "You know I've never forgiven myself. Not for a second. For leaving. For abandoning them. And you."

"You didn't abandon us, Nathan. Father pushed you to go."

"If I had been there I would have never let them go out into the square. I knew ways to get around. Mr. Loracyk's apartment led out onto the rooftop of the house next door. It was an easy jump. We could have sneaked across it and then gotten out in the next building onto Cimilianska Street."

"And then what? Run from basement to basement like criminals until someone turned us in? They would never have gone, Nathan. You know that. In the end, everyone in the ghetto was sent somewhere. Their fate would have been no different." She tried to brush the sadness off his face. "They only looked at you with pride, big brother. They always loved you and had the highest hopes for you. That was our *only* hope in the end. That whatever would happen to *us,* at least you had made it. *You* would survive. And now look . . ." Tears edged into her eyes. "You're *here* . . . in this camp. The same as all of us. What was the point?"

"The point is that we are both going to make it out, Leisa." He took her hand. "You and I. You will see."

"Just like Chaim was coming to save me?" She pushed up on an elbow. "I went to him, Nathan. Just like you asked me to. I had nowhere else to turn. And do you know where he was? On a slab. In the morgue, at Gestapo headquarters. To be tossed into a mass grave. Things happen, Nathan, things even you can't control. It's time to let Mama and Papa go.

"But enough of that. I have something to show you," she said, her face lighting up. "I think you'll like it." She took her shoe and slipped off a crack in the fake heel. She took out a small, tightly folded scrap of paper and gently unfolded it. "It hasn't left me since the day you left. I've hidden it, even in here. Do you remember, we promised each other . . ."

He stared at it.

It was her half of the Mozart concerto for clarinet she'd torn in two on the fire balcony the night before he left.

"Of course I remember," he said, and took it into his hands.

"The Mozart A-major. We were never supposed to be without it until . . ."

"Until we saw each other again." He looked at her contritely. "Leisa, it's been a long road, moving to America, and then thinking you were gone. I'm afraid I—"

"Nathan, I know." She put her hand on his cheek. "It's okay. Don't worry. I understand . . ."

"I'm afraid that's why I had to hide it very carefully myself," he said with a widening grin, reaching into the lining of his uniform and coming out with a similarly folded square, which, when opened, became the matching half.

"You are a devil, Nathan!" Leisa crowed ecstatically.

"I've never been without it for a day myself. It's been my lucky charm. I just never ever thought we'd ever be able to do this again."

They put the torn halves on the cot and fit them together until they formed a seamless match.

Leisa's eyes grew liquid with joy.

"I can hear it in my head. La-la, la-la-la, la-la . . ." Blum sang, waving his hand as if conducting. "I can see Master Bernheimer himself as if he were here now."

"Yes. Mr. Baggypants." Leisa giggled too. "He always looked like a rumpled character straight out of a Tolstoy novel. I can see him too."

"I bet he's dead now," Blum surmised.

"Yes. I heard he was among the first to be taken." Leisa nodded. "Most everyone we knew is dead now."

He clasped her hand. "But, sister, tomorrow you will wake up, and it will all have been like a dream. This place. All that was bad. All left behind. We'll be in England.

"*England?*" She blinked at him incredulously. "How?"

"I told you. There is a plane. It will land nearby. Tonight. I'm going to get us on one of the overnight work details. You will pretend to be a boy. I know it doesn't seem so easy, but it will be night and the line will be crowded. It will work. At oh thirty hours there will be an attack by local partisans. That will provide the cover for our escape. If all goes well, they will take us to the plane."

Her eyes expanded with awe. "How are you part of all this, Nathan? You're a soldier now?"

"Yes. After a year in school, I enlisted in the U.S. Army. They sent me back here on a mission. I'm here to take out an important scientist who is needed for the war effort."

"A scientist . . . ?"

"The truth is, I don't even know what he does. Only that it's all extremely vital to the war effort. You won't believe this, Leisa, but the mission was approved by the President of the United States himself."

"*Roosevelt?*"

"Yes." Blum nodded.

"You've met him?'

"No. But I spoke with him on the phone. From London. He wished me luck."

"The president called *you*? And what did you say?"

"I told him that I was honored. But that I didn't need any luck . . ." He picked up his half of the sheet music. "As long as I had my good luck charm from my little sister."

"Oh, stop. I'm sure that's exactly what you said . . ." Leisa rolled her eyes. With her shaved head and sunken features she reminded Blum of the little girl he had always remembered. "You are very brave, Nathan. Mother and Father, they would be so proud of you. Imagine, the *president* . . ."

"Yes, she would probably have baked him an almond cake and sent it to the White House."

"And Papa would ask what size hat he wore and send him one. Perhaps a very nice bowler."

"I think he prefers fedoras. Or maybe a Panama in the summer. I've seen that in the newsreels."

"Whichever, it must be firm and resistant, Papa would say," Leisa said, mimicking her father's deep voice.

313

"But never stiff," Blum added.

"No, no. At all costs, never stiff."

The prisoner across from them stirred, his eyes glazed, and then turned the other way.

"And what if it all doesn't, Nathan . . . ?" Leisa's eyes dimmed with worry. "Doesn't go so well?"

"What do you mean?"

"Tonight. What if your plane doesn't arrive? What if the Germans find us? What if the guards notice that I am not a man? You should leave me here. You know the kind of risk you are bringing on yourself and this man to get me out and take me along with you?"

"Then it will all have been worth it, my little sis. Coming back here. Finding you. No matter what fate has in store. I have never felt such joy as the moment I followed the sound of that clarinet and saw that it was you." He took his half of the torn music sheet and refolded it. "You and me, we are whole once again. I would never leave you here. No matter the risk. Or the outcome. Not again."

She leaned across and hugged him a long time.

"But anyway, this is all nonsense," Blum said, patting her on the back with affection. "Because we *are* going to make it. Soon we'll be putting these two halves back together in America. And you'll be playing your clarinet at Carnegie Hall."

"And you'll be with me?" She pulled away and looked at him. He saw that she'd been crying.

"Of course. Right on stage. Next to you." He wiped a tear off her cheek. "Still trying to learn my scales."

That made her laugh.

"But now you must pretend to sleep. There are a few things to attend to. Don't worry, you'll be safe here. For the time being, you hold onto these." He handed her the two folded music sheets. "We are a whole again. That's all that matters. We've only a few more hours here."

"Okay." She wedged the music sheets back in her shoe.

"And so as not to surprise you, there is someone else who is coming out with us tonight. He's a boy, the professor's nephew. He's a very smart lad. He's only a year or two younger than you."

"There are four of us then?" Her tone carried a measure of worry.

"Yes." Perhaps something on his face conveyed that the same concerns were running through his mind too. "But do not worry. We're going to make it, Leisa." He squeezed her hand tightly. "God wants us to. How else would I have gotten this far?"

"I'm not sure God is watching," Leisa said. "If he was, this place wouldn't exist."

"Well, then one way or another *I'll* get you out. How's that?" Blum winked at her.

"Yes, you, my brave brother. Now, that's something I *can* believe in." Leisa smiled, throwing her arms around his neck once more.

FIFTY-EIGHT

Josef Wrarinski looked around the dark room and knew his time had come. Low-pitched groans emanated from the small, closed row of cells behind him. Instruments were hung on the walls, instruments, Josef knew, whose only purpose was to inflict pain. His hands were bound behind him. Two officers stood in front of him: one the camp commandant, with a handsome but falsely sympathetic face; the other a balding colonel with impatient but purposeful eyes who wore the markings of an intelligence officer.

A beefy sergeant with fat lips and short, thick hands stood off to the side, his uniform jacket unbuttoned, his sleeves rolled, as if waiting to be called.

If he was here, Josef said to himself, they clearly knew.

He could delay things, he figured. He could deny everything; declare his innocence until he was hoarse. He could get down on his knees and sing *Die Holzhackerbaum,* "The Happy Lumberjack," and hoist a fucking beer with them. But it would all be for nothing. He had chosen this path, and now he must walk it. Josef knew he would never leave here on his feet.

He would never see his family again.

"Herr Wrarinski, welcome to Block Eleven," the commandant said with a deliberate and falsely accommodating smile. "By all means look around, take in a whiff. I think you understand the kind of place this is and what goes on in here."

Josef didn't reply.

"So let us not waste time or play around. Time is short for us. I'll tell you why you're here. First, let's not pretend you are simply a baker, any more than as the Lagerkommandant of this camp, I am running a fancy spa for the fanciful rich. Two days ago, someone made their way into this camp. We believe he flew in on a plane and that a group of partisans, you among them, picked him up and placed him the next day on a work detail inside this camp. Colonel Franke, here, who as you can see is from the intelligence corps in Warsaw, believes this man's mission here is to extract someone from inside the camp. We believe their escape is set for tonight so, as you see, this doesn't give us the time for the usual cat-and-mouse questioning. Am I understood? So the question I put to you, Herr Wrarinski, if you ever hope to walk out of here again, is, who is this man? And how is he set to leave tonight?"

"I don't know. I don't know what you're talking about." Josef shrugged. As a lieutenant in the Armia Krajowa, he was prepared to take whatever they had to give. They'd all sworn they were. He knew the risk long ago, and now he must face it.

"And that is your response?" the commandant asked.

"My only response, since I don't know the answer to what you're looking for." The partisan nodded.

"Well, that is a shame." The intelligence colonel stood up with a sigh, unbuttoning his sleeves. "Because it means, either you or your cousin, Herr Macak, who is still our guest in the cell behind you, is a liar. Because he has specifically told us it was you who came to him and placed this person on his work team the other day. *Cousins . . .*" He shrugged, slowly rolling his cuffs. "Who can figure out precisely where their competing loyalties lie? But since we are short of time, we will have to assume you both are lying. Now, we can go about it in several ways, finding out who is telling the truth and dealing with the other. I can ask Sergeant Dormutter here to apply his skills, and I am told, he is a very stubborn and persuasive questioneer."

Josef glanced at the sergeant, who was smirking against the wall.

"Or I can ask you the question again . . ." Franke sat on the desk across from Josef and opened a file. "This time pointing out that you also have a wife and two lovely children at home, Karl and Nikolas, correct? Not even teens yet, and I am saddened to think how they would fare if Major Ackermann here picked them up and relocated them here—for argument's sake, say, tonight. Sadly, many people, women and children among them, I am told, seem not to last a single day."

Josef looked at the sergeant with the meaty arms and the ready smirk, and the steely-eyed intelligence officer, who now got up, came over to where Josef was sitting, and dropped the file on the chair next to him, so that a photo of Mira and his boys edged out a bit, just far enough for Josef to see.

"Shame"—the colonel shrugged, scratching his brow—"for them to have to pay for your silence." He sat on the edge of the table and stared, not unsympathetically, Josef thought, but with a resolve that was clearly unmistakable. "Your time is over, Herr Wrarinski," the German said. "The only question still to answer is, what of your wife and children?"

FIFTY-NINE

Alfred spotted Zinchenko, the Lithuanian *kapo* who generally organized the overnight work details, weaving through the yard with his ever-present club, as they served the evening meal.

"A word, *kapo* . . . ?" Alfred went up and got his attention.

"If it's quick." The Lithuanian had a hair-trigger temper. Alfred had personally seen him club dozens of men senseless for seemingly nothing more than just the pleasure of it, or more, just because he could. Alfred didn't even like going up to the man because you couldn't predict what mood you'd get in return, nonetheless having to barter with him for his fate.

"I was hoping you could arrange for me to be on the tracks detail tonight," Alfred said, leaning close to him.

"*You?*" The *kapo* gave him a sniff of amusement.

"Why not?"

"Why not . . . Have you ever held a pick or a shovel in your life?" the *kapo* asked with a smirk. "Look at you, there's not a scrap of muscle left on those bones, if there was ever."

"Maybe. But there's enough to do the work for the extra meal, if you'd indulge me."

The nightly work detail was formed mainly by *kapos* going from block to block and rousing from their bunks those who had just come off their own twelve-hour shifts. To keep them from dropping in their

319

tracks, a second bowl of soup was served on a short break after midnight, and then they could generally sleep after breakfast the following day. Still, it wasn't exactly a plum assignment. The guards on the overnight shift were always grumpy and quick-triggered, and every morning, a few who went out the night before on their own feet came back as crumpled, twisted corpses wheeled in a cart.

"There's a few bucks in it for you, if you agree. British pounds . . ." Alfred said, finding a spark in the *kapo*'s mercantile eyes.

"What do you think I am?" The Lithuanian glowered back at him. "I could put a dent in the back of that overstuffed skull of yours just for asking that."

"Sorry. I meant nothing of it," Alfred said. "Just a meal."

"A meal." The *kapo* spat. Then he looked back up. "*Pounds,* you say . . . ?" Alfred knew it was like putting out the evening garbage under the nose of a kitchen mouse. "Teams are put together seven thirty by the clock tower," the Lithuanian agreed.

"Thank you, Zinchenko. I'll be there."

"And don't puke out on me, Professor. This isn't just a meal ticket. You come, you work, same as everyone. Or else."

"I understand," Alfred said. "And listen . . ." He took a step after the *kapo* as he began walking away. "I also know a couple of others who were looking for the same privilege."

"Others?"

"One of them is Leo. You know him. He's the chess champion in camp."

"Don't press your luck, old man. Or they may be wheeling you back in a cart, the hell with your meal."

"I only thought pounds are hard to come by in here . . . Same price, of course."

At first, the *kapo* started to walk away. But the inner workings of his mind were as transparent as the slow tick-tick of a cheap watch. "You say sterling, huh . . . ?"

"Brand-new notes. Taken off a new arrival. What other use do I have for them?" Alfred shrugged. "My vices are all behind me."

"Ten pounds a head." The *kapo* rubbed his nose.

"Ten? That's double the rate in marks."

"That's the price. Go through the kitchen trash then if you want more to eat."

"I could buy the finest dinner in Vilnius for that," Alfred appealed to the *kapo*'s Lithuanian place of birth, as if he had fleeced him dry.

"Then by all means, feel free to go to Vilnius. On me." The *kapo* began to walk away.

"Okay, okay. What choice do I have? We'll be there."

"Wait at the end of the line," the *kapo* said with a greedy smile. This night would keep him in vodka for a month. "And come with the cash. I'll find you there."

SIXTY

When Martin Franke was a boy in Essen, his father, who was an iron-worker in the mills of the Krupp Ironworks, acted as if he only had one son.

Yet there were three.

His father was a sullen, irascible drunkard, and every night after his shift, while his wife sat in the bedroom and made quilts, he drank at the kitchen table until he staggered his way to bed, rarely exchanging words with his children. His particular brand of harshness was not the type designed to inspire his boys to improve their station in life through education or hard work. His intent was simply to belittle them, to remind them of the dark, sweltering furnace that awaited them, where he trudged off to every day, and the scant, scraped-together life that he had handed them and that he had failed to pull himself up from.

Hans, the oldest, was a local football standout in his youth, and their father readily threw his achievements in Martin's face—Martin never having the same physical stature as his older sibling. At the family table, it was as if Hans was an international star, already a mainstay on the German team, even though he had never gotten farther than the local playing fields.

"Why are you such a little twig?" His father would look at Martin with shame. "Look at your brother. He has a future ahead of him.

What will you be able to offer anyone at the factory? Germany needs tall firs to build its future, not spindly twigs."

Ernst, the middle son, wasn't blessed with much between his ears, but in a brawl, you could always count on him to be the last one standing. When Ernst looked in the mirror with his father behind him, the old man saw an image of himself as a youth, someone tough, good with his fists, who had dreams maybe, until the reversals after the Great War had forced him into the mill. How often Ernst left Martin holding the bag for scrapes and transgressions at school or beer missing from the family icebox. He had the smug, self-righteous bravado of someone who knew he had nothing to contribute in life yet who everyone sought to line up with and who pretended he had it all. Even to this day, when Martin brought him to mind, all that came was the image of his brother's flat nose and thick lips in a perpetual, supercilious smirk.

Martin was the silent one, more of a watcher than a doer from an early age, never blessed with the agility or brawn of his older brothers. But he did have a methodical mind. Yet, his high marks in school produced more of an indifference than a badge of honor in his father's beer-dulled eyes. No one ever went anywhere from their town except into the mill, which was like a giant furnace eating up youth like a forest of timber. After graduation, Hans, whose football skills never progressed further than a few mentions in the local paper, became a smelter at the ironworks. He worked alongside his father. In 1942, as a forty-six-year-old, he was drafted when they were throwing anyone who could walk into uniform, and word came even before the telegram that he had frozen to death in Stalingrad a year later. The bully, Ernst, was recruited into the SA in 1935 as Hitler rose to power and went around smashing windows at synagogues and kicking in storefronts and beating up Jews, his fists in high demand. In 1938, he was found dead in an alley in Dortmund with a knife in his khaki uniform and a Jewish star stuck to his chest.

Martin meanwhile went on to the local police academy after graduation. His steady, watchful way gave him the skills of a standout investigator. Over ten years he worked his way up to becoming the most decorated inspector on the Essen force. In 1937, he was recruited by the Abwehr with the rank of captain. He was rewarded with a posting in France in 1940 and then a station at the embassy in Lisbon in 1942, and a promotion to his present rank.

But by then his father had died in a lathe accident on the job, and he never saw a single medal on his son's chest.

And that was what Martin Franke was thinking of in the Lagerkommandant's office that night, as he waited to catch his prey. How surprised his father would have been, if he was sober enough to even see, that by night's end, his little twig of a son who could not stand up to his drunken old man would have unearthed a plot that all the big firs in Berlin would have to take notice of.

"So where is this orchestra member?" Ackermann said to Lieutenant Fromm as his aide came into his office. "You've had three hours."

"We have found two women, but according to our witness," the young lieutenant said, "neither is the one. The third, the clarinet player—her name is Blum—did not show up for her performance this afternoon upon the return of the work details."

"So then pick her up. What is the delay? Bring her to me," Ackermann insisted.

"That is the problem, Herr Lagerkommandant. We went to her block, Thirteen, in the women's camp, but she was nowhere to be found. In fact, she has not been seen since."

"Since this morning . . . ?"

"Since apparently a repair detail was sent to her block in the afternoon. The block matron claims she was seen talking with one of them. It was assumed at the time to have been a conjugal visit."

"Conjugal? I don't understand."

"A water pump team was brought in. Though no one seems to have officially requested it."

"So there you have it!" Ackermann turned with excitement to Franke, who was at the table nearby. "I think we know now who your truffle hunter has come here to find."

Franke slowly stood up. He shook his head skeptically. "To find a

324

sister? No, I do not think so, Major. That is not why he was flown in by plane and was able to connect with the local underground. No, I am certain there is a bigger prize that awaits us in here. We will see."

"The escape of a single prisoner is a big enough prize for me," Ackermann said. He instructed the lieutenant, "Find me the repair chief of this team. I want him in front of me immediately."

"Yes, Herr Lagerkommandant . . ." The aide cleared his throat, but still remained.

"Go, Fromm. Why are you still standing there?"

"Because I think I already know where to find them, Herr Lagerkommandant," the SS lieutenant said.

"Out with it then. Or are you waiting for them to send you a postcard from London after they escape?"

"Something unusual turned up from the men's roll call this morning. It did not surface until a short while ago." The lieutenant cleared his throat.

"I'm waiting . . ."

"One of the prisoners in Block Twelve used the name Fisher. A Pavel Fisher was recorded among the list of deceased. Yesterday. The Blockführer has confirmed that he was the only Fisher in his block."

"And what was *this* Fisher's number?" Ackermann pressed his aide.

"Today's? A22327, Herr Lagerkommandant." The lieutenant found his notes and read it off.

"*And* . . . ?" Ackermann waited. "I'm trying to determine if this Fisher's number matched the dead man's number, Obersturmführer Fromm, if you please?"

"It did not, sir," the aide said nervously. "In fact, the number A22327 belonged to an entirely different prisoner."

"Who?" Ackermann stared impatiently. He snapped his fingers. "Quick, Fromm. We are pressed for time."

"Rudolf Vrba." The lieutenant swallowed hesitantly.

"*Vrba.*" Ackermann stood up; the color draining from his face. The name was known, of course. Known to everyone in the camp, both guard and prisoner. He now knew if this got out, without the immediate apprehension of all involved tonight, things would not go well for him when Hoss returned and the conversation turned to his career. No matter what numbers he reached.

"What is it?" Franke asked.

"You are right, Colonel. This *is* far, far larger than someone who is simply here to rescue his sister. Bring out the entire block!" Ackermann said to Fromm. "Every fucking yid in there. I want it scrubbed and gone over so that even the fucking bed lice are accounted for. Do you understand me, Lieutenant?"

"Yes, Herr Lagerkommandant. I understand." The SS aide came to attention and moved to leave.

"Wait, Lieutenant . . ." Franke motioned for the aide to remain. "Major, there is more than just this man and an escape that is at stake. It is imperative we also find out precisely who he is here for."

"And what do you suggest, Colonel?"

"I suggest we let it all play out."

"Play it out? Why take such a risk?" Ackermann said. "We know where he is. We have them now."

"It's only a small risk, don't you agree? The work teams are assembling shortly, are they not?" Franke checked his watch. A part of him flashed back to an image of his father—dull-eyed, in a sleeveless undershirt in the kitchen, hunched over a beer. His two shining sons now gone in shame, while his twig of an unworthy offspring was about to blow the lid off an Allied plot that might even put an Iron Cross on his chest. "I say let it all proceed as planned. In a few minutes, we know precisely where they will be."

SIXTY-ONE

As the minutes passed, Alfred sat among the spent and exhausted workers in his bunk. He'd had his evening meal—his last at the camp, he hoped. Of all the things he had experienced and hoped to forget, the rancid swill they served twice a day that barely kept them alive would be near the top of the list.

His mind drifted to Marte and Lucy.

How they had both talked of one day making it to America. To settle in some beautiful, bustling city with an esteemed institution there. Maybe Chicago. With Fermi. Or Berkeley in California with his old friend Lawrence. Or New York. He'd been there once to share a paper at the Atomic Science Symposium in 1936. To continue his work in a place that was safe and not hostile to the Jews would be a dream.

It had been *all* their dreams, when they had crossed from Poland to Holland to France, papers in hand.

But now it would just be him going on. If that was to be his fate. This pale, undernourished shadow of himself, so thin Marte might look at him twice and still not recognize him.

He and this boy.

It was just like Heisenberg's theorem, Alfred reflected. Uncertainty is the only certainty in this world. The only thing you can completely

327

measure. Even on the small scale of the atom, there were inherent limits to how precisely events could be known.

And clearly on the grander scale of life as well.

It made him smile, recalling what the great Einstein was said to have muttered when told that it was his theory, $E = mc^2$, that had opened up this new world and unleashed the radioactive consequences of mass and energy.

"Ist das wirklich so?" Is that really so?

Even as vast a mind as Einstein never imagined the consequences that resulted from his random musings on a notebook page.

The unknowable was the beauty of life, Alfred now knew. And also its greatest sadness.

If you identified the position of a particle, he recalled, say, by allowing it to transfer through a zinc-sulfide screen, you changed its velocity and thereby lost its information. If you bombarded it with gamma rays, you inalterably changed its path as well, so who could then measure precisely where it was? Any new measurement always rendered the one before it, even an instant before, uncertain. And then the one after that and the one after that, so said Heisenberg.

Only the wholeness of everything leads to clarity.

And when does one ever get to see that? When do we ever get to see the whole picture?

You see it now, don't you, Marte? And Lucy? I know you do. And I am going on, for as far as God lets me.

With this boy.

The only moment of true clarity is at the end.

He got up from his bunk, slipped his blue and swollen feet into his hard clogs. He carefully folded the thin, hole-ridden cloth that had acted as a blanket these past months and placed it neatly on the foot of his mattress.

"Leaving, Professor?" Ostrow, the forager, who slept across from him inquired, noticing Alfred tidying up.

"Just hungry," Alfred said. "I intend to find myself a meal."

"Of what? Some bits of stale bread? A little grizzle perhaps? Boiled to perfection. Maybe a lump of fat?" The forager chortled.

"No." Alfred looked at him. "I was thinking crumpets, actually."

"*Crumpets?*" The cobbler watched as Alfred made his way to the front of the block, sure that with all those numbers and theorems clouding his head, the old man had finally lost his mind.

"I'm working on the night shift tonight out on the tracks," Alfred advised Panish, the Blockführer.

"*You?*" Panish's eyebrows arched up.

"And why not? Is it so strange I would do my share of work?"

"No, not strange, just . . ." The Blockführer thought to himself that it must be suicide. That, as many did from time to time, the old man was finally tossing it in. "Goodbye, Professor. God's grace to you."

"Thank you, Panish. I will need it all."

The Blockführer made a note in his book that bunk number 71 would need to be filled.

At the door, Alfred looked at his block for what he knew would be the last time. Bent, spindly shapes, more bone than flesh. Goodbye. Only wholeness leads to clarity, he thought. They will see that tomorrow. We only know bits and pieces. Fragments. What the universe allows us to see. The rest . . . The rest is just things flying around. Uncertainty.

"*Ist das wirklich so?*" He smiled, and stepped out into the night.

SIXTY-TWO

Blum sat on the edge of the cot where his sister lay sleeping and stared at her.

He put his hand on her shoulder, feeling her steady breathing beneath him, her lungs going in and out, and he wondered if, in her dreams, there was a faraway place she escaped to, a place of safety and trust, far beyond the odor of death that penetrated everything here. He brushed his hand along her cheek.

Doleczki.

He reminded himself why he was there. Why he had come back to this country that had only the cruelest of memories for him. Why he had put on this striped smock, snuck into this pit of hell, faced immediate death if it came out who he was and what his mission was.

He knew now it wasn't to help win the war for his new country, or even to get back at the Germans for what they had done to his parents.

No, that wasn't it.

It was to bury the shame he had long felt for being the one who left. To pay the debt in his heart for those he had left behind.

And now, as he stared lovingly at his sleeping sister's face, he realized he had repaid that debt in the most remarkable way.

He felt expansive.

One of the first pieces Leisa had ever played at recital was from

Orpheus in the Underworld. By the German Offenbach. It told of the grieved, desperate lover who ventured down into the underworld with his lyre, passing the ghosts and anguished souls of people unknown; charming Cerberus, the guardian of the deep with his three gnashing heads until even the cold heart of Hades melted just enough and he allowed Orpheus's love, Eurydice, to go back to the world above with him.

Whatever you do, don't look back was the underworld ruler's only condition.

And in a way Blum felt like that lyre player himself. Seducing his way into Hell, cheating death not once but twice; past the wires and the guards, until the beautiful sound of music somehow lured him to her.

Except this time he would not leave her behind.

This, not the calculations of some professor, was why God had sent him here.

"Leisa," he whispered, squeezing her on the shoulder. "Wake up now."

His sister stirred with a start and then, as if reassured that Nathan still was beside her, smiled. "I had the most troubling dream," she said. "We were back in Krakow. I was hiding. In the attic of Father's shop. You remember how we used to play up there, amid the rows and rows of hats and size molds?"

"Yes."

"Except this time I was locked in. It was dark, and no one could hear me when I called, and for a moment I was really scared. So I played. Somehow I had my clarinet, and I had to play louder and louder. I was sure no one would ever come. That I would be lost up there forever. But then you came. You found your way in. You rescued me, Nathan."

"I know," he said with a smile. "I was having similar thoughts myself. Just like today."

She turned to him. "We're going to make it, aren't we, Nathan?"

"Yes. We will."

"No, I mean, really. You can tell me. Because I couldn't go on if I was causing you danger. I'd rather die here, Nathan. I—"

"Hush now." He squeezed her arm. "No one's going to die. You remember the vow I made to Papa when he held you in the window . . . ?"

"I remember you telling me about it." Leisa smiled. "I was just an infant."

"Just know that my promise to keep it is even stronger now. So yes, we will make it. I promise." He looked at the man sleeping in the bunk across from them. "Now, put this on." He handed her his cap and tucked it down over her brow. He put his hands in the gravel near the foundation and smeared a bit of dirt from his thumbs onto her cheeks. "Now you look like a tough young man."

"Not such a flattering thing to say, Nathan."

"Maybe. But today it will save your life. So let's go." He pulled her to her feet. His heartbeat picked up with urgency. "It's time."

SIXTY-THREE

NEWMARKET AIR BASE, ENGLAND

Strauss was on the tarmac briefing the flight crew that was preparing to leave when a radioman ran up and said he had an important call. He followed the man back up to the communication center.

It was Donovan. Back in Washington.

"So tonight's the big night, Peter?" the OSS chief said.

"Yes, sir, it is."

"I'm sure this is a stressful time for you. Have we heard anything more?"

"Only what I've patched along. Blum's inside. The plane crew is preparing their flight plan. We have diversionary bombers set for Hamburg and Dresden. The partisan attack will go off as planned in five hours."

"Well, you've done your job well, son. You should be proud, whatever the result. I just called to tell you good luck."

"Thank you, Colonel."

"How is it you say that in Hebrew, Captain?"

"*Beh-hats-la-khah*, sir," Strauss replied. "Literally, it means *in success.*"

"In success . . . ? You know, it's generally not a good thing in this trade to set your hopes too high. There's always more on these things that can go wrong than right and dash them. In this case, a lot more. We both knew from the start the odds of success were long."

"I understand, Colonel. But I'm thinking my man might just surprise you in this case."

"Well, nothing would make me happier than to inform the president so. So let's say we both put in a little hope on this one."

"Thank you, sir. I appreciate that."

"*Beh-hats-la-khah* then." The OSS chief stumbled over the word. "You know, *mazel tov* would be a damn sight easier."

Strauss laughed. "Yes. We'll see about that then, sir. A bit later."

"I'll be at my desk as long as it takes awaiting the news."

"Yes, sir. I'll inform you as soon as I know something."

Strauss put down the phone. It was hard to stop his heart from pounding. He had a good feeling inside him. Hell with the odds, he smiled. He felt certain tonight they were going to buck them.

SIXTY-FOUR

At just before 1930 hours, the work line formed under the clock near the main gate. About thirty to forty prisoners stood in an irregular formation. Most, including many who had already worked a full day and had been roused from their naps, showed little desire to be there. Blum came up with Leisa and settled into the ragtag line. On Blum's instructions, she kept her eyes down and her cap low on her brow. With her dark features and dirt smeared on her cheeks, she didn't look much different than any teenage boy. Darkness had fallen. Four or five of the SS guards stood around, keeping order. Others ringed the area around the front gate armed with submachine guns. Dogs barked and tugged at their leashes, as if the scent of Jews trudging off to work reminded them that it was mealtime.

Alfred and his nephew came up and melded into the queue.

"Is everything done?" Blum asked.

Mendl nodded. "But who is this?" he asked, surprised to see Blum with someone else. His face reflected what Blum already knew: That three was one thing, but now four, whoever this addition was . . . Four would be harder to conceal as they tried to lose themselves in the attack. Four was one too many.

"You said you wouldn't leave behind your own flesh and blood," Blum said, gesturing to Leo.

"Yes, but . . ."

"Well, neither would I. Leisa, this is the man I came here to rescue."

"*Leisa?*" Mendl stared at her, his eyes widening in confusion.

"My sister," Blum said under his breath. "An unanticipated development. But she's coming along. Any issues?"

"*Your sister?*" Mendl saw there was no wavering on Blum's face. "No issues at all," he replied. And no time to argue anyway.

"I'm Leo," Mendl's nephew said. "We'll all watch out for each other."

Leisa nodded back a nervous smile.

Blum pressed some bills in Alfred's hand. "Here. At the going rate, enough for four."

A few stragglers arrived. "Stay in line!" Guards and *kapos* pushed everyone together. Slowly the line began to move forward. The dogs barked, snarling at prisoners as they shuffled past, held back only by their straining handlers. Blum watched as Mendl made eye contact with a *kapo* who was traveling down the line wielding a truncheon.

"Ready for a hard night's work, Professor?" The shifty-eyed *kapo* seemed to recognize him.

"Hopefully, it won't be as bad as all that. This line is for the rail tracks, right?"

"Yes, the rail tracks." The *kapo* nodded.

Alfred reached out and pressed the bills Blum had given him into the *kapo*'s palm. Zinchenko shifted his eyes down and seemed surprised. "It's now four of us," Alfred said.

"Four?"

"Why do you care? Someone else came along. It's all been paid for."

The *kapo* glared at him with contempt but put the cash in his pocket. "Stay in line or I'll make sure your bell is rung good." He raised his club at a prisoner in the row behind them.

Trucks pulled up outside the front gate. The camp labor fed various work sites. Some for the rail tracks that went up to Birkenau and various ditches beyond the camp gates, used both for sewage or as a mass grave for those who didn't make it to the ovens, which were only a short ride away. Others—the IG Farben facility and a munitions plant— were situated a mile or two to the west by Auschwitz 3. The trick, as

336

when Blum first arrived here, was to make sure they were positioned in the proper line; otherwise it all was pointless. The attack would come and they'd be in a different location. They'd be stranded here.

"Remember, run toward the river," Blum said into Alfred's ear. "As soon as the shooting starts. Not to the woods. They will provide cover for us."

"I will get him there," Leo said.

"You will do just as we discussed," Alfred rebuked him sharply. For the first time Blum saw just how doubtful the old man was that he'd be able to run amid the shooting. Still, everything depended on him getting there. And alive.

"You stay by me," Blum said, posting himself between Alfred and Leisa. Now he had two to protect.

"What if we are out there and the attack doesn't come?" Alfred asked. "What if all we get is our ladle of soup and then we're marched back in?"

"Then you are no worse off than when you woke up this morning." Blum shrugged philosophically. "But I won't be able to say the same."

Leo pointed toward the front. "We're going."

The line began to move, an officer at the front counting off those who passed before him. Alfred and Leo merged in behind.

"There is something I must tell you," Mendl said close to Blum's ear, "in case I don't make it."

"You'll make it."

"It's about Leo."

"Your nephew? Don't worry, I'll do my best to watch out for him as well. I give you my—"

"No, that's not what I meant. I—"

Suddenly the officer taking numbers at the front of the line yelled, "*Vierzig! Vierzig nur. Nicht mehr.*"

Forty. Forty only.

He counted each prisoner and tapped them on the head as they went by.

Blum froze. He scanned up ahead. Maybe fifteen or twenty had already passed through. There had to be an equal number still in front of them. A knot twisted in his stomach. "We're going to be left behind," he said to Mendl, worry setting in. If they were sure to make it through, they'd have to move up three or four rows in line.

"Zinchenko . . ." Mendl got the eye of the *kapo* he had bribed. "They said just forty only . . ."

"A meal's a meal, Professor," the *kapo* replied indifferently. "There are other lines."

"Those other details are more like death marches," Mendl pressed him. "We paid your price. A deal's a deal, Zinchenko. Honor it."

"You want to argue, Professor?" The *kapo* reared his club. "Here's the court of appeals." The bastard clearly didn't like to be challenged.

Panic reared up as Blum looked ahead and saw the work line nearing its last ten, the officer counting aloud. *"Thirty-one, thirty-two . . ."* He tapped the head of each prisoner he let through.

Fifteen or so were still in front of them.

"We're not going to make it," Blum said, his alarm mounting. Could it now be all for nothing? The plane might already be in the air. The attack . . . It was tonight or never. They had to move up.

"There's more where that came from, Zinchenko," Mendl whispered to the *kapo,* seeing the same outcome taking shape. "I can get it for you."

"Dreiunddreißig, vierunddreißig . . ." the officer called. *Thirty-three, thirty-four.*

Ten still in front of them. And only six more spots.

"Zinchenko . . ." Alfred hissed.

"Here! More grist for the mill tonight," the *kapo* called out, pushing the professor and Leo forward and grabbing Blum by the neck of his uniform. Blum held onto Leisa. The kapo threw the four of them forward toward the front of the line, grunting to the officer who was counting them off. "These four are on me tonight. Top workers, all of them."

"None of them look like they can even hold a spade," the German replied, looking them over. Then, back to his counting as if it was no matter. "Thirty-five, thirty-six, thirty-seven, thirty-eight . . ." The officer pushed each of them on the shoulder until they passed. "Only

338

two more," he said to the row behind them. "Everyone else, keep your lines. There will be more details."

They'd made it through.

Relieved, Blum squeezed Leisa's arm as they made their way slowly through the main gate, which was ringed by guards staring blankly ahead as if the prisoners were cattle, not men. Many in line grumbled about their rotten fate. Roused out of their bunks, deprived of a night's sleep. And just their luck, Hauptscharführer Scharf was in charge; he had a hair trigger even when he'd had a good night's sleep. Tarps were cleared from the bays of the trucks and those in the front of the line began to climb in, guards checking numbers and pushing them along, dogs snarling, barking loudly, a reminder to anyone who might have a thought of escape outside the wires.

Blum's heart pounded with anticipation. It was one thing for him to sneak through with only Mendl, but Leo and Leisa made it far more challenging. But they were almost there. Only one more checkpoint. Ahead, another guard was taking down workers' numbers. Getting Leisa through would be the final hurdle. With her hair shaved and dirt smeared on her cheeks, in truth, she looked no less a man than Leo. "Just say your name and show your arm," Blum whispered in her ear. "And don't look him in the eye. Keep your head down. You'll be fine." She nodded bravely, but Blum could feel her nervous heart beating briskly.

Mendl was first up. He recited his name and number. The guard dutifully waved him past. Then Leo. The same result. Blum was up next. He pushed Leisa in front of him and held onto her arm.

"Blum," she muttered in a low voice, showing her forearm.

"A390207," the guard read off. Leisa kept her eyes down.

Blum eyed the Luger strapped to the guard's side. If he stopped Leisa, if this was it, that was where Nathan would lunge. They would be dead in an instant, of course. But he wouldn't let them be taken, tortured. He would not go without a fight like his parents.

"Next."

Leisa stepped through.

It was done.

"Mirek. A22327," Blum said.

"Mirek. A22327 . . ." the guard confirmed. Then his gaze went past Blum to the one in back of him. "And you . . ."

They had made it. Their line was now climbing up into the truck. Blum squeezed Leisa's shoulder. It was all going as planned. All they would have to do was work the line for a couple of hours and wait for the attack. When it came, with machine gun fire and maybe a grenade or two, there would be chaos. Smoke. People running about. There was always the last hurdle, of course, to sneak away amid the pandemonium and make it to the river. And now with four of them, that would be a harder feat. But if he had to, Blum was prepared to disable one of the guards; everyone would be distracted in the confusion. It would be risky, of course, that was clear. But the hardest part had passed. He had made it inside, managed to find Mendl, and Leisa too. It was all going to work, he was sure. He felt it in his heart. In a few hours, the plane would land and they'd be on their way to London. And then to America. The thought of Orpheus bringing Eurydice back from the dead came into his head—he was going to do it. And then Hades's own warning passed through his mind:

Whatever you do, Leisa, don't look behind.

Just a few seconds more.

About half the work team had climbed into Truck Number One. The tarp was lowered and secured, and the rest were directed to the one next to it. Slowly they began to file in. Five, then ten, guards herding them quickly into the cargo bay. *"Schnell! Schnell!"*

It was almost their time now. Blum's heart surged. A guard pushed each one up who stepped forward. *"You. You."* Now it was their turn. Leo put his foot on the step and jumped in first. He reached back to help Alfred, who awkwardly put a foot on the step, took Leo's hand, and hoisted himself up with a quick but satisfied look that seemed to say, *Thus far, so good.* Blum put his face close to Leisa's ear and whispered, "I'll help you up. We're almost there. It's only—"

The guard blocked them with his arm. *"Alt!"*

An instant later, bright lights flared on; everything was flooded in a blinding glare. Blum shielded his eyes, dogs barking, lunging out of the darkness, all teeth and gnashing jowls. The piercing wail of a warning siren.

What was going on?

To Blum's horror, the commandant he had seen at roll call this morning came around the side of the truck. Closely followed by the Abwehr colonel he had seen as well, his Mauser drawn.

How were they here? What the hell had gone wrong?

Someone pinned him by the shoulders, amid voices in German shouting. "These four!"

The intelligence colonel stood in front of him, his eyes alight with satisfaction. "So our truffle hunter, at last . . ." he said in English. "And which of you is the prize?"

The commandant greeted Alfred. "Herr Professor."

In that instant Blum saw in a flash that everything was lost. The mission. Mendl. Leisa. All lost. His blood surging, he lunged for the colonel's pistol, trying to rip it from his hand. He knew it was a futile act. At any second, he would likely be shredded by machine gun fire. He knew he had cost his sister her life, just as he had tried so valiantly to save it. But still he leaped. He got his hands as far as grasping the colonel's gun, focused only on the fact that he would not go like his parents had gone, accepting and scared, when someone struck him in the back with a hard, blunt object and, knees buckling, he fell to the ground.

Leisa ran over to him and screamed, covering Nathan and shouting his name.

"Leisa, no, no . . ." Blum pleaded. He looked up at her with heartbreak in his eyes, knowing he had failed her. Failed them all.

"Ah, and our missing clarinet player as well . . . !" the commandant said. Leisa's cap was off her head now and she was totally exposed. "You can be sure you will be properly serenaded by your friends on your way to the gallows." He nodded and a guard struck her in the back with a rifle stock. With a whimper, she crumpled to the ground.

"*Leisa, no!* Don't hurt her. *Please!*" Blum reached out for her.

"And let us see who this is," the commandant said. A guard yanked Leo down from the truck.

"I'm sorry, young man," Mendl said as a guard dragged him down, pummeling the old man on the back and head with the stock of his gun.

"Alfred!" Leo ripped his arms free and ran to the old man and received a rifle butt across the head, sending him to the ground as well.

Blum was dragged up to his feet and squinted into the bright light. "Let her go," he said, not even able to make out the faces in front of him. "You have me. Please, let her go."

Then something firm and blunt made contact with the back of his head, and the sight of his sister being dragged away unconscious was flooded over by a wave of darkness.

SIXTY-FIVE

"In a faraway world . . ." Greta read to the barely conscious man on the cot who stared up blankly, "through the veil of mist you see an image of beauty . . ."

She came here and read most every afternoon. Today, after what Kurt had done earlier, she couldn't go home. As hard as it was to see the withering, disfigured shapes, more bones than flesh, many in their last throes of life, it was also one of the few places that made her feel whole. Made her believe in life again. To see a brief flicker of a smile or twinkle in the eye of someone on the edge of death, whose mind was now set free. She wasn't permitted to tend to the sick, since she wasn't a trained nurse, nor was it appropriate, Kurt insisted, for the wife of the Lagerkommandant to touch the Jews directly or, even more so, to try to mend them. So she did what she could.

Which was to speak soothingly to those who were dying, assure them that they weren't alone. No one should leave this world without someone holding their hand or sitting by their side. Once she smuggled in precious sulfanilamide to treat a patient with gangrene, which was generally a death sentence in here. And once, when a young female prisoner who tended the sick and kept her pregnancy hidden gave birth—in a state of abject fear, as it generally meant death for both mother and child, because Kurt would insist this wasn't a nursery, and bringing a Jewish life into the world was not worth the milk

343

it would take to feed it—she took the newborn baby and arranged for her housemaid, Hedda, to smuggle it out of camp. And she prayed with all the hope still in her that though she had not brought a child into the world herself, somewhere there was one still living because of her.

One against all who had died.

Mostly she just read. Rilke. Heine. Holderlin. Most of the people she sat by were already more corpse than living. Three days, and then they shipped you to the crematorium and your fate was sealed. But she knew they liked to hear the sound of a woman's voice, momentarily transporting them to a place of calm and rest. And as she helped a few let their final thoughts fly over the dark cloud and wire back to their homes and families, it made Greta feel, at least for a brief time, less trapped and alone herself.

Almost free.

"*Pani* . . . " the patient she was reading to reached out and touched her arm. His lips quivered. He indicated he would like a sip of water.

"Just rest. I'll be right back." She marked the place and got up to pour him a small cup.

That was when she heard the sound of the siren.

An unmistakable, repeating wail, penetrating the entire camp like a blade through the ears, designed to alert the guards in the case of an escape or emergency and to signal to the prisoners that a capture had been made, since no one ever got beyond the second row of electrified wire.

In her heart, she always cheered for those brave enough to try.

But now she feared, from what Kurt had told her, that they had found the intelligence officer's mole. It demoralized her that they had won again, just as Kurt had predicted.

Still, for just a second she hoped that maybe this time they hadn't won. Maybe this one time someone had made it free.

She put the cup of water to the patient's lips and let him drink, then she excused herself and went outside.

Guards were hurrying, weapons in hand, in the direction of the front gate.

"Rottenführer Langer," she called, seeing the corporal coming from that direction. "What is going on?"

"An attempted escape," he announced.

"*Escape* . . . ?" Then maybe the mole hadn't been caught yet. There was still hope.

"But do not worry, Frau Ackermann," Langer said, sarcasm showing through. "You will be pleased to know that it has not succeeded."

Pleased . . . She would have been pleased if anyone had made it beyond the wires, if only for a moment, to die there, as many did, just to end the misery for good. But whoever these escapees were, she knew they would not face such a quick death. "Excellent, Corporal," she replied, transparently enough that even a dull rod like Langer could see right through.

"But I think you will be particularly interested, Frau Ackermann, to know the identity of one of the escapees . . ." The Rottenführer's eyes lit up with kind of a gloating grin. "The young boy, I'm afraid," he clucked.

"*Boy* . . . ?" Her heart rose up in alarm.

"Your chess partner, Wolciek, Frau Ackermann."

"*Leo?*" Greta's blood stopped cold.

"I always knew the little prick had a devious side," the Rottenführer sniffed, "and with all the kindness you graciously bestowed on him. Anyway, you should make sure he didn't rob you blind before we put him out of his misery."

Leo.

Her heart felt like it was tied to a weight and cast into the sea. For a moment she thought that maybe Kurt had set it up himself. She knew how much he resented their intimacy. And what had he told her, *My hands are tied.* He could not protect him anymore. She knew he would do anything he could to hurt her. This was right up his alley.

Leo.

She felt shaken. He was a dead man now, she knew. Worse than dead. Kurt would always find something special for those caught trying to escape as a warning to any who harbored the same thoughts. And this one he would apply himself to with relish. How he would gloat later, with that repulsive, self-assured, I-told-you-from-the-start smirk. *"As I recall, Greta, I warned you not to open our house to a Jew and let your defenses down."*

"Yes, you are right," Greta said back to Langer. "I will check." Though inside her heart was torn at the devastating news. "And where have they taken him, Rottenführer?" she asked, though, of course, she knew.

"Where they are all taken, Frau Ackermann." Langer snorted with a cynical laugh. "To give them a fond welcome back to camp. Not to matter, by breakfast he will be on the gallows for all to see as they pass by. An example must be made of such vermin, do you not agree?" he asked. *He* who had dragged Leo visit after visit to her door and had been told to wait outside, who was now seemingly delighting in the pain he knew it caused her.

"Yes, Corporal." Greta nodded. "An example for certain."

The corporal excused himself with a smirk and hurried off, cackling inside. No doubt the entire guardhouse would be laughing over it within the hour. *An example,* he had said. Yes. An example indeed.

Greta headed back to her house. Leo was the only thing of goodness she had ever touched in here.

But for once the Rottenführer was right.

That is precisely what needed to be made of these people. *An example.*

SIXTY-SIX

Water was splashed on him. Blum came to. Suspended by the arms from hooks in a cell, his feet dragging the floor. It was dark. His arms ached. The cell stank of feces and urine. His head still felt fuzzy from the blow he had taken. He wanted to ask, "Where are they? *Leisa? Mendl?* What have you done with them?" But then he realized his mouth was taped. Two men stood in the cell in front of him. One he recognized as Sergeant Major Scharf. *Avoid that one, a born killer,* he'd been warned. The other was Zinchenko. He had no idea how much time had passed. Hours, maybe. The plane, it had likely come and gone by now. His only way out of here.

What did it matter now?

He would die here shortly anyhow.

"Herr Vrba." The German laughed, grabbing his wrist. "A22327. Welcome back. We had no idea how much you actually missed it here."

They took him down from where he was hanging.

"Excuse us, we have to pretty you up a bit for your interview. You're looking a little ragged," the SS sargeant said. Then he drove his fist into the pit of Blum's stomach, forcing whatever air was inside him from his lungs, doubling him over. Zinchenko picked him up and Scharf hit him again. Every cell in Blum's body screamed out in pain for air. He felt the urge to vomit. "This is only the start. Get used to

347

it, yid," the SS guard said. "We've got all night. For me, this isn't even work. It's pleasure." The next blow was to his kidneys. Paralyzing pain, rocketing through him.

Then they let him go and he crumpled to the soiled concrete floor.

Where was Leisa? Dead already, likely. They didn't need her, so why keep her around? All she was, was just another escaped prisoner. *Thousands die every day.* Someone had betrayed them. Josef, maybe, the partisan. Who knew? What did it even matter now? The mission was over. He was done. When they were ready they would do what they could to find why he was here. Torture him likely. This was child's play. Beat his heels. Stick wires in him. He didn't know if he could stand up to much abuse. And in the end, what did he really know? Not much. That's why they never told him the full picture, Strauss said. *In case . . .* In the case that he ended up just as he was now.

It was a suicide mission, they had all known it. From the start.

"C'mon, Jew, you've got people to see. Get your ass up." Scharf ripped the tape off his mouth.

Blum's thoughts went to the cyanide capsules sewn into his collar. *Bite,* Strauss had said. *It will do the trick.* In seconds. He had to believe it was still there. How had Strauss put it: *It might just be the best alternative, if you're captured . . .*

If he just clamped down on his collar and didn't have to go through the ordeal.

They dragged him out and down a row of cells, his legs unable to hold him. The light got slightly brighter—harshly emanating from an exposed bulb. At the end of a hall he saw a table. A German leaning on it. The intelligence colonel, he recognized. And Ackermann, the commandant, behind it in full dress as if he had an appointment with the Führer. Three wooden chairs in front. Two had bodies slumped in them, their arms fastened behind them. He saw they were Mendl and Leo. Faces bruised, puffy. They didn't look any better than he. Mendl particularly. His head was bowed; he was breathing very softly. Leo was doing his best to look brave, a welt on his face, but inside, Blum knew he must be shitting bricks.

Because *he* was.

"We've saved you a seat!" the intelligence colonel announced, his face brightening. "So glad you could make it, Herr Blum. That is your name, is it not? I did get to meet your sister. So sad not to hear her play."

"Where is she?" Blum looked up at him accusingly.

"Please, please, we'll get to that later," the colonel said. "In the meantime, let's focus on what we have here."

They threw Blum into the left-hand chair, twisted his arms behind it, and bound them with a rope. With seeming relish, Scharf pulled the knot as tight as he could. Blum looked toward Mendl and Leo. "I'm sorry," he said. He tried to suck needed breath into his lungs.

"No matter." Mendl drew in a labored breath himself and tried to smile. "I'm not sure my stomach was fit to have enjoyed the food on the outside anyway. It's Leo I'm actually sad about . . . My fault to include him from the start. And of course, your . . ."

Sister, he decided not to say. Who knew where she was or what fate she had already suffered?

"Don't listen to what he says," Leo said to Blum. "He's an old man. His head doesn't work right sometimes."

"Defiant to the end." Mendl smiled fondly at him. "Always did hold you back as a student."

"So, shall we get started?" the balding colonel said, his palms together as if announcing the commencement of a party.

"I want to know where my sister is," Blum said in German to the dark-featured commandant behind the table. He had a small riding whip in his hands.

"I would not worry about her right now." He shook his head. "Her fate, I'm afraid, is sealed. Only you can make it"—he tapped the whip in his palm—"more acceptable, if you understand what I mean."

"Tell me what you've done with her," Blum said again. "I want to see her."

"Do you now . . . ?" The commandant sniffed kind of grudgingly with a smile of amusement.

349

"I am Colonel Franke," the intelligence officer said, sitting down on the edge of the table, facing them. His gaze came to rest on Blum, soft, gray eyes both seemingly pleased that he had found his prey and at the same time calculating, calmly methodical. "I know you've only been in the camp a handful of days, but I think you have seen, and certainly your friends here can verify if you need, that Major Ackermann here is quite capable at a number of things, and one of them I have noticed is inflicting as much misery on a man as can be tolerated. He and his aide here, Hauptscharführer Scharf. Which is precisely what will happen, I assure you, if what we discuss is not fruitful."

The beefy sergeant looked at him with a smug gleam in his eye.

"Let me start with what we do know. You'll be interested to know I've been following your journey for a long time. We know you were dropped in on the morning of May twenty-third, three days ago. Your accent is very good, Herr Blum. You are Polish, I presume? Czech, maybe?"

"I want to see my sister," Blum demanded again.

"You'll soon tell us." Franke ignored his plea. "Or one of your associates here will, I assure you. I know you were picked up by the local underground and came into the camp as part of a construction team. The foreman of that team has, I'm afraid, met with a sudden work-related accident that has halted his construction career. His skull was bashed in. I know you were sent in here to locate someone within the camp, and it seems we have found him," the colonel tapped his finger on the table, "the professor here . . . and to take that person out. But to where, Herr Blum, if you don't mind? If you want to see that sister ever again. Back to England maybe? Your area of specialty was what, Professor Mendl? Mathematics? Physics . . . ?" He waited. "Not talking . . . ? No matter. We will soon know. And the others . . ." He turned to Leo. "How do you fit in, young man? I hear you are quite the chess prodigy. I used to play myself. It will be a shame not to have the challenge. No takers yet?" He nodded, smiling, as if unruffled and checked his watch. "Ten thirty . . . It is still early. We have all night. There is a lot that can be done to make someone talk when you have all night."

"Let's get on with it, Colonel." The commandant tapped his watch impatiently. "Enough talk. Hauptscharführer Scharf here is growing impatient. And so am I. These are my prisoners, not yours. We'll interrogate them as we please. But sadly, there is a train arriving shortly that will interfere. And, espionage aside, there is still a business here to manage."

"Go to your train, Herr Major. You will answer to Göring himself if what they know does not come out before your sergeant here bludgeons the life out of them. So who *are* you . . . ?" The colonel turned back to Blum. "Why Mendl? Why are *you* so important, old man, that someone would come into the den of hell here to get you out? And to where . . . ? And *you,* my young friend . . ." He turned to Leo. "You seem fond of the old man. Start talking, or I'll have the sergeant do his work on you if your friends here are too stupid to comply."

"We're dead anyway." Leo shrugged, meeting his gaze. "We were dead the day we walked through those gates. It was only a matter of when."

"Let them go," Blum said. "Leisa and the boy. Promise me as an officer they will not be harmed. And I will tell you what I know."

"Then start speaking, Herr Blum." The intelligence colonel got up and sat in front of him. "My car is outside. I can have them at the Romanian border in hours."

"No one is going anywhere," Mendl interrupted him, fighting to summon the breath to speak. "In fact, none of us will even be around tomorrow. Even if the colonel here gives you his word, the minute he leaves, they'll be a bullet in the back of their heads. Or maybe something far less 'acceptable . . .' Isn't that right, Herr Lagerkommandant? We are all already dead but the final blow."

"As I said, the choice is yours," Ackermann said, with a nod that indicated let's get on with this waste of time. "I say one by one we put them up on the rack, let Scharf have a go at them. In a minute, they'll be cackling like geese."

"You see, I can only save you for so long," Franke said. "Otherwise, what happens is out of my hands."

There was a noise at the door and a guard came in from the outside. "The train, Herr Lagerkommandant. You asked to be notified . . ."

Ackermann nodded. He drew in a breath. "Half an hour. An hour tops, I will be back." The commandant stood up. "No one leaves the block. No one goes anywhere. On my orders, understood, Scharf?"

"Of course, Herr Major." The sergeant came to attention. "Perfectly understood."

"*Kapo* Zinchenko, you can join me. And if you don't have what you need when I come back . . ." He glared at Franke. "We'll do it my way. And you, my little chess player," he turned to Leo with an icy smile, "when I return, you and I will have to have a much more personal discussion about just how you came in the possession of these . . ." He took out the photo of Greta Leo had taken and placed it on the table and put the white rook she had given him on top of it. He smiled. "I look forward to such a talk." He tossed his riding stick on the table and went out the door.

"You heard the man." Franke threw up his palms in frustration as if to say he no longer had control. "He has a very difficult job. Yet in some ways, he might be right. I've always been told I have too much patience. So what is it you know?" He came around the table and went up to Alfred. The old man's eyes were dropped and his mouth hung open slightly. "Why did they send this man in to find you? What do you know, Professor, that is so vital?"

"Just that the density of a gas is directly proportional to its mass," Mendl said with a slight smile. "Isn't that right, Leo?"

"Yes, Professor, it is," the boy replied. "At least, that is what I'm told."

"Very brave, very brave. Don't you think, Scharf? Such a show of daring. So you are the truffle . . ." Franke said to Mendl, taking his Luger from his holster and dangling it in his hand. "And that makes you the pig." He looked at Blum. "And you see what happens to little pigs in here, don't you?" He took hold of the gun and put it to Alfred's side. "Why did he come here to get you out?"

"If you think the prospect of a bullet frightens me after six months in here, you have greatly underestimated this rat's nest," Mendl said.

"Is that so, Professor?" Franke squeezed the trigger.

There was a dull report, the acrid smell of burnt fabric and flesh. With a groan, Alfred rocked back in his chair, a twisted grimace on his face.

Leo shouted, *"No!"*

A flower of blood spread on Alfred's uniform.

"The next one is to his kneecaps, boy. And then his balls. You know about the balls, don't you, son? If it doesn't bother him, I know it does you. So why the good professor here? I know you know. And where were you headed? Speak up, boy." He put the Mauser to Mendl's knee. "Only you can stop it."

"Don't." Mendl turned to Leo and shook his head. He looked at his side, blood matting against his uniform. "Do you hear me, Leo, don't."

"Yes, Leo, listen to him." Franke wrapped his finger tightly around the trigger. "What is your tolerance to watch him suffer, boy? You only have so much time. No answer . . ."

The colonel pulled the trigger again.

Mendl thrashed in his chair, the bindings holding him down. He arched his head back and writhed in pain. Blood ran from above the knee.

"Stop!" Leo begged.

"I say it again, son." The colonel took his pistol and drew it back one more time. He held it to where Alfred's legs joined. "I'll give you to the count of five . . ."

"No, lad," Mendl said, shaking his head. The color had drained from him. "Not one word."

"Two, *one,* boy . . ." Franke stiffened his hand on the gun. *"Now!"*

"He is a physicist!" Leo shouted. *"Stop!* Please! In electromagnetic chemistry. He has an expertise in a process called gaseous diffusion. It's about the displacement of gases inside an enclosed space."

"And why is that important?" Franke urged him. Again he pressed the muzzle to Alfred's groin. "I'll take him apart piece by piece, I promise. Why did he come here?" He motioned to Blum. "Who is behind it? The British? The Americans? Where were they taking him back to? Don't press me, boy, he only has so much time."

"Do it to *me*!" Leo twisted in his binds. "Leave him. Shoot *me*! Can't you see he's dying? Shoot me!"

"Last chance." Franke's gaze fell on Leo as he pulled back the pin.

"For God's sake, no," said Blum, straining to get out of his binds. The SS goon behind him came up and smacked his gloved fist heavily across Blum's head.

"He's taking him to America!" Leo shouted. "America."

"*America!*" Franke gasped, eyes wide.

"It's for a weapon. I'm sorry, Alfred, but I can't sit back and watch him just kill you. I'm sorry . . ." Leo looked at the colonel and began to sob. "Shoot me. You can shoot me. Can't you see you're killing him!"

Franke pulled back his gun. Blum could see his brain putting together that the stakes had now grown to something far larger than even he had first imagined. "What kind of weapon?" he said to Leo. "What *kind*?" This time he put the gun to Alfred's head. "Or I swear this is only the beginning of what you will see. Tell me, or I will splatter his brains all over your lap."

"I don't know! I don't know what kind! I swear. I don't know anything about the weapon. That's all he's told me. Just don't hurt him. I'm sorry, Alfred, but I can't watch them kill you like that. I can't . . . I can't . . ." The boy hung his head and wept.

"It's all right, son," Alfred muttered softly. He turned to Franke. "That's all he knows. You've gotten everything you can get." The flower of blood on his side had spread. "It's all I've told him."

Franke sat back down on the edge of the table, this time in front of Blum. "All right . . . So now it's you, truffle hunter. Your turn." He put the gun to Blum's knee. "Somehow I don't think anyone is going to rush to save you."

"Probably right," Blum said back to him. He bent his head to reach the two pills sewn into his collar. Strauss had said, even through the material, enough of the poison would get into his system to do the job. And why not now? There was no mission anymore. Leisa was likely dead; they all would be in a matter of hours. He lifted his shoulder up so his collar was close to his teeth. *Why not now?*

"Except there is one person . . ." the colonel said. He nodded to Scharf. "One person who still might persuade you. Bring her in."

SIXTY-SEVEN

They dragged Leisa in from the last cell and ripped the tape off her mouth. She sucked in air and cried out, "Nathan!"

It was hard to look at her. Her face was swollen; her eyes puffy and bruised. Staring at her, Blum was filled with sorrow. But all he could do was helplessly shake his head. "I'm so sorry."

"Nathan, don't be." Leisa looked at him, her eyes flooding with tears. "I'm only sorry you are here."

He smiled through the tears that streamed down his cheeks. Tears of anguish, powerlessness. He fought with his bindings, desperately trying to wrench his arms through the knots for what purpose he wasn't sure, almost ripping his right arm from its socket. "Do not ever touch her again," he seethed at Franke in German, "or I will find a way to end your life."

"You will, will you? Very daring, Herr Blum. You are quite the protector. And so very touching." The light reflected off the colonel's shiny brow. "Don't you think so, Sergeant Scharf?"

"I do, Colonel," the SS henchman chuckled, as if things were about to heat up very nicely for him.

Franke said, "I've heard about your little reunion at the wire. One question. Did you know your sister was here, or was it just providence that you found her while looking for the professor?"

Blum didn't reply.

"I assume the latter. All the more, it tugs at one's very heartstrings, right, Sergeant?"

"Indeed, it does, sir." The Hauptscharführer grinned amusedly.

"Well, now we'll see just how very touching it gets." Franke picked up his gun and softly ran the back of his hand across Leisa's face and neck.

Blum glared, his blood boiling over. "Leave her alone."

"Who ordered you to come here and locate the good professor? How were you planning on getting him back? First to England, I presume? Or maybe Sweden? Across land? Or is there a plane?"

"Professor, how are you holding up?" Leo asked, leaning across.

"Not so well, I regret . . ." Mendl's head sank back. It was clear the man was slowly dying.

"Don't you worry about him. Tell me about the bomb the lad was talking about." Franke sat over Blum, running the muzzle of the gun along Leisa's cheek. "I've heard of such things—heavy water, harnessing the power of the atom. How far along are the Allies in development? Cat got your tongue? Maybe I can loosen it just a little." He moved the Mauser to Leisa's head. "How will it be to watch her brains blow into your lap? Very messy, I think. Only you can stop it."

Leisa shook her head, tears flooding into her eyes. "Nathan, don't. Not a word. We're all dead anyway. Don't give him what he wants."

Blum screamed and struggled with everything he had to free his bound hands. Just to put them around Franke's neck, if God intervened for him, and then be bludgeoned by the bloodthirsty sergeant. She was right, they were all dead anyway. "I don't know what kind of bomb," he shouted. "Please! Let her alone."

"I wonder what it must be like to watch your sister die. The sister you so daringly rescued from the women's camp. And now to see her so close to death. And you are the only one who can save her. With just a word. Merely a squeeze of my finger and . . ." Franke tensed on the trigger.

"I swear, I don't know about the weapon!" Blum screamed, his eyes desperate and begging. "I was just sent here to get him out. That's all I know. I swear it."

Leisa met his gaze, imploringly. "Nathan, don't."

"Why *you*?" The colonel kept at him. Blum writhed in futility at the bindings. "Tell me, or she'll be dead in her next breath."

"Because I spoke the language. And looked the part. To fit in here."

"You are a Pole?"

He nodded. "Yes."

"And where did you come from prior to this mission? From England? The United States?"

"From the United States!" Blum looked at Leisa, shaking his head with despondency.

"*From America!*" Franke's eyes lit up. "America. And how did you get there?" He raised the gun again. "Don't go silent now . . ."

"I escaped from the ghetto in Krakow in 1941. I enlisted in the Army a year later."

Leisa looked at him, calmness replacing fear on her face. Suddenly he saw it. All the while, she had thought the opposite. Yet in this moment, with him unable to do anything to stop it, or save it, he saw, with her so willing to die, that she was stronger than he. She was beautiful. "Nathan, I release you from your vow," she said with a knowing smile. "It's okay now. It's okay to stop."

"So why did you come back?" Franke pressed. Blum's eyes stung with tears and he shook his head. "Whatever vow she is talking about, it can't be worth watching her die. You'd gotten out. You were safe. Why did you risk it all to come back? To find your sister?"

Nathan shook his head. "No. I thought she was dead."

"For your new country then . . . ?" Franke said. He kept the Mauser's muzzle pressed to Leisa's temple. She turned her head away.

"No." Blum shook his head. "Because I was ashamed. Ashamed I had gotten away." Blum looked at Leisa and his eyes filled with tears. "Because everyone else, my parents, and I thought my sister, were dead." His gaze settled on Franke. "Because I was the one who would go."

"See, they always talk. They want to play the big hero but they always talk." The intelligence officer smiled. "You wanted to avenge your parents' deaths. And so how do you feel now, Herr Blum, knowing what you've done has had just the opposite effect? That it has essentially gotten the person you loved most, who was alive, killed?"

"We would have all died anyway, *Myszka*." Leisa looked at Blum. "This only makes it quicker."

"How do I feel . . . ?" Blum said. In the distance he heard the sound of marching music. Ackermann's train disembarking. He smiled at her, bringing forth an image of her as a child, maybe just a glance or a mischievous wink while they were doing their lessons, and then looked back at the colonel. "I would do it again. In a heartbeat." He thought that maybe these would be the last words she would ever hear. "She is half of whoever I am. You cannot separate us. I would rather die with her than live, not knowing." Then he looked back at Franke and shrugged. "So how does that touch you?"

"Let me show you," the colonel said, and extended his arm at Leisa's temple.

He was distracted by the sound of the outside door opening. A woman came in. Pretty. In a patterned dress and a raincoat. Blond hair pulled back in a tight bun.

"Frau Ackermann!" Sergeant Scharf said in surprise.

Leo looked up.

"I have never been in here before," she said, scanning the room where such grave deeds were said to be done. "I've only heard . . ."

"Frau Ackermann, with all due respect, this is not the place for a woman." Franke put down his gun. "As such, I must ask you to—"

"I have something to say," she said. Her gaze turned to Leo, at first with a ray of affection as she noticed the photo and alabaster chess piece on the table, then just as quickly seemed to harden. "I treated you with respect. I gave you food, presents. I said I would watch out for you . . . And this is how you betray my trust."

Scharf, behind Leo, held back his smirk.

"These people are worthless, madame," Franke said. "Show them a little kindness and they behave like . . ."

She lifted her hand out of her sweater and removed a gun.

"*Frau Ackermann!*" Franke's eyes stretched wide. He took a step toward her.

Her hand was a bit shaky at first—it was clear she had never held a gun—but steadily she extended both arms and leveled the weapon directly at Leo, strapped into his chair. "I took you under my wing. I gave you hope. You shamed me." She pulled the hammer back.

"Madame, I'm sorry." Leo looked at her and hung his head, waiting.

"Don't be." Greta twisted her shoulders and shifted the gun toward Franke. He stared in shock. "They behave like *what*, Colonel . . . ?"

She fired, Franke's jaw opening in a bewildered, wordless reply, and a dark hole appeared between the Abwehr man's eyes. He dropped like a weight onto the floor.

His smirk erased, Scharf struggled at his waist for his own gun, and Greta fired twice into his chest, the impact hurtling him back against the wall, where he slowly sank, in a smear of his own blood, and slid to the floor.

At first there was only silence. The smell of lead and burnt flesh. For a moment, everyone was simply too stunned to fully comprehend what had just taken place.

"Quick," Greta said, "there is little time. The train will occupy them only for another few minutes." She ran over and undid Leo's bonds. "Do you have a way out?" She directed the question to Blum.

"Yes. I think so." Still a little stunned.

"Then you can change." She pointed to the intelligence officer's uniform. "His car is outside. There's a driver in it. But you must hurry."

"Nathan!" Leisa ran over and undid the knot that bound Blum's wrists.

Blum swung his arms out of the rope and threw them around Leisa, having thought he would never hold her again. Then he quickly ran over to Franke on the floor and did as Frau Ackermann suggested, unbuttoning the officer's gray jacket, pulling the dead man's arms through. They heard the far-off sound of music playing and the din of new arrivals on the train platform. People were no longer being separated to the left or to the right but all in one line, quickly processed, likely to their deaths, that very night.

Blum wished he could warn each one of them. But right now they were the best cover he could ask for.

As soon as Leo was free he hurried over to Mendl. The old man's face was white now. He had lost a lot of blood; the wound had bled completely through his striped tunic. Yet there was kind of a calm and clarity in his eyes even as his strength ebbed away. Blum flung on the German officer's jacket as Leo untied Mendl's arms. "Professor, please get up," he said. "You are coming with us."

"No." The old man shook his head. "It's too late now. I'm not going anywhere. You can see, I'm done."

"No, you are not done," Leo pleaded. "Not yet, Alfred. You must come."

Blum pulled off the dead man's boots and tore off his trousers. "I think you know more than anyone, sir, how much depends on it." He thrust his legs through the pant legs and pulled on the black boots, perhaps a size or two too large, but his feet went through without difficulty.

Leo tried to help his friend up. "Alfred, please . . . you must try. We can take you."

"No. I can't. I can't . . ." His breaths had now grown heavy and harder to draw. He looked to his side and put his hand there, and when he brought it back up his palm was smeared with blood. He shook his head forlornly. "I will only die on the way and slow you down. Let me stay."

"Impossible," Blum insisted, dressed in Franke's Abwehr uniform now. He didn't look like the colonel, of course. Not a stitch. He was half his age and with darker features. But at night, in the uniform, with his cap low on his brow—an instant was all they would need. "Get up, sir. I was sent by the president of the United States to bring you back, and as long as there is breath in you that's what I will do. You more than anyone know what is at stake in getting you out. I will carry you if I have to. It's only to the car."

"Blum, please . . ." The flower of blood had seeped wider on Mendl's side. There was only a resigned and fading glimmer left in his eyes. "I can't."

"*You must*! I will not leave you behind. Not after what we've risked to find you, Professor. Not now." Blum knew they had only seconds to

361

get out of there. Ackermann had said he'd be back in half an hour. That could be any time. Blum looked at the white-faced physicist, fearing with every passing moment that he would expire and all would be lost: the mission, his oath, Roosevelt's own voice sounding in his head, *Do not fail us,* not knowing what to do.

"I'm afraid God had in mind a different ending," Mendl huffed, giving the faintest smile. "But there is still a way . . ."

"*A way* . . . ? The only way is out that door, sir. What is it you mean?" Blum knew that in minutes the man he had risked his life for might well be dead.

"Leo," the professor said. He reached out his hand, almost blindly, and the boy grabbed it. Mendl looked at Blum. "He's not my nephew at all. I lied. I'm sorry, I know how it might have slowed us down, but it was for this very eventuality. The boy . . ." Mendl coughed, then winced, wiping blood off his lips with his sleeve. "He knows it all. Everything I know. Every proof. Every formula. On what it is you need. I've taught him it all these past months."

"You've taught him?" Blum stared at Leo, his mouth agape. "Is this for real?"

"Yes," the boy said. "But—"

"He has it all, Blum. Every bit." A flame flickered in Mendl's eyes that confirmed it. "Even more than if I gave you my own notes to take back with you. I give you my oath on this."

Blum turned to Leo. He didn't have a pad or a notebook with him. Not a thing. And nothing with him when they attempted to leave the camp. "How? *Where* . . . ?"

"Tell him, Leo," Alfred said with a smile, nodding. "Go ahead."

The boy tapped the side of his head. "In here."

"In your head?" Blum gaped and looked back at Mendl.

"Remember, I told you he was a remarkable young man . . ." the professor said, though each new breath seemed to take even more out of him. "He's as good as an encyclopedia with what he has in there. I knew it the second I met him. Trust me, Blum, what a joy it would be for me to go and reunite with some old friends; to present my work at last. But I would only slow you. You know as well as I do, none of us would make it then. So now go," he smiled weakly, then coughed, blood on his tongue, "you no longer need me."

"Quick, you must hurry," Greta said. "You hear the orchestra? The crowds are starting to move. Kurt will be back shortly."

"They're playing Beethoven's 'Ode to Joy,'" Leisa confirmed to Blum. "That means they are being moved off the platform."

Leo's eyes filled with tears. "Alfred, please, come . . . You must."

"No, son. It's your path to go, Leo, not mine. That's why God sent you to me. I see it now. It's the only thing of which I'm certain."

"I cannot leave you behind."

"Yes, you will, Leo. You must leave me. You promised you would. You owe me that oath."

Blum took Leo by the shoulders and peered into his eyes. "This is all true? You know this? Just as he says. Every bit of it? I need to know this with absolute certainty."

"Yes." He hesitated at first, then nodded with conviction. "I swear it."

"Then we must go. *Now*." He took Franke's Mauser from the floor. "Professor, I wish there was something I could say. God owes you a far better fate than simply for us to leave you here to die."

"My fate is in good hands," he said with a resolved smile. "My girls have been waiting for me a long time."

"And madame . . ." Blum turned to Greta. "There is room. Will you come?"

"Thank you." She shook her head. "But I will stay with him."

"Please, come . . . ," Leo said, imploring her. Everyone knew what fate awaited her upon her husband's return.

"No." Greta smiled at him. "The professor knows it correctly. It's not my fate either. And anyway, you may all need a few moments of diversion when my husband comes back here. So go."

Blum nodded. "Then whatever impelled you to do what you did for us, you have my heartfelt thanks."

"You must hurry." She looked deeply into Leo's eyes and put a hand on his cheek. "Go. The guards will be coming back from the platform any time. God watch over you."

"And you, madame," Blum said back. "Leisa, wrap yourself in that cloth." Blum pointed to a folded blanket on the floor. "Leo, you will follow behind me once I give you the signal that it's safe. You say his car is right outside?'

"Yes." Greta nodded. "When I came in, his driver was having a smoke."

"Well, let's hope that he's done with it and back in the car." Blum checked the Mauser. "Otherwise, his war is about to end and we'll have to make a run for it in the car as best we can. Leo, is there any chance you know how to drive?"

"No." He shook his head. "I don't."

"Me either, sadly. So let's both hope he's back in that car. Professor . . ."

Mendl didn't answer. His head was tilted, his mouth open, his lips white and crusted, muttering something. He was dying.

"*Alfred!*" Leo said, anguish tearing him inside. Again, he seemed unable to leave.

"Leo!" Blum grabbed onto his shoulder. "You have to leave him. It's time to go."

"I'll stay with him," Greta said. "He will not die alone. Your friend is right, you must leave without delay. But Leo . . ."

"Yes, Frau Ackermann . . ." Leo turned at the door.

"Greta." She smiled. "And you would not embarrass a lady to have so easily forgotten, would you . . . ?" She held out the photo of her in the boat he had taken along with the white chess piece. She went over and wrapped them in his hand and gave him a fond kiss on the cheek. "Good wins out, Leo. Every once in a while. Remember that. Even in here. So you make it, live out your life. If only just for me."

"I will, madame," he said, tears winding down his cheeks. "I will."

"Then go." Greta went back over to the professor and took his hand. "He needs to hear a soothing voice now."

"Thank you again," Blum said, and opened the cellblock door a few inches. He peered out. He saw the large car only a few yards away. It all looked clear. "Are you ready?" He glanced at Leo and Leisa. They both gave him a nod. *This was it, then.* He took one more look at Alfred and then smiled at Greta a last time. "To good, then. Seems as right as anything."

"Yes. To some good."

Blum drew the colonel's cap down over his eyes and stepped outside.

SIXTY-EIGHT

Luck *was* with them outside. No guards were visible. A huge din and the sheen of bright lights came from the direction of the train platform near the front gate. Franke's driver was in the front seat of a large Daimler sedan, the driver's door open.

"Come." Blum, holding Leisa in a blanket in his arms, waved to Leo.

The driver jumped out to open the door.

"Remain in the front," Blum snapped officiously in German. He had Franke's Mauser in his hand and was prepared to use it if the driver didn't comply. Fortunately, the intelligence colonel must have been enough of a taskmaster that the driver merely snapped back to attention, uttering, "Yes, Herr Colonel," and remained behind the wheel.

Blum twisted the latch on the Daimler's trunk and a large hatch opened. He tucked Leisa inside. "Now." He looked around and waved Leo out of the door. The boy ran out and climbed in the trunk as well. Blum told them, "Stay quiet. I will get you both out when we are safely away."

He shut the latch and came around the side. "Start the engine," he barked, climbing in the backseat, the colonel's Abwehr cap pulled low. "We head back tonight. Let's go."

366

The driver turned around. "Back to Warsaw, Herr Colonel . . . ?" It was already close to midnight and it was a many-hour drive.

His eyes widened in shock.

Blum had the Mauser at his face. "If you want to live, you'll just drive. Once we are past the gates, I will let you out. But if you say one word or give even the slightest signal that something is wrong, that will be the last thing you ever do. Are we understood?"

The driver, a corporal in a gray Abwehr uniform and soft, peaked cap, at most a couple of years older than Blum, nodded and turned back around. "Yes, sir, I understand." He turned the key and the Daimler's engine rumbled to life.

"Keep both hands on the wheel so I can see them. And as you can hear, Corporal, my German is perfect, so no games. Be assured my gun is at the back of your head."

"Yes, Colonel." The driver nodded nervously.

"Drive."

He turned the car around and headed slowly back toward the main gate. No one seemed to take notice or come after them. Blum could see guards in the watchtowers behind machine guns, but their attention seemed directed toward the tracks, not the fancy officer's car below. There was a lot of activity ahead as the train had let off its cargo. Floodlights glaring, music playing. A festive Slavic dance. Guards barking orders. Blum could see a huge crowd, thousands, like a black wave, congested on the railway platform.

Likely none of them would be alive to see the light of the next day.

"Stop at the gate, as normal," Blum instructed. His heartbeat began to pick up. He saw two or three guards manning the entrance. "And let me say again, one wrong word and it will be the last breath you ever take."

"Yes. I hear you." The driver nodded.

"Good."

They slowed on the brick approach and pulled up to the front gate, the very one Blum had been brought through three days earlier. The clock on the tower read twelve oh eight. Another hour and a half or so until the plane was scheduled to land. *If* it would still land. Blum suddenly pushed back a tremor of concern, thinking how he and Mendl would not be there at the river as planned when the attack took place, twenty minutes from now. A guard stepped out of the guardhouse and came up to the Daimler. The driver rolled down his window. Blum pulled the action back on the Mauser so the driver could hear it. "Remember, I'm listening to every word."

"Leaving so late?" the gate guard asked, with a look around the car.

"Back to Warsaw," the driver said. "Urgent business, I'm afraid."

"Herr Colonel . . ." the guard acknowledged, perfunctorily peering in the back.

Blum, sitting deep in the darkness of the rear seat, gave him a wave in return. The gun was hidden by the colonel's greatcoat draped over his arm.

His heart almost beat out of his chest.

"Well, watch out for the fog, then," the guard said, and signaled the guardhouse. "It gets bad in the valley at night."

"I will. Thanks," the driver replied. The gate slowly rose and the guard stepped away.

Blum let out a deep exhale.

The Daimler pulled ahead. As they passed through, Blum glanced behind and watched the guard take his place back in the guardhouse. The gate lowered again. His heart began to resume its normal cadence.

He had spent three days inside the worst hell on this earth.

And now they were free.

SIXTY-NINE

Ackermann knew something was wrong as soon as he and Fromm approached the cellblock.

Whistles sounded. Guards were running all around, shouting. Lieutenant Kessler stood ashen in the doorway and came to attention as he approached.

"What has happened?" the Lagerkommandant asked, a nervous feeling grinding at his belly.

Kessler just motioned inside.

Ackermann stepped in. His jaw tightened sharply as he took a look around.

Franke was dead. *Impossible*. On the floor. A dark hole in his forehead. His eyes as wide as a two reichsmark coin.

And Scharf . . . He was sitting upright against the wall, looking as startled as a man can appear, two red holes in his chest and a trail of blood smeared where his body had slid.

Greta turned to him. In a blue print dress and raincoat. She was holding a gun.

"What's gone on here?" he said, aghast, though the answer was irrevocably clear.

"They're gone, Kurt. That what's gone on." Greta smiled, though not with humor. "Your precious mole. His sister. Oh, and my little

369

chess player. All gone. The professor . . ." Mendl sat in the chair with his head back, eyes blinking at long intervals, a large bloodstain on his stripes, muttering something. "He stayed with me."

"What the hell is he saying?" Ackermann asked, not sure why he cared.

"He's speaking German, Kurt. You should understand. Something about '*Ist das wirklich so?*'"

"Is that really so?" Ackermann said, bewildered.

"Maybe he's as amazed as you are, Kurt, at what he sees."

"Greta, put down the gun. Please."

"No, Kurt. I won't." Instead, she raised it at him.

Fromm went for his pistol, but Ackermann held his arm.

"I could kill you as well, Kurt. But why would that even matter now?" There was pleasure in her eyes and voice. "Your career is done. Everything you worked so hard for. All your precious numbers. And I don't even need to pull the trigger. You're already dead. As dead to them now as you are to me. Dead to everyone."

Ackermann stared at her in horror and then slowly looked around. "Greta, what have you done?"

"What have *I* done?" She laughed. "The question is, Kurt, what is it *you* have done? What have you all done? They were people. Your precious numbers . . . Not digits, Kurt. They were mothers. Husbands. Little children. They had lives. Hopes. Just like we did once. People."

"I did what I had to, Greta. If not me, someone else." He took a step forward. "Fromm, go sound the alarm. I want those three brought back now."

"Yes, Herr Lagerkommandant." The aide slowly backed away to the door, aware of the gun in Greta's hands, which never shifted from her husband's chest. He hurried out.

"We're going to catch them, Greta. It will all be for naught. We'll catch them, and you already know what we will do to them. Now put down the gun."

"I'm afraid I can't, Kurt. It's too late. We both know that. Not now.

And one last, little thing, my darling husband . . . something you should know."

"What is that, Greta?" He looked at her, rage building up in him. She was right. His career was ruined. Their lives. What else was there?

"You were right. I did fuck the little Jew."

The Lagerkommandant's jaw twitched in anger.

"I let him do to me willingly what you had to force on me."

He gritted his teeth. "Greta, give me the gun."

The old man had stopped muttering. His head hung to the side. His mouth was open. But his eyes seemed clear. A last, deep exhalation came out of him.

He was gone.

"I think I know what he means, Kurt. *Ist das wirklich so?* Anyone who has lived in this hell would know. I think he sees his wife and daughter. As I now see something . . ."

"What do you see, Greta?"

"I see beyond this. You still have to believe in something. Even in this hell, right?"

"And what do you believe in, Greta?"

"What do I believe in . . . ?" She smiled at him thinly. "I believe in the sky, Kurt. The big blue vastness of the sky."

"Greta!"

She raised the gun to her head and squeezed the trigger.

After Greta's body slumped to the floor, she was able to lift herself up. She no longer felt bound by a place of ugliness and death. She walked right by Kurt, still staring in horror and disbelief, as if she wasn't there. The door was open. She went past the barracks, one after another, in their geometric sameness, and the grim, red-bricked crematorium. Guards running around. Past the bitter smell and the heavy cloud that always hung so low you could never see the blue behind it, even on clear days.

But now she could see the sky. Infinite and beautiful. She could see stars, galaxies. She could see all the way to a faraway place she had read about. Of grass and rivers and beauty. It all seemed so close, just up ahead of her. It made her smile. Through the mist. It was always just an arm's reach away, she thought. Always so close.

Just beyond the wire.

SEVENTY

"Head for the town of Rajsko," Blum told the driver as soon as they were clear of the camp. The road sign said it was to the southeast, twelve kilometers. "Remember, there's still a gun to your head."

"Please," the young driver said. "I'll do what you say. Just don't shoot me. I was just married four months ago."

"Then just drive. And two hands on the wheel. At all times."

The drop location had been a field three kilometers south of the hamlet of Wilczkowice, and the landing site was on a farm road cleared just enough to accommodate the Mosquito a quarter mile to the north. Josef had pointed it out when he picked Blum up.

"What time do you have?" he asked the driver.

"Time? Zero zero fifteen hours, sir," he answered, glancing behind.

The attack on the work crew was set to take place in fifteen minutes. The plane was well on the way. But when there would be no one at the river, Blum's fears now turned to whether it would even land at all. He only prayed there would still be people at the landing site. They had to clear the field and light the way. They would be in radio contact with the plane.

Now he just had to locate the site.

"What is the mileage, Corporal? On the odometer."

373

"The mileage? Seventy-eight four two nine," he read.

"Seventy-eight four two nine," Blum repeated. "Thank you." For the first time he sat back.

The road was dark; after midnight there was almost no one on it. He wondered how much of a head start they had until they were discovered. Until Greta Ackermann was discovered. At first the Germans wouldn't know for certain which direction they had taken. But they likely had checkpoints at each town, and, in a fancy Daimler, they would be spotted in a flash.

"Hit the lights," Blum ordered the driver.

"But, sir, the road is dark. It's dangerous."

"Trust me, not as dangerous as if you don't." Blum put the gun to the back of the driver's head. "Hit the lights."

The driver switched off the headlights.

Blum's thoughts went to Mendl and Ackermann's wife. He was probably dead by now; and she, who knew. He only prayed that what the professor said was true. That all he knew was safely locked away in Leo's brain. Everything depended on that now.

Rajsko, three kilometers.

"Slow down. We'll be making a left-hand turn up ahead."

"A left? I thought you said you wanted to go to Rajsko."

"There'll be a kind of mill on the right-hand side, and there should be a dirt road on the left. Take it. Go slow, or you'll pass it." It was one of the back roads Josef had taken to avoid detection on his way to Brzezinka the night Blum arrived.

Up ahead, he suddenly saw headlights in the distance coming toward them. "Quick, pull off the road now."

"Here, sir?"

"*Now!* In this gully to the right." Blum put his gun to the driver's head again. "And don't even think of flashing your lights as they pass unless you want to make that new wife of yours a war widow."

"Yes, sir." The driver nodded. He swung the Daimler, its lights off now, into a clearing to the side of the road. The oncoming headlights grew brighter. Blum saw that it was a truck. Heading toward the camp. As it passed, his heart stood completely still. He leaned forward, the gun at the driver's head.

"Not a move."

As it passed, Blum saw it was a troop truck—*filled*. He knew there was a detachment in Rajsko. So likely the word had gotten out. He held his breath as he watched the truck pass by and keep on going, its taillights fading into the night.

Blum let out a breath. "Okay, let's get going again. And keep your eyes out for that turnoff."

They found the road and skirted the sleeping town. It wound past dark farms and cottages, their inhabitants asleep. The road was rutted and uneven, fit more for a farm truck or a tractor than a heavy Daimler built for cruising. He felt bad for what Leisa and Leo must be going through in the hatch.

Finally it let them out onto the main road again.

"Which way now?" the corporal asked.

"Left. Toward Wilczkowice."

The driver took the turn, and for a few kilometers the only vehicle they came upon was a chemical truck heading east, likely for the IG Farben facility. Blum searched for anything even remotely familiar. There was nothing, but, to his joy, a couple of miles down they came up on the train crossing where the guards had stopped him and Josef three nights ago, now deserted and quiet. Blum knew he was on the right path. But now was where it began to get tricky. He, Josef, and Anja had been talking, and he hadn't paid attention to the way. It never occurred to him he'd need to find his way back. He knew he was looking for a back road, unpaved, off the main thoroughfare. *But where?* He passed a farm with a conical silo. Yes, he thought maybe he'd seen that before. Perhaps. "Keep going."

Farther along, they passed a darkened farm road blocked by a fence. "*Stop!*"

The driver applied the brakes.

"What is the mileage now?" Blum asked. "On the odometer?"

"Seventy-eight four fifty-one," the driver read off.

They had driven twenty-two kilometers. *Fifteen miles.*

This had to be the road.

"Get out, and pull back that gate," Blum instructed him. "Make one move to run and I'll shoot you in the back. I don't need you now."

"I won't. Don't. Please."

"Hand me your gun."

"I don't carry a gun," the driver said. "I'm only a mechanic. See . . ." He lifted up his jacket. As he said, there was no gun strapped to his belt.

"Okay, then quickly." Blum stepped out of the car with him. "The gate should unlatch."

The corporal ran over, fumbled with the lock for a few seconds, then finally threw open the gate, all the time Blum keeping his gun trained on him. It was pitch dark. Blum wasn't 100 percent sure about the road. But the gate had to be the one Josef had flung open on their way to Brzezinka. They hadn't passed another that fit. And the mileage seemed correct.

"Now go back and open the hatch," Blum instructed him.

"Okay," the driver said, his palms raised to his shoulders. "Just don't shoot." He opened the trunk of the car. Leo and Leisa peeked their heads out, uncertain.

"Where the hell are we?" Leo inquired.

"Close to where we need to be. Climb on out."

Leisa looked around. "Is everything all right, Nathan? Do you know where we are?"

Blum gave her a positive wink to convey it was all okay.

"What do we do with him?" Leo said, speaking of the driver, who was starting to look at them with an anxious concern.

"We'll decide. For now, climb in. Leo, you're in front."

They continued down the dark road, headlights on now. Blum focused at every stretch and turn, trying to find something that looked familiar to him. A barn. A farm gate. A sign.

Nothing.

"What's the time?" he asked the driver again.

"Zero zero forty," he said. *Fifty minutes to landing.* If they missed the plane, it didn't matter if they were right or wrong. Or where they were. They had no other way to get home. There was the safe house back in Rajsko, but that would entail driving around in a vehicle every Nazi in Poland probably knew of by now. Plus, their escape plan had been infiltrated, that was clear. Who knew if the "safe" house was even still safe?

They suddenly came to a fork.

The driver turned around. "Which way?"

Three kilometers west of Wilczkowice, Josef had said. "That way," Blum said, pointing left.

Here, the road seemed to wind along a ridge of dense trees.

"How will the plane even land?" Leisa asked, looking around. "It's all forest here."

"Hush!" Blum cautioned. He saw the driver's head turn.

"Are you sure of where you are?" Leo questioned from the front.

"I don't quite have your memory," Blum said tersely, "but it is somewhere near."

He damn well prayed it was.

They continued on, another mile or two. The night was so thick and dark they could see nothing but the glare of their own headlights and bugs smacking against the windshield, virtually blinding them. The Daimler bumped along the uneven path. A rabbit ran across in front of them. The driver stopped for it. Then a fence of wire blocking in a field that Blum thought perhaps he had seen before. Then a house in the distance, a dog barking. A hand-scrawled sign: NIE WCHODZIC NA POLA. *Keep off the fields.*

His heart picked up. He was sure this was near where he had landed. "Pull up here."

The Daimler came to a stop.

"This is it?" Leo looked around doubtfully. There was nothing. Nothing but fenced-in fields and more woods.

"It's close enough. Everyone get out."

There wasn't a light or a landmark to fix on anywhere. Blum estimated they had driven at least two miles from the main road. The nearest dwelling was at least several hundred yards away.

The driver looked at them nervously, his hands raised.

"Now what?" Leo turned to Blum, questioning.

Blum looked at the driver. "Now we deal with him."

SEVENTY-ONE

"Give me your watch," Blum instructed the driver.

"It belonged to my father," the German protested.

"My apologies to him then. Mine was shot by the Nazis." Blum waved his gun at him. "Come on now."

The driver took the watch off and handed it over. It was ten of one. Forty minutes now. *If* the plane was still set to land. The attack would have already taken place on the camp work detail and the partisans would know that no one had come to meet them.

Blum's heart raced anxiously. He didn't see a sign of anyone around.

"So? What do we do with him?" Leo finally asked.

"He says he's just a mechanic," Blum said.

"I am," the driver insisted, overhearing the word "mechanic," which was the same in Polish. He was maybe a year or two older than Blum, no more. With a new wife. If he was being truthful. His eyes kept flitting around, maybe searching for an escape route to take off on, if it became necessary.

"Well, he's heard things," Leo said. "And mechanic or not, he's still got that eagle on his chest." He pointed to his Abwehr insignia.

"It's just a uniform," the driver pleaded to Blum, needing no translation. "I was drafted."

"You two go on ahead." Blum pointed to a dark clump of trees a couple of hundred yards away. "Wait there. I'll take care of him."

"You have to kill him," Leo said in Polish. "Or else he'll alert them all."

"Maybe it's just as he said," Leisa said, coming to the driver's defense.

Blum nodded. "You both go on. I'll catch up in a while."

The driver was trying to figure out just what was being said and didn't seem to like what he was hearing.

Leo and Leisa started off through the deep grass toward the trees. Blum waited until they were fully out of sight.

"Please, I won't tell anyone," the German pleaded, sensing what was happening. "I'm only a mechanic. They ordered me to make this drive. The uniform means nothing to me. They make me wear it. I don't believe in what they do."

"Just walk." Blum motioned with the gun. There was a spot of high grass under a tree. "Over there."

"Please, I did what you asked. You said you would let me go. I won't tell a soul. I promise," he begged nervously.

"You heard about the plane."

"I didn't hear a thing. What plane? I don't speak a word of Polish. My wife's expecting in three months. Don't shoot me. Please . . ."

"I'm sorry. Bad things happen in war. No one told you? Move over there." The driver took a step back. Blum knew what the right thing was to do. He remembered what Strauss and Kendry had asked him back in England, "Can you kill?"

I'm a soldier. Of course I can kill.

"On this mission it may mean the difference between life and death. You will have to do far worse than kill a cat."

So do it then. Now.

The driver stood there, fear pooling in his eyes.

Blum said, "The Nazis murdered my father and my mother simply because they were near where one of their own was gunned down." He tightened his finger on the trigger.

"I didn't do that," the corporal pleaded. He looked into Blum's eyes. "Please."

"Take a step back."

The driver swallowed fearfully and did as he was told.

Blum wanted to shoot him. For his father and mother's sake. For all the pain and monumental suffering he'd witnessed in the past three days. For all of that, it felt fitting to hold this gun and watch a fucking *szkop* German, a moment or two from execution, begging, as anyone might, as thousands of Jews must have begged already, for his life.

Blum pointed the Mauser at the driver's chest.

Now.

Instead, he lowered the gun. "Go on. Get the hell out of here."

The driver looked back in bewilderment.

"Go on! And remember that it's a Jew who gave you back your life when I could have taken it. Do something good with it. That's in the Talmud."

"Yes." The corporal grinned and nodded, grateful for his stroke of luck. "I promise. I will."

"Get in those woods over there and remain there until we are gone." Blum waved the gun at him. "Or I'll change my mind."

"Yes. Of course. Don't worry, I will."

He calculated it would be at least two miles on a dark truck path back to the main road to flag down a vehicle. And if he ran to some farm house, all the way out here, unarmed . . . Who could be sure where any farmer's loyalties would lie? *"Go!"*

"Yes. Thank you," the young corporal said, nodding. "Thank you," he said again. He trudged off, looking back once, picking up his pace, and disappeared into the brush.

Blum fired a shot into the ground. Then another.

Then he hurried back through the high grass to where Leo and Leisa were waiting.

"Did you do it?" Leo asked.

Blum nodded grimly.

"It was the right move. And *now* . . . ?" Leo looked at him doubtfully.

One a.m. He wasn't sure if he had made the right decision letting the driver go. But the plane would be there in half an hour. Too soon, Blum was sure, for the man to make his way back and find his countrymen.

A quarter mile southeast of the drop site.

Blum pointed in that direction. "Now we go on foot."

SEVENTY-TWO

At Newcastle, Peter Strauss leaned over a radio operator who was communicating with the Polish resistance.

"Truffle Hunter One to Katya," the radioman said in Polish to their contact on the ground. "Please confirm that you have our delivery. The truck is close by."

The Mosquito had left three hours ago. It had maintained radio silence for most of the journey, but now, according to the timetable, it was deep inside Poland and approaching the landing site.

If it all went well, Blum should be on that plane with Mendl in half an hour.

Strauss wasn't a religious man. Law school and the bitter war had long cured him of that luxury. His father, the cantor, hardly recognized the secular man with two young kids who ran around in Yankee caps—not even Dodgers!—and barely knew the meaning of the High Holy Days. Nonetheless, Strauss felt himself praying a bit tonight. A year had been spent trying to get this one man out of Europe. A year in which operatives had died; where they were blocked at every turn. In which hope had turned to despair at least a dozen times.

And now, at last, they were within minutes. "As close as Exodus is to Genesis," the cantor would say. Every cell in his body seemed to be at attention. Strauss had gone through six cigarettes in just the

383

last hour. The attack on the work detail outside the camp would have already taken place. He should be hearing from those on the ground at any second. If they had them, if Blum and Mendl were safely in their hands, all that was left to do was land.

"*Anything . . . ?*" he pressed the operator, searching for any sign of contact.

"Nothing yet, sir."

"Just keep trying."

"Truffle Hunter One to Katya. The truck is in the neighborhood. Let us know if you have our goods."

0010.

"*To Katya,*" the scratchy voice finally came back in Polish. *This is Katya.*

"I have contact, sir!" the operator said. "Katya, the trucker wants to know if you have our delivery."

"*Negacja,*" the voice came back. Negative. "No truffles. Only beets today, I'm afraid."

The radioman didn't even have to translate. *Beets.* That was the predetermined response if the escape didn't go as planned.

Strauss's stomach plummeted. It should all have happened close to an hour ago. He checked his watch, though in the past ten minutes he had checked it five times.

Fucking beets.

He sat on the edge of the radio table.

"I'm sorry, sir. Do we still land?" the radioman asked him. "The pilot wants to know."

Do they still land? What was the point of risking a plane and its crew in the middle of occupied Poland if their "cargo" was not there to be picked up. On the slim hope that they had managed some other way out? Be real, there was no hope. It was a year—a year of planning, every detail, every possibility, wasted. And Blum . . . Strauss muttered a prayer in Hebrew. He'd had the highest hopes. God bless him. God bless us all, he said, for what he'd done. He blew out a disgusted breath and rubbed his brow.

"Sir, the pilot is asking if they should still land?" The radio operator turned around.

Strauss had an urge to say, *Yes, Goddamnit, do it anyway. Land.* A flicker of hope had still burned. Blum was a resourceful man.

"Call it off," he said. He put the headset down. He looked at his watch. "Have them remain in the area until the extraction time, and then head back."

It was suicide from its conception, Strauss ackowledged to himself. Donovan had said that. They all had. A one-way mission from the start. He prayed that Blum was somehow okay, even if he hadn't made it out. Spending the war in that camp. He just plain liked the bastard, and admired his courage. But the cold truth of it was, they would likely never know.

"Get me OSS headquarters in D.C.," Strauss told the operator after he'd delivered his message to the plane. Donovan.

The president had asked to be informed about the mission.

He should know the bad news.

SEVENTY-THREE

The three of them thrashed through the woods and dense brush in the direction Blum was certain Josef had pointed to him where the plane was set to land.

It was dark; only the moon lit their way. Leisa and Leo's feet were bare. They stayed out of sight as best they could. As they hiked, Blum prayed over and over that the hope he still clung to that the plane would come was not futile and that the landing site was somewhere close. He knew someone had given them up; that much was clear. Was it Josef? Or the foreman, Macak? Or even Anja? And how much of the plan had that person divulged? Blum realized that if the partisans' attack on the work column had taken place as planned, what would they think now except that he and Mendl had not made it. That he was either dead or captured. What then? Who knew if they had already radioed that information back? If the plane would even come now as planned? Or if it had turned around and was on its way back to England.

If there was anyone even ahead of them to meet them here?

"Are you sure we're right?" Leo looked back, exasperation on his face as if they were traipsing around on a wild goose chase.

"Yes, it's just through the next fields," Blum said. "I'm sure."

He had to believe himself.

And what if it didn't come? The plane. And there was no one to meet them. Blum remembered the safe house in Brzezinka . . . That option was now likely completely lost. It was miles away. Every checkpoint in the area would be searching for Franke's Daimler. Soon the woods would be littered with Germans. There would be no way they could ever reach the town on foot.

Blum knew it was this or nothing. "Keep going," he exhorted them, as if trying to convince himself as well.

"Nathan, can we rest a moment?" Leisa asked, trying to catch her breath. Her bare feet were cut and sore.

He checked the watch. It was 0110 now. Twenty minutes to landing. Nothing looked familiar. No sign of anyone around to meet them. The only light they had to guide them was the bright, full moon.

Maybe the next field.

"No, we have to go on. Here, let me help, Leisa. I'll carry you."

"No, I'll make it," she said, continuing on ahead.

"You remember how we used to play hide-and-seek in the fields at our country house?" He tried to take her mind off of their situation.

"Yes, but that was always during the day. And there was our little cousin, Janusz, who always gave your hiding places away."

"You had to bribe him with cakes to shut him up, otherwise you were a dead duck."

Lesia giggled. "What a brat. No wonder he became such a little tubby."

"Yes, I think he and that cat, Phoebe, were in cahoots and—"

They heard a sound. Coming from behind them. Even Leo turned. Blum's heart stood still.

It was dogs. Barking. Not the kind of dog who was watching over a farm and roused at night.

Multiple dogs. The sound was far off, but clear. Coming from behind them.

"Stop!" Blum said, grabbing Leisa's arm. He put out his palms for them to be still.

In the distance, there were voices too. A shout.

"*Shit.*" It had to be. The Germans were after them.

"How could they be here so soon?" Leisa said in a forlorn voice that conveyed, *What hope was there now?*

"I don't know. I don't know . . ." Blum shook his head, unsure. Could it have been the driver? So quickly? Leo was right, of course. He should have shot the little bastard for sure. It had been wrong to let him go.

Or maybe whoever had given them up to begin with had also given up the landing site.

What did it even matter? They were behind them now. Maybe half a mile.

"Run!" He took Leisa's hand and sprinted through the high field. "It's up here, I'm sure of it," Blum urged them farther on. *A quarter mile southeast from the drop site.* It had to be around here. But he wasn't supposed to get them to the spot—the partisans were. So it was all unfamiliar.

They ran until they were almost out of breath.

"Where the hell are we going, Nathan?" Leisa finally said in exhaustion. "We'll never outrun them."

"They're only minutes behind," Leo said. "By the time we—"

Suddenly he stumbled and let out a shout. Ten feet ahead of them, he had tripped over something and landed on his side. "What the hell is this?"

He held something up.

"It's a lantern," Blum said. Unlit.

"Here's another," Leo said, crawling a few feet away. "And one more."

Then Blum came upon one, running up ahead.

There were dozens of them. In two parallel lines. Set at ten-meter intervals.

"It must be a road of some kind," Leo said. Dirt, of course. Cleared out of the uneven field. Bumpy. It seemed to stretch on for quite a ways. Wide enough for a truck or a tractor. *Or a . . .*

They looked at each other with joy and realized they had found it.

"Good lord, it's the landing site!" Blum said. It had to be.

He looked at his watch. They'd made it! *Fifteen minutes to the plane.*

Blum spun around and wanted to cheer in with elation, but the Germans were only minutes behind them. "Now we have to—"

As if out of nowhere a hand wrapped around his mouth, yanking back his head. A knife went to his throat. "*Nie ruszaj sie,*" someone whispered in Polish. *Don't make a move.*

People came out of the dark woods holding guns.

Leo and Leisa put their hands in the air.

"How are you fucking here?" the man with the knife hissed in Blum's ear.

"We escaped. From the camp. We've brought you truffles," he said, using the code word he had used with Josef. "I've come a long way . . ."

The person released his neck. Blum spun around to face a bearded man in a hunting jacket and cap. He put his knife in his belt.

And Anja. The girl who had picked him up with Josef. Her blond curls coming out of a knit hat. Holding her Blyskawica submachine gun.

"Where's Josef?" Blum asked.

"Josef's dead."

"*Dead?*"

"He was picked up. By the Germans. We assumed you gave him up."

"Me? Not a chance. Never."

"Then why were you not on the work detail as planned?" the bearded man demanded. "We went through with the ambush. No one was there."

"We tried. We were all caught at the gate. Someone gave *us* up. They threw us in a cell."

"It was a trap," spat the man in the beard, who seemed to be the leader. A cadre of ten others dressed in dark clothing came out of the trees and brush. "We lost six good fighters."

"A trap . . . ?"

"They were waiting for us. What happened to the old man? You were supposed to just be two."

389

"He didn't make it. It's just us," Blum said. "But the mission is still alive."

The leader looked at them, suspicion and resentment flickering in his gaze. He stared contemptuously at Leo. "I hope, whoever the fuck you are, it was worth the life of our friend Josef. He killed a lot of Germans."

"What about the plane?" Blum asked them. "The Germans are right behind us."

"We'll handle the Germans this time." He signaled to his men in the woods, and they began to spread out in the brush. "And as for the plane . . . ? Lucjan, bring me the radio again. Truth is, we didn't think we'd be seeing anyone here. I need to call back your ride."

Strauss had no sooner started to contact Donovan to deliver the bad news when the radio operator grabbed his arm. "You may want to hold a second, sir. There's another transmission coming in."

"Truffle Hunter One. Katya here . . ." The operator translated the Polish. "You'll be pleased to know that we have your truffles after all. Three big ones. Ready to be picked up. Come get them, as planned. And fast, please, as there are other buyers nearby."

We have your truffles. Come get them!

"We're back on!" Strauss shouted, seizing the operator by the shoulders, almost knocking his headphones off. He grabbed hold of the mic and contacted the circling plane himself. "Water Dog One, Water Dog One, we're back on! Repeat, they are there. Get down and get them as fast as you can. And you may have some excitement on the ground. We're back on as planned!"

The Mosquito copilot came back scratchily. "Roger. Going in now."

Strauss sat back. Elation coursed through him. He was reserved by nature, a cantor's son, but he made no attempt to hold back at all. "Cancel that call to Donovan," he said to the operator, slamming the table, papers flying onto the floor. "We're back on! They're there!"

390

However the hell Blum had done it, they were there!

Then he stopped and for the first time thought on what the parti-san leader had just told them. He sat down on the edge of the table and muttered, quizzically, wrinkling his brow, *"Three . . . ?"*

SEVENTY-FOUR

They hid in the woods while the band of partisans disappeared into their cover. Anja and another ran out into the field and lit the lanterns.

In minutes, the landing strip became clear.

Now all Blum had to do was pray they could hold the Germans at bay.

Five minutes.

"The plane is in the area," Janusz, the partisan leader, said. "Unfortunately, it looks as if we'll have a local welcoming committee as well."

The yelps of the search dogs could be heard advancing through the dark fields, closer than just minutes before. Shouts in German. Lights flashing haphazardly.

Blum checked his Mauser. His blood was surging. It was clear they were going to have to fight it out.

Above them, they suddenly heard the sound of an engine in the night sky.

"Hear that?" Blum said to Leisa, exultantly, and pointed toward the sky. "Who else has a plane coming to pick them up? In a few hours, we'll be in England."

For the first time since he had found her today by the orchestra, he saw the bright smile on her face and the trusting eyes he remembered from their youth.

"Yes. I hear it, Nathan."

"See, Leo." Blum pushed the boy triumphantly. "I told you this was the spot."

"I never doubted." Leo grinned back. Then he cast a nervous glance in the direction the German shouts were emanating from.

Another minute and the rumble above them grew louder. The plane would land without lights, Janusz explained, the lanterns guiding them in.

"*There!*" Leo pointed to the sky.

Barely a shadow above the horizon, the only light coming from the cockpit, the plane descended from the north. Soon it was only a couple of hundred feet off the ground, its wings swaying in the wind.

Blum said, "She's coming in fast!"

"Get ready. She'll be on the ground in thirty seconds," Janusz said. "When they are, we'll—"

Suddenly they heard the sputter of machine gun fire. A Czech ZB-26. The partisans had surprised the Germans and were trying to push them back from the site. All they would need was to hold them off for another minute or two.

Blum could see dark shapes, soldiers, advancing in the same field he, Leisa, and Leo had come through minutes before, and the yellow flashing of submachine gun spurts.

"Get down!" Janusz instructed them. "We're going to take some heat." The Germans were now returning their fire, mostly toward the woods where the resistance fighters were spread out. The ground firing was so loud, it wasn't clear whether they had yet made out the plane.

"There are a lot of them." Janusz pulled back the bolt on his Blyskawica. "Once it lands, you will have to move quickly and whatever you do, do not stop."

Blum nodded, taking hold of Leisa's hand. "I understand. *You?*"

"Yes." She nodded, the worry clear in her eyes.

"Get ready then. Take my hand."

Anticipation coursing through him like a river spilling over its banks, Blum followed the path of the Mosquito as it swooped above the field and came in. Now you could see its wings dipping from side to side, lower and lower, and the cockpit light descending below the trees, and then it touched, its wheels hitting the ground and then bouncing high, once, then twice along the bumpy, improvised strip.

Janusz said, "Get set, it's down!"

Propellers whirring, it came to a stop at the far end of the field and immediately turned back around. It settled a couple of hundred yards away from them, preparing for a swift departure.

A hatch door in the fuselage opened.

Janusz gave them the thumbs-up. "Get going—*now! Go!*" The fighting had gotten even closer. "Good luck!"

Cocking her Blyskawica, Anja said to Blum, "I was wrong. You do look like a fighter now."

He smiled back at her. "As do you."

Nodding to Leo and taking hold of Leisa, Blum shouted, *"Run!"*

They sprinted into the field, legs pumping as hard as they could. Behind them they heard the concussive sound of a grenade exploding nearby. Then a flash. Recoiling from the noise, Leisa stopped and screamed. Blum retook her hand and pulled her. "Go on!"

The fighting grew closer now. The Germans, now aware of the plane, had shifted their attention to the three of them. As they ran, rounds sprayed at their heels, the zinging *phht, phht, phht* of bullets hitting the earth close behind them.

Blum shouted again. *"Run!"*

The plane was about a hundred yards away from them. An airman crouched in the opening, waving them on. Leo ran ahead, Blum, clinging to Leisa's hand, ten yards behind. "Don't stop, either of you! *Run!*"

He heard an explosion not far behind them. A grenade landed directly where Janusz and his men had been firing from, bodies flying in the yellow blast. The concussion almost shattered their eardrums. Anja stepped out from the brush. She stood there in the open field, covering them, discharging her submachine gun until it was empty, and then Blum heard a spurt of return fire and Anja crying out and falling.

"*Anja!*" He wanted to go to her, but they couldn't stop now. "Leisa, Leo, keep running!"

Suddenly a German came up on the side. Blum let Leisa go and ran off four shots on his Mauser, emptying Franke's clip. The soldier fell back.

Blum turned and ran.

The airman was waving them in now. *Twenty yards*. Bullets sprayed, scraping the ground behind them, clanging loudly off the fuselage. *Ping, ping, ping, ping*.

"Leisa, keep going! Don't stop!"

They were going to make it. *Ten yards*.

Finally they reached the plane, bullets popping loudly against metal all around them. "You first!" Blum said to Leo.

The airman put out his hand. "Who the hell are these?" he shouted. "Where's the old man?"

He hoisted Leo into the plane. Then he reached down for Leisa.

"Mendl's dead," Blum said. "Leisa, get in now!" The ground fire had grown more intense. Bullets *pinged* like heavy hail against the fuselage. The airman had a bullet graze his shoulder and grunted, "*Shit!*" ducking back inside.

Leisa screamed hysterically, ground fire tearing all around her.

"Leisa, now, you must go!" Blum pushed her up, the airman scampering into a crouch and grabbing onto her arm. He pulled her inside. The engines revved loudly and the propellers began to whir.

"Nathan, come on!" she screamed back to him.

Now it was Blum's turn. The airman grabbed onto his hand, bullets blistering all around the fuselage door.

"Nathan, give me your hand!" Leisa turned back around to help him. *Leisa, no . . .*

He reached out and touched her, catching a glimpse of the beauty and love she had for him in her fierce, determined eyes.

That was the instant he felt something hot and searing slam into his back. Like a prize-fighter's punch. Only harder. His insides on fire.

"Nathan!" his sister screamed.

Then another, straightening Blum up, his fingers slipping out of the airman's desperate grasp.

Maybe one more.

The next thing he knew he was on the ground. He looked up at the plane. He couldn't hear any sound, only the airman shouting silently for him to get up. Leisa, her face twisted in helplessness and horror, screaming his name over and over, just no sound, desperately lunging with her hand, fighting the airman off to climb down to get to him.

Nathan, get up.

He tried to pull himself to his knees. He tried with every bit of strength he had. But it was like the heaviest weight he had ever felt had pinned him to the ground. Kept him there.

Get up.

He rested his head back on the soil. It felt good there. He blinked once or twice. He looked at his hand on his chest, and it was covered in blood. Things began to grow hazy. You have to get up, he told himself. *Up.* He felt an explosion to the left, close to the plane. A grenade, maybe. The earth threw him up for a second. Then back down.

He could see the airman and Leisa shielding themselves from the incoming fire.

They'd better get out of here fast, Blum said to himself. *Go.*

You have to go now, Leisa. Now.

He put his head back down. He heard the sounds of the propellers whir. The only regret he felt was that he wished he had done what he intended to do and shot the damn driver.

SEVENTY-FIVE

"Nathan!" *Leisa screamed.* "Nathan!" *staring down at him in hor-ror. She tried to hurl herself back out of the plane to get to him, but the airman grabbed her by the torso to rein her in, fighting against her desperate attempts to wrestle out of his grip.* "Nathan, no, no, no!"

"We have to go!" *the airman shouted, trying to get to the door. Bul-lets shrieked into the fuselage and he ducked to the floor.* "The fire's too intense." *You could see Germans advancing in the field now. Only fifty yards from the plane. The airman reached to throw back the door handle.* "We have to go now!"

"No! No!" *she kept screaming, fighting him with every ounce of strength she had.* "Nathan! Nathan! We have to get him."

Before he shut the door, she peered down at him, in helplessness and horror, blind to the incoming fire. I saw him there. His eyes had become still and glazed. I don't know, maybe I saw some life still in him. Not fear. Not even a glimmer of it. Regret, maybe. At seeing her go. If it doesn't sound crazy, I would almost say there was a smile on his face.

"We can't!" *The airman pulled her back inside.* "He's gone."

"No!" *She tried to tear herself away from him.* "He's not gone! He's not!"

"He's gone!" *the airman shouted, and threw the door closed.*

"No . . . !" She was screaming, sobbing, as the realization that he was left behind became clear now. "No, no," she kept repeating, tears running down her face. "It was supposed to be me. Don't you understand, I was the one who was supposed to die. Not him! Me . . . !" She ran to a small window and continued to shout his name, looking down at him, as bullets peppered against the outside door. "Nathan, get up, please . . ."

"We've got to get out of here now!" one of the pilots shouted back to us. "Hold on!"

The propellers whirred faster and faster and the engine rumble intensified into a drone. We started to move.

"Don't you understand? I was the one who was supposed to die," she kept sobbing. "Not him. Me! Nathan!"

"You both have to strap yourself in!" the airman said. "We're taking off now. Hard."

"No, please, don't leave!" She scrambled back to the door. "Don't! Don't," she said as the speed picked up. "Don't leave him . . ." She dug her fingers against the door.

I grabbed her and brought her over with me to the makeshift seat. There was no time to strap anyone in. The plane was already moving fast. I felt the g-force tug as the Mosquito picked up speed over the bumpy landing strip.

So I just held onto her as tightly as I could. She was crying, sobbing against me, saying his name over and over.

I held her against me, and I vowed then to never let her go.

SEVENTY-SIX

So this is what it is like . . . Blum said to himself.

The plane door was closed. Leisa was safe inside. He heard the rumble of the engines revving, the *ping, ping, ping* of bullets clanging off the plane.

It's not so bad at all.

Go, he said. *Go. Now. You have to go.*

The droning of the engines grew louder and louder.

Then everything became very quiet.

Whatever light there was, even only the halo of the moon, intensified into a bright glare, luminous as a star exploding. He thought maybe he heard the whine of the plane as it took off from the bumpy field. And that it swooped around, maybe just one time, dipping its wings, to say goodbye.

Or maybe he was just imagining that.

Either way, he felt pride, somehow. Leo was on his way to England. With everything he held in his head. Strauss and Donovan would be pleased. He had done what he said. He had fulfilled his mission.

And *Leisa . . .* She was safe too. He had watched over her. Just as he'd always promised. He had kept his oath on that as well.

Doleczki. He smiled. He had seen those dimples one last time as she smiled at him in the woods. *Don't be angry with me.* That was my vow all along. Our Mozart fit together one last time. Remember that. Keep it that way. Together.

No, it's not so bad at all.

He heard shouting. He couldn't tell if it was up close or far away. Or if his eyes were even open or closed. What did it matter now? *Aliyah*. Why did that of all words come into his mind? The first time he went up to read from the Torah. He'd made a promise to return one day. To the Holy Land.

"A man may compel his entire household to go up with him to the land of Israel," Rabbi Leitner had said to him, "but may not compel a single one to leave."

He dug his nails into the soft earth around him.

Papa, I told you, I will not leave.

It had been dark the night he went away; nerves grinding in his stomach. He stood somewhere between a boy and a man. "I don't want to go," he begged his father as he dressed to go on his journey. "If I do, who will take care of her?"

"You *must* go," his father told him. "I release you from your vow, Nathan. You can't protect her any longer."

"But I can," he said back defiantly.

"No. You can't." His father shook his head. "Not any longer. With what is to come, only God can protect her now. But you have something even more important you can protect. You will take the *Mishnah* to a new home. In that way, you will protect us all, my son. Our history. Our tradition. Not only Leisa. Us all. For that, you have to go."

"But, Papa . . ."

"What is good cannot be known in the short term, Nathan. Remember?" his father said. "It is a great honor." He put his hands on Nathan's shoulders. "And they chose you, my son. *Here . . .* " His father took off his hat, his goose-felt bowler, and placed it on Nathan's head, adjusting it so that it sat just right. "This is rightfully yours now. Now you are really a man. And remember, a hat is not just a thing to wear, it's what you stand for. Who you are."

A feeling as proud as the day he first stood at the bimah and read from the Torah ran through him. His father's goatee curled into a smile. He put his hand on Nathan's cheek. "Do you understand all this, my son? What I've told you."

A soldier ran up to him on the ground. He pointed his rifle at Blum's chest, his finger on the trigger.

"Yes, Papa." Blum stared into his father's eyes. "I think I understand."

SEVENTY-SEVEN

THE EDWARD HINES, JR., VETERANS ADMINISTRATION HOSPITAL

"So I guess you know now"—the old man shifts in his chair and looks at his daughter with hollow, bloodshot eyes—"that the woman I held in the plane was your mother."

His daughter nods, her hand firmly wrapped over his, tears forming in her eyes. "Yes."

"I vowed never to let her go. And I didn't. I didn't let her go for sixty years."

"Oh, Pop," she says, taking his hand and bringing it softly against her cheek.

"She used her middle name, Ida, when we came to the States. And I guess it just stuck. All these years. As you understand now, there was a lot that took place there that we wanted to leave behind. We moved to Chicago just like her brother had. It was the only family either of us had."

She's never heard this, any of this, the true story of how her father and mother met. She has only heard, without much explanation, that it was "in the camp."

"Oh, Daddy." She squeezes his hand.

It is after midnight now. The floor staff had let her stay on. The night nurse had looked in on them from time to time, taking his tray, bringing him his pills, but they let him finish his tale. He has been sitting up this whole time, years pouring out of him, years he had kept to himself, completely hidden, stopping only for a few sips of water when his throat grew dry.

Then he just sits there, and there is nothing more to say.

"So you see, I'm no hero. I couldn't even save the one man who saved me. This photo . . ." He picks up the one of the military officers presenting the Distinguished Service Cross. "This wasn't given to me. They were presenting it to his sister. To your mom. The only surviving family he had. You probably missed somewhere in that box, there's a little plaque, 'To Nathan Blum, Lieutenant, U.S. Army.' He was the hero." The old man shakes his head. "Your uncle . . . Not me."

"I'm not sure, Pop." His daughter shakes her head too. "From what I heard, I think you both were."

"I don't know . . ." Her father sits back. "But I did give him the greatest honor I could think of . . ." He takes her hands. "And that was to give his name to you, pumpkin. At least I can finally tell you who you got your name from. Natalie."

A sensation of pride surges through her. Her eyes glisten. She had never known. Natalie. After Nathan. Her uncle. "Thank you, Daddy." She nods.

"I'm so sorry . . ." He shakes his head again as a tear winds down his cheek.

"Sorry for what?" She squeezes and kisses his hand.

"Sorry that all these years I couldn't tell you what was in my heart. What was always here. Every day." He taps his chest. "In here."

"That's okay." She grabs a tissue to dab his eyes. "You did now."

"We made a pact, your mom and I. I never picked up a chess piece again. And she . . . Well, as you know, maybe she played a little piano over the years. The clarinet . . ." He shrugs. "It just reminded her of everything she felt responsible for and wanted to leave behind. She did bring this back, though." He reaches inside the cigar box and takes out the two halves of the Mozart Clarinet Concerto, which had been taped back together. "So now you see, they're one. Seventy years it sat in there . . ." He looks at her and smiles. "You know that he was the real love of her life, her brother, not me."

"That's not true. She adored you, Pop. You know that."

"Well, she used to say that I had my own heartthrob too . . ." He picks up the white chess piece and holds it in his hand. "You know, there hasn't been a day when I haven't thought of her. When I haven't been heavy in my heart. All these years. That's the reason. You understand what I'm saying, don't you?"

She nods, tears welling in her own eyes. "Yes."

"She said to me, 'Good wins out, Leo . . . Even in here.' Even in that hell we came out of. 'Live out your life,' she said. 'If only just for me.' And I have." He looks at his daughter. "I've been a good father, haven't I, sweetheart?"

"Of course you have, Daddy. The best."

"And a good husband?"

"Yes." She takes his hand. "Sixty years."

"And I provided for you all? We built a family. You, Greg, and the kids . . ."

"A beautiful one, Pop. You did."

"That was the vow I made. In that plane. And I tried to live up to it every day." He looks at the picture of the pretty blond woman in the boat, the rim of her white sailor's cap folded up and that beautiful smile. "None of us would have been here if it wasn't for her. You never would have been born. All the good things in my life would never have happened. I would have died there. So I guess she was right, in the end, about good."

"Yes." His daughter looks at the dog-eared photo. "She was right."

"Here. You can keep this all now." He hands her back the photo and the chess piece. "Maybe you'll tell the kids one day. When I'm gone. But now I'm a little tired. I think I've earned that nap. I think this is the latest I've stayed up since your mom and I took that cruise to the Caribbean and I won twenty-eight hundred bucks in the ship's casino."

"I never heard about that one." His daughter laughs with surprise.

"Your mom was mad. Never let me near a casino again." He curls a smile. "But I always could count the cards pretty well."

He tries to stand, and she takes him by his arm and helps him, a step at a time, over to the bed, where he eases onto his back and lets out a satisfied sigh. "Just move it down a little for me, pumpkin. The switch is over there. You know, when I finally get out of this place"—he winks at her—"we ought to pick up one of these for the house."

"Of course, Pop. We'll put it on the list." She depresses the lever and gently eases him back down.

"That's good." He closes his eyes for a second. When he opens them, he catches her staring at him. "What?"

"It's just that I've loved you every day of my life, Daddy. But I've never been prouder of you than I am now."

He nods, a satisfied smile creeping onto his face. "It's good to hear you say that, pumpkin. But now I'm gonna get my beauty sleep, if it's okay."

"Of course it's okay." She bends down and gives him a kiss. "I'll be back tomorrow."

She takes her things and puts everything neatly back in the cigar box, staring a second at the photograph of the woman in the boat, whom she now had a name for, one last time. "Thank you," she whispers to her softly.

Then she puts the photograph into the box with everything else and closes it, closes the story that their lives had sprung from, and goes to the door. She stops before turning out the light. "So I have to ask one more thing, Pop. Was it true?"

"Was what true, pumpkin?" he asks with his eyes closed.

"About your memory. We always knew you had a good one. I mean, you could certainly recite the entire Illinois Code of Civil Law by heart."

"Was it true? Well, let me see now . . . As I recall, you were born on January twenty-second, 1955." He puts his fingers to his forehead. "That was a Saturday, I think."

"Of course it was a Saturday, Pop. I heard a million times, how I kept you from going to the Cubs game that day. You had front-row seats."

"Oh. All right, all right . . . Guess I've gotten a little rusty in my old age."

She smiles, about to reach for the light. "And you didn't tell me about all the formulas you brought back. Mendl's work. What happened to all that? Did it have the impact they hoped for?"

"Did it have the impact . . . ?" He shrugs. "They said it changed the course of the war. History, for that matter. At first they were a little unsure what to do, what with Alfred and Nathan not being there. They brought me out to this place in New Mexico and I just started rattling things off . . . They had a staff of people taking things down fast as I could say them. Turns out, in the end, however, the Germans weren't quite as close to a bomb as anyone thought. Still, you know what, honey . . . ?"

"What, Pop?"

Her father turns to her. "I never understood a single thing that old man said to me. I just took it all down and put it in here." He taps his head. "Gaseous diffusion . . . Never made a lick of sense to me. Now, tax law, that I understand." His words begin to grow faint. "Trusts, wills . . . Those things make sense. Know what I'm saying, hon . . . ?"

She stands at the door for a while and he closes his eyes. In a few seconds he is asleep.

"Yes, Pop." She turns out the light. "I think I know."

EPILOGUE

On the wall of the Bradbury Science Museum in Los Alamos, New Mexico, there is a large plaque, just behind the life-size statues of General Leslie Groves and Robert Oppenheimer, in his iconic, soft brimmed hat, commemorating the scientists who as part of the Manhattan Project helped oversee the development of the atomic bomb and changed the course of modern history.

There are 247 names on the wall. Some are names everyone knows who has studied this chapter of history. Einstein. Fermi. Bohr. Teller. Others, Kistiakowsky, Morrison, Neddermeyer, Ulam: theoretical physicists, chemists, mathematicians. People of uncommon brilliance, whose contributions were essential yet whose names are not widely known.

Of all the names, only one never actually worked on the Manhattan Project. He died in Europe during the war, in a concentration camp, far from the laboratories of Los Alamos or Oak Ridge, Tennessee, and the circumstances of his passing are cloudy. But his contribution, on the matter of gaseous diffusion, brought back by people of uncommon bravery, was thought by those who erected this tribute to be just as vital to the project's success as that of those who toiled every day in Los Alamos.

You can find him, if you kneel down, between McKibben and Morrison near the bottom of the third row.

Alfred Mendl.

AUTHOR'S NOTE

My father-in-law, Nathan Zorman, was raised in Warsaw, Poland, and, in a shift of fate that no doubt saved his life, he left in early 1939 to come to the United States, just months before the war.

He never heard from anyone in his family again.

In 1941, when America entered the war, he enlisted in the U.S. Army and, because of his knowledge of languages, was placed in the Intelligence Corps.

Sadly, he died months before this novel's publication, at ninety-six, but like many survivors, never spoke a word about his experiences either during the war or while he was growing up in Poland. Bringing to mind the faces of the family he never saw again was simply too painful. Over the years, he never even made an attempt to find out his family's fate. I always wanted to find a way to put his anguish in a book—the grief and the loss—the guilt at having survived, which, I thought, in spite of many blessings in his life, had left him detached from inner happiness for seventy-plus years.

Much of the story you have read was based on truth. Alfred Wetzler and Rudolf Vrba were indeed real, and their depiction of Auschwitz after their remarkable escape was circulated in the highest channels of the U.S. government and brought the horrors there out of the darkness. The meetings with President Roosevelt and his war cabinet on this very subject were based on truth, as his war chiefs reviewed several proposed plans to stop the genocide, such as raids on the camps or bombing the railway tracks leading into them, but ultimately rejected them all. The compelling saga of the Vittel Jews with their forged Latin American identity papers is true as well, as was their fate—after being betrayed by a Jew from the Warsaw ghetto, they were all shipped to Auschwitz in January 1944, all 240 of them, and never heard from again.

While looking into my father-in-law's past, I came across the massacres that took place in Lvov, Poland (now part of Ukraine), in June–July 1941 under the German occupation. At the time Lvov had a thriving university and the third-largest Jewish population in Poland. In what was termed an act of "self-purification," the university there was brutally purged by both Nazis and Ukrainians, and thousands of Jewish intellectuals—professors, scientists, and artists—were rounded up and either shot on the spot or sent off to the death camps of Treblinka, Sobibor, and Auschwitz. From there, it wasn't too much of a leap for a novelist to ask: What if one of these esteemed thinkers carried some kind of vital knowledge that could change the outcome of the war or, even beyond that, the course of human thought? Something that needed to get out, or would, like a buried secret, die along with him.

It was with this idea in mind that I came across the figure of prominent Danish physicist Niels Bohr. Considered one of the founders of atomic theory, Bohr was awarded the Nobel Prize for Physics in 1922 and was among the most revered scientific figures of his time. In the book I describe his harrowing escape from Denmark literally a day before he was to be arrested and likely sent off to a death camp and his even more harrowing voyage to London strapped into the bomb bay of a British Mosquito. A year later he was a member of the British mission to the Manhattan Project in Los Alamos. In addition to being a father figure to many of the other physicists there, as late as 1945 Robert Oppenheimer credited Bohr with making an important contribution to the modulated neutron initiators that were crucial to the bomb's triggering device. Bohr's vast knowledge never assisted the Nazis, but it was not too much of a stretch to imagine how, had

Bohr been sent to the camps or even forced to succumb and aid the German war effort, the course of the war might have been decidedly altered or, at the very least, the outcome delayed.

Sadly, Alfred Mendl is not a real figure (and his mention in Los Alamos is fictional too). But the science he taught Leo—the gaseous diffusion process, whereby highly enriched uranium-235 is separated from its more common and nonfissile cousin, U-238—did become the most efficient separation method for the first atomic bombs. It was also not a European physicist who was at the forefront of this process in 1943 and 1944 but scientists from the University of Minnesota and the University of California at Berkeley. For that research I am highly indebted to several books (listed in the bibliography), but principally Richard Rhodes's compelling and monumental study, *The Making of the Atomic Bomb*. It was also very helpful to speak with Robert Kupp, a chemical engineer who actually worked on the Manhattan Project in Oak Ridge.

While researching this book, I also came across the real-life story of Denis Avey, a British soldier captured in North Africa and sent to a POW camp in Poland, who actually snuck inside Auschwitz for a night and then back out to tell a firsthand account of the horrors there. His remarkable story can be read in his memoir: *The Man Who Broke into Auschwitz* (Da Capo Press, 2011). So it was not such a leap to imagine that Nathan actually could have gotten in and out.

I've tried to remain as true as possible to the actual history around the events described in this book. (Filip Müller's testament, *Eyewitness Auschwitz*, Ivan Dee Publisher, was one of several indispensable firsthand accounts.) Never for a second did I think of writing the definitive book on Auschwitz—the atrocities there have already been ably recorded on far more graphic and personal levels than mine. Still, the subject matter is sacrosanct, and as a Jew, I respect that history as much as anyone. But I did take what I hope will be seen as a few small liberties with the actual truth in the following areas: One is that after 1942, the women's camp was situated at Auschwitz's sister camp, Birkenau, a mile and a half to the northeast. And although my story takes place in 1944, the train tracks leading through the gates of Birkenau were already completed by then. Other than that, I tried to remain as accurate as possible in my retelling of the place and the acts there. Several people, especially Morris Pilberg, recounted personal stories of their experiences that are included in the narrative. I was also lucky that my neighbor, Joanna Powell, shared two extraordinary memoirs of her family members' Shoah testimonies to draw from on Jewish life in prewar Poland and then under the occupation. Their stories helped me enormously. Lastly, the Abwehr Intelligence Command was always a thorn in Hitler's side, the upper ranks populated by non–Nazi Party members. The Abwehr was believed to have been involved in several assassination attempts on Hitler's life and possibly in unauthorized negotiations with the Russians. Hitler finally shut it down in February 1944 (and its head, Admiral Wilheim Canaris, was arrested)—literally during the timeline of this book, in the months between the deportation of the Vittel Jews to Auschwitz and the bulk of the action that takes place at the camp. Therefore, I decided to push the date forward just a couple of months for the sake of the narrative, and I do hope you'll forgive me for this slight.

As I said, once the United States entered the war, my father-in-law enlisted in the Army and, because of his facility with languages, was placed in the Intelligence Corps. As with his upbringing in Poland, whatever it was he did in the service has never been spoken of to any in his family. What you've read is my story, not his. But if I could somehow have pushed through his pained and brooding expressions when urged to speak about his past; through his inability to articulate the long-held-in burdens of guilt and loss; if he was able to tell his own story, the whole tale, of his past in Poland and the role he played during the war, I always imagined it would read something like this.

ACKNOWLEDGMENTS

When you do something people don't expect from you, something way beyond the margins of your resume, one thing you learn quickly is who will come along for the ride and who will take a pass. One of my favorite quotes, from Henry Ford, is, "Some people think they can and others think they can't, and they're probably both right." This book, one so close to my heart, yet so different from anything I've ever attempted before, represents about the 6,532nd time I've asked people to take that ride along with me over a handful of careers. I guess I'm just one of those who perpetually think that they can—and I hope this book, in the humblest of ways, bears that out.

There are many to thank, some already mentioned in the Author's Note, who have helped make this effort seem far more accomplished and well-researched:

Robert Kupp, a nonagenarian in his own right, and who was a chemical engineer assigned to the Manhattan Project, for talking me through the tricky edges of atomic science, someone who barely muddled his way through eighth-grade Earth Science.

Joanna Powell, my neighbor, for digging into her boxes and sharing two extraordinary family memoirs, which painted a rich tableau of Jewish life before and during the war.

Steve Berry (and his wife, Liz), who made it clear at their kitchen counter in Florida that this was the next book I needed to write. And for his patience and plotting acumen in nursing it through a couple of early outlines.

My friend Roy Grossman, who always adds enough clarity that I seem to keep putting my Work in Progress back in front of him.

The many people over the years who have shared their Holocaust stories, especially Auschwitz survivors Magda Linhart and Morris Pilberg, whose harrowing tale of the gun that kept jamming at the back of his head I used in the book. I pray I've done some small justice to all of them.

My agent, Simon Lipskar, who challenged me over and over to firm up the background and historical antecedents to the story. And who didn't do a half-bad job of finding the right home for it.

To my new team at Minotaur Books and St. Martin's Press—my editor, Kelley Ragland, Andy Martin, Sally Richardson, Jen Enderlin— for seeing the virtue in an outline when many didn't and for giving it the kind of enthusiasm and unity of effort an author rarely feels from his publisher. I pray that outline has become an even better book.

And to my wife, Lynn, who has stood next to me through many such rides, believing in them (mostly), this being just one more. Your partnership in life is evident within these pages.

BIBLIOGRAPHICAL SOURCES

A number of books and firsthand accounts, some already mentioned in the Author's Note, helped enormously in the writing and preparation of *The One Man:*

FDR AND THE HOLOCAUST

FDR and the Jews, Richard Breitman and Allan J. Lichtman (Harvard University Press, 2013).

"Orthodox Ends, Unorthodox Means: The Role of the Vaad Hatzalah and Agudath Israel during the Holocaust," David H. Kranzler. In *The Goldberg Commission Report: American Jewry during the Holocaust,* ed. Maxwell Seymour Finger (1984, 2011).

Saving the Jews: Franklin Delano Roosevelt and the Holocaust, Robert N. Rosen (Thunder's Mouth Press, 2006).

Those Angry Days: Roosevelt, Lindberg, and America's Fight over World War II, Lynne Olson (Random House, 2013).

JEWISH CULTURE

American Prometheus: The Triumph and Tragedy of J. Robert Oppenheimer, Kai Bird and Martin J. Sherwin (Vintage Books, 2006).

THE MANHATTAN PROJECT

Jewish Literacy, Rabbi Joseph Telushkin (William Morrow and Company, 1991).

The Adventures of a Mathematician, S. M. Ulam (The University of California Press, 1991).

The Making of the Atomic Bomb, Richard Rhodes (Simon and Schuster, 1986).

The Physics of the Manhattan Project, Bruce Cameron Reed (Springer-Verlag, 2015).

AUSCHWITZ

Eyewitness Auschwitz, Filip Müller (Ivan R. Dee, 1979).

Inside the Gas Chambers: Eight Months in the Sonderkommando of Auschwitz, Shlomo Venzia (Polity Press, 2009).

The Man Who Broke into Auschwitz, Denis Avey with Rob Broomby (Da Capo Press, 2011).

True Tales from a Grotesque Land, Auschwitz, Sara Nomberg-Przytyk (University of North Carolina Press, 1985).

POLISH LIFE IN WWII

The Polish Officer, Alan Furst (Random House, 1995).